USA TODAY bestselling author **Heidi Rice** lives in London, England. She is married with two teenage sons—which gives her rather too much of an insight into the male psyche—and also works as a film journalist. She adores her job, which involves getting swept up in a world of high emotion, sensual excitement, funny and feisty women, sexy and tortured men and glamorous locations where laundry doesn't exist. Once she turns off her computer she often does chores—usually involving laundry!

Melanie Milburne read her first Mills & Boon novel at the age of seventeen, in between studying for her final exams. After completing a master's degree in education she decided to write a novel, and thus her career as a romance author was born. Melanie is an ambassador for the Australian Childhood Foundation and a keen dog-lover and trainer. She enjoys long walks in the Tasmanian bush. In 2015 Melanie won the HOLT Medallion, a prestigious award honouring outstanding literary talent.

Also by Heidi Rice

Claimed for the Desert Prince's Heir
A Forbidden Night with the Housekeeper
Innocent's Desert Wedding Contract

Passion in Paradise collection

My Shocking Monte Carlo Confession

The Christmas Princess Swap collection

The Royal Pregnancy Test

Also by Melanie Milburne

The Return of Her Billionaire Husband

Once Upon a Temptation collection

His Innocent's Passionate Awakening

Wanted: A Billionaire miniseries

One Night on the Virgin's Terms
Breaking the Playboy's Rules
One Hot New York Night

Discover more at millsandboon.co.uk.

ONE WILD NIGHT WITH HER ENEMY

HEIDI RICE

THE BILLION-DOLLAR BRIDE HUNT

MELANIE MILBURNE

MILLS & BOON

First Published in Great Britain 2021
by Mills & Boon, an imprint of HarperCollins*Publishers* Ltd,
1 London Bridge Street, London, SE1 9GF

www.harpercollins.co.uk

HarperCollins*Publishers*
1st Floor, Watermarque Building,
Ringsend Road, Dublin 4, Ireland

ISBN: 978-0-263-28250-4

06/21

MIX
Paper from
responsible sources
FSC™ C007454

This book is produced from independently certified FSC™ paper
to ensure responsible forest management.
For more information visit www.harpercollins.co.uk/green.

Printed and bound in Spain
by CPI, Barcelona

ONE WILD NIGHT WITH HER ENEMY

HEIDI RICE

MILLS & BOON

To Daisy.

I love you, and your little dog too!

H x

PROLOGUE

'YOU CANNOT BE SERIOUS, Ashling! I can see my nipples in this thing. And it feels far too...'

Dangerous? Exciting?

Cassandra James cut off the errant thought. The dress her flatmate and BFF Ashling Doyle had sourced for her to wear to an *über*-hip celebrity wedding in San Francisco, in exactly fourteen hours' time, was not dangerous, or exciting, it was—well, frankly, it was indecent.

Her boss, Zachary Temple, had asked her to go to the wedding to check out Luke Broussard of Broussard Tech, in what Temple had referred to as 'his natural habitat', before kicking off a two-week trip to the West Coast to scope out investment prospects for Temple Corp in the buoyant US technology market.

As Temple's trusted executive assistant, Cassie had done some of the groundwork before on his investment decisions—crunching numbers and rigorously fact-checking industry credentials when she wasn't doing all the usual admin her job entailed... She enjoyed the rare chance to branch out, and she knew she'd impressed Temple with her work and her recommendations.

He'd given her this assignment after she'd voiced her concerns about Broussard's background check. And it was a huge opportunity to stop being a glorified gopher and move up the corporate ladder. The only problem was that up till now she'd always worked in the comfort of Temple Corp's HQ in London, not by attending a glittering society event an ocean away, full of super-cool people.

She hadn't told Temple of her concerns when he'd given her the assignment out of the blue, because it would have made her look and feel pathetic. And it was only a wedding, for goodness' sake.

Plus, she had been right to suggest Broussard might need closer inspection. She hadn't been able to discover anything about his origins or his background online… It was almost as if the details had been deliberately erased. The extensive internet research she'd done on him had offered up a ton of glowing reviews on the stratospheric rise of his company from innovative start-up to global player in less than a decade, and a few furtively snapped paparazzi shots of Broussard himself with an assortment of beautiful women on his arm. But not a lot else…

Going to San Francisco to see if she could discover more about him in person made sense. And asking Ashling—who had a quirky eye for fashion and had always been the coolest person Cassie knew—to source a dress for the wedding had seemed like the perfect solution to calm any residual nerves…

But then Ashling had produced this glittering gold creation which clung intimately to every one of Cassie's curves.

'You can't wear a bra with that dress, Cass,' Ashling reiterated, standing at Cassie's shoulder. 'It'll ruin the shape.' She stepped back, the sparkle in her blue eyes taking on an assessing gleam. 'You look amazing.'

'Seriously, Ash? I can feel my boobs swaying.' Cassie placed her hands on her breasts for emphasis—and some much-needed support.

Ashling's lips pursed into an adorable pout, which Cassie knew her friend could use like a lethal weapon—as she had so often when they were growing up together. As the daughter of their housekeeper, Ashling had quickly become Cassie's ally and her best friend. Someone who could tempt her into the best adventures and out of the shell created by her father's disapproval.

Cassie had always adored her childhood friend for her free spirit. But she was loving that free spirit a lot less at the moment. Because she did not have the time—or the talent—to find an alternative dress before the car arrived to take her to Heathrow.

'If you wear a bra with that dress you'll be committing a major fashion faux pas,' Ashling said, still pouting—and totally missing the point. 'This dress is perfect for a fancy celebrity wedding in San Francisco…'

Ashling paused as the colour flared in Cassie's cheeks. And the anxiety Cassie had kept ruthlessly at bay ever since Temple had dropped his bombshell so casually about this trip threatened to strangle her.

'Cass, what's wrong?' her friend said, her voice rich with concern.

'Nothing,' she said automatically. But then she breathed in. *Damn.* If she couldn't tell Ashling how she really felt, who could she tell? 'I just do not want to go to this thing.'

There—she'd said it.

'Why?' Ashling asked.

Cassie frowned. 'Lavish social events aren't my forte.'

She could still remember the time her father had asked her to host an important soirée when she was eighteen. It had felt like a test—a test she'd been desperate to pass and had comprehensively failed. He'd never asked her again.

'And, anyway, Temple's not sending me to socialise. He wants me to check out a tech entrepreneur called

Luke Broussard while I'm at the wedding.' Cassie stared at herself in the mirror again. 'And this dress feels like too much.'

Ashling's blue eyes softened, and the fierce solidarity Cassie had relied on so heavily throughout her childhood was ringing in her voice when her friend banded her arms around her waist and rested her chin on Cassie's shoulder. 'It's not. It's gorgeous. You look like a sex goddess. Which makes it the perfect dress to wear to conduct some industrial espionage. You'll dazzle this Luke dude into giving up all his secrets while he's ripping it off you in a passionate frenzy.'

Cassie gulped as she recalled the pictures of Luke Broussard which she'd pored over maybe a bit too forensically. A slightly hysterical laugh slipped out as she conjured up the far too vivid image of Luke Broussard's large hands tearing glittering gold *lamé.*

'"Passionate" is not what I'm looking for,' she announced, as firmly as she could, while fighting to ignore the weight now sinking into her abdomen.

Good grief, trust Ashling to put that totally inappropriate thought into my head.

'And this trip is not about industrial espionage. I'm just going to help Temple suss out some potential investment opportunities and I don't want to mess it up. I need to blend in with the crowd,' Cassie added, pretty sure that Ash's dress choice was going to make her stick out like a sore thumb. Albeit a gold-plated one.

Ashling grinned and spread out her arms as if she were introducing Cassie to a crowd of admiring onlookers. 'Then my work here is done.'

Cassie sent Ashling what she hoped was a stern look, but then her phone buzzed and her worries about the dress got hit by a more immediate problem as a message from her assistant Gwen popped up.

Cassie, so sorry, my back's playing up. Won't be able to do the tux pick-up today.

Cassie swore softly under her breath.

'What is it?' Ash asked.

Cassie lifted her head to find her friend sending her a quizzical look. 'Ash, could you do me a humungous favour?'

'Of course—what's the favour?' Ash said, and Cassie wanted to kiss her despite the dress debacle.

'Could you pick up Temple's tuxedo from the dry cleaners this afternoon and deliver it to his place in Mayfair by six? He has a big event tonight and Gwen's just bailed on me. I can text you his address on the way to the airport,' she said, as she frantically tried to find the zip on the dress.

'Can't he get his own tuxedo?' Ash replied, surprising Cassie.

'Um…no. And I need someone I can trust to pick it up for him.'

Ash wasn't always super-reliable, but if she said she'd do something she would. And she would go to the wall for Cassie, so surely…?

'Seriously? There isn't anyone else you could ask?' Ash said.

'Not at such short notice,' Cassie said, confused by Ash's continued resistance—her friend was usually so helpful. 'Ash, what's the problem?'

As far as she knew Ash had never met Temple, and she'd never detected any animosity from her friend before about her boss. That said, they were total opposites. Because Ash was warm and sweet and slightly kooky, and Temple… Well, Temple so *wasn't*. But…

'It's fine. I'll do it.' Her friend cut through Cassie's thoughts, bending her head to work on the dress zip. 'I'm just not keen on being a billionaire's handmaiden, that's all. It's nothing personal.'

'Okay…' Cassie studied her friend a moment longer. Was Ash blushing? 'Are you sure?'

Ashling rolled her eyes so hard Cassie was surprised she didn't dislocate her eyeballs. 'Of course. My yoga class finishes at three-thirty. I'll have plenty of time.'

'Right… Great…' Cassie said as her friend eased down the zip.

The dress slipped over her hips, triggering a rush of sensation. She dived for the T-shirt she'd left on the bed, far too aware of a strange feeling of exposure… And vulnerability?

What was with *that*?

Okay, so she was technically still a virgin—thanks to a couple of really lacklustre dates at university—but she was hardly a complete novice. She'd kissed her fair share of guys. And the only reason she'd never gone the whole way was because her career had always been more important than her sex-life.

Was that where her concerns about this event really came from?

She pulled the T-shirt over her head.

No, that couldn't be it. Maybe she wasn't that comfortable without her professional armour firmly in place, but she had never been intimidated by men like Broussard—rich, powerful men—because she'd spent the last three years of her life working in close proximity to Temple.

'Now, you need to pack this dress and get going, if you're going to make your flight.' Ash scooped the dress off the floor. 'And try to enjoy your trip, even if it is work. There's no harm mixing business with pleasure occasionally.'

That trickle of anxiety returned at Ashling's teasing remark—and joined the swelling in Cassie's throat and a few more disconcerting parts of her anatomy.

No more overthinking, Cassie. It's just a job.

But the gold *lamé* still felt dangerous—and exciting—as she folded the dress into her suitcase.

CHAPTER ONE

You were right about the dress, Ash. I'm not even the most naked woman here… But what happened with the tux? You had one job, Ash!!

LUKE BROUSSARD TOOK another sip from his beer and continued to watch the woman standing on the opposite side of the arbour as she finished texting, switched off her phone and tucked it back in her purse. Her gold dress shimmered in the dusky orange light as the sun sank into San Francisco Bay, accentuating her high breasts and slender neck.

He'd spotted her twenty minutes ago, busy fending off all the eligible heterosexual bachelors, as soon as he'd arrived at this wedding in the Botanical Gardens. That stunning dress and the even more stunning figure it displayed had been turning heads ever since.

But it wasn't her body which had snagged *his* attention. Not entirely, anyway.

He sipped the cold brew again, to douse the low-grade fire in his pants which was calling him a liar.

Nah, the thing that had *really* intrigued him was the fact that he didn't recognise her. And he was pretty sure he knew all the available women on the West Coast scene, because he'd either dated them or they'd hit on him.

Who the heck is she?

At first he'd wondered if she'd crashed the event. He'd crashed enough of these things himself, when he'd been starting out and trying to get funding for Broussard Tech's first prototypes, to make the thought fire his imagination and his libido.

As he'd observed her, though, he'd discarded that idea. She looked way too elegant and aloof to be here without an invitation.

Which only made her more fascinating.

Her unattainable, ethereal beauty reminded him of the girls he'd never been good enough for in high school. The rich, fancy, privileged girls from the *right* side of the tracks who had been eager to make out with him after-hours on a game night, but had ignored him the next day in class because he'd lived in a trailer park, had a deadbeat for a father, worked two jobs and still hadn't been able to afford the latest high-tops.

Those memories amused him now he was worth billions and change.

But could that explain why the woman in gold had captured his attention? Did she represent a chance to relive those old high school humiliations and win? No woman was unattainable to him now. Not even one as stunning as her.

He gulped his beer as he noticed her chewing her bottom lip. Maybe she wasn't as aloof and composed as she seemed. He continued to study her. She actually looked kind of tense. Not aloof so much as uncomfortable.

Interesting. He hated these types of events, too.

He would never usually attend something like this, because if there was one thing he hated more than being on display, it was being on display in a monkey suit.

He tugged at his shirt collar and dragged off the tie which had been strangling him ever since the happy couple had said their vows five minutes ago. He shoved the tie in his pocket. If the two grooms hadn't once saved him from complete social isolation in college he wouldn't have come to this event either, but now he was here he was glad he hadn't dodged it. And not just because hearing Matt and Remy make their vows had been so touching.

When was the last time a woman had demanded his attention?

The mystery lady in gold stopped chewing her lip to chew the edge of her thumbnail, then stiffened. She drew her hand down to clutch the purse resting on her hip.

Another guy approached her. Luke tensed.

Back off, buddy, she's mine.

The possessive thought came out of left field.

Not cool.

He'd stopped letting his libido make decisions for him ever since those nights under the bleachers. These days he had his security team check out anyone he was considering dating to ensure he didn't hook up with women who were more interested in his platinum credit rating than his make-out skills.

The only problem was, that had taken all the fun out of the chase.

His heartrate spiked as the mystery girl gave the guy—whom he recognised as a rival tech company's CEO—the brush-off. For the first time in a long time he felt the heady adrenaline rush which meant he wanted to stop watching and start finding out more about this woman… A lot more.

He dumped his beer on the tray of a passing waiter, scooped up a couple of glasses of fancy fizz and strode past the arbour towards her.

To hell with the security check.

Whoever she was, she was the first woman to snag his interest in way too long for him to remember—which gave her considerable cachet in the jaded world of billionaire hook-ups.

Plus, there was nothing he loved more than a mystery that needed to be solved.

As he drew closer she looked directly at him, like a deer sensing the approach of a hunter. Their gazes collided and her eyes—hazelnut-brown shot through with flecks of gold that matched her dress—popped wide. With recognition or surprise or arousal, he couldn't be sure.

The shimmering gold fabric hugged the round weight of her breasts, making them look even more spectacular up close.

Is she wearing a bra?

His breath backed up in his lungs.

She really was exquisite—much more refined and beautiful than any of the girls he'd hooked up with in high school. He forced his wayward gaze back to her face. The flush of reaction—and guilty knowledge—highlighted her pale cheeks.

Arousal for sure, then. And recognition. And something else he couldn't decipher—but he would.

Lust fired through his bloodstream and hit his groin like a missile.

Well, damn...

'Hi.'

He handed her the champagne glass and gave himself a mental high-five when she took it. He wanted her more than he'd wanted any woman in a while. And before the night was over he intended to have her—after all, his make-out skills had improved considerably since high school, and he'd never had a problem getting any girl he wanted even when he'd been the boy good girls were warned to stay away from.

But first he was more interested in uncovering all the

fascinating secrets lurking in those big, beautiful and guarded eyes.

'Drink up, *cher*,' he said, laying on the Cajun manners his mama had drummed into him as a kid. 'Whatever you said to Dan Carter to send him packing,' he added, clinking his glass against hers as he mentioned the CEO she'd just given the bird, metaphorically speaking, 'I salute you. The guy's an entitled jerk. I have it on good authority.'

Luke Broussard! In the flesh.

'You… You do?' Cassie spluttered, taking a gulp of the champagne the man she'd been discreetly trying to locate in the crowd had just handed to her.

'I do.'

He tapped his nose, his firm, sensual lips stretching into a grin so full of laid-back hotness she could feel the effect right down to her toes—even in the heeled sandals which had been punishing her feet for over an hour.

Funny thing… She couldn't feel the pain any more as she became fixated on that seductive smile—full of confidence, and heat, and rueful amusement…and directed squarely at her. As if they were sharing a particularly good joke.

Although that couldn't be right.

She tried to get her jet-lagged brain back into gear.

Was this actually happening? Or was she imagining it out of desperation and fatigue and the Aperol Spritz she'd chugged down too quickly as she'd struggled to relax enough to make small talk?

She'd been at the wedding for what felt like an eternity, and there had been no sign of Luke Broussard and no one who knew him had seemed willing to talk about him. But Ashling's dress choice had worked its magic—or rather its curse—because she'd been approached by a selection of increasingly pushy guys, the last of whom had asked her point-blank if she'd like to spend the night on his yacht.

She'd met enough American men in business to know they could often be staggeringly forthright, but the leer in that man's eyes had made her feel unclean.

Luke Broussard's eyes, though—a striking emerald changing to a deep forest-green around the rim of his irises—were full of something a great deal more dangerous to her peace of mind… Not to mention her breathing… Because the look in them had triggered an urge to step closer to him, to gather the hint of his clean scent—pine soap overlaid with man—and bask in the mocking approval in his expression. Which could not be good.

His husky American accent sounded different from the others she'd heard this evening too. Slower, deeper, less sharp, the soft purr brushing over her skin and making it tight and achy.

The snapped, mostly blurred shots she'd found of him on the internet hadn't done him justice. He'd seemed conventionally handsome in those pictures, but in person his features were more rugged and a great deal more breathtaking. The strong jaw, darkened with the first hint of stubble, was matched by a prominent nose and chiselled cheekbones. His left brow was rakishly bisected by a piratical scar, and his dark wavy hair looked as if he'd missed his last few appointments at the barbers.

The hint of a tattoo on his collarbone—was that barbed wire?—revealed by the open collar of his shirt, only added to the aura of raw masculinity, untamed and defiant, and as out of place in this exclusive setting as she was… But for entirely different reasons.

The shock of having him walk up to her so boldly gave way to curiosity—and that odd yearning which she'd have to examine later. *Much later.*

For goodness' sake, Cassie, say something smart and erudite. Draw him out. Don't stare at him like a dummy.

She took another sip of champagne to buy some time and think up something coherent to say. Why did this feel like a strange exotic dream—both dangerous and exciting—rather than a golden opportunity to further the interests of Temple Corp?

'I'm not sure if Mr Carter is a jerk,' she managed, having finally grasped enough of the conversation to actually participate, 'but he was certainly very forward.'

'Forward, huh?' Broussard's scarred eyebrow arched and his lips quirked as if she'd said something amusing. 'What was his pick-up line?'

'He invited me to spend the night on his yacht. Apparently it's very big.'

His lips quirked some more. 'Classy,' he murmured. 'What did you say?'

'I told him the truth—that it probably wasn't a good idea as I can get seasick on a pedalo.'

His eyes sparkled, the tantalising curl of his lips making her breath thready. What was it about his smile that made it seem dangerous and precious at the same time?

'A peda— what, now?' he asked.

'A pedalo. It's like a small paddle boat with pedals you use to propel it, usually on a boating lake…' She babbled to a stop as those beautifully sculpted lips tipped up even further at the edges.

Shut up, Cassie, why are you composing an encyclopaedia entry on pedalos for him?

'Interesting,' he said, even though they both knew what she'd just said wasn't interesting in the slightest. 'You're British, right?'

'What gave me away?' she asked, and the appreciation

in his eyes added a spurt of exhilaration to the tangle of nerves in her belly.

She took another hasty sip of the champagne to calm them. It didn't work.

'The cute accent,' he said, with that dangerous gaze roaming over her face. 'And the peaches and cream complexion.'

Her peaches and cream complexion heated accordingly.

'You blush real prettily too, *cher*,' he added.

Her cheeks promptly ignited.

The sun had dipped behind the headland in the distance and a row of flaming torches was now lighting the gardens edged by a lavish arboretum—expertly planted with everything from Mesoamerican ferns to African impatiens, according to the plaques Cassie had read while trying to pluck up the courage to talk to strangers. But even in the glow of twilight Luke Broussard had to be able to see her blush. The fact that he seemed to be enjoying her gaucheness wasn't making Cassie feel any less out of her depth.

'What does that mean?' she asked, trying to steer the conversation back to neutral territory and give herself time to get her breathing back on track. *'Shar?'* she asked, struggling to pronounce the word he'd used. 'It sounds French.'

'Cher?' he said again, and she nodded. 'It's Louisiana French, or French Cajun. I'm from the bayou originally—a sleepy little town just outside Lafayette.'

It was more information than she'd been able to glean about him online, but as she tried to think of a follow-up question his emerald-green irises darkened to a rich jade.

'And *cher* is Cajun for *cherie*...which is what you call a lady when you like the way she blushes.'

'Oh,' she managed, and her next question was drowned out by the thunder of her heartbeat.

Was Luke Broussard hitting on her? It seemed so outside the realms of possibility that she didn't know what to do with the information. Other than pray it didn't send her pulse-rate any further into the red zone. Passing out would definitely not be good.

She knew she wasn't a troll, and that Ashling's dress was doing its best to advertise every single one of her assets. But right now she really wished she had a lot more sexual experience than a few unimpressive kisses at college… For example, was the heavy weight now wedged between her thighs and pulsing in time with her heartbeat normal?

She'd always assumed she wasn't a sexual person. And she had always thought she preferred it that way. Her career was all she needed, because it defined her and motivated her and gave her life meaning and purpose.

But that had been before she'd stood in the glow of firelight, inhaled the scent of salt water and rose petals and pine soap carried on the summer breeze off San Francisco Bay, and felt a strange thrill charge through her system as Luke Broussard's attention—and those playful green eyes—focussed solely on her.

She couldn't think clearly…couldn't feel anything but the prickle of sensation awakening every one of her nerve-endings…and couldn't say anything except, 'That's…very sweet.'

Broussard's brows shot up, and he barked out an astonished laugh. 'Fair warning…' His gaze darkened as he traced his fingertip over her burning cheek. 'No woman has ever accused me of being sweet, *cher*.'

The casual endearment sounded anything but sweet in his deep, husky purr, and the torturously light touch ignited the weight between her thighs.

'My name's Luke Broussard,' he said. 'Of Broussard

Tech,' he added, as if there was any need—surely everyone in San Francisco knew who he was?

'I know,' she said.

'That leaves me at a disadvantage. Because I don't know who you are.'

'Cassandra James. I work for Zachary Temple at Temple Corp as his executive assistant.'

She bit her tongue the minute the words were out of her mouth. Should she have told him that? After all she was supposed to be here incognito, until Temple made a decision on her investment report's recommendations.

To her relief, he seemed unfazed by the information.

'Temple Corp, huh? I've heard of them,' he said.

She remembered he had no way of knowing yet that Temple was considering investing in his company. Her panic downgraded a notch.

Until he asked, 'So how do you know Remy and Matt?'

Anxiety kicked in as she struggled to recall the story she'd invented on her eleven-hour flight. But then something Ashling had once said to her—after they had sneaked out of her father's stultifying house one Saturday, for a day of adventure in Soho, and ended up getting interrogated by her governess—rippled through her consciousness…

'If you have to tell a lie, I've heard it's better to stick to the truth as much as possible.'

'Actually, I don't know the grooms,' she confided. 'I'm here as Temple's representative. He wanted to pay his respects, but he couldn't make it himself.'

Which wasn't actually a lie. Temple Corp *was* one of Remy Carlton and Matt Donnelly's biggest clients, because Temple always preferred to use their boutique hotels whenever he travelled, and his invitation to the wedding had been entirely genuine.

Broussard nodded, but a small frown appeared on his brow. 'That's a thing now?'

'What's a thing?' she asked, panicked again by his sceptical look. She really was not cut out for industrial espionage, however slight. It was already hard enough to keep hold of the conversation when the sensation now sprinting up her spine was turning her nipples into lethal weapons.

Please don't let him notice I'm not wearing a bra.

'Getting your executive assistant to stand in for you at social events,' Broussard supplied, then gave another of those rough chuckles which tickled her right down to her toes. 'I need to get me an executive assistant like you. I hate being sociable.'

'Are you kidding? You're a lot better at it than I am,' she said bluntly, her guilty conscience loosening her tongue.

This time he threw back his head to laugh, giving her a glimpse of the strong column of his throat and the tattoo peeking above the open collar of his shirt.

That strange bubble of exhilaration burst in her chest when that dangerous green gaze met hers again and she saw approval in his eyes.

'Has anyone ever told you you're super-cute, Cassandra?'

Efficient? Professional? Smart? Boringly conventional? Yes. Super-cute...?

'Um...no, never.'

He continued to chuckle, his playful grin making his rugged features look almost boyish. 'Have you ever been to the city before?'

'No, I've never been to Frisco before,' she said.

'I can tell,' he said, wincing theatrically.

'How?' she asked, mesmerised all over again by the approving look.

'If you'd ever been before you'd know what the locals think of that nickname.'

'Frisco is bad?' she asked.

'Frisco can get you a one-way ticket to Alcatraz. I found that out the hard way when I moved here.'

'Good to know.' She grinned.

Were they flirting? Why had she never tried this before? It was actually fun. And she wasn't as horrendous at it as she had assumed.

'How about we get the hell out of here?' he said as he lifted her now empty glass from her numb fingers. He placed it and his own on a wooden bench. 'Seeing as being social really isn't our thing, I could show you the city they don't call Frisco.'

The husky intimacy in his tone, and the intensity darkening his gaze to a rich emerald, made it clear that the offer was loaded with all sorts of possibilities—not one of them safe.

For a fleeting moment it occurred to her that accepting Luke Broussard's offer would be the perfect opportunity to find out more about him for Temple… But she knew that wasn't why she wanted to say yes.

She felt light-headed, detached from reality. Every practical and pragmatic consideration in her head was becoming soft and fuzzy and insubstantial as a heady shot of adrenaline powered through her veins.

She studied his outstretched hand—capable, tanned, scarred—and the reckless streak she hadn't even known she had shot through her like a drug.

And then she remembered what Ash had said what seemed like a million years ago in London.

'There's nothing wrong with mixing business and pleasure occasionally.'

Why not take him up on his offer? There was no reason she shouldn't enjoy herself while she found out a bit more about him. *It's just a drive.*

She raised her gaze to Luke's and had the strangest sensation that she was about to step off a cliff. But before she could second-guess herself, she placed her hand in his. 'Yes, I'd like to.'

His hand wrapped around her fingers and he lifted them to his lips. The chivalrous gesture was comprehensively contradicted by the heated purpose in his gaze when he murmured something in heavily accented French.

'Laissez les bon temps rouler.'

She had no clue what the words meant. But as he led her through the crowd the jolt of adrenaline became turbo-charged.

CHAPTER TWO

Spellbound.

That's what he was.

Luke figured he probably ought to be disturbed by how much he had wanted Cassandra James to say yes. But as he placed his hand on her lower back and handed his ticket to the valet, and she shuddered violently, he found it hard to give a damn.

He hadn't discovered a thing about her except that she was British, and she worked for a British billionaire investor whom he'd heard of but didn't know much about. But that didn't stop his yearning to place his lips on the nape of her neck below her hairline and inhale her scent.

Even gilded by the dusk, that killer blush still ignited her cheeks. Cassandra James presented a challenge—a challenge he hadn't even known he wanted. She seemed unable to hide her physical response to him, and he sensed she lacked the sexual confidence of the women he usually dated.

He had no idea why he found that so refreshing. He wasn't a guy who had ever prized honesty when it came to dating—everyone had their secrets, him most of all, and he respected that, understood it. Sex didn't mean intimacy—certainly not where he was concerned—but she excited him on more than just a physical level.

The valet pulled up at the kerb, riding the vintage 955cc motorbike Luke had reconditioned himself last winter.

Cassandra swung her head round, her golden eyes widening to saucer-size. 'You're not serious? I can't ride that.'

He chuckled—he couldn't help it. Her shocked expression was as hot as her slight pout of disappointment.

'Sure you can. I have a spare helmet,' he said, as he handed a hundred-dollar bill to the valet.

'How much change do you need, sir?' the boy asked.

'None, kid. I'm trying to impress the lady here.'

The boy grinned as he pocketed the cash, the flush of pleasure on his face more than worth the money. 'Yes, sir, and thank you, sir. That's the biggest tip I've had all night.'

'I'll bet,' he replied. 'Working service jobs for rich folks never tips as good as it should—am I right?'

'It does now, sir,' the boy said, still grinning as he saluted him before heading off to deal with another couple who had just arrived in the parking lot.

'That was very generous of you,' Cassandra remarked.

'Like I said, I was trying to impress you,' he replied, and her gaze was so rich with appreciation it suddenly didn't feel like a joke any more.

'You succeeded,' she said, but then she tilted her head to one side and added, 'But that's not why you did it. You enjoyed putting that smile on his face. Did you work a lot of service jobs before you founded Broussard Tech?'

It was a probing question—the kind he usually avoided answering. He never talked about his past. He also didn't much like being figured out so easily. Since when had he become so transparent? But, even so, her expression—perceptive but also impressed—had the truth coming out.

'My fair share. And my takeaway was, the richer the customer, the more invisible you become.'

'But not to you?'

He hesitated, taken aback not just by the appreciation in her voice, but by the way it made him feel. His heart pulsed too hard in his chest. He braced himself against the uncomfortable sensation.

Time to get this seduction back on track. He didn't need to impress her—he just needed to persuade her to get on the bike. Hot and giddy was what he wanted…sincere and genuine not so much.

He unbuckled the bike's saddlebag and pulled out the helmets. 'Here you go,' he said as he offered her one.

She tucked her bottom lip under her teeth, sending another jolt of heat straight through him.

'I really don't think I can… I've never ridden a motorcycle before. Isn't it dangerous?'

Yeah, but not in the way you think.

'That's all part of the rush,' he said.

She still looked unsure, her hands clasped behind her back as if she were determined not to take the bait, however much she might want to.

Inspiration struck.

'How about we try this?' he said, then plucked the pins out of her hair.

'Oh!' Her hands flew up to save her hairdo, but it was already too late, and the fragrant mass was tumbling down over her bare shoulders.

He laughed. 'How about, if you come for a ride on my bike, I do something I've never done before, too?'

She frowned, her confused expression only making her more adorable.

'Well, I don't see how that's going to work. I bet there isn't anything you've never done.'

Smart girl.

'Not true.' He stifled a chuckle as he racked his brains

to think of something that would work. 'I've never let a lady ride on my bike before. How about that?'

'Really?' she said, and he could see the astonishment in her eyes, and then the pleasure.

The reaction should have made him uncomfortable. He didn't like to give a woman the impression she was special or different, because it might lead to misunderstandings. But the truth was he'd never wanted a woman on the back of his bike before now.

He got a kick out of riding the vintage machine through the city solo whenever he was in town. He'd always been a loner. But wanting to share it with her didn't have to mean anything. He needed to kick her out of her comfort zone, so he had no problem taking a small step outside his own.

'Yeah, really,' he confirmed. 'You'll be my first passenger.'

The emotion on her face made his heartbeat uneven as he waited for her answer.

'Okay, you're on,' she said, with a determined expression which was half-excitement and half-terror. 'Give me the helmet,' she added, holding out her hand.

'Let me,' he said, scooping her chestnut locks into his fist, no longer able to resist the desire to touch her. Her hair whispered against his palm, soft and silky, but he had to let it go after he'd placed the helmet on her head, to clip the chin buckle and adjust the straps for a snug fit.

'I bet I look completely ridiculous,' she said as he put on his own helmet.

'Not at all,' he said, stifling the urge to kiss her.

He needed to take this slow. He knew anything worth having was worth working for. And Cassandra James definitely ticked that box.

The sea breeze fluttered the ends of her hair peeking out from underneath the helmet and she shivered. He shrugged out of his tux jacket and placed it over her bare shoulders. 'Here, put this on—it might get chilly.'

She wasn't a short woman, but even so his jacket engulfed her. Sadly, it covered up her magnificent breasts in that clingy material, but he forced himself not to sulk. If his luck held tonight, and their chemistry proved as strong as it seemed, he would get a much better look soon enough.

'Now I *know* I look ridiculous,' she said, rolling up the sleeves. 'But thank you.'

He climbed aboard the bike, adjusted the throttle and kick-started the engine.

She jumped and he grinned. 'Don't worry. I promise it won't bite.'

Even if I do.

'I don't even know how to mount it,' she said, all practical as she chewed off the last of her lipstick.

He had to force his gaze off her reddened bottom lip and ignore the swift kick to his gut.

Whoa, buster, no dirty thoughts while driving or you'll wipe out.

'Gather your gown up,' he said, 'and tuck it under your knees when you get seated. We don't want it snagging on anything. There's a pedal there to stand on and mount up.'

She nodded, her frown making his lust kick again. He was treated to an impressive display of long, toned thigh before she put one foot on the pedal and flung her other leg over the bike. Grasping his shoulders, she bounced up behind him.

'Hang on tight,' he said, and her slender arms banded around his waist.

Her soft breasts flattened against his back, and the kick burned down to his crotch. Heck, he needed to get his response under control, or this ride was going to be torture.

Her helmet clicked the back of his.

'Oops, sorry,' she said. 'Are you sure you want to do this? I'm a complete novice.'

Her thighs hugged his butt, and it was all he could do not to weep.

'Positive,' he groaned.

Revving the engine, he settled his hand on her bare knee and gave it a reassuring squeeze—then he let her go, before the sizzle against his palm could add to the torture.

'Just remember to lean with me on the turns. I'll take it slow at first, until you get the hang of it. If there's a problem, yell.'

Her helmet clicked his again as she nodded.

'All set, *cher*?' he asked.

'As I'll ever be,' she yelled, above the rumble of the bike's engine.

He peeled the bike away from the kerb and heard her shocked gasp, felt her breath hot against his nape, her arms locking tighter around his waist.

The grin that split his face as they headed down the street made him wonder why the heck he hadn't thought of taking a woman for a ride on his bike before now.

'Oh, my goodness,' she said, as she clung on and he whipped around the traffic on Lincoln Way.

She tightened her grip again when he hung a left on Clayton. Her intoxicating scent mixed with the aroma of exhaust fumes and stale weed as he slowed the bike to a crawl to turn at the busy intersection into Haight Street.

'This is Haight-Ashbury!' he yelled over his shoulder. 'Where the tourists come to celebrate the Summer of Love a half-century too late.'

She giggled, the light musical sound floating on the night air. 'I feel like I should start singing a Bob Dylan song!' she shouted back.

He laughed as a shiver of sensation shot down his spine.

And suddenly he knew why he'd never offered another woman a ride on his bike. Because no woman had ever captivated him the way she had.

And he hadn't even tasted her yet.

Cassie caught her breath as they entered the old hippie neighbourhood she'd read about in a guidebook on the plane but never imagined she'd have a chance to visit. Neon signs announced tattoo parlours, thrift stores and record shops, while young people spilled out of bars and restaurants dressed in a rainbow of psychedelic colours.

She absorbed every detail, astonished that even fifty-plus years after its heyday the area could still seem edgy and exciting. But as the muscles in Luke's back tensed, she wondered if that edgy feeling came from the neighbourhood or simply from the thrill of being on Luke Broussard's bike as they rode through Haight-Ashbury.

Unlike Ashling, she'd never been the cool girl at school, or anywhere else for that matter, but she felt like the cool girl now. For one night only.

As they left the born-again hippies of Haight-Ashbury behind, the bike climbed up a hill that cut through a lush, surprisingly untamed park.

Luke slowed the bike to a stop when they reached the top and pulled off his helmet, then glanced over his shoulder. 'Hop off. I've got something to show you.'

'Okay…' She scrambled off the bike. Her pulse started to pound again as he unclipped her helmet and hooked it over the bike handles with his own.

'Where are we going?' she asked breathlessly.

'You'll see,' he said, sending her a sultry smile that had all her pheromones going haywire again. How did he *do* that? Was the guy a sex whisperer, or something? Because she'd never felt this giddy before in her entire life.

She stored the thought away as he gripped her hand and led her past a sign that announced the park as the oldest in San Francisco. They took a path that led into the greenery.

'Should you leave the helmets on the bike like that? Won't they get stolen?' she asked, trying to find some semblance of her usual practicality.

He sent her a wry grin, as if she'd said something cute, then shrugged. 'We won't be long—but anyhow I've got others.'

Well, of course he has. The man's a billionaire, Cassie, for goodness' sake.

She tried not to fixate on the heat now running riot through her body as they reached a clearing. Then he gripped her shoulders, stood behind her and twisted her round.

'Check that out,' he said.

But her breath had already caught in her lungs.

The city was laid out before them in a carpet of lights, just starting to wink on as night fell. The staggering view spread across the dark expanse of the bay, where the white lights of the Golden Gate Bridge shone like a runway leading to the opposite shore.

'Wow!' she murmured, so awed and humbled that all she could feel was the clamour of her heartbeat in her throat. 'It's so beautiful. You must adore living here,' she managed, desperately trying to keep talking to curtail the foolish spurt of emotion.

No man had ever shown her something so magnificent. And she'd only just met him.

But why had he?

'I don't live in the city,' he said, his voice so low and husky she could feel it rippling down her back and detonating in her abdomen.

'You don't?' She twisted to see his face, illuminated by the glow from the sunset. 'But why not? It's wonderful.'

'I keep an apartment here,' he said. 'But it's not my home.'

'Where is your home?' she asked, suddenly desperate to know more about him. Much more. And knowing that it had nothing whatsoever to do with her report, because she'd stopped thinking about what Temple had asked her to do a thousand giddy heartbeats ago.

'I own an island off the Oregon coast.'

He frowned, and she got the impression he hadn't meant to tell her. But before she had a chance to worry about whether she had probed too much he took her hand again and led her back down the path they'd just climbed.

'Where are we going now?' she asked, feeling like a child—carefree and excited—which was rather ironic, given that as a child she'd always been the opposite… weighed down by worries and anxiety.

'I've got something else I think you'll enjoy,' he said, without revealing much at all.

She climbed back aboard the bike, her heartbeat skipping and jumping as he put her helmet on again. She clung to him, feeling like a pro now at leaning on the turns as they headed off into the dusk.

The bike made its way back down the hillside, winding through steep residential streets lined with San Francisco's signature bay-fronted wooden terraced houses, eventually coming to a busy two-lane road that headed through another park.

As they travelled down towards the bay, dodging cars and lorries in the snarled evening traffic, it occurred to her that she'd never allowed herself to be led anywhere before now. But as she clung to Luke's broad frame, and inhaled his clean, masculine scent, the thrill of rebellion intoxicated her.

Darkness descended as they entered a traffic tunnel, and when they emerged, her heartbeat slammed into her tonsils.

The Golden Gate Bridge towered above them, the lights from the evening traffic giving the magnificent steel structure an eerie red glow, silhouetted against the dying day. An eighteen-wheeler rumbled as they flew past it, and she stole a glance over her shoulder to see the city stacked like children's building blocks on the hillside behind them.

She sheltered behind Luke's broad back and imagined them taking flight across San Francisco Bay into the erotic dream which had blindsided her.

She wasn't Cassandra James, smart and supremely efficient executive assistant who always kept her mind on business any more. She was Cassandra James, free spirit and all-round badass.

The journey seemed to take for ever and yet no time at all. Hills shaped like sleeping giants formed the dark shoreline ahead as the suspension bridge's final supporting strut passed over their heads. They took a series of twists and turns off the main road, through manicured parks and down dark roads, to a marina covered in mist.

Luke parked the bike at the end of the point and the engine powered down as they sat in the darkness alone together, next to a small grove of palm trees. The light from a waterfront diner and the distant beat of dance music spilled into the quiet night.

Luke lifted off his helmet and hooked it over the handlebars, then twisted round to unclip hers.

'Hop down,' he said, and she suddenly wondered if she'd done something wrong, because his voice was no longer relaxed, and the playfulness had vanished from his eyes.

She had to hold on to his shoulder to get her leg over, dismounting in a tangle of gold *lamé* which only made her feel more self-conscious.

She stood shivering in his jacket, the warm weight of it reminding her of the heady scent which had engulfed her when he'd draped it over her shoulders what felt like a lifetime ago. On that other girl. The dull rule-follower who would never have got on a bike with a guy she'd just met in a million years.

She waited for him to dismount and tuck the helmets in the saddlebag, wrapping her arms around herself to stave off a shudder of inadequacy.

'Is something wrong?' she asked.

His head rose and his eyes flared. 'Yeah, actually there is.'

Then, to her utter surprise, he snagged her wrist and drew her into his arms. Suddenly she was surrounded by his warmth, his heat, the heady scent of soap and man and sea water. A pulse of need throbbed viciously as his gaze raked over her and one strong hand cradled her face.

'I want to kiss you so bad I can't think straight…'

The husky murmur was so full of need and intensity it seemed to reverberate in her sex.

'And I sure as hell can't drive.' His mouth hovered over hers and he whispered, 'Tell me you want to kiss me too, Cassandra.'

She could have said no. Maybe should have said no. But it would have been a lie.

'Yes.'

In less than a heartbeat his mouth found hers. The kiss was warm, firm, uncompromising. But where she would have expected him to be demanding he was coaxing… where she would have expected practised moves she got the thrill of desperation.

No man had ever kissed her before with such fervour, such yearning. His tongue delved deep, dancing with hers, licking and feasting, tasting and tantalising, until she was clinging to him even tighter and harder than she had as they'd flown across the bay.

Sensations bombarded her—all of them novel and intoxicating—and this time the weightless sensation in her stomach became swifter, sharper and more brutal, the longing so real and vivid it was painful.

He tore his mouth away first, then opened the lapels of his jacket to wrap his arms around her waist and draw her against his body. The insistent edge of his erection pressed into her belly through their clothing. But what would once have shocked her only excited her more.

Why did this feel so right? So new and exciting? Why did tonight feel like a night out of time? Was it the jet lag? That one Aperol Spritz and those few sips of champagne? The tour of the city? The beauty of that magnificent view and the wild ride that had followed? Or was it simply the heady feeling of being wanted so desperately and knowing she wanted with the same urgency in return?

'My seaplane's docked here. I can call you a cab back to your hotel, or you can come with me to Sunrise Island tonight.'

He ran his thumb down the side of her face and the whisper of sensation intensified the longing now charging through her veins.

'One night,' he said. 'And I'll bring you back tomorrow morning.'

The implication was clear. This didn't mean more to him than slaking this raw, shocking need which had sprung from nowhere.

She stifled the foolish sting of disappointment and whispered, 'I've never done anything like this before.'

'Like what?' he asked.

Had a one-night hook-up... Or any hook-up at all, for that matter.

The answer seemed too compromising—and embarrassing. Would he change his mind if he knew she had no experience?

'I've never done something so spontaneous,' she said, settling for a less revealing answer which was no less true.

He chuckled, that low, husky laugh she had begun to adore.

'Then you're way overdue, *cher*.'

He lifted her hand to his mouth, spread open her fingers and bit gently into the swell of flesh beneath her thumb. The sharp nip sent sensation tearing through the last of her self-control.

Her fingertips skimmed the rough stubble on his jaw as his gaze locked on hers, dark with desire.

'If we do it right,' he said, 'the only consequence will be *bon temps*. Good times. I swear.' His gaze remained locked on hers. 'And I *know* we're gonna do it right.'

Before she could give herself too long to think—to plan or regret or become that dull rule-follower again—she nodded. 'I'd love to go with you.'

'Good,' he said, and excitement dropped like a stealth bomb into her heart.

CHAPTER THREE

'I'VE NEVER BEEN in a seaplane before!' Cassie shouted into the microphone attached to her helmet above the rumble of the plane's engines as the floats skipped over the water and the aircraft gathered speed. 'Does that mean you owe me another first?'

Luke sent her a smile. 'Nope—because I've never had a woman in this plane before either.'

She wasn't sure she believed him, but still her heart-rate bumped in her chest as the plane rose from the water.

She gasped, and awe pressed against her ribs as the aircraft lifted over the Golden Gate Bridge. The plane tipped to the right, giving her a panoramic view of Oakland and San Francisco sprawled across the hillside, and she squinted to pick out the places he'd already taken her tonight.

Her heart catapulted into her throat for about the tenth time that evening. But it wasn't the amazing views as they headed out onto the open water, leaving the city lights scattered like stars behind them, that was taking her breath away.

The plane's wing lights lit Luke's frown of concentration as he handled the controls with practised efficiency.

Ashling would die of shock if she could see me now.

She choked off a slightly hysterical laugh. Luke turned,

pinning her again with that intense green gaze and making her insides purr along with the plane.

'All good?' he asked.

'Wonderful,' she said.

Why had she never done anything like this before?

'The coastline is breathtaking in daylight,' he said. 'Green and rugged and untamed.'

'It looks amazing at night, too,' she said, as captivated by the man beside her as she was by the breathtaking view. 'How long does it take to get to your home?' she asked, not wanting the ride to end, but at the same time eager to kiss him again and feel his hard body against hers.

If a person was going to lose her mind for a night, she couldn't imagine a more rewarding way to do it. This was so much better than trying a contraband cigarette at boarding school, or handing in an essay three hours late, or getting your flatmate to deliver your boss's tuxedo and then discovering the fallout far too late to do anything about it.

Cassie sighed, remembering the tsunami of text messages she'd found on her phone when she'd turned it on at the airport. Tons from Gwen, from her sickbed, because she'd obviously been harassed by Temple when his tuxedo had failed to show—and one from Temple.

The tux has finally landed. Don't get your flatmate to run errands for me in future.

Ashling going AWOL on her was nothing new, but by the time Cassie had found out about the problem it had been two in the morning in the UK and there had been no point in ringing Temple to apologise profusely, or calling Ashling to give her hell for screwing up such a simple task.

So Cassie had sent Ash a text from the wedding—which

her friend would get in the morning—and then switched off her phone.

Thank goodness Temple wasn't the sort to hold a grudge. But it was funny to think that ever since Luke had approached her she'd completely forgotten about Ashling's latest *ditzkrieg.*

'It'll take about an hour to get to Sunrise Island,' he barked out over the headphones.

'I… I can't wait to see it. Is there a reason why you decided to settle there?' she asked, making desperate small talk again, trying to ignore the sudden drop in her stomach.

Am I actually doing this? Travelling to a private island for a one-night stand?

The hum of the engine cut through the silence. She turned to look at him, wondering at the sudden pause in the conversation, only to realise he had the same frown on his face he'd had back in the park, when he'd told her about his island home.

'I like my privacy,' he said at last.

The rest of the journey went by in a haze of stunning night-time views as the coastline meandered north. The lights marking their way in the darkness turned from clusters into sprinkles as they journeyed into Oregon. But as Cassie stared at the coastline the buoyant sensation which had been driving her decisions all evening turned into a leaden lump in the pit of her stomach…

'I like my privacy.'

What was she actually doing? Taking him up on the offer of a one-night stand when the reason she was in San Francisco, the reason why she'd been at the wedding of his friends in the first place, wasn't as it appeared to him?

Should she tell him about Temple's interest in investing in Broussard Tech? Wouldn't it be hopelessly unprofessional to bring up work now?

Yeah, Cassie, almost as unprofessional as climbing aboard his bike, kissing him senseless and agreeing to spend the night with him on his private island?

She blinked into the darkness, her newfound adventurous streak tempered by a cold, harsh dose of reality. And the spontaneous choice she had made at the marina didn't seem quite so simple any more.

After landing Jezebel on the sheltered east side of Sunrise Island, Luke drove the plane into the small secluded cove below the house. The right float bumped against the dock as a sprinkle of rain hit the fuselage.

'A storm's brewing.' He glanced at his passenger, who had been silent for the last half-hour of their journey. She hadn't been the only one.

Why the heck had he invited her to Sunrise? It had been a spur-of-the-moment decision driven by an organ other than his brain—and by the transparent wonder on her face when he'd shown her the city view from his favourite spot in Buena Vista Park.

Something about her unguarded, refreshingly artless reaction had made him want to show her more. And the next thing he knew he'd been heading across the bay towards Sausalito.

He had a penthouse condo in San Francisco less than a mile from the Botanical Gardens. A nice place—sleek and modern and expertly furnished at an eye-watering cost by an award-winning design team in one of the city's snootiest neighbourhoods. It was the place he always took the women he dated.

But once they'd got across the bridge the feel of her wrapped around him like superglue had driven him a little nuts, and he'd found himself taking the road to the marina where he had his plane docked.

Now her small white teeth worried at her bottom lip and the heat landed back in his lap.

Not much point trying to figure out the dumb decision to bring her to Sunrise now. With a storm brewing they were stuck here for the night, so they might as well make the most of it.

'We should probably get inside before the storm hits,' he said, unclipping his belt. 'The weather in this region can get nasty fast,' he added, unfastening her belt too, because she'd made no move to do it herself.

He turned to open the door to the aircraft and she grasped his forearm.

'Wait, Luke. I need to tell you something,' she said, and the glare from the plane's interior lights illuminated the shadows in her eyes before her gaze darted away. 'Something I should have made clear to you before I agreed to come here…'

She looked more than worried now. She looked guilty and freaked out.

The heat twisted and burned in his gut. But a kick of disgust at himself wasn't far behind, reminding him of a man he had always despised.

'Hey, Cassandra,' he said, touching her chin and lifting her head so their gazes connected. 'There's no pressure here.' His gaze dipped to take in the hint of cleavage revealed by his open jacket as he reminded himself what tonight was really all about. 'I'm not gonna lie…' He took a deep breath, deciding to give it to her straight. 'I want to explore every inch of you tonight, and make you moan and sigh and gasp a lot more…' His lips quirked as hot colour flooded into her face. 'And make you blush so hard your cheeks feel like they're on fire.'

'Actually, they already are,' she murmured.

The wry rejoinder surprised a laugh out of him in the

middle of his big speech. He touched his thumb to her burning cheek and grinned, happy to be back on solid ground. Their chemistry was real and immense—this invitation wasn't about anything more than that.

'Yeah, I can tell,' he said. 'But here's the thing,' he added. 'You don't owe me anything. There's five bedrooms in my home and no expectation that the one you sleep in tonight has to be mine. You got that?'

He forced himself to drop his hand. If she was having second thoughts he wasn't going to pressure her either way—because that would make this more than it was.

'I…' She blinked, looking taken aback. 'That's very gallant of you,' she said.

Gallant? What the...?

He choked out a laugh, relieving some of the tension snapping in his gut.

'What's so funny,' she asked, her clear-eyed pragmatism something he was becoming addicted to.

'That's another first for me,' he said. 'No woman's ever called me gallant before, either. Now you owe *me* a first.'

'Are you sure?' she asked, looking genuinely surprised. 'I suspect a lot of less gallant men *would* have expectations after flying a woman several hundred miles for a hook-up.'

Another laugh escaped on a spontaneous bark of amusement, but beneath it was a strange feeling of uneasiness. 'Yeah, I'm one hundred and one per cent positive no woman's ever even *thought* of me as gallant before,' he said.

'Then they were fools,' she said, outraged on his behalf.

'But you still owe me,' he said, to keep things light as the weird clutching sensation he'd felt earlier—when she'd been so impressed with his hundred-buck gratuity, and again when she'd looked at him as if he'd given her something precious in Buena Vista Park—returned.

He wasn't gallant—not even close. And he didn't want

to be. He took her hand in his and lifted her fingers to his lips. Time to get the night back on track. If she wanted gallant, he knew how to fake it.

'So, are we good to go?' he asked, lifting his eyebrows in a deliberately lascivious way that had her choking out another of those musical giggles.

'I don't think that was ever in doubt,' she said, but then the blush seemed to intensify again. 'But that's not what I wanted to talk to you about. It's to do with my work for Zachary Temple and Temple Corp.' She tugged her fingers from his, stumbling over the words. 'I'm here to—' He touched his finger to her lips to cut her off.

'Shh…' he said. 'It doesn't matter,' he added.

He'd heard of the British billionaire businessman's reputation as a smart investor. Once upon a time Luke would have had to go cap in hand to a guy like him. But not any more. Not since he'd taken his company global and pushed his income and his industry cachet into the stratosphere. Thank the lord.

Perhaps she figured he was planning to prise information out of her about her boss? Or pitch for investment.

He should be insulted. He didn't need investment, or to impress men like Temple any more. And he sure as heck didn't need to mix business with booty calls. Broussard Tech had taken the tech industry by storm because it produced quality, innovative, unique products. Not because he used sex to further his business interests.

But, strangely, he wasn't insulted—he suspected her hesitancy wasn't because she was judging him, but because she was judging herself. He'd never met a woman before who was such a knockout but seemed so unaware of it.

He guessed it was one of the things he found so refreshing about her. But he did not want her nerves getting in the way of their booty call. Especially with the rain lashing against the fuselage as the storm arrived in earnest.

'Are you sure?' she said. 'I don't want to sleep with you under false pretences.'

Oh, for the love of...

'Cassandra,' he said, trying to sound firm, when the words 'sleep with you' in that prim UK accent had made the heat pounding in his pants hit critical mass. 'There's gonna be nothing false about tonight. As far as I'm concerned we left our professional interests back in San Francisco. Anything that happens tonight is between us and only us. You got that?'

She tugged at her lip again with her teeth, torturing him for one more excruciating moment, but then she nodded. 'Okay…if you're sure.'

'I'm sure.' He grasped her hand and tugged her across the console. 'Now, let's get up to the house before we drown.'

Cassie raced up the slick stone steps cut into the cliff-face behind Luke.

She was soaked through in seconds, but it was a warm, revitalising rain, washing away the guilt and the hesitation and leaving behind a freshness, a newness, and a woman committed to making tonight a memory to savour.

The relief was immense—but not nearly as immense as the tidal wave of excitement which swept over her as Luke's house appeared out of the mist and rain, lit by the same solar-powered flares illuminating the steps up from the dock.

The Pacific Ocean churned below them as the wind picked up its pace and the storm arrived in all its glory. The sleek modern structure of glass and steel, redwood and granite, rose out of the rock face in stacked terraces, blending into the surrounding landscape of dense forest and millennia-old volcanic rock.

Oh... My.

She imagined the structure would be glorious in the daylight, when the waves crashed against the rocks, framing its magnificent view over the ocean, but at night it looked dramatic and daring.

Her heartbeat bumped into her throat, and her breathing turned into staggered pants as they reached an arched doorway. Sheltering her with his body, Luke tapped out a code on a security panel. The rain dripped off his brow and soaked into his shirt to reveal the shadow of chest hair and the bulge of muscle and sinew beneath.

The steel entrance door slid open. He dragged her in behind him and flicked a switch. A series of low lights revealed the cathedral-like drama of the living area—two storeys high and fronted by a wall of glass—at the end of the short redwood entrance hall. Cassie glimpsed sunken sofas surrounding a granite firepit, a state-of-the-art kitchen area and an open staircase leading up to a mezzanine.

Luke Broussard's home made a statement, like the man himself. Both were unique and bold and breathtaking.

The entrance door slid closed, shutting out the roar of the storm, and all she could focus on was the distant rattle of water cascading down glass and the staggered sound of her own breathing. And his.

Luke tugged her round to face him. Her gaze became fixated on the magnificent contours of his torso revealed by the translucent shirt.

'You good?' he asked, as his thumb wiped the water from her lips.

'Yes.' The vicious shudder which racked her body had nothing to do with the clammy feel of her soaked clothing, and everything to do with the fire his touch ignited. 'You have an incredible home,' she added, dislodging his hand, desperate to fill the charged silence.

'Glad you approve,' he said, his wry tone turning the shudder of need into something absolutely terrifying.

What on earth was she doing here? She didn't know the first thing about having epic sex. Or even about having one-night stands. She'd never even made love with anyone before, and certainly not with a man as overwhelming as this man.

Had she set herself up to fail? Spectacularly?

What if she disappointed him? What if she disappointed herself?

Seriously, Cassie, what the heck were you thinking? You're not a free spirit. Or a sexual adventurer. You're a boring workaholic who doesn't know the first thing about satisfying herself, let alone satisfying a man like Luke Broussard.

'Hey.' Grasping her chin between his thumb and forefinger, he brought her gaze back to his. 'I can see you overthinking again.'

A laugh escaped. 'It's what I do best,' she said.

His hand slid down to capture her neck. He nudged her back against the wooden wall of the entrance hall. She could smell him, heat and arousal and pine soap, above the scent of wood resin and fresh rain. Her hands settled on his waist, absorbing the tension in his abs and sending a shock of longing straight to her sex.

His mouth lowered to hers. She stared at his face, the yearning as intense as the fear now.

'Close your eyes, Cassandra,' he demanded, and she obeyed.

Then his lips were on hers at last. She let out a small

sob, welcoming him in instinctively. He cupped her cheeks and angled her head so he could delve deeper.

And as he devoured her, every thought, every feeling blasted out of her head bar one.

I want this. I want him. It doesn't matter if I muck it up.

The liberating thought loosened her tongue to tangle with his. Fire spiked in her sex and at every point where their bodies touched as she gave herself permission to fail, for the first time in her life.

He dragged his sodden jacket off her shoulders and dropped it on the hall floor. Grasping her waist, he lifted her, his mouth leaving hers to growl, 'Wrap your legs around me.'

Again she did as she was told, clinging to his broad shoulders as he marched them both across the living area and up the open staircase.

The rain pounded the glass in undulating waves, like the tsunami of sensation battering her body. Hunger surged as they reached the mezzanine level.

A flash of lightning outside revealed a staggering view of the inlet below them and the storm-tossed forest. The trees bowed and buckled against the wind. The turbulent weather and the magnificent sight of nature reaching its nadir was almost as dramatic as the clatter of her heartbeat.

She usually hated the dark. A silly lay-over from childhood which had always embarrassed her. But the usual anxiety failed to materialise now, as her excitement spiked.

He barged backwards into a room off the landing and shouted. 'Lights on!'

The sudden glare illuminated a stunning if sparsely furnished room, dominated by a view of the ocean and the distant sprinkle of lights along the Oregon shoreline miles away. Then Cassie caught sight of her reflection in the dark glass. She buried her face against his neck to hide her burning blush. With her clothes and hair drenched, she was a total mess.

But the moment of panicked vanity lasted less than a second when he murmured, 'Lower...' and the lights dipped to a shadowy glow.

He put her down, still holding her waist. Her legs wobbled, unsteady, unsure. But then his mouth returned to hers—firm, commanding, uncompromising—telling her in no uncertain terms how much he wanted this. How much he wanted her.

He took control, his hands exploring her curves, and exploiting the dazzle of sensation across her chilled skin. She followed his lead, threading her fingers into his wet hair, loving the feel of his hard body against hers.

Thank goodness someone knew what he was doing.

He broke away and his questing fingers paused. He stared at her, his face shadowed by the soft light but fierce with need, and she felt a residual flicker of panic. Had he already figured out what a fraud she was?

'How the hell do I get you out of this thing?' he asked.

The frustration in his voice had a laugh popping out alongside her relief. 'Here,' she said, and lifted her arm to locate the tab.

But before she could lower the zip he took charge again. 'No, let me. I've been dreaming of peeling you out of this all night.'

She nodded and let go, exhilarated by the sharp concentration on his face as he eased the zip down. He skimmed his fingertips over her shoulders to push the dress's straps off. The flash of hunger and desire that darkened his expression only vindicated her more.

No hesitations, Cassie. No regrets.

The gold *lamé*, heavy with water, dropped down and snagged at her waist, leaving her breasts bare.

'No bra…'

He groaned, the sound deep and feral. She crossed her arms over her nakedness instinctively.

'Don't…' he murmured, the word half-command, half-plea.

Taking her wrists gently in his, he lifted her arms free, his gaze branding her. Her nipples—already pebbled from the cold—squeezed into painful peaks. He swore, and circled his thumb over one, then the other. *'Belle...'*

She shuddered, her emotion as powerful as her desire when his gaze locked on hers. Naked need echoed deep in her sex.

'You cold, *cher*?' he asked, the gruff question making it sound as if he were having trouble speaking English.

She shook her head, speech deserting her completely.

If this is just a one-night stand, why does it feel so intense?

Cradling her heavy breasts, so sensitive now that she couldn't stop shivering, he sent her a lazy smile, but fierce passion filled his eyes.

'Let's warm you up anyhow,' he said.

Then he bent his head and captured one engorged peak between firm lips.

She sobbed, her fingers sinking into his hair to drag him closer, and to keep her knees from buckling as he drew the nipple deep into his mouth. Heat cascaded through her, flooding into her core, the sensation becoming overwhelming as he feasted on the swollen flesh.

He suckled strongly, one breast then the other, until she was weak and aching with need, every point on her body desperate for something more.

At last he released her from the torture and shoved the sodden dress the rest of the way to the floor.

Kneeling, he bent his dark head to touch her belly. Then

he eased off first one sandal, then the other. He skimmed his thumb over the raw spot where the leather had rubbed her heel.

'Ouch,' he said.

But she couldn't feel the pain any more…had stopped noticing it hours ago.

Then he hooked his fingers into her lace panties and eased the damp scrap of material down her legs.

Holding on to his shoulder, she stepped out of her underwear, naked now, while he was still fully clothed.

She'd never felt more exposed, more vulnerable, before in her life. But as he stood up the yearning only pulsed harder in her sex. Her head barely reached his collarbone.

'You're wearing too many clothes,' she managed, folding her arms over her breasts, still damp from his lips.

He nodded, his eyes glassy with desire, then ripped his shirt loose from his trousers, dragged it over his head without unbuttoning it to reveal the sculpted beauty of his naked chest. The strong lines bunched as he moved. The tanned skin was marked by several small scars, and the black ink which ringed his collarbone was not barbed wire, she realised, but a tangle of thorns.

He had other tattoos. One on his bicep of a bird of some kind, and a line of text in French—or probably French Cajun—arrowing into the dark line of hair which bisected his six-pack. But before she could read the words, or attempt a translation, he kicked off his shoes, unbuckled his belt, ripped open his fly and shoved off his trousers and boxers.

Her mind blurred as his magnificent erection—hard, thick and long—stood proud from the thicket of hair at his groin.

Moisture flooded her sex and dried in her throat. She reached out to run her fingertip down the thick length.

He made a tortured sound and the massive erection jerked against her touch. But then he grabbed her wrist to pull her hand away. 'Don't…'

'I'm so sorry,' she blurted out, meeting his eyes. 'I didn't mean to…'

'Don't apologise,' he said, his tone raw. 'But we'll have to take a rain-check on the foreplay.'

A rain-check? There's going to be a next time?

Something that felt disturbingly like joy burst in her chest, but then he scooped her up and placed her onto the bed. She bounced on the coverlet, the tumultuous feeling only intensifying as the storm continued to rage outside, matching the thunder in her chest.

He knelt over her, trapping her under his big body as he reached into the bedside table and located a foil packet. He tore it open with his teeth, and she watched him sheath himself with the protection.

She braced herself, ready for him to plunge deep into her yearning sex, but instead he moved down, cradled her hips in strong hands and sank his face between her legs.

He trailed his tongue up her inner thigh, sipping and licking, and she bucked off the bed.

'Ahh…' she cried, the sound as incoherent as her thoughts, her feelings.

He parted her with his thumbs and blew on the molten bundle of nerves already throbbing painfully. Then he swirled his tongue through the slick folds.

'Please…' Her cries became louder, as she begged, so shocked by the pleasure battering her body she could hardly breathe. 'Just…'

'Just what, *cher*?' He looked up, his smile as devastating as the crash of thunder outside. 'You know you taste even better than you smell?'

'I… *Really?*' she asked, then realised how ridiculous

she sounded when he gave a deep, husky laugh. But before she could become embarrassed he licked her again—right…*there.*

She shuddered…sobbed. Then he closed his lips over the swollen nub and flicked his tongue across it. She bucked, writhed, desperate to escape the torture, but just as desperate to have it never end. He held her steady, held her open as he worked the tender nub. The wave gathered—strong, fast, too furious to bear.

Everything inside her clenched tight, bearing down. She moaned, her body arching up, bowing back, straining, desperate. Then she flew apart. The orgasm shattered her, cascading through her body like the waves crashing onto the rocks below.

She sank back to the bed, her body floating on a golden tide of afterglow.

His face appeared above her. *'Encore,'* he demanded.

He angled her hips, his erection butting against her sex. And before she had a moment to brace herself he plunged home.

She flinched, the penetration immense, the full, stretched feeling too much.

He stopped, embedded to the hilt as she struggled to adjust.

'So tight, *cher…*' he murmured, the gruff tone tortured. 'You okay?'

She nodded, her sex pulsing around the thick intrusion, the slice of pain thankfully receding.

'You're not a virgin, are you, *cher*?' he asked, and the frown was back, his tone rough with astonishment.

She shook her head vigorously, suddenly desperate not to have him know the truth or this moment would take on a far greater significant than it already had.

He waited, searching her face as he held her hips, and didn't move.

'Really, I'm not…it's just been a while,' she finally managed, hating the lie, but hating the miserable feeling of inadequacy that she remembered far too well from her childhood more.

He nodded, and at last he began to move. But emotion scraped against her throat.

The pleasure ignited again—a flicker, then a throb in the deepest recesses of her body. It built and built as he rocked his hips, finding a rhythm that propelled her with staggering speed back towards that terrifying edge.

She clung to him as she had on the bike, her fingers slipping on his sweat-slicked skin. He grunted, growing huge inside the tight sheath. Her throat closed, and she felt the emotion gathering in her chest to form a fist, punching against her ribs.

The pleasure turned to exquisite pain, hurtling towards her. So fierce, so furious, she couldn't think any more. All she could do was feel… Until the wave rammed into her at last and he made her fly once more.

CHAPTER FOUR

Ash. Help! I slept with Luke last night! Luke Broussard of Broussard Tech. The guy I'm supposed to be checking out for Temple. What do I do now? I'm freaking out. You have to help me. You so owe me, Ms Don't-Wear-a-Bra-with-That-Dress. xx

LUKE PROPPED HIS shoulder against the kitchen doorframe and watched Cassandra furiously tapping with her thumbs and chewing on her bottom lip while she typed what looked like a novel into her cell phone. She kept pausing and looking into the middle distance, then tapping some more. But he could tell by the pucker on her brow that she wasn't seeing the ocean beneath the cove, quiet now, and gilded by a bright new day after last night's storm.

His body tightened. As it had so many times during the night. He eased himself upright, careful not to make a sound. He didn't want to alert her to his presence—not yet—only too aware of the storm in his gut which still hadn't been tamed. And the storm in his chest which refused to go away.

Jesus, how could she look even more stunning, with her tangled, sleep-mussed hair tumbling over her shoulders, her bare legs going on for miles under the T-shirt she must have snagged from his dresser while he was comatose?

Heat bloomed in his gut and he tensed. By rights he should be well satisfied and still comatose. From the angle of the sun, filtering through the forest behind the house on the east side of the inlet, it wasn't much past nine. But when he'd woken up, he'd reached for her and found her gone. And then he'd seen the spots of blood on the bed sheets. And he had wondered, just as he had suspected when he'd thrust heavily inside her last night and felt her flinch… Had she been a virgin after all?

And, if so, why had she lied?

Waking up with an erection was nothing new. But why did the possibility of her virginity make it seem more intense? She might be inexperienced, but she was a grown woman. How the hell she might have managed to stay untouched for so long, he had no idea, but it was her choice—he hadn't pushed or pressured her—in fact he'd gone out of his way to do the opposite. She'd even accused him of being 'gallant' for the first time in his entire life.

He hadn't exploited her or taken anything from her she hadn't been willing to give.

And if she *had* been a virgin, it didn't make him a bad guy.

But, as he continued to watch her unobserved, something told him that for the first time in his life, with Cassandra James, all the usual rules didn't apply. She'd changed them. And he didn't like it. Because normally after a one-night booty call he'd be looking to find a way to get her out of his home without things getting too awkward. But instead all he could think about right now was walking up behind her, wrapping his arms around her waist, inhaling that glorious scent which had invaded his dreams last night and finding out if she'd picked him to be her first lover. And if she had, why had she?

But how could he do that without making this even more

intense and awkward? Even more weird? Why had he broken his own rules with her, bringing her here?

Would she expect something from him now? Something more than pleasure? Even though he hoped he'd made it clear he couldn't offer her more?

He felt a strange contraction in his chest as he imagined her turning round and opening her arms to him with the same enthusiasm and spontaneity she'd shown last night.

He frowned.

How did she do that? How did she make him forget that this situation was now all kinds of screwed up? He couldn't touch her again. It would only make him feel more invested.

Whatever happened now, he needed to lay off her until he could get her off the island.

Perhaps she was expecting him to ask again about her virginity—but he wasn't falling into that trap.

Why did it have to be a big deal? They were both adults. And the sex had been incredible. She'd been so responsive, so cute and sweet and hot and uninhibited. No reason to make this anything else than what it had always been intended to be. And if she brought it up—which she probably would eventually, because why else would she have kept her virginity a secret other than to use it at a later date—he'd tell her the truth: that her virginity was her business and had nothing to do with him.

She finally stopped tapping on her phone and placed it on the countertop. The sharp click of metal against granite echoed in the silent room. But she continued to stare at her phone as if it might leap up and bite her. Kind of the way she'd stared at the bike helmet the night before, until she'd decided to take it.

He cleared his throat, deciding it was time to stop thinking and start doing. He needed to get past the awkwardness so he could get her off his island.

She spun round. A blush blazed across her cheeks and hunger fired through his gut on cue.

He forced a smile to his lips. *Relax, man.* 'Good morning, *cher*,' he said.

Her gaze dipped to his naked chest, then shot back up again as the blush climbed to her hairline. After everything they'd done last night, he wouldn't have thought it was physically possible for her to continue to blush so readily. Unfortunately, it only confirmed what he already knew. Virgin or not, she had not been as experienced as she'd made out.

He crossed the kitchen, then sank his hands into the pockets of his sweats in order to resist the powerful urge to cradle her cheeks and feel the heat from her skin seep into his palms.

You're not gonna jump her again. Remember?

'How you doing?' he asked, because she looked hesitant—in a way she hadn't been last night.

'I'm…great, thank you,' she said, her bright tone brittle.

He let it slide and fisted his fingers in his pants' pockets to resist the powerful urge to touch.

'The storm has passed,' she said, turning to study the view as if her life depended on it.

'Yeah,' he said, studying her instead. So they were going to talk about the weather. 'Not too much damage done.'

'Do they usually?' she asked, her eyes widening as she turned back towards him. 'Cause damage? The storms? It was so overwhelming last night. I wouldn't be at all surprised.'

He wondered if they were really talking about the weather, or something else entirely, as her blush continued to glow.

'I'll need to do a thorough check before I know for sure,' he said.

The splash of colour on her cheeks went scarlet.

Nope, not talking about the weather at all.

He braced himself, waiting for her to address the huge elephant in the room.

But all she said was, 'I see.'

Her gaze skimmed over his bare chest again, and the heat in his gut blossomed. He tensed, but then his stomach rumbled loud enough to be heard in Washington State.

At least this was one hunger he could satisfy.

'You want some breakfast? I could make pancakes?' he said, then frowned.

When was the last time he had offered to cook a woman breakfast? Probably never. Especially when he was supposed to be trying to get rid of her.

'That would be wonderful, but I really don't want to put you to too much trouble before we fly back to the city.'

The casual mention of their trip back surprised him. Truth was, it should have relieved him. If she wasn't going to make a big deal about last night that was good, right? But it didn't relieve him. Somehow it just annoyed him more. She'd dropped a bombshell into their casual one-night booty call and now she thought she could just ignore it? Seriously?

'No trouble,' he said. 'Why don't you grab the eggs and milk out of the fridge?' he added, needing to keep things short and sweet.

He'd cook her pancakes and then take her back to the city. End of. That was what they'd arranged.

She returned with the fixings and he set about making the batter.

'Do you need me to do anything?' she asked.

'No, I've got this,' he said, cracking the eggs into the

bowl one-handed and trying not to notice the way his old T-shirt inched up her thighs when she perched on one of the stools at the breakfast bar.

The sudden blast of heat as he recalled having those long, supple limbs hooked around his waist had him scattering the flour a bit too generously as he added it to the mixture.

'You're very good at that,' she said.

'Yeah,' he murmured, still distracted by the smooth, toned skin as she crossed her legs. 'I was a short-order cook in a diner the whole of my sophomore year in high school,' he added, to distract himself from the heat starting to pound again in his pants.

'Was that one of those minimum wage jobs you were talking about yesterday?' she asked. 'In the small town near Lafayette?'

'Sure, but this was *in* Lafayette. Nobody would hire me in my hometown,' he said, trying not to get fixated on the memory of how sweet she'd tasted when he'd...

'Why not?' she asked, sounding upset, and the indignant tone interrupted his wayward thoughts.

'Because of my old man's reputation.' He picked up the whisk and dragged his gaze away from the danger zone.

You're not jumping her again, Broussard, this booty call is over.

'That seems very unfair.'

'Huh?' he said, having totally lost the thread of their conversation.

'Why should you be blamed for your father's bad reputation?'

He stared at her sympathetic expression as the guileless question registered and the slow throb of his pulse became a gallop.

Hang on a minute? He'd told her *that*? What the...?

He *never* spoke about his father, or that time in his life. Certainly not to a hook-up. Because he'd gone to some pains to cover it up when he'd been starting out. He hadn't wanted his father's crimes tarnishing his company the way they had tarnished so much of his childhood and adolescence. But now, as she stared at him, the concern in her gaze had his ribs feeling tight. The way they had during the night, when he'd held her in his arms as they'd both dropped into sleep.

His galloping pulse charged into his throat.

Hell, no. They were not going to have this conversation. Talking about his old man was off-limits.

'How about you go find yourself something to wear in the housekeeper's annexe while I get these done? Mrs Mendoza's about your size—you can get to it through the mud room.'

He had to get her out of that thigh-skimming T and into something a lot more substantial before he got so damn distracted he ended up blurting out his whole life story.

'I'm guessing the gold dress is a write-off,' he added.

'Um…yes—yes, it is.'

Her eyes widened, and a flush rose up her throat—making him almost feel bad for changing the subject so abruptly. *Almost.*

'Won't Mrs Mendoza think it's a bit odd that I came all this way with no clothes,' she asked, as the blush hit her cheeks.

And then he figured out the cause of her embarrassment. This had to be the first time in her life she'd ever done the walk of shame after a booty call.

His ribs contracted again. *Bingo, buddy!* Now you feel even more invested. *Terrific.*

'Mrs Mendoza's not here,' he said, his tone gruffer and

more impatient than he had intended. 'I get the staff to vacate when I'm on the island,' he added. 'Like I said, I prefer my privacy. Take whatever you need and I'll make sure she's reimbursed.'

'Oh, okay…'

Her gaze flickered away from his face and he felt like a jerk, which didn't improve his mood at all.

She slipped off the stool, and her unfettered breasts bounced enticingly under the soft cotton of his old T. A shaft of heat hit him square in the gut. It came with a brutal side order of regret that he wouldn't be able to feast on those ripe, responsive nipples again.

'I'll go and see what I can find,' she said, flicking a thumb over her shoulder. 'And be back ASAP.'

'Don't rush on my account,' he said, going the full jerk and trying not to care. Better she knew this was the end of the road. 'The batter needs to sit for a while before I start flipping.'

She'd complicated things with her possible virginity. Made him feel responsible in a way he never had before and blurt out stuff he'd never told anyone. Not to mention deal with the worst case of FOMO known to man as his gaze tracked the sweet, sultry sway of her hips under the butt-skimming T-shirt as she headed for the mud room.

The journey back to the city in his seaplane, surrounded by her scent and tortured by memories of last night, was going to be an hour-long lesson in sexual frustration.

He'd just sprinkled some more flour into the egg and milk mixture, trying to concentrate on getting through the next couple of hours without losing what was left of his mind, when he heard a rattling hum and spotted Cassandra's cell phone, vibrating against the granite countertop. He picked it up, intending to switch it off, but caught sight of the notification that flashed onto the home screen.

His brows drew down as he read the message from someone identified as 'Ash'.

His stomach twisted into a painful knot and suddenly sexual frustration was the least of his worries, as the cruel wave of betrayal washed through him like acid.

CHAPTER FIVE

'WOULD YOU LIKE a hand with the pancakes?' Cassie asked, trying to sound calm and casual and totally cool.

Not easy when she felt anything but.

Especially after Luke had caught her earlier in nothing but his T-shirt and her knickers. He'd been tense and guarded and *off*, somehow, and what had been exciting and freeing last night—a sexual adventure to be proud of—now just made her feel exposed… And unbelievably awkward.

Still, at least she had some clothes on now. Even if they did belong to someone else. She had drawn the line at borrowing his housekeeper's underwear, but she'd managed to find a pair of jeans and a baggy T-shirt and sweater and some boots and socks.

She'd left a thank-you note on the housekeeper's kitchen table in the annexe, with a promise to have the clothes returned once she'd had them cleaned.

With her hair tied in a knot after she'd taken a quick shower in one of the guest bathrooms, she still felt hopelessly exposed, though. She didn't have on any of her usual armour. She didn't even have her make-up with her… Or a bra!

Gee, thanks, Ash.

Luke sat on a kitchen stool, his head bent over something. He hadn't heard her offer to help—probably a good thing, she decided, seeing as she knew next to nothing about making pancakes.

She took a moment to absorb the sight of him. A sight that still had the power to stagger her.

Her breathing became ragged. Again.

She still couldn't quite believe everything that had happened…or how immense it had seemed. That a man who looked like he did, who oozed heat and passion and sex appeal from every pore, hadn't just noticed her, but had seduced her so thoroughly, with such power and passion and such dedication to her pleasure as well as his own.

One thing was certain. However grumpy he might be in the mornings, Luke Broussard came into his own at night.

A small smile tilted her lips, but then wavered and flattened as she caught her reflection in the window glass and the awkwardness returned.

Unfortunately, while she looked less than her best, Luke Broussard, even in nothing more than a pair of sweatpants, looked drop-dead gorgeous. The smooth tanned skin on his bare chest and broad shoulders gleamed in the sunshine coming through the floor-to-ceiling windows, highlighting the tattoo of thorns that ringed his collarbone.

The thousand and one thoughts that had been bombarding her ever since she'd woken up that morning, to find him fast asleep beside her, her body aching and her mind a mass of confusion, began to batter her all over again.

Not one of those thoughts, though, was calm or cool or casual.

All the problems with what she'd done—what *they'd* done—had only increased her confusion and anxiety in the past twenty minutes, while she'd taken a shower and tried to get a handle on how to deal with the awkwardness of her first ever morning-after…

She had no doubt last night had been about chemistry and fun for Luke, but she could see now that it had been about more than that for her. And that was without even factoring in the lie she'd told him about her virginity.

She'd tried to tell herself it wasn't a big deal. But when he'd treated her so dismissively this morning it had hurt when it really shouldn't have. Why hadn't she thought this through? Being stuck on an island with the guy you'd had your first ever sexual encounter with was bound to be awkward. Practicalities-wise, it was a nightmare. Not only had she been forced to borrow his housekeeper's clothes, she couldn't leave under her own steam. She was completely reliant on him flying her out of here.

She coughed, trying to clear the swell of anxiety from her throat.

Luke's head lifted sharply.

What she saw on his face had her drawing in a sharp breath. This was more than impatience. Much more. His jaw was rigid with tension as he stared at her, his gaze flat and hard…

'You're back,' he said.

His voice was as harsh and flat as his gaze, the husky purr which had intoxicated her all through the night gone.

'You've got some explaining to do.'

The accusing words came out like brittle staccato punches, confusing her more. Until he lifted the hand he had on the counter and she spotted her smartphone.

'Tell me, did Temple tell you to screw me while you were spying on me? Or was I just lucky?'

'I…? What?' she choked, shocked by the barely leashed fury in his tone—and the crude accusation. 'I wasn't spying on you…'

'Cut the BS. I've got evidence.'

He got off the stool and stalked towards her, the fury

on his face becoming thunderous. Snagging her wrist, he slapped her phone into her palm.

'Read it,' he sneered, the command in his voice low with disdain. 'Then explain yourself.'

She clicked on the touch screen to find a notification of Ash's reply to her earlier text…

You slept with the fella Temple sent you to spy on???
OMG! The dress was even more deadly than I thought.

Cassie stiffened. And wanted to die on the spot.

A thousand and one ways she could defend herself against Luke Broussard's claims flashed past. She'd never asked him for any information about his business. She'd tried to tell him why she had originally been sent to San Francisco by her boss and he'd shut her down.

But the fury and disgust on his face and the rigid stance of his body made all the denials freeze on her tongue. Because they reminded her of all the times she had tried to defend herself against the disapproval of another man. Suddenly she was a little girl again, bullied and belittled by her father and always, *always* found wanting.

'No wonder you were so damn interested in my old man's reputation,' he sneered. 'All part of the background check for your boss.'

She curled her fingers around the phone and shook her head. 'I wasn't asking for Temple. I just… It seemed so unfair. And I—'

'Yeah, right…' He cut her off again. 'And to think I thought you were a virgin there for a minute.'

Cassie recoiled at the bitterness in his accusation. How had he guessed the truth?

'That's one hell of an act you've got going,' he added.

She stepped back, away from the fury emanating off

him. She knew he wouldn't hurt her—not physically… that wasn't the kind of man he was—but she could see he was only holding on to his temper with an effort. And she couldn't engage with it. Because it would make her feel small and insignificant and defenceless, the way she had felt so many times as a child.

'I didn't come here to spy on you,' she said again, her hands shaking now. How ironic that she hadn't wanted him to know about her inexperience, and somehow he'd found a way to use it against her anyway. 'I should go,' she said.

'Ya think?' he sneered.

She needed to get away, humiliated now by the heat and longing still rippling through her body. How could she still respond to him when he had changed from the man she'd thought she knew to someone cruel and suspicious and judgemental?

But before she'd gone five steps his voice tore through her.

'Just so you know,' he added, 'when we get back to the city I'm gonna be talking to my lawyers.'

She swung round. What was he saying?

'I… I don't understand,' she said, keeping her voice even while her insides were turning into a gelatinous mass. How could she have put her career, and everything she'd worked for into so much jeopardy?

'You snuck in here to get insider dope on me and my business for your boss. No way am I letting you use what you learned against me.'

The brutal pressure in her chest increased as the heat of his fury emanated off his skin, making his biceps bulge as he planted his hands in the pockets of his sweatpants. Unfortunately, that shifted the waistband of his pants lower, revealing the line of his hip flexors and the text of his tattoo—which read *Laissez les bon temps rouler*, she had discovered that morning, when she'd woken up in a sleepy haze and found him lying next to her.

Heat pulsed and glowed at her core. Damning her even more.

'But I didn't find out anything compromising about you,' she blurted out, ignoring the painful tightening in her chest. 'And even if I did, I would never use it against you. Not after—'

'How dumb do you think I am?'

She heard it then—the insecurity beneath the anger—and suddenly she knew that the high school boy who had been ostracised in his hometown because of something his father had done still lurked inside this man, defensive and guarded. She couldn't talk to this man, couldn't make any of this right. The only thing to do now was to leave and hope she could repair what was left of her career and her self-respect. She'd fallen into his arms far too easily, given him something of herself she had never intended to give, and ended up being punished for it.

'I'll meet you at the plane,' she said, feeling stupidly raw because she had given him so much ammunition… And for what? For a passing moment of physical pleasure…the chance to throw caution to the wind for the first time in her life. It had been exhilarating and exciting, and so much more than she had ever expected. But now she would be forced to pay the price for her naivete and her stupidity. 'I think it's probably best we leave as soon as possible.'

His biceps flexed, making him even more imposing. Dark brows lowered over those blazing green eyes, drawing her gaze to the small scar she'd wondered about several times during the night. But then the hard line of his jaw tightened.

'At least that's one damn thing we can agree on,' he said.

Turning away from her, he stalked back to the kitchen

island, the rigid line of his shoulders suggesting he wasn't as calm and collected as he was trying to make out.

Unfortunately, that wasn't much comfort for the pain digging its claws into her belly as she headed across the kitchen on unsteady legs towards the stairs.

The last of her once glorious adventure had disintegrated, the hideous reality of it revealed, as humiliation and anxiety tangled in her gut.

And one miserable thought reverberated in her head.

How on earth am I going to survive an hour in a tiny plane with him when he hates my guts?

'We can't leave.'

Thirty minutes later Cassie stood on the dock with her evening purse and the torn gold dress stuffed into a backpack she'd borrowed from the housekeeper's annexe. Her whole body was shaking as she tried to absorb what Luke had just barked at her.

'What do you mean, we can't leave?' she said, trying to keep the tremble of panic out of her voice.

Surely she could not have heard him correctly? He wanted her gone as much as she wanted to be gone. She needed to be gone, like, yesterday if she was going to have any chance whatsoever of preserving the remnants of her tattered dignity until this dreadful day was over.

'The plane's damaged. The Wi-Fi went down last night and the cell phone service went out twenty minutes ago, while I was talking to the mechanic,' he said, his face implacable.

'But...'

But I can't stay on Sunrise—not with you...not now. Not after the things you accused me of.

'Don't you have a boat?' she asked, becoming more frantic by the second.

Her phone had lost its service too, but she had actually been grateful for it, having no idea what she was supposed to say to Ash now.

Ash's jokey text had landed her in trouble with Luke, but she knew Ash wasn't the one to blame for her predicament. Not even close. Eventually Luke would have found out the truth about Temple's interest in his company and assumed the worst.

Their one wild night had been brought about by pheromones and insanity—on her part, at least—and she hadn't stopped to think about how it would all play out because she hadn't really cared at the time. Luke Broussard had unleashed feelings she had never known she was even capable of, and she'd ridden that adrenaline rush to its inevitable car crash conclusion.

She could see that clearly now. She should never have taken the risks she had with a man she barely knew. A man who clearly had serious trust issues she knew nothing about. But she had at least hoped she might be able to mitigate the worst of the fallout from this disaster when she got back to San Francisco.

She had come up with a course of action while raiding Mrs Mendoza's living quarters a second time. She would simply tell Temple the truth—or as much of the truth as was required. That she had lost her objectivity with Luke Broussard, but that she knew he wasn't interested in attracting investors.

Temple had in no way been committed to investing in Broussard Tech…this had simply been a fact-finding mission. She still had time to come up with other investment opportunities in the Bay Area, using the contacts he'd given her.

She had planned to use the flight back to the city to soothe Luke Broussard's temper and get him to call off his plans to sue. She knew how to handle difficult billionaires after three years working for Temple—although she had to admit Temple was considerably less volatile than Luke. But she'd never been drawn to her boss the way she'd so stupidly been drawn to this man. Surely she could use that, somehow, to make Luke see he was being unreasonable? That following through on his knee-jerk reaction after seeing Ash's inflammatory text would be expensive and unnecessary if Temple dropped any interest in his company?

But all her plans would come to nothing if she was stuck on Sunrise Island for any length of time, without being able to contact her boss or do the job he'd sent her to San Francisco to do.

Not only that, she didn't think she could hold herself together if she had to spend any more time alone with Luke Broussard.

A surge of distress at the prospect made her heartbeat ricochet into her throat.

'Yeah, I have a speedboat,' he said, grinding out the answer as if she had no right to even ask. 'But the power's out by the boathouse, which means I'm gonna have to hand-crank the doors to get it out, and I don't like the look of the weather.'

He thrust his fingers through his hair, then glanced up at the sky just as a dark cloud crossed over the sun.

'It's an hour's ride to the mainland from here,' he added. 'And I'm not risking the journey just to please you when another storm could drop any minute.'

'Right…' she said, feeling her own jaw tightening. Really? Did he have to be quite so much of a pill? Hadn't he given her enough grief already? 'So are you saying we might be stuck here for another hour or two?'

His flat gaze met hers. 'We're stuck here until I say it's safe to leave.' Each word was drawn out to make it abundantly clear he was the one in charge. 'Which could be days, not hours.'

'You can't be serious…' she murmured, shock reverberating through her body.

Days? Dear God.

'Don't get your panties in a twist. This is a hell of a lot worse for me than it is for you,' he said, disgust dripping from every word.

'How can it be worse for you?' she began. 'You're not the one who has been accused of—'

'Stop bugging me and go back to the house and wait,' he said, slicing her distressed defence right down to the bone, the way he had done earlier. Without giving her a chance to explain.

Bugging him? How dare he?

Her temper sparked and sizzled as she opened her mouth to snap back at him. But when his eyes flared, the challenge in them unmistakable, she swallowed down the retort.

He *wanted* her to argue with him. So he could feel superior and vindicated and display more of his temper. She refused to give him the satisfaction.

As a child she'd always backed down in the face of her father's disdain, and it had left her feeling hollow and inadequate. But now, as she forced herself to nod and swung round to make her way back to the house, she didn't feel cowed—she felt righteous. Confronting him about his snotty attitude was not going to help her cause.

Unfortunately, though, the moment of righteousness didn't last long as the truth of their situation began to sink in as she climbed the stairs from the dock. Panic and anxiety turned into a brick in the pit of her stomach as she reached the porch and stared out across her island prison.

The view across the inlet had distress churning under her breastbone.

Last night's storm was visible in the bent and broken branches of the lush evergreens which grew from the rocky crags that formed the cove. A rainbow shimmered over the headland as the bright morning sun hit the mist clinging to the shoreline.

Her throat thickened. The staggering beauty of Luke Broussard's home drew forth memories from the night before which had been haunting her ever since she woke up.

Luke's hands on her, his lips, his mouth, touching, tracing, tempting, tormenting… Helping her to discover pleasures she'd never even known her body was capable of.

But it wasn't just the sex that had seduced her, she thought miserably. It was the way he'd held her afterwards, stroking her hair, murmuring nonsense into the darkness…

Nonsense he probably said to every woman he slept with.

She blinked and blocked out the staggering beauty of the landscape, attempting to block out the memories still torturing her, too—memories that were all false. She'd imbued last night with a significance it had never had. It had been about sex and only sex. Nothing more than a cataclysmic physical connection which had blindsided her because she had no experience whatsoever of physical intimacy.

She'd been much more vulnerable than she'd realised last night—which had to explain all the foolish, reckless, wrong decisions she'd made. Decisions which, ultimately, she had to own.

Yes, Luke was behaving like a domineering, bad-tempered jerk, but she needed to suck up her disdain and make the best of it. And hope like hell he could find a way off the island quickly… Because spending another night here with him was not something she wanted to contemplate, let alone actually negotiate.

At least with him busy she would have a little respite from that judgemental glare—and super-snotty attitude.

Her stomach grumbled as she dumped her borrowed backpack in the entrance hall. She pressed her hand to it. Her rising irritation was not sitting very well with her hunger and her anxiety. First things first: she needed to eat.

Opening the fridge, she spotted the pancake batter he'd made earlier but never had the chance to use. She blinked away the sting in her eyes, stupidly reminded of his offer to make her breakfast—before he'd spotted Ashling's text and turned into Cro-Magnon man.

Ignoring the sealed container, she reached for some cold cuts. She'd never been very good in the domestic sphere. She'd never had to learn more than the absolute basics when it came to home catering—cereal and takeaway—so making pancakes was out. Which was a good thing. Because having a congenial breakfast with the man was also not going to happen now.

She poured herself a cup of the lukewarm coffee dregs sitting at the bottom of the state-of-the-art coffee maker on the counter. *Terrific.* She was probably going to need an engineering degree from NASA to figure out how to use that, too.

After hunting down some sliced rye bread, she began slapping pieces down on the countertop with a lot more force than was strictly necessary, while indulging in a stress-busting fantasy of slapping the bread against Luke Broussard's granite-hard skull.

But then an idea occurred to her. And she seized on it for no other reason than it allowed her to feel a little more in control… A little more herself again after twenty-four hours of losing herself and becoming someone she didn't even recognise—that crazy lady who had decided to take a motorbike ride and then a plane journey with a guy who fired her senses but had the manners of a Neanderthal.

The only way to take back control of this disaster was to be the bigger, better person. She was not going to rise to Luke Broussard's outrageous accusations, or lower herself to the level of having a temper tantrum over something that could not be changed.

And, to prove it, she would have a magnificent sandwich waiting for him when he came in. Because they would both need to eat before they could take a boat to the mainland…and never see each other again.

The charm offensive she'd planned for the plane journey was not a good idea until they actually got on their way, because it was going to be a titanic effort to maintain it while he was being so difficult. And, knowing him, he'd probably misconstrue her motives and think she was using her nefarious seduction skills to prise precious information about his company out of him.

The jerk.

She scoffed loudly, knowing that no one could hear her. For goodness' sake—if he only knew how ridiculous that scenario was. How the heck could she be Mata Hari when she had so little experience of sex and no experience of seduction whatsoever? But she'd be damned if she'd defend herself against those ludicrous accusations.

And the truth was, on careful consideration, she would much rather he cast her in the role of scheming *femme fatale* than simpering virgin. How much more compromised would she feel right now if he knew she had chosen him to be her first lover? Or how much those moments had meant to her?

The guy already had an ego the size of Oregon.

She slapped slices of baloney and cheese onto the bread,

then slathered the sandwiches in mayonnaise and mustard, even more determined to take the moral high ground and extend this olive branch to him—thus treating his snotty attitude with the contempt it deserved…even if it killed her.

Swallowing her temper now, in a way he had been unable to swallow his, wouldn't just make her the better person, it would show him he hadn't rattled her or upset her—far from it… Unlike her father, he didn't have the power to hurt her. All he had the power to do was infuriate her. And if she didn't show him how infuriated she was, he wouldn't even have the satisfaction of doing that.

Ultimately, by rising above his sulky behaviour she could take a huge chunk out of his superiority complex. And on a professional level her strategy was a win-win, too. Because saving her job mattered. Stopping him from suing her or Temple Corp mattered. What had happened last night and what he thought of her did not.

She finished making his sandwich, then left it with a curt note on the countertop before taking her own sandwich to eat in one of the guest bedrooms.

She would learn from this experience, and next time she got offered a ride on a seaplane to a private island for one wild night of pleasure, by a volatile, super-hot, brooding billionaire with a chip on his shoulder the size of a redwood, she would run full-tilt in the opposite direction.

Her stomach continued to churn, though, as she forced herself to consume every bite—while the brick in her belly resolutely refused to go away.

Please, please, don't let me be stuck here for another night.

CHAPTER SIX

LUKE TRUDGED UP the stairs carved into the rock wall that led from the dock as sunset burst over the horizon. He barely spared a glance for the spectacular light show of reds and oranges bleeding into the cerulean blue of the sky, so dog-tired he was ready to face-plant on every agonising step.

And more frustrated than he had ever been in his life.

No way was he getting his overnight guest off the island any time soon.

He'd managed to crank open the doors to the boathouse, only to discover the boat's hull had been damaged in last night's storm too. Not only that, but when his cell service had come back for a half-hour he'd checked the local shipping forecast and seen a number of weather warnings that made any attempt to make it to the mainland in the next couple of days—even if he fixed the boat—not a good idea.

Exhaustion dragged at his heels and made his shoulders sag.

Jezebel was a write-off too, until he could get a plane mechanic out here—and that wasn't happening for the next few days either, because of the weather forecast.

After confronting that reality he'd kayaked to Pirates' Cove on the opposite end of the island and taken his daily swim, trying to calm himself down enough to function again. Even in summer the water had been satisfyingly freezing. Then, to keep his mind off the woman now camped out in his house—and his head—he'd spent the rest of the day circumnavigating the island's ten miles of shoreline to check for any more damage.

His home was the only major structure on Sunrise, and it had survived unscathed, and he'd repaired some broken shingles on the boathouse roof before heading home to give himself time to think.

As much as he wanted Cassandra gone, the fact that he couldn't get her off the island in the next few days meant he had a couple of options. He could take time out from his hard-earned vacation time to repair the boat's hull himself…or he could do what he'd originally intended to do before he'd met Cassandra James—spend the week getting some much-needed downtime on his private island, and she would just have to stay the hell out of his way.

His eyes stung as he brushed sea-matted hair off his forehead, and heat pulsed beneath his wetsuit on cue. He drew in a harsh breath and shoved open the door to the mud room. *Damn it.* Even though he was exhausted, she still had the power to make him ache.

A vision of her as she had looked ten hours ago in his kitchen—wearing his oversized T-shirt, her hair tied on top of her head in a haphazard knot—blasted back into his brain and he tensed.

She hadn't even tried to defend herself. Hadn't even had the decency to admit what she'd done and apologise. If anything, she'd doubled down on her scheme—which was exactly why he wasn't going to let her screw over his vacation. She'd already screwed *him* over enough.

He could control his desire if he put his mind to it.

He needed this break before the product launch.

He and his team had been working on the prototypes

for two years, and he hadn't taken any vacation time in almost as long.

Indignation seared his throat as he sat down on the bench and tugged off his board shoes, heat still pulsing defiantly in his lap. And the memories he'd managed to keep at bay throughout most of the day, through sheer force of will and hard physical activity, cascaded through his tired body.

Cassandra draped over his bed, her erect nipples begging for his attention, her eyes dazed with passion, her body flushed with need, her scent intoxicating him as he thrust heavily inside her.

He shivered violently. But it wasn't from the cold, clammy neoprene as he peeled it off.

Jeez, Broussard, forget about last night, already. She's the enemy now.

Everything had been fake: the sweet, sultry smile, the forthright expression, the live-wire response which had so intoxicated him, the empathy when he'd let that nugget of information about his past slip, even the possible evidence of her virginity. She'd been playing him the whole time to get what she wanted for her boss.

The heat pulsed harder and he frowned.

Okay, maybe not *everything* had been fake. No one could fake a response like that. She'd been as turned on as he was, the memory of her sex gripping his as she came so vivid it made the ache in his crotch painful.

Maybe some guys couldn't tell when a woman was faking an orgasm, but he could tell Cassandra hadn't been faking *that*.

But she'd still played him. And he'd let her.

He picked up the wetsuit and dumped it into the rinsing sink with a loud splat.

Get over it.

It wasn't as if he'd been emotionally invested in their booty call. All he'd wanted out of their night together was great sex, and they'd both got that. So why was his stomach still jumpy and his throat still raw at the thought of her this morning, her chin thrust out, tendrils of wet hair framing her high cheekbones and her translucent skin still reddened from his kisses? Her toned thighs had been rigid with indignation while she'd stared him down and refused to admit how far out of line she was…

Why should he care if she didn't have the decency to come clean and beg for his forgiveness? Business could be dirty. He'd done some things himself he wasn't proud of in the past, to push Broussard Tech to the place it was now.

Temple was obviously a wolf. He got that. He could be ruthless too, when his business was at stake. But to use an employee to seduce him…

Unless…

Was she Temple's lover?

His stomach twisted into a knot at the unbidden thought and something dark and violent rushed through him.

He strode naked into the mud room's power shower and flicked on the jets. But then the memory of how tight she'd been when he'd entered her that first time came echoing back. And the shock and awe on her face when she'd climaxed. She'd looked overwhelmed.

He didn't trust her, but she'd have to be an award-winning actress to fake *that* response.

His shoulders relaxed a little.

The hot, needle-sharp spray pummelled his cold skin, but as he scrubbed away the salt and sweat of the day's activities the strident erection refused to subside.

Pressing his forehead against the glass bricks, he took himself in hand, jerking his stiff flesh in fast, efficient strokes. Trying to keep Cassandra out of his head, though, proved impossible, the memory of her body caressing his length still vivid as the seed exploded in his hand.

He washed away the evidence, feeling like he had as a teenager after those nights making out under the bleachers—used and dirty.

Not the same thing at all, he told himself. At least those experiences had made him wise to women like Cassandra James ever since. Those girls had shown him that no one could be trusted…that sex was a bargaining chip, just like everything else. He'd finally figured out he didn't need their approval or their affection. And he didn't need Cassandra's.

Nor did he need her to admit what she'd done. All he needed to do was make sure she didn't do his company any damage. Keeping her here for the next few days, maybe even the whole week, didn't necessarily have to be a bad thing. At least if she was stuck on Sunrise, with no cell service, it would save him the trouble of having to brief his legal team to get her to sign an NDA.

He dried himself off and dressed in the sweats he kept in the mud room.

With the edge taken off his need, and the shower having revived him, it occurred to him that he was ravenous. All he'd had since breakfast was a couple of energy bars and a flask of coffee.

He headed into the kitchen.

He had staff for the house—as well as Mrs Mendoza the housekeeper he also employed a maintenance woman and a forester—but, as he'd told Cassandra, he always had them vacate when he was on the island. He hadn't lied when he'd told her he preferred his privacy.

He huffed out a tortured breath.

The irony would almost be funny if it weren't so damn aggravating.

The truth was, the main reason he'd bought Sunrise and built the house was so he could be alone here. He liked his solitude. The outdoor activities available when he needed downtime were a great way to stretch his body as well as his mind. And when he was working on a particularly tough or troublesome new design this was the perfect place to hole up and get it done without any distractions.

Right about now, though, he wished Mrs Mendoza and the rest of his staff were in residence, because he could use a cooked meal without having to do it himself. And having a buffer between him and his resident spy would also be useful.

The sunset cast a reddening glow over the kitchen's granite surfaces, highlighting a mound of something on the main countertop, draped in a paper napkin. He lifted the napkin to find a mountain of bread and cheese and baloney, drenched in enough condiments to sink a battleship.

What the...?

His hollow stomach growled, but not with any particular enthusiasm. Then he noticed the passive-aggressive note jotted down on the napkin.

I made you a sandwich.
You can thank me later.

This mess was supposed to be a sandwich? It looked barely edible. Not only that, but it had clearly been sitting on the counter for the last eight hours. He pressed his finger into the bread to test it… Yup, hard as a slab of concrete.

Wrapping the whole mess in the napkin, he dumped it in the trash can.

He might be starving, but he had standards. And if she thought that pathetic attempt at a peace offering was going to go any way towards appeasing him after what she'd done, she was living on another planet.

By rights she should have taken the damn initiative and cooked them something decent for supper. The house was fully stocked, and she'd been sitting on her butt all day, doing nothing, while he'd been out trying to work out a way to get them off the island. Maybe that wasn't going to happen any time soon, but he'd be damned if he'd let her freeload for the rest of her stay.

If he was going to be forced to keep her here—to keep his company safe from her shenanigans while he took a well-earned break—she could damn well make herself useful.

'Cassandra!' he shouted up the stairs. 'Get down here now. You're on kitchen duty tonight.'

'But I already made you a sandwich.'

Cassie stared at Luke Broussard's hard, handsome face and cursed the flush spreading across her collarbone. She'd figured out several hours ago that they wouldn't be leaving the island tonight. So she'd spent the time trying not to let her anxiety go into free fall while she'd scoped out a bedroom for the night and hunted up a nightlight.

She had raided Mrs Mendoza's closet again for more clothing, just in case Luke's threat of being stuck here for more than one night played out. She did not plan to be unprepared for whatever he might throw at her. She'd also taken the opportunity to do some snooping.

To her astonishment, while looking through the wardrobes in his four guest bedrooms, she hadn't managed to find any leftover clothes from previous girlfriends. Perhaps Luke had actually been telling the truth when he'd told her he'd never brought a woman to the island before… Not that it meant anything. The women he hadn't brought here were the lucky ones—at least they hadn't ended up stranded here.

Satisfied with her haul from Mrs Mendoza's wardrobe, she'd headed to Luke's study in a futile attempt to find an internet connected computer, or at the very least a phone charger in case the coverage returned, because her phone had now died. Unfortunately, the only chargers she'd found were for Broussard Tech phones, and all the computers had elaborate security systems so she hadn't even been able to turn them on, let alone access the internet.

Seriously…who did that? Who had several layers of security on their computers when they were in a study in a locked house on a private island that no one could get to without a plane or a speedboat? Paranoid much?

After nearly an hour spent trying to crack his security, Cassie had returned to the guest room and dropped into a deep, exhausted sleep. She'd woken up about an hour ago, groggy and raw, still feeling the effects of the sweaty erotic dreams which had chased her in sleep…

Beyond grateful that the star player in every one of those dreams was still out of the house, she'd managed to figure out the coffee machine and made herself a cup to enjoy with the view of the sunset from her bedroom.

She'd spotted him coming up the stairs from the dock about twenty minutes ago, his head bowed and his body looking far too buff in a clinging wetsuit, his damp hair dishevelled, the way it had been last night when they'd come in from the storm.

Don't think about last night.

As he'd entered the house, the surge of longing had convinced her to stay well clear of him for the night. Confronting him was pointless—all it would do was make her more aware of the desire that would not die, or more anxious about her predicament, because they clearly weren't going to be going anywhere tonight.

She'd managed to find some crime novels on his bookshelves… They should keep her entertained, and might even contain a fiendishly clever and undetectable way to murder a man in his sleep.

But then she'd heard him calling her to come downstairs… Not calling her, *summoning* her—as if she were an employee instead of a hostage.

Ignoring him had been impossible, and it would have made her seem weak. So she had steeled herself against the inevitable surge of heat and forced herself to remain calm. Or calm-ish…

But then he'd demanded she cook them both dinner, because—as he'd put it so charmingly—'I don't like freeloaders any more than I like spies.'

That was when she'd reminded him of the sandwich.

'I threw the sandwich in the trash,' he replied now.

What the actual…?

A blush rose up her throat, combining with the surge of temper that she'd been keeping carefully at bay ever since his many hissy fits that morning had threatened to blow her head off.

'You… You…' she stuttered, so shocked at the sneering tone and the complete lack of gratitude for her titanic effort that morning in taking the high road that the words got stuck in her throat. 'You did *what*?' she blurted out at last.

'I threw it in the trash. Next time you make me a sandwich, don't drown it in mayo. I hate the stuff. And don't leave it sitting on the counter all day, so all that's left of it when I get a chance to eat are its fossilised remains.'

She gasped—she actually gasped—so aghast at his audacity and his total inability to show any appreciation for her effort whatsoever that she was actually struggling to draw a decent breath. *'Next time?'* she spat the words out. 'You have got to be joking. There isn't going to be a next time. I'd be more willing to make a sandwich for my worst enemy than you.'

'I *am* your worst enemy right now, and you still owe me,' he shot back, his tone dripping with sarcasm. 'I've been out all day working my butt off and I'm starving, so a sandwich—even if it were actually edible—isn't going to cut it. Let's see what else you've got,' he finished, before stomping past her.

She gulped, a sudden spurt of panic chipping away at her fortifying fury. 'What do you mean, what else I've got?' she asked.

Although she had a horrid feeling she already knew.

He wasn't kidding about expecting her to cook him supper.

A *hot* supper, with *actual* ingredients, from *scratch*—something that didn't come out of a ready meal container or off a takeaway menu.

He stopped and stared down his nose at her. 'What else you've got in your repertoire of go-to meals. Other than prehistoric sandwiches,' he added.

But the dig didn't even register this time as her panic started to consume her.

But I don't have a repertoire.

It was what she wanted to say. But she couldn't say it because she knew it would make her look pathetic. Because it *was* pathetic.

She didn't know how to cook anything. Not anything complicated. Nothing other than maybe beans on toast, or scrambled egg, or warmed-over soup from a tin. And she was fairly sure that wouldn't cut it with this man any more than her 'fossilised sandwich' had—because he could whip up a pancake batter from scratch and had been a short-order chef in a diner when he was still a teenager.

The truth was, she had no excuse. She should have learned how to cook for herself a long time ago. But she'd avoided learning, avoided even attempting to learn. And the reason for that was even more pathetic.

She hated being in a kitchen and doing any kind of domestic chores because it reminded her of the day she had discovered exactly how much her father disapproved of her…

Not even disapproved of her, really. Because disapproval required some kind of emotional input. And the truth was Aldous James hadn't cared enough about his daughter to put in any emotional effort.

He hadn't disapproved of her. He hadn't even seen her. And the day she had discovered exactly how little he cared had haunted her every day since—whenever she spent any time in a kitchen.

For five years—from the day Ash and her mother had come to live in the servants' quarters at her father's house on Regent's Park West—the kitchen had become a place of solace and sanctuary for Cassie. A place of vibrancy and life and excitement, for good times and good feelings.

Until the day her father had chosen to change all that without telling her.

The heat in her cheeks exploded as she recalled that day in vivid detail.

She had raced down the stairs brimming with exhilaration because it had been the first day of October half-term. She had known Ash would be up early, having her breakfast while Ash's mother, Angela, put together her father's breakfast tray. Her friend would already be concocting some marvellous new adventures for them both for the holiday. Because Ash always came up with the best adventures.

But it hadn't been only Ash's latest mad plans that Cassie had been anticipating as she'd shot down the back stairs in her family's ten-bedroom Georgian town house—a house that had felt like a prison to her—a prison full of ghosts—until Angela had appeared one day in the staff quarters and introduced Cassie to her daughter.

'Sure, you two are about the same age. I won't mind a bit if you want to come down and keep Ashling and I company while your father is busy.'

She hadn't just been excited about spending some quality time with her best friend again after weeks and weeks of boring school, when they'd only got to see each other for a few hours a day because of the endless hours of homework Cassie was set by the posh private school she'd attended. She'd also been anticipating basking in the homely atmosphere Angela and Ash had created ever since they'd come into her life.

She'd loved all of it. The comforting wittering of Angela Doyle's conversations about fairies and crystals and other nonsense, the sound of Ash's slightly off-key singing as they sang along to her favourite show tunes while sharing the headphones from Ash's MP3 player, the tempting aroma of the scones and breads Angela baked from scratch and the scent of lavender floor polish.

She'd burst through the kitchen door that crisp October day when she was thirteen with the wonderful feeling of belonging, of friendship, bursting in her heart—only to find the room cold and empty and silent.

And Ash's hastily written note on the table telling her they'd been forced to leave.

A cold weight sank into her stomach all over again,

joining the sharp twist of inadequacy as she recalled the conversation in her father's study later that day.

'Angela Doyle is no longer in my employ. We don't need a housekeeper any more as you will be boarding at St Bride's after half-term and I can simply eat at my club.'

'But, Father, what about Ashling? She's my best friend.'

'Ashling is a housekeeper's daughter. She is hardly a suitable companion for you.'

Cassie pushed past the recollection, disturbed by the realisation that her father's callous words that day and his blank expression—impatient and vaguely annoyed—still had the power to make the muscles in her stomach clench into a knot.

How pathetic that she could still recall that day in such vivid detail. Especially now, when the last thing she needed was to give Luke Broussard more ammunition.

For goodness' sake, Cassie, get over yourself.

How ridiculous to let the devastation of that day still control her all these years later… Maybe her life had been more colourful with Ash and her mum living in the staff quarters. And, yes, it had been thoughtless and insensitive of her father to wrench them away from her without a thought to how she might react. But to think she had avoided learning to cook because of that one painful memory…?

Seriously, it was beyond pathetic.

Especially when she considered that everything she'd thought she had lost that day had never really been lost at all. Ash was still her best friend. They'd made sure never to lose touch during all those miserable years Cassie had spent at St Bride's. They had been sharing a flat together for the last four years, ever since Cassie had finished uni and begun her career at Temple's as a graduate associate.

It was all good. Give or take the odd bra-less dress debacle and tuxedo *ditzkrieg*.

Cassie cleared her throat.

Except for one glaring problem. She did not have a 'go-to' meal repertoire which she could use to whip up something now and impress Luke Broussard. Not even close. Which meant the only course of action open to her—as her tormentor continued to stare at her with utter contempt—was to bluff. Because she would actually rather die than let him know she had allowed that easily bruised, painfully lonely child to continue to lurk inside her for so long.

'Cook your own supper,' Cassie said, drawing herself up to her full height—which was still a lot shorter than his—and trying to draw on the outrage of a moment ago. 'I'm not your personal chef.'

She swung round to make what she planned to be a dignified and speedy exit.

Too late.

'Not so fast, Miss Priss.' He grasped hold of her elbow to tug her back.

A spike of adrenaline shot up her arm, adding shocking heat to the twist of pain and inadequacy already festering in her belly.

To her horror, instead of accepting her perfectly reasonable rebuttal, Luke Broussard tilted his head to one side, studying her in that strangely unsettling way he had that made her feel totally transparent.

'You can't cook, can you?' he said.

It wasn't a question.

'How do you…?' She stopped, her pulse tripping into overdrive as the weight in her stomach grew to impossible proportions. 'Of course I can,' she said, scrambling to cover the gaffe.

'Uh-huh?' he said. 'Then prove it.'

'I don't have to prove anything to you,' she managed, but she could tell from his expression that the game was up.

'What are you? Some kind of princess?' he said, contempt dripping from his words now. She should have been prepared for it. She wasn't. Especially as she didn't even have anything resembling a decent excuse. The weight in her stomach twisted and throbbed on cue.

'No, it's just… It's not a skill I've ever needed. Particularly…' she said, desperately trying to cover her tracks. Bluffing hadn't worked. Maybe bluster would.

'Why?'

'We had s-staff when I was little, and I went to boarding school.'

She stumbled over the word 'staff', because she'd never thought of Angela as her father's employee. Angela Doyle had been the closest thing she'd ever had to a mother. Which was why she had been devastated when her father had let her go—as well as Ash.

But Luke didn't need to know any of that. Playing the privileged spoilt princess made her feel stronger, somehow, than the truth… That she'd been a needy, lonely child, looking for affection from people who had been paid to care for her. Angela had never made it seem that way, but that was the reality.

'You had staff…' he said, cursing softly under his breath. 'That's the excuse you've got for not learning a basic life skill?'

'Well, it can't be that basic if I've survived perfectly well without it,' she said.

'Until now,' he said, sounding exasperated with her incompetence. 'I mean, *damn*. What about your mama? Didn't she teach you something? Anything?'

'No, I was only four when she died.'

As soon as the words were out of her mouth she wanted to take them back. Because his eyes darkened and what she saw on his face, instead of distrust or anger or even heat—which seemed to be his go-to emotions where she was concerned—was pity.

'That's tough, *cher*.'

It was the first time he'd used the endearment since discovering Ash's text, and to Cassie's horror the growled condolence had an effect she couldn't mitigate or guard against, brushing over her skin and making her heartbeat slow and her ribs squeeze, cutting off her breathing.

She stiffened and re-inflated her lungs with an effort.

'You're weak, Cassandra, that's your problem.'

Her father's voice slashed across her consciousness. She forced herself to keep breathing past the pain in her chest and the boulder in her throat.

Don't you dare cry—not in front of him. You're just tired and stressed. This is not a big deal.

'Not really. I don't even remember her,' she lied. 'And, anyhow, that's a little sexist, isn't it? To assume my mother would teach me how to cook?' she added, trying to regain at least some of her self-respect and the fighting spirit she'd worked so hard to create over all the years of her father's indifference.

Men like Luke Broussard saw a weakness and exploited it. That was what they did.

Luke shrugged, but his expression didn't change, his clear mossy-green eyes still shadowed. 'I guess it could have been your papa,' he said, the French inflection on the word sounding strangely intimate. 'I just asked because my mama taught me. She always said I needed to know the basics…' He counted them off on his fingers. 'Gumbo, Jambalaya, crawfish étouffée and pancakes.'

'I only know what one of those things even is,' Cassie supplied, stupidly relieved as the knot in her stomach loosened a fraction.

As much as she might want to stand up to him, handling

confrontation head-on had never been her strong suit—just ask her father.

Luke swore again, but she felt the knot release a little more. Maybe he despised her, but at least she wasn't going to have to fake any cordon bleu cooking skills now.

Always an upside.

'Well, we've both gotta eat tonight. And I'll be damned if I'm gonna do it all. If you want, I can show you how to cook my mama's Jambalaya?'

Warmth blossomed in the pit of her stomach alongside a burst of astonishment. But then she got a grip and saw the pity still shadowing his eyes.

The off-hand offer wasn't really meant as an olive branch—she totally got that. He was quite possibly only doing it to demonstrate to her exactly how pathetic she was. But somehow she couldn't bring herself to tell him where he could stick his offer.

Unfortunately, she was fairly sure her inability to tell him no wasn't just because she was so hungry she was more than ready to eat anything—even humble pie—but also because darkness was closing in outside the window, and spending the evening with him without having to argue with him would be better than spending it alone in the guest room.

'I think I could probably manage that,' she said cautiously, hating herself a little bit for folding far too easily, but deciding she could always go back to standing up to him tomorrow. Tonight, she was too stressed and exhausted and famished. 'If you tell me exactly what to do.'

The quirk of his lips took on a wicked tilt—and suddenly she was fairly sure he wasn't thinking about cooking any more. Because neither was she.

'Don't worry, I'm real good at giving orders.'

Don't I know it? she thought, but didn't say. Because

with the thought came a blast of unhelpful memories about the orders he'd given her the night before, and how much she'd enjoyed obeying them without question.

Way to go, Cassie. Why not turn a catastrophe into a sex-tastrophe? Because this isn't already awkward enough...

'Go grab the bag of crawfish from the freezer,' he said, the teasing glint instantly gone again, 'and then I'll show you how to make Jambalaya.'

She was so relieved that he seemed as disinclined to flirt as she was, that she was halfway across the kitchen before she thought to turn around and ask, 'What does a crawfish look like?'

He paused while grabbing a pan from the rack above the kitchen island, a low chuckle bursting out of his mouth. 'Hell, *cher*, don't you know anything?'

Apparently not. But suddenly not being able to cook didn't seem like her biggest problem, when the rusty rumble of spontaneous laughter rippled over her skin and made the ever-present weight in her stomach start to throb.

Hello, downside, my old friend.

Whose dumb idea was it to give her cooking lessons?

Luke watched Cassandra's forehead crease as she shook the skillet. The sizzle of frying scallions and garlic was doing nothing to mask the smell of his pine shampoo on her hair. She scraped the pan with the spatula.

Oh, yeah, your dumb idea.

'Just tease it,' he said, wrapping his fingers around her wrist to direct her movements.

Her pulse jumped under his thumb and she jolted. The stirring in his groin, which he thought he'd taken care of an hour ago in the mud room shower, hit critical mass. He let go of her wrist as if he'd been burned. Because that was what it felt like—as if she were a live electrical socket which he couldn't resist jamming his fingers into.

'That's it…you got it,' he said, regretting his spur-of-the-moment decision even more as he got another lungful of her clean scent over the pungent smell of frying garlic. His burgeoning erection hardened and he stepped back, far too aware of the urge to press it into the curve of her backside.

He cursed silently.

By rights he should be exhausted.

By rights he should have taken care of this yearning in the shower and during twelve hours of chores and outdoor pursuits.

By rights he should want to have nothing whatsoever to do with this woman.

She'd lied and cheated and had intended to use the connection between them to spy on him for her boss. So why couldn't he get his hunger for her under control? And why had the look on her face when he'd demanded she cook him supper, then asked her about her mama, torn at his insides?

When she'd come back from the cellar where he kept a chest freezer, holding a bag of frozen crawfish aloft like a fisherman with a prize catch, the smile of accomplishment which had split her face had hit him square in the chest. And he'd known he'd made another major error of judgement. Because spending any time with her, let alone teaching her something she should have been taught long ago, was going to be pure torture.

Why did she have to look so hot in Mrs Mendoza's jeans? And why had the truth about her mama made him aware of her fragility instead of her duplicity?

He set about dicing bell peppers and then instructed her on how to sift and rinse the rice and make the broth. All the while trying to persuade himself that he had been played again.

How did he know that the brave, motherless girl act wasn't as much of a con as the forthright, artless sex goddess act of yesterday?

But somehow, as she worked diligently to follow his instructions to the letter and make as little eye contact with him as possible, he couldn't shake the memory of the look of devastating loss which had shimmered in her eyes when he'd harassed her about her cooking skills.

And somehow he knew, even though he wanted to recapture his previous cynicism and harden his attitude towards her, that Cassandra James wasn't that good an actress.

He'd touched a nerve somehow. A nerve he'd never meant to expose. And he couldn't quite bring himself to exploit it.

Picking up the rice she'd sorted, and the sausage he'd fried earlier, he chucked it into the skillet on top of the vegetables.

'Is your mother still alive?' she asked carefully over the sizzling of the food.

'No, she died when I was sixteen,' he said, not only surprised by her decision to break their truce, but also by the pulse of connection he felt. Just because they'd both lost their mothers when they were still kids, it didn't make them friends.

'I'm sorry,' she said. 'She was very beautiful.'

'How would you know?' he asked, pushing his cynicism back to the fore. *Damn*, was she still spying on him?

'I saw a picture of the two of you on your desk,' she said, her forthright expression daring him to make a big deal out of it.

'What were you doing in my office?' he demanded.

'Trying to find a phone charger so I can save my career,' she shot back, but then her gaze softened. 'I'm so sorry for your loss,' she added, and he could see she meant it. 'I didn't see any photos of your father, but I hope—despite his bad reputation—he was still...'

'I never met him,' he lied smoothly. 'After she died I was on my own. But that was the way I wanted it.'

'Then why are you so worried about people finding out about him?' she asked, her expression open and uncomplicated. 'Surely his reputation can't hurt you? Not after everything you've achieved?'

He swallowed, but the lump of anger in his throat, that was always there when he thought of his father had faded. 'I'm not worried about it any more,' he said, astonished to realise it was true. 'Now, stop snooping and start stirring,' he added, suddenly desperate to change the subject before the compassion in her gaze got to him.

She stiffened at the curtness in his tone, but did as she was told. The recollection of how she'd followed instructions last night, too, sent a shaft of heat through his overworked system. But this time he welcomed it as he set about defrosting the crawfish in the microwave.

He didn't want to care about her loss—didn't want to feel any connection to her grief or recall how much he had needed his own mom growing up, and how much he'd missed her when she was gone.

His mother had been the only person to stand by him through all those years of being despised, being kicked around and treated like dirt because of his old man. He definitely didn't want to think about how much it had hurt when he'd lost her too soon.

But as he peeled the crawfish it reminded him of how he'd watched his mother doing the same task in their trailer. And the words she'd spoken to chastise and console him.

'Don't go getting yourself into more fights—you hear

me? It won't change a thing. All it'll do is give them an excuse to judge you more.'

She'd been right, of course, and eventually he'd listened. But what would it have been like to have none of that guidance, none of that care and compassion when you needed it most, no one to tend you when you were hurting, to teach you what you needed to be taught?

The tightness in his chest increased.

Not the point. She still used you. Just because she lost her mama young, it doesn't make her someone you can trust.

He breathed deep, to calm the pummelling of his heart and the low-grade pulsing in his pants. Leaning closer, he poured the broth into the pan. It spat on the hot metal and made her flushed face glow.

Heat slammed into him again. 'You can stop stirring,' he said.

She dropped the spatula and edged away from him, obviously finely tuned to how volatile his feelings had become—which just made the feeling of connection more acute. *Damn her.*

'It'll take a while to cook now,' he said, placing the lid on the pan so the food could steam. He glanced her way, taking in the gentle sway of her breasts, which he could detect even under the housekeeper's sweater, and making him far too aware of how much he wanted to cup the plump flesh…

'I'm afraid we're gonna be stuck here together for a couple of days at least,' he murmured.

Her eyebrows rose up her forehead, and the flush on her cheeks intensified, but the argument he'd been expecting didn't come.

'I assume it's unavoidable?' she said.

'Yeah, it is,' he said. Even though it wasn't…entirely.

Truth be told, he could get her back to the mainland sooner rather than later if he was prepared to spend the next couple of days fixing the speedboat's hull. Or, when the cell service came back—which it would—pay to have a mechanic flown out to fix Jezebel…

But he was forcing himself to stick to the plan of action he'd decided on earlier. Why should he ruin his vacation or spend a small fortune just for her convenience?

Plus, keeping her here until the product launch was good insurance.

He knew she was right in what she'd said—his father's sins had never been his. Why should he keep them hidden any longer? Didn't that just give the bastard a power over him that he had never deserved?

His gaze flicked over her breasts and back to her face as the heat continued to pulse in his groin. But just because he still desired her, and she'd made a good point about his old man, it didn't mean he was going to let this attraction get the better of him.

She was watching him with those guarded eyes, and he had the weirdest vision of a young doe bracing itself for the hunter to shoot when she said, 'I'm sorry this happened. I really didn't intend to spy on you…'

She swallowed, and he realised he wanted to take her words at face value.

'I'll be sure to stay out of your way until I can leave,' she added.

'You do that,' he said, annoyed at the pulse of regret he felt when she stiffened at his surly statement. 'If you need food, Mrs Mendoza leaves stuff in the freezer that you can nuke,' he added, to soften the blow while also making it crystal-clear that no more impromptu cooking lessons would be forthcoming. 'I'll shout once this is ready and you can eat in one of the guest rooms,' he finished.

'All right.'

She walked away, and the strange pang in his chest increased. But then she turned back.

'Thanks for teaching me how to make your mother's Jambalaya.'

'Not a problem,' he murmured.

Even though he knew it *was* a problem—*she* was a problem—which he had a bad feeling he now had even less of a clue how to fix.

CHAPTER SEVEN

CASSIE STEPPED OUT through the back door of the housekeeper's annexe wearing the raincoat she'd borrowed from Mrs Mendoza's dwindling supply of clean clothing.

Sun shone off the dew clinging to the ferns and rhododendrons lining the path and burned away the last of the morning mist. After a whole day yesterday spent hiding out in her room, in between sneaked trips to the kitchen to heat up food whenever the coast was clear—which had been most of the time, because Luke seemed to be avoiding her with the same dedication with which she was avoiding him—she was going stir crazy.

She zipped up the raincoat, settled the borrowed backpack on her shoulders and set out along the path which, according to the map, led to a trail that circumnavigated the island.

Worrying about her inability to contact her office—or anyone, for that matter—and how long it might be before she got back to San Francisco, not to mention the job of avoiding her reluctant host and any more too revealing heart-to-hearts at all costs, wasn't helping with her sleep deprivation. Or her stress levels.

She needed to get out of the house. Perhaps she was not the outdoors type, but the only way to take her mind off Luke and the things she'd learned about him two days ago was to fill her time with something else. And a hike was pretty much her only option.

From what she could remember when they'd flown into the bay three nights ago, the island was more than big enough to contain both of them without there being much chance of her bumping into him. She'd managed to find a small guidebook to Oregon's bird life. She would tour the area, scope out the terrain, and see if she could spot some of the birds indigenous to the Pacific Northwest. Because staying holed up in his house all day yesterday had given her far too much time to mull over the conversation they'd had about his childhood.

'After she died I was on my own. But that was the way I wanted it.'

Did he really believe that? She frowned. And why did she care whether he did or not? She'd had no business probing, or offering him advice about a relationship with the father he'd never known, when her relationship with her own father could best be described as barely functional. She couldn't even sort out her own daddy issues, so what made her think she could sort out his?

One thing she did know, though: keeping busy had always kept her sane—especially when she was dealing with a problem outside her control, such as the loneliness she'd fallen into when her father had pushed Ashling and Angela Doyle out of her life without any warning, or the fact that she'd got stranded on a taciturn billionaire's private island and started to delude herself into believing they had something in common, when they clearly did not.

Avoidance had always been her great go-to strategy. So, having stuffed the backpack with the bird book, some energy bars, a bottle of water, a map and a pair of binoculars, she was all set to make the best of things. Plus, physical exhaustion might help with her sleep issues.

Wisps of moisture still clung to the headland as the path meandered past the dock and into the forest. She breathed in, the air so crisp it hurt her lungs. A bracing walk and some bird-spotting would do her the world of good. Not that she knew the first thing about bird-spotting, but how hard could it be?

Two hours later Cassie wheezed to the top of another steep incline on the cliff path. She bent over to catch her breath, stunned again by the startling natural beauty of Sunrise Island… And by how chronically unfit she was. Who knew two spin classes a year weren't enough to prepare you for a ten-mile hike?

After drawing in several deep breaths of the clean air, she stood to admire another staggering view.

The outcropping of volcanic rock she stood on formed a natural archway, revealing a hidden cove eighty feet below her. The black sand beach, scattered with driftwood from the recent storm, curved around the headland, edged by the vivid green of the towering redwoods and pines on one side and a sheer rock face on the other. Her breathing slowed and her heart swelled. The scent of salt water carried on the breeze and tempered the heat of the midday sunshine.

She pulled the map out of her pack and located her position.

Pirates' Cove.

An apt name, given who owned it.

A jolt of awareness took her tired body unawares.

Not thinking about him, remember...?

She pushed the unhelpful thought to one side as she spotted a bird offshore, its large wingspan holding it aloft on the sea air. She scrambled to dig the bird book and the binoculars out of the backpack, then focussed the binoculars on the magnificent creature.

Was that an eagle or a hawk?

She flicked through the book to the pages she'd dog-eared during the many breaks she'd taken, to give her unconditioned legs some downtime in between the more strenuous climbs. She studied the pictures. Then lifted the binoculars again. Surely it was an eagle? Wasn't it too big to be a hawk?

Her heart beat a giddy tattoo as the bird swooped straight down into the waves, then climbed again with a small silver fish clamped in its beak. As it skimmed above the surface of the water, carrying its prey back to its nest, she followed its progress, marvelling at its speed and dexterity, but then she saw it fly over something in the water.

For one moment she thought it might be a seal, but then the dark shape ploughing through the waves morphed into something sleeker and more defined.

A swimmer in a wetsuit.

Luke.

She focussed the binoculars on him, her gaze fixed on the solitary figure, and all the thoughts she'd been keeping so carefully at bay during her gruelling hike flooded back.

He seemed oblivious to the violent action of the waves as he moved towards the shore, battling against the retreating tide, each tumble of surf dragging him back out to sea. He kept heading in the same direction, unfazed, uncompromising, ruthless, resilient and totally focussed on his goal.

Was he in danger? What if he was drowning and she was just watching?

The visceral fear faded, though, before she had a chance to act on it, as he found his footing and stood in thigh-deep water.

Her heart pulsed hard as she thought of the sixteen-year-old boy, left alone but unafraid. Determined to survive and make a staggering success of his life, despite what must have been impossible odds.

The tide continued to buffet him as he made his way through the rolling waves, but he seemed oblivious to its energy, arriving on the sand moments later undaunted. His dark hair lay plastered to his head, curling slightly around his neck, and his tanned face was burnished by the sun as he stood with his legs apart, his hands fisted on his hips, the clinging suit creating a powerful silhouette. He closed his eyes to tilt his head back and the sun gilded his features once more, making him for one fanciful moment look like a sea god, confident in his ability to command the ocean and win.

Cassie's breathing slowed, and then accelerated as relief that he was okay, that he was safe, sent a well of emotion through her tired body.

He looked magnificent. Powerful and intimidating in his masculine beauty. The yearning which was never far away flowed through her again. The same giddy exhilaration which had blindsided her in San Francisco was somehow more intense now, and even more overwhelming—despite twenty-four hours of avoidance and several more hours of his disapproval.

He shifted, twisting his arm up his back to grab the strap which dangled down. He tugged the zip tab to peel off the wetsuit.

Look away. Look away now.

She was invading his privacy—and only making the agitation she'd been trying to control the last couple of days worse again. But she couldn't seem to force herself to lower the binoculars…couldn't stop looking.

Her gaze was riveted to the taut contours of muscle and sinew as he freed his arms from the suit. She absorbed every inch of exposed skin, her fingers trembling as they tightened on the binoculars. She studied the curls of hair around his nipples that meandered in a line through his abs. She didn't move—couldn't move—as he shoved the wetsuit off his hips and down his legs. Her gaze clung to the tensed muscles of his flanks, sprinkled with hair, then honed in on the dark thicket at his groin. The tattoo which curved over his hip pointed her to his sex, which hung limp but still looked remarkably impressive despite his cold swim.

A hot weight sank like a fireball between her tired thighs and made her own sex throb.

But it wasn't just the memory of their intense physical connection that first night which had her throat thickening.

It was the memories of the man she had met in San Francisco—playful, demanding, flirtatious, so into her before he'd turned against her. The man who had wanted her as desperately as she'd wanted him. Who hadn't judged her, hadn't despised her.

Why did her throat hurt so much as she remembered that man now? The man she'd thought she'd glimpsed again when he'd offered to teach her how to make Jambalaya and had shared things she never would have expected him to share with her?

Why should she still be moved by that man when she wasn't even sure he was real?

Kicking the suit away, Luke picked up a towel resting on a piece of driftwood and began to dry himself. Still Cassie watched, unable to deny herself the pleasure and the pain of those memories and the glorious sight of her first lover.

The fact that Luke Broussard would always be her first lover shouldn't really have any great significance. That was what she'd told herself at the time. What she still wanted to believe. But how could it not?

She swallowed, aware of raw desire and the sting of

tears. She had to stop looking—had to walk away. She had a long trek back to the house and she needed to get there before he did and get a grip on her wayward emotions. Which really made no sense whatsoever. What had happened between them that first night wasn't going to happen again. He'd made that abundantly clear. And anyway she didn't want it to happen again.

Did she?

Hadn't the emotional fallout from that mistake already been devastating enough?

But just as she made the decision to stop looking his head jerked up, his gaze locking on the exact spot where she stood. For a second she stood frozen, still staring back at him through the binoculars. Caught. Trapped. Unable to escape from that hard, magnetic gaze. Then she lowered the binoculars and scrambled back, snapped out of her trance by panic and guilty knowledge.

She hid for a few precious seconds, long enough to get her breath back, before she finally she got up the guts to take another look.

The spurt of terror and guilt—and adrenaline—faded as she watched him head to a pile of clothing and dress himself with slow deliberation. Without the binoculars he was little more than a speck on the landscape… He couldn't possibly have spotted her all the way up here, unless he had better eyesight than the eagle.

But the relief that he hadn't caught her spying on him like a besotted schoolgirl didn't last long as she headed back into the forest.

Why had she stared at him like that? What was wrong with her? Where was Cassie the boring rule-follower when she needed her? Because she did not need that wild woman back again. Not in any shape or form. That woman had caused her more than enough trouble already…

* * *

So, Cassandra James is full of...

Luke cursed under his breath.

She'd lied to him. Hadn't she promised she'd steer clear of him? And here she was spying on him again.

Even before he'd seen the tell-tale glimmer of sunlight reflected on glass giving away her position—probably shining off the lenses of his own binoculars—he'd felt the zap of awareness on his chilled skin.

How long had she been standing there? And what the hell had she been doing? Other than getting an eyeful of him naked…

Luke tugged on his jeans and buttoned his fly—not easy as that prickle of awareness arrowed down.

Pirates' Cove was his sanctuary, and she'd invaded it. His cold morning swim was the only way he had to contain and control the hunger which was still driving him nuts.

And she'd ruined that too, now.

But alongside the burst of anger and frustration had been the rush of something worse when he'd spotted the flash of light and realised she was watching him. Something giddy and light-headed and kind of demented, which he now recognised as…

Anticipation.

What the hell?

He swore again, viciously. Infuriated with himself as much as her.

He'd caught her spying on him. And instead of being furious, which he had every right to be, for one split second he'd actually been *pleased*.

Was he some kind of glutton for punishment now? Even when he'd been a teenager, treated like dirt by girls he'd thought liked him, he had never been a sucker. He'd stifled his need to be accepted, to be liked, and got over himself.

And over them. They'd never really hurt him because he'd never let them.

No one's approval was worth losing your dignity over, or your pride. If the girls he made out with at night didn't want to acknowledge him in the daylight, they could go right to hell. He was in charge of his own destiny now.

He couldn't even remember their names any more, and their faces were just a hazy memory. He'd never had any trouble moving on from those long-ago betrayals… Even as a sex-starved, untried kid, denied the one thing every kid yearned for in high school: acceptance.

But even as he congratulated himself on his ability to preserve his dignity back then, another voice and another memory beckoned.

His mama, her head high as they walked past those guys who'd always sat in front of Cunningham's Deli, holding his hand too tightly while the wolf whistles followed them down the sidewalk.

'If you can put out for a felon, honey, why don't you put out for me?'

'How about I give you some sugar, sweet thing? You ain't going to be getting none from Gino for another five to ten.'

His fingers curled into fists.

How he'd hated those men, and the way they'd spoken to his mama—as if she were a piece of meat instead of a human being. But none of them had been the man he'd hated most of all.

'He doesn't give a damn about us, Mama. When are you going to figure that out?'

The memory of the feel of his mother's open palm slashing across his face made his cheek sting all over again, and his chest tightened with the same impotent, futile rage that had tortured him as a teenager.

'Don't you disrespect your papa. He loves us. And when he gets out he's gonna take care of us again.'

It was the one thing his mama had always been dead wrong about. Gino Leprince hadn't loved either one of them. If he had he wouldn't have ended up in the penitentiary, doing time for grand theft auto and aggravated assault—without a thought for the heavily pregnant seventeen-year-old girl he'd left behind.

But Celestine Broussard Dupuis had been too starry-eyed, too sweet and gullible and idealistic to see it.

He shook the memory loose, felt the shudder of long forgotten anger racking his body replaced by irritation.

Jesus, where had that come from?

He wasn't a sap, like his mom.

He had loved her dearly, but he'd always been aware of Celestine Dupuis's faults. The most glaring of which had been to mix up sex with emotion—to think that making love with a guy meant he cared about you. That he would protect you and provide for you.

Love had been a trap for her, and ultimately for him, because it had anchored them both in a place where no one had respected them thanks to the crimes of someone else.

It had been the only upside of growing up as the son of the town's biggest screw-up—learning to be cynical about the starry-eyed hogwash called love that robbed you of your common sense, your dignity and self-respect.

Had his conversation with Cassandra shaken all that loose again? Because if it had, he had even more reason to be mad with her.

He flung his towel and his wetsuit over his shoulder and headed round the point to where he'd anchored his kayak.

He shoved the boat off the rocks and jumped in.

Cassandra James had messed with his head two days ago and now she was doing it again.

Well, that ends now.

He'd given her space and she'd taken advantage of that. Coming out here and spying on him when she'd promised not to. Why was he even surprised she hadn't stuck to her word? It was just one more example of how he couldn't trust her.

He sliced the paddle into the water, picking up speed as the kayak rode over the surf and caught the tide.

He could see a new storm gathering, and the sun was starting to sink behind the point. She had a long walk back to the house—and once she got there he would be waiting.

CHAPTER EIGHT

CASSIE TOOK THE steps two at a time, with the long shadows chasing her all the way to the back door of the imposing wood and glass structure.

She pressed her forehead against the cold steel, stupidly pleased to have got to the house before the last of the light faded on the horizon. The sun had set less than five minutes ago, but even so the familiar vice around her chest tightened.

She forced herself to even her breathing. *Grow up. You're fine...you're safe...you're back now. You did not have to spend a night lost in the forest.*

She had always had an idiotic fear of the darkness, and had been forced to sleep with a light on at night ever since she was a little girl.

Except when…

The recollection of strong arms cradling her, a hard body cocooning her against the storm, protecting her after dark, pushed against her consciousness… And the disturbing truth occurred to her for the first time.

Except when I fell asleep in Luke Broussard's arms.

She blew out a breath, pushed the unhelpful thought away.

Wonderful, Cassie. Just what you need to make you feel even more pathetic.

She rubbed her open palms down her jeans, inhaled and exhaled several more times.

She'd got lost on her way back from Pirates' Cove—probably because she hadn't been able to think about anything except Luke Broussard and his naked body.

Her map-reading skills were rusty at best—when was the last time she'd been outside of London, let alone hiking in an Oregon island wilderness?—so it had taken her several wrong turns before she'd finally found the coastal path that would take her back to Luke's house.

But she'd still been a good two miles away—according to the map—when she'd noticed the sun starting to dip ominously towards the horizon and the wind beginning to whip away the last of the day's warmth.

Suddenly getting caught eyeballing Luke Broussard's very delectable naked body had been the least of her worries…

She pressed the code into the control panel so she could enter the house, and stepped inside just as the drizzle which had soaked through her clothing an hour ago turned into fat drops of rain. The metal door slid closed behind her, shutting out the beginning of the storm. Her tense shoulders finally relaxed.

She shivered, stripping off her damp sweater and boots, feeling the underfloor heating sending some much-needed warmth through her tired, overwrought system.

The lights in the entranceway emphasised the gathering darkness outside and her heart did a panicked two-step. The utter exhaustion—both mental and physical—which she had been holding at bay with sheer force of will for the last mile of her hike began to make her overused muscles ache, and the tension headache at the base of her skull turn from a whisper into a shout.

No more indiscriminate hiking. Or extra-curricular bird

watching. Especially not less than three hours before dark and/or in the vicinity of Pirates' Cove.

To avoid Luke from now on she would have to venture out with extreme caution.

She dropped her backpack, headed through the mud room, and flicked on the lights before taking the steps down to the basement.

Her hollow stomach howled in protest. She needed food. A hot shower. Some painkillers and bed. In that order. At least tonight she shouldn't have any trouble sleeping.

She rummaged through the chest freezer for one of Mrs Mendoza's ready meals and found a vegetable lasagne in a glass container. Carrying the dish under her arm, she headed back upstairs and scanned the dark open-plan living space.

Only the lights in the kitchen were on. The clenched muscles in her stomach relaxed.

Empty. Luke must still be out and about.

She'd been more than ready to forgo the first part of her To Do list and starve herself until morning if she had found Luke already there. She might be famished, but she did not want to face him tonight. She simply didn't have the mental bandwidth to deal with his overbearing presence when she was already exhausted and perilously close to tears.

Not only did Luke Broussard have the ability to look right into her soul and discover all her secrets without even trying, there was no way on earth she wanted to risk seeing him with the vision still in her head of him naked and gorgeous and indomitable in Pirates' Cove.

The kitchen's lighting glowed on the clean granite work surfaces. She tiptoed into the quiet space, finding the fierce patter of the rain almost soothing as she placed the container on one of the surfaces without making a sound and set about programming the microwave.

She'd heat up the pasta dish and head upstairs to her room with a plate. Safe for another night.

'Sneaking around comes real natural to you, doesn't it?' a deep voice purred from the darkness.

Cassie let out a high-pitched squeak and swung round so fast the lasagne dish launched off the counter like a missile. The sound of glass shattering blasted away the last of her calm.

She steadied herself against the countertop as Luke Broussard's tall, broad and uniquely intimidating silhouette rose from one of the sunken sofas in the living area.

She gulped in a few desperate breaths, then pressed her palm to her chest to steady her rampaging heartbeat and control the vice now tightening around her ribs with the force of a starving anaconda. How long had he been lying in wait, ready to scare the bejesus out of her?

'Are you actually trying to kill me?' she managed—not easy with the adrenaline now pumping round her body at warp speed.

He stepped into the light.

Heat powered through her exhausted system.

He'd showered and shaved since she'd left him in the cove. And put on a few more clothes. *Thank goodness.*

Unfortunately, the black cashmere jumper did nothing to disguise the sleek musculature of the chest she'd been admiring four hours, five miles and one major coronary episode ago.

Look away from the six-pack.

She forced her gaze to his face and noticed a muscle tensing in his jaw. And the flat, disapproving line of his lips. Apparently he hadn't been lying in wait to scare her for a laugh.

She should be grateful that he hadn't enjoyed seeing her

learn how to levitate, but somehow she wasn't—because his displeasure was having a far more devastating effect.

'I'm not trying to kill you,' he said. 'But if I did, I reckon a judge would consider it justifiable homicide.'

He ground out the words, and it occurred to her that Luke Broussard was absolutely furious. Possibly even more furious than he had been when he'd read Ash's text two days ago.

Just as she was trying to figure out what she could possibly have done, he supplied her with the answer.

'You get a good enough look this afternoon?'

Shame combined with panic, and the inappropriate shaft of heat climbing up her torso.

'You *saw* me?' she blurted out, before she realised how incriminating that sounded.

He stepped closer, making her even more aware of her height disadvantage in the woolly socks. The subtle scent of pine soap filled her senses and she saw the glint of fury turn the mossy green of his irises to emerald fire.

'Uh-huh,' he said, almost casually.

But she could see what the semblance of control was costing him in the rigid line of his jaw and the vein pounding in his temple.

'Next time you're going to use binoculars to check out my junk, don't stand facing the sun.'

'I… I wasn't checking out your junk… Precisely…' she said, but even she could hear the weakness in her denial. And feel the tell-tale blush warming her cheeks.

'Then what *were* you doing… *Precisely?*' he snarled.

'I was watching an eagle… Or… Or possibly a hawk.' She hesitated, hopelessly flustered. 'I'm really not sure what it was.'

Shut up, Cassie. Rambling incoherently about the bird

you couldn't identify before you got fixated on his junk is not going to make you look any less guilty.

'I couldn't find it in the book,' she added, so jittery now that she was incapable of obeying even her own instructions. 'But it was big… *Very* big.'

Her gaze drifted south, entirely of its own accord, then shot back up so fast it was a miracle she didn't break her neck. The blush exploded.

The muscle in his jaw remained as rigid as pre-cast steel. And about as forgiving. 'Why did you track me to the cove? And why were you spying on me there?'

The questions sliced out on a grim murmur of suspicion.

'I didn't track you to the cove. I didn't know you would be there. And I wasn't spying on you.' She fought back, trying not to see all his naked beauty in her mind's eye, but guilty heat glowed on her face regardless.

His eyes narrowed, but then his jawline relaxed, his lips quirking in an arrogant smile that only made her feel more insecure… And volatile.

'Damn…you got a kick out of it, didn't you?'

'I… I don't know what you mean…' she said, but the flush had become radioactive.

'You know, for a corporate spy you're a real crummy liar, Cassandra,' he said.

He stepped closer, crowding her personal space, making her more and more aware of the heat flowing straight to her core and turning her heartbeat so frantic her tired limbs became animated. Energised. A flash of lightning from outside blinded her for a moment, and electrified the sexual tension already sparking between them.

'If you want sex, why don't you just say so?' he growled, the low, husky tone of his voice both provocation and promise. 'No need to sneak around and spy on me. I can't think of a better way to pass the time now we both know exactly where we stand.'

The spark leapt and sizzled, searing her nerve-endings, burning down to her core. But she jerked back a step, her bottom hitting the counter, even as her body clamoured for her to get closer, to take him up on his insulting offer.

She couldn't give in to this yearning again. However powerful, however intoxicating. Not after everything he had accused her of. She had to control the chemistry, the yearning, or she would be lost.

'I don't want sex from you—not any more,' she said.

'You're lying,' he said, so confident, so arrogant, so sure.

'No, I'm not,' she said, but the denial came out on a shattered sob, daunted rather than decisive.

How did he do that? How did he make her want him when she knew she shouldn't?

She lifted her hands, palms out, determined to shove him away, to preserve what little was left of her dignity. But just as her palms flattened on his broad chest a lightning flash and a deafening crash of thunder plunged the house into darkness.

She gasped, blinked, but the black veil was so impenetrable it grabbed her by the throat and yanked her down into a bottomless abyss.

Fear thundered through her veins, weakening her knees and catapulting her heart into her mouth.

She couldn't see, couldn't feel, couldn't breathe.

A whimper escaped. Was that her? How could it be? It sounded like a trapped animal a thousand miles away.

Panic consumed her, turning her into a frightened child, cowering, terrified…and so, so alone…

Until her fingers acknowledged the warm, solid wall she touched and the strong, steady beat of a heart.

The urge to cling to the only human thing in the darkness overwhelmed her. She threw her arms around the broad body, cowered against its strength, folding into herself, fear choking her.

'Please…' she begged, taking great gulping breaths of the clean pine scent as she tried to escape the terror chasing her.

'Cassandra… It's okay, it's just a power outage,' Luke said, concerned by the choking sound and the whimpering cries coming from this woman who had been turning him on to the point of madness one minute—he'd found her guilty, outraged expression as captivating as every other damn thing about her—and then literally collapsed into his arms the next.

As soon as the lights had cut out.

The rush of shock as her whimpers echoed in the darkness transformed into the swift rush of compassion and Luke wrapped his arms around her trembling body, aware of her nails scraping at his back in desperation.

'Shh… It's okay, I've got you,' he murmured.

Her fingers released their death grip, but still she seemed to be curled into him, her body racked by violent shudders. Was she even aware of his presence?

He sank his face into the rain-soaked, citrus-scented hair that haloed around her head and stifled the jolt of desire. How could she be driving him nuts one second…and be so defenceless the next?

That desire shamed him now—the way it had in the cove, when he'd spotted her watching him. But for very different reasons.

He'd wanted to goad her, he realised. Wanted to make her as angry and frustrated as he was about the chemistry that would not die when he'd found her sneaking into the kitchen.

And he'd succeeded.

But that impulse had gone south pretty quickly. Because he'd seen the same shocked arousal, the same vicious awareness in her eyes, that had tormented him for days.

And then the lights had gone out and she had retreated somewhere he couldn't follow.

All he could do was hold her until she found herself again.

He wanted to deny her sudden switch from hot, aggravating woman to terrified child—wanted to dismiss it as another trick, another game, another act to garner his sympathy or his co-operation. But she'd never tried to elicit his sympathy before. She'd stood up to him, even offering him comfort when he hadn't asked for it.

'Please don't leave me.'

The hoarse plea pierced through the last of his cynicism.

'I… I can't be alone…not in the darkness,' she added.

Her voice was so small and scared it crucified him.

'I won't,' he said, finding her face in the darkness, tracing his thumbs over her cheeks. Moisture coated his fingertips, the tears almost as shocking as her fear. 'Just hang on. The emergency generator will kick in any second.'

He'd wanted her at his mercy—wanted her to admit she was as tortured by the relentless desire as he was, as desperate, as close to the edge… But having her in his arms like this, so vulnerable, so terrified, so dependent, did something to him.

None of it good, all of it disturbing.

They stood together for seconds which felt like hours as he willed the lights to come on, aware of the shivers still racking her body.

Sympathy and sadness assaulted him. What the hell had happened to her, to make her so afraid?

At last the lights flickered back on and the sound of the rain died to a soft patter. The storm had passed as quickly as it had come. But the storm of emotion gripping his chest continued to bite as she shifted out of his arms.

Blinking against the bright, brittle light, she turned away and braced her hands on the countertop, holding herself together with a force of will he had to admire, even as he watched her try to shove the last of her fear back into the shadows.

'I'm sorry,' she murmured, as if there was something to apologise for. 'I need to go to bed.'

He should let her go. Whatever had just happened, it wasn't his concern. But as she passed him, hightailing it towards the staircase, his hand reached out of its own accord to curl around her bicep.

'Hold on.'

She stopped instantly, her shudder of reaction almost as disturbing as his surge of desire. He forced it down. Again.

'Please, I just…' She stumbled over her words, her head bowed, her humiliation so complete it made his ribs hurt. 'I'm sorry,' she said again, sounding so hopeless that the drawing sensation in his chest cinched tight.

He tucked a knuckle under her chin, lifted her face to his. 'What have you got to be sorry about?' he asked, because suddenly he wanted to know.

The shattered look in her eyes, before she could mask it, turned the golden brown to a rich caramel. She looked away, the glow on her cheeks highlighting the reddened tracks of her tears.

He could see her exhaustion.

He hadn't noticed it earlier, because he'd been so mad—about everything. But he could see it now, in the weary line of her shoulders, the smudged shadows under her eyes, that bone-jarring shudder when she sighed. So she hadn't been getting any more sleep than he had these last couple days…

'I'm sorry for making such a ridiculous scene.'

She raised her head, the direct stare somehow brave and bold, a valiant attempt to deny her obvious fatigue and the remnants of her anxiety attack.

'I don't want you to think I'm weak, because I'm not,' she added. 'That was just a…a blip. I'm not used to being anywhere that gets so dark at night.'

He found his lips softening at the prim, carefully chosen words, the unconvincing defence. He was captivated, even though he didn't want to be. And relieved that whatever had been terrifying her had been conquered.

Part of him wanted to ask where the 'blip' had *really* come from. What had caused it? Because her explanation was garbage. People didn't react with that level of fear and panic just because they normally lived in a metropolis with a lot of light pollution. What he'd just witnessed was a fairly major phobia was his guess. One she'd somehow managed to keep hidden the first night they'd been together.

How come she'd been okay in the darkness when she was tucked against his body?

He sliced off the thought and stopped himself from asking the question burning in his gut. Increasing the intimacy which was already making his chest hurt would not be a smart move. But somehow, even though he knew he should let her leave, he couldn't seem to loosen his grip on her arm.

His lips quirked and she stiffened.

'What exactly is so amusing?' she snapped. The prickly tone dispelled the last of shadows in her eyes, easing the pressure on his chest.

He let go of her arm, enjoying her show of strength. 'That's gotta be the dumbest thing you've ever said to me,' he replied truthfully. 'Whatever you are, you're not weak.'

Her eyebrows rose up her forehead and he could see the observation had surprised her? Why?

'Okay…well, thanks,' she said, her tone a fascinating mixture of embarrassment and indignation.

He was glad. Because the broken child was finally gone, replaced by the smart, forthright woman whose armour was almost as beautiful to him as the furious light in her eyes which had added streaks of gold to the rich caramel.

His gaze drifted down, entirely of its own accord, and snagged on the front of her T-shirt, where her breasts rose and fell, full and high and untethered. The nipples were clearly visible, puckered into hard peaks beneath the worn cotton of the Portland State logo of the shirt, which he was pretty sure he'd seen a few times on his fifty-something housekeeper.

Funny…that old T-shirt had never looked hot on Mrs Mendoza.

He raised his gaze with an effort, and the flush of indignation on her cheeks did nothing to stem the renewed pulse of desire.

So he went with it.

Desire he understood—it made sense, unlike the pressure in his chest, which still hadn't disappeared.

'Did you get a good enough look?' she demanded, but even he could hear the husky tone under the snark.

She wanted to be offended. But she wasn't. She was turned on.

'Not as good as the look you got this afternoon,' he shot back, rising to the challenge, glad to take the opportunity to meet her on her own terms. 'Seems to me, we're not even close to being even,' he added, unable to resist the provocative statement.

Her expression flashed with the same heat he could feel building in his groin. Hot blood flooded through his system, rich and fluid and familiar, burning everything in its path.

So what else was new?

'Fine,' she announced.

Then she reached down, gripped the hem of his housekeeper's old T-shirt and dragged it up and over her head. She flung it over her shoulder. Her bare breasts bounced, and the sight of ripe reddened nipples, the scent of firm soft flesh, turned the heat in his abdomen to raw fire.

'How's that?' she demanded. 'Are we even yet?'

He swore as his erection thickened so fast it hurt.

Jesus, she was so damn perfect. So exquisite… Her sweet flesh was as soft and succulent as he remembered it. He looked his fill, then lifted his head and saw the same desperate passion that was turning his sex to iron reflected in her eyes.

'Not even close,' he gritted out, then reached to glide his thumb under one plump, puckered nipple.

She gave a shattered gasp and he gripped her hips, dragged her close to lift her. She wrapped her arms round his shoulders and plunged fingers as needy and desperate as his into his hair.

The pure, heady rush of adrenaline made his arms shake. She slanted her mouth across his and he devoured her moan of surrender.

To hell with it. What were they waiting for? They both wanted this... Both needed this...

He thrust his tongue past her open lips, feeding the heat, and explored the recesses of her mouth, starved for the taste of her after two never-ending days and sleepless nights.

He spied the best available horizontal surface—a couch—and headed towards it with her in his arms, determined to get the rest of her naked before he lost what was left of his mind.

He couldn't wait one more minute to bury himself deep inside that tight, wet heat once more. And to forget about everything but making her scream with pleasure.

This is insane. This is madness.

The thoughts surged into Cassie's head as she gripped Luke's cheeks and sucked on his invading tongue. Then surged right back out again as she welcomed everything he had to give her and demanded more.

Ravenous, desperate, frantic.

Not weak. Not sad. Not alone.

Strong and in command of her own pleasure at last.

He tasted so good, so right. The staggering pain and humiliation of her fear was replaced with hot, unstoppable desire as she clamped her legs around his hips and felt the hard, thick ridge of his erection rubbing against the melting spot between her thighs.

She could have this—could have him. Anything to finally destroy the last of that pitiable, frightened child who had been so exposed, so vulnerable, only moments before.

She didn't want him to think of her like that.

She wanted him to know her like this.

She needed to take the power back, to own it again. The way she had never been able to before him.

He dumped her on the sofa and she shivered—not from the cold, but from the staggering rush of sensations already battering her body, waking it up and making it crave. She resisted the urge to cover herself from his searing gaze as it raked over her.

'Fire on,' he murmured as he stripped off his sweater and threw it away.

Flames leapt to life in the firepit, gilding his tensed muscles in an orange glow, highlighting the dark curls of hair arrowing down to his groin.

She watched transfixed as he undid his belt, stripped off the black jeans and boxer shorts. His erection sprang up, taunting her, tempting her. His penis was longer and thicker than it had been that afternoon, and even more magnificent. The flames from the firepit seemed to lick at her sex, where the throbbing pulse was swelling the sensitive nerve-endings.

'Lose the pants, Cassandra,' he demanded, and the gruff murmur reminded her of how his voice had dragged her out of the abyss minutes before.

'Shh... It's okay, I've got you.'

She blinked, shuddered, and then jerked into action, ruthlessly trying to contain the warmth swelling in her chest.

Don't think about that.

She scrambled to undo the borrowed jeans, shoving them down her legs, taking one woolly sock with them in her haste, frantic to banish the foolish, misguided emotions.

Still about sex. All about sex. Nothing more.

'Now let's lose the panties,' he added, his gruff chuckle reverberating at her core as he hooked his fingers in the waistband and tugged the lace down her legs.

She lifted her bottom to help him, shaking uncontrollably when he flung her panties away and knelt between her legs. He cradled her bare bottom in large palms, sending sensation reeling, and then leant forward to capture one turgid nipple between his teeth.

She bucked off the sofa cushions. His soft nip was like touching a live wire to her breast as sensation slammed down to her core. He feasted on each tortured peak, tugging and tasting and tempting, licking and sucking, then blazed a trail down her belly to blow on the curls of her sex.

She moaned, gasped, propped herself up on her elbows to watch as he parted the wet folds with his thumbs and feasted.

She threw her head back as the focussed attention of his tongue, so devious, so perfect, so sure, made an inferno rip through her.

The orgasm hit with staggering speed and intensity, slamming into her like a freight train. And she flew, remembering the flight of that eagle…soaring over the waves.

As she came down, floating in afterglow, his dark shadow rose over her, his broad shoulders blocking out the orange glow from the firepit. But she wasn't scared any more. She was alive.

She held on to his shoulders, widened her knees to cradle his hips. She needed him to plunge deep and take away the shudder of emotion, that raw feeling of connection.

'I don't have a condom,' he said, his voice strained.

'I wear a contraceptive patch,' she managed, never more grateful for the period pains which had blighted her life for so many years before she'd found the solution.

'I'm clean,' he said. 'I get a test each year for my insurance and I've never gone bareback…before now.'

It took her dazed mind a moment to work out that there was a question in his statement. 'You're my…' She stopped dead, realising she had almost revealed the truth of their first night. 'I haven't slept with anyone for a while. Not since college,' she added trying to make the lie convincing.

'Yeah?' he said.

He tilted his head, considering, and she thought for one horrendous moment she'd been busted. But then his expression became fierce.

'Good to know.'

His fingers firmed on her hips and the huge head of his erection butted her sex. She had a moment to register the self-satisfied tone, and a moment more to panic that she might have exposed herself again, but then every thought flew out of her head as he pressed home.

He surged deep, filling her to the hilt. Then he began to move. Rocking out, surging back, rolling his hips to conquer every part of her.

Her surge of emotion combined with the shock of sensation. Sharpening, twisting, torturing…

Her shattered sobs matched his deep grunts, her thundering heartbeat echoing in her chest as they moved together in blissful unison. The wave gathered and built like a tsunami this time, so much bigger and bolder than before.

Reaching down, he found the heart of her pleasure, his touch triggering a massive release. The wave barrelled through her and sent her soaring into the stratosphere. She flew free for what felt like an eternity, her body shimmering with bliss. Then collapsed, exhausted and spent, back to earth.

Luke braced his hands on the sofa cushions to stop himself crushing her. He eased out of her tight sheath, grunting as her muscles gripped him, massaging him through the last vicious throes of his orgasm. And hers.

He let out a ragged breath and touched his forehead to

hers. 'That was intense,' he said, in what had to be the understatement of the century.

'Hmmm...' she said, her eyes closed, her voice barely a murmur.

He forced himself to lift off her and sit up, suddenly raw and confused. For a moment he'd thought she'd been about to say she had been a virgin after all, and something brutally possessive and protective had surged through him—was still surging through him. Which made no damn sense.

He perched on the edge of the sofa, then glanced over his shoulder to watch her. She rolled away from him, tucked her hands under her cheek and settled into the couch cushions, her naked body given a golden sheen by the light from the firepit.

A few moments later he detected the steady rise and fall of her ribs.

She'd crashed out on him.

A part of him figured he should probably be annoyed she'd dismissed him so easily, but as he studied her—the delectable curve of her bare butt, the elegant line of her spine, the tangle of hair down her back—he couldn't muster much indignation.

If the orgasm had shattered him, it had destroyed her.

Standing, he dragged his boxers back on, far too aware of the renewed pulsing in his groin. But no way were they doing that again tonight, or it would probably kill them both.

A wry smile tugged at his lips, despite the unsettling direction of his thoughts. After three days of hard physical activity and very little sleep, was it any surprise that he was ready to face-plant after finally addressing the sexual tension that had tormented him? Why should she be any different? That was all this was. Nothing to see here.

He tugged on his sweater, then found a throw rug on the opposite couch to cover her.

But after tucking the soft blanket around her naked body he heard the distant rumble of thunder from the retreating storm. He couldn't leave her alone down here. What if the lights went out again and she woke in the dark?

The tension in his groin moved up to constrict around his heart.

'Ah, to hell with it…' he murmured, then hunkered down and scooped her into his arms, wrapped in the throw.

'Mmm…' she said, groggy and dazed, but then she shifted to snuggle against his chest, as trusting and defenceless as a child.

His heart bobbed as he toted her towards the staircase. 'Come on, Cassandra, let's go to bed.'

He reached the mezzanine, but instead of heading down the hallway towards the guest bedroom she'd been using for the last two days, he walked into the master bedroom.

She wasn't his responsibility… But he didn't ever want to see her fall apart that way again.

He laid her gently on his bed, still covered in the throw rug. One of her feet peeked out of her cocoon and hung over the edge of the mattress. She was wearing one hiking sock.

He frowned, mesmerised and stupidly touched by the sight.

Just a sock, man, get real.

He tugged the dangling sock off, then tucked her slender foot back under the blanket and headed to the bathroom for a cold shower.

When he returned to the bedroom she hadn't moved a single muscle, so deeply asleep he would guess she wasn't going to move till morning.

He climbed into bed behind her and placed a hand on her hip, needing that connection and not even knowing why.

Being mad at her hadn't worked—maybe losing themselves in the electrical connection they shared was the answer? Perhaps they could get it out of their systems while they were stuck here together. But *then* what did he do with her?

He sighed, his brain knotting around the unsolvable problem of Cassandra.

Whatever.

Tomorrow would be soon enough to figure out what the heck was going on here. And what the heck he was supposed to do about her.

But, for tonight, what he needed most of all was the sleep he'd been denied.

'Dim lights,' he murmured, burying his face in the citrus-scented puff of hair peeping out of the throw. 'Stop,' he added, leaving a slight glow to prevent plunging the room into total darkness. Just in case.

Letting his hand drift over her curves, he anchored her safely to him, then dropped into a deep dreamless sleep.

CHAPTER NINE

CASSIE'S EYELIDS FLUTTERED open the next morning. Her body was rested, her stomach grumbling loudly, but when she moved she felt the tug of yearning, and a slight discomfort between her thighs.

Cocooned in a blanket, it took her a moment to register the blaze of mid-morning sunlight coming through the signature windows she recalled from three—no, four mornings ago, opposite the bed.

The scent of sea salt, wood resin and pine soap had her letting out a cautious breath.

She was back in Luke Broussard's bed—which had to be why she'd slept so peacefully.

She rolled over, scared to look. But the bed beside her was empty, the room quiet except for the accelerated sound of her own breathing. She stifled the foolish sting of disappointment.

The events of last night came tumbling back in fits and starts—the stark shock of Luke's presence in the kitchen, the crippling fear brought on by the power cut, the humiliation of how she'd clung to him in the darkness and then... His mocking smile, her bold challenge... The panic when she'd nearly revealed the truth about her virginity... And then the sex—raw, desperate, frantic, mind-blowing...

But that was all she remembered.

How had she ended up in Luke's room?

She wriggled off the bed, keeping the blanket wrapped around her naked body, and shuffled towards the bedroom door, surprised at how rested she felt. More energised and clear-eyed than she could remember feeling since she'd landed in San Francisco and this whole disaster had begun.

She crossed the spacious room, her bare toes sinking into the thick pile carpet. But then she spotted a thick white sock, neatly folded on the dresser. Shrugging off the blanket, she reached out to stroke the wool.

It was one of the pair she'd been wearing yesterday. Had Luke taken it off her after carrying her upstairs?

A strange choking feeling constricted her throat. She swallowed convulsively and lifted her hand, bundling herself securely back in the blanket.

It's just a sock.

At least they hadn't made love after he'd brought her up here, because that would be even more humiliating. She was pretty sure she'd jumped him downstairs. Although he certainly hadn't objected.

But why had he brought her to his room instead of hers?

She shook off the unhelpful question and opened the bedroom door to peek out. Whatever the reason, she did not want him to catch her in here now.

The buttery, syrupy smell coming from downstairs had the rumbling in her empty stomach turning to insistent growls.

Pancakes? Is he trying to torture me?

Tiptoeing to her own room, she headed straight into the en suite bathroom, dropped the blanket and darted into the shower.

She scrubbed the scent of him off her skin. She needed to get past the memories of last night, erase them from her consciousness before she confronted him and tried to make some sense of what she'd done… What *they'd* done… *Again…*

And figure out how on earth she was supposed to deal with it.

Ten minutes later, she made her way down the open staircase. The buttery aroma was almost as tantalising as the sight of Luke in baggy sweats and an old MIT T-shirt, busy flipping pancakes like a pro.

His head rose and his gaze locked on hers. 'Hey,' he said, his voice as raw as she suddenly felt.

She wrapped her arms around her midriff, thankful for his housekeeper's jeans and baggy sweater. She pressed a hand to her damp hair in a foolish moment of vanity, then dropped it.

'Hi,' she managed round the thickness in her throat.

And to think she'd thought their first morning-after had been the most awkward moment in her life… *Hello, awkward* times a thousand.

He switched off the heat under the pan and slid the pancake he'd been cooking onto the pile warming on the hot plate. 'Grab a seat,' he said, nodding at the breakfast bar.

And she noticed the neatly prepared place-settings—knives, forks, plates, rolled napkins, glasses of orange juice, butter on a dish and a bottle of maple syrup.

Had he been waiting for her to wake up? Had he cooked breakfast especially for her? Why did the thought make the boulder in her throat swell to asteroid proportions?

Luke Broussard as an angry, demanding jerk was manageable.

Luke Broussard as a good guy was catastrophic.

'Thank you,' she managed, as she perched on one of the stools.

With the sizzle of frying pancakes no longer filling

the silence he had to be able to hear her stomach—which was so empty it was practically inside out—doing its best mountain lion impression, but he didn't comment as he brought the loaded plate to the table.

'I'm famished,' she said, just to make him aware that she appreciated the effort.

'Yeah, I can tell,' he said, the rueful quirk of his mouth doing nothing to mitigate her embarrassment.

Hadn't she devoured those firm, sensual lips last night, like a starving woman?

That would be a yes.

He served himself a stack of expertly cooked pancakes, added a slab of butter, then doused them in a lake of syrup. 'Dig in before they get cold,' he prompted.

She didn't need any more encouragement.

At least if they were eating she wouldn't have to speak… Which was good, because she still did not have a single clue what to say about last night.

She concentrated on helping herself to three pancakes, swirling syrup over every inch of them, then slicing off a hefty triangle.

A low moan escaped her as the sinfully delicious combination of fluffy pancake, salty butter and sugary syrup melted in her mouth.

'Bon?' he asked, the quirk of his lips now a definite smile.

She nodded enthusiastically. 'Delicious,' she said, then covered her mouth, which was still full of pancake.

He gave a low chuckle and she set about demolishing her stack and filling the empty void in her stomach.

Five minutes later she placed her knife and fork across her plate, her belly so full she was surprised it hadn't burst. She raised her gaze to find him watching her. He was leaning back on his stool, his empty plate in front of him. Apparently he'd finished a while ago.

The colour leapt into her cheeks on cue.

Yo, awkward—how about company?

'Sorry, you must think I'm an absolute pig,' she said.

His eyebrow quirked, but then he smiled. One of those lazy, easy-going smiles that filled his emerald gaze with heat and approval. She recognised that smile because it was exactly the same smile he'd treated her to so many times on their first night—accepting, appreciative, impressed, aroused—before their first morning-after.

She swallowed, brutally aware of the effect that smile could still have on her as the warm glow—rich and full and misguided—shimmered right down to her toes.

'Come here,' he said, his gaze drifting to her mouth as he beckoned her towards him with his index finger.

She leant forward without thinking, and he glided his fingertip under her bottom lip.

She let out a small, shocked gasp and pulled back, but it was already too late. The light, fleeting touch brought with it a barrage of sensations.

His devastating smile widened as he brought his fingertip to his own lips and licked off the errant drop of syrup he'd captured.

The jolt of awareness in her too-full stomach became a lightning bolt.

'I'll clear up,' she said, lifting the two plates, suddenly frantic to find something—*anything*—to dispel the sexual tension building again at breakneck speed.

His hand clamped on her wrist, sending a lightning bolt deep into her abdomen. 'Leave them,' he said.

'But it's only fair…' she began to babble, trying not to notice the sizzle of sensation where his thumb stroked her wrist. Could he feel her pulse going haywire? 'If you cooked, I should—'

'You can do them later,' he interrupted, the smile disappearing. 'First we need to talk.'

He released her wrist, and the reprieve made her light-headed. *Talk?* He only wanted to talk. Surely she could handle that without bursting into flames… Or begging…

She sank back onto her stool, grateful for the granite breakfast bar between them, and let go of the plates. She dropped her hands to her lap, just in case he could see her pulse still going nuts.

'What do you want to talk about?' she asked with as much guilelessness as she could muster, while frantically rubbing the spot on her wrist where his touch still burned.

He frowned. 'You know what,' he said, pinning her with that intense gaze which had always had the ability to slice right through all her denials. And all her defences. Not that she'd ever really had any with him.

'It shouldn't have happened…' she said, her frantic pulse almost as insistent as the look on his face. Because what else could she say?

'*What* shouldn't have happened?' he asked.

'You know what.' She threw his words back at him, feeling the pancakes starting to dance in her stomach as her pulse continued to jiggle and jive.

'No, actually, I don't,' he said. 'Are we talking about when you came apart in my arms when the lights cut out, or when you came apart after they came back on again?'

She stared at him, quite sure her cheeks were so bright now they were probably visible in San Francisco. Was he actually for real, or was he just trying to ram his point home? That she'd been a basket case last night in more ways than one?

'It's a serious question,' he said.

Fabulous, so now he's a mind-reader, too.

'Both, I suppose,' she said, giving him the only serious answer she had. 'If you want me to apologise again for my behaviour, I will.'

Although she didn't feel apologetic. She just felt… Pathetic. The way she always had as a child, looking for the approval she was never going to get.

But with Luke she'd taken that sad, desperate streak one step further and added hot sex to the mix.

Way to go, Cassie. You really know how to make yourself feel like a total loser.

He didn't say anything, just continued to study her with that steady, inquisitive gaze.

She popped off the stool and reached for the dirty plates again. 'I'll do the dishes,' she said, fairly sure their 'talk' was over.

'Sit down,' he said, before she could pick up the plates.

She plopped her bottom back on the stool, obeying him without question, and then wanted to kick herself for being such a doormat.

But then she spotted the shadows in his eyes and the pancakes flipped over in her stomach.

Was that pity? The same pity she'd seen last night? She tried not to let it humiliate her. But somehow she knew she deserved it. She'd lost her cool last night, exposed herself to ridicule and worse, and then tried to regain some semblance of control by igniting the explosive chemistry they shared.

She owed him an explanation…

She just didn't want to give him one.

'I really am sorry,' she said.

'Cassandra,' he replied, his tone firm enough to make her gaze shoot to his. 'What the hell makes you think I want an apology? For any of it?'

* * *

Luke watched conflicting emotions march across Cassandra's expression in quick succession—surprise, guilt, shame, caution, confusion—and wondered how he could ever have mistaken her for a spy.

The woman was an open book. Even when she wanted to, she couldn't hide what she felt or thought.

But what should have pleased him and reassured him only disturbed him more. He shouldn't have taken what she'd offered last night, and he sure as hell shouldn't have carried her up to his bedroom and slept with her in his arms the entire night, acutely aware of every shift, every sigh, every moan.

Where had the desire to protect her come from?

She wasn't his responsibility, and certainly wasn't his problem.

But they'd both crossed a line last night that couldn't be uncrossed. And the worst thing was he was pretty sure he didn't even *want* to uncross it any more.

He'd set a number of precedents with Cassandra, right from the first moment he'd met her—maybe even before that. When he'd spotted her standing on the other side of the arbour at the wedding party in that stunning dress and been captivated.

Wanting her was one thing—he'd desired women before her. Maybe not with quite the same level of passion and urgency, or the same staggeringly intense results, but when had he lost sight of an objective so easily before?

He never brought dates to the island. This was his sanctuary, his safe place, but he'd brought *her* here after knowing her for precisely an hour.

And, what was worse, once he'd believed her capable of industrial espionage, instead of getting her out of here by whatever means necessary, he'd made all sorts of excuses to allow her to stay. He'd used reasoning he could see now was deeply flawed, because what he'd really been doing was encouraging an intimacy he'd believed himself immune from.

But he didn't feel immune. Not now. Not after last night.

She'd got to him. Not only as she'd clung to him in fear and then passion, but before that—when he'd spotted her watching him in the cove and a part of him had wanted her to look her fill.

Having her stay here any longer was fraught with all sorts of dangers. Dangers he needed to guard against. He'd been dumb thinking he could indulge himself, indulge her, and not worry about the consequences. Letting her get any closer would be a mistake.

'I feel like an absolute fool,' she said, her voice breaking on the words. 'I'm glad you don't require an apology, but that doesn't make what happened any less…' She huffed out a breath. 'Mortifying.'

The emotion he'd been keeping a tight rein on swelled in his chest, making his ribs ache, but he was ready for it this time.

She'd always been able to captivate him with her candour—even when he'd wanted to doubt her, he'd struggled to doubt that—but maybe it was time to use her transparency to his advantage, and finally get answers to the questions which had tortured him every time she'd stirred during the night.

'Do you know where it came from?' he asked. 'Your phobia?'

She glanced up, her eyes widening. 'It's not a phobia. That's… That's ridiculous. I just don't like the dark. And it was exceptionally dark. Living in London, I'm not used to that.'

It was the same excuse she'd given him last night. He

could have left it at that, let her get away with the lie. But the feel of her collapsed in his arms, clinging, scared, not herself, was still far too fresh. He hated thinking of her like that, vulnerable and afraid, because it reminded him of demons from his own childhood.

'Cassandra, you went totally to pieces,' he said. 'That's not you. You're tough. But even strong people have no control over irrational fear if it's the result of trauma. I know. When I—' He stopped abruptly, clamped his mouth shut, then thrust his fingers through his hair, shocked that he'd almost shared something he'd kept secret for so long.

This was about Cassandra—not him. And while he might trust her more than he had yesterday, he wasn't dumb enough to trust anyone that much.

Luckily, she seemed too lost in her own misery to have noticed his slip.

'If that's not a phobia, I don't know what is…' he finished.

She continued to stare at her fingers, clasped tightly in her lap. But finally she nodded. 'I suppose I never thought of it like that, but I guess you're right,' she said, so softly he almost didn't hear her. 'I always thought I had a handle on it, that I could manage it. It's humiliating to realise it was just waiting to hijack me all this time.'

The honest, forthright statement, the admission of weakness, of doubt, and the bravery required for her to speak about it aloud, had his heart swelling to press against his larynx.

He swallowed. Forced the feeling back where it belonged. Mostly…

'So you *do* know what caused it?' he asked carefully, not sure any more if he should be taking this route, but unable to stop himself now.

She nodded again, then met his gaze, her rich caramel

eyes so open and candid and her expression so frank and yet defenceless it made his heartbeat slow to a crawl.

'The night my mother died…'

He watched her throat contract sharply as she swallowed.

'I lied when I said I don't remember her. But what I do remember isn't much. I was only four. And she was ill for a long time. My nanny used to take me in to see her. I used to love lying on the bed beside her, just listening to her voice. It was so calm. So full of love, I suppose. But as she got sicker her smell changed, and she couldn't speak any more. I hated that smell—chemicals and sickness and a too-sweet scent which I realised years later was morphine. That last night…' She hesitated. 'The night she died… The room was shadowy and dark and scary. I didn't want to sit with her. She wasn't my mummy any more. I cried. I don't think she knew what was happening…'

She coughed, and he could hear the sandpaper in her throat.

'Gosh, I hope she didn't know. But my father was very angry with me. He called me weak. Pathetic.'

'You were just a little kid—what the heck did he expect?' Luke said, his anger for that small child blindsiding him.

She looked up, her gaze dazed and unfocussed, lost in memory. 'He was grieving. I don't blame him. After that night…after she was gone… I couldn't sleep unless I had a light on in my room. I knew how much he disapproved.'

Her father was clearly almost as much of a bastard as Gino Leprince. But Luke forced himself not to make the comparison. He'd already let too much slip. Anyhow, his father's crimes, his own past, weren't relevant to her trauma. And they sure as heck weren't going to make this thing between them—whatever it was—any less disturbing.

She pressed a hand to her hair, pushing the damp strands behind her ear, drawing his gaze to her clear skin. The lack of make-up made her look so young and vulnerable.

He clenched his fingers until the knuckles whitened, trying to resist the urge to capture her chin in the palm of his hand and kiss the lips he had feasted on the night before.

Things had got way too serious, way too fast. It was time for some damage limitation. He didn't know what he'd expected to happen when he'd quizzed her about her phobia. But it hadn't been the terrifying feeling of connection that was now all but choking him.

She'd been open with him; it was time he was open with her in return.

'Listen, Cassandra… The Wi-Fi signal returned this morning. I'm staying here for another five days on vacation and flying back to the city on Saturday. But if you need to leave I can call you a water taxi back to the mainland today.'

'If you need to leave...'

Luke's offer was such a shock it took Cassie several pregnant moments to process it…and her knee-jerk reaction. *But I don't want to go. I want to stay here, with you.*

Which was totally insane. Of course she should leave. He was offering her a way out of the predicament which had caused her so much anxiety since Saturday morning.

If she left now she would be able to do a much more comprehensive report for Temple—after all that was the only reason she was even in the US. But she couldn't seem to concentrate on her responsibilities to Temple Corp. All she could focus on was the deep yearning that had nothing whatsoever to do with her career and everything to do with the unreadable expression on Luke's face as he waited for her answer.

And that was the weirdest thing of all…

Her career had always been such a huge part of who she was. It was the one thing—the *only* thing, really—that had ever made her feel entirely whole. She'd devoted so much of her life to it. Not just to prove to her father she had value, but to prove it to herself. And she'd sacrificed so much to get where she was now, in a trusted executive position at Temple Corp which had the potential to be so much more.

She'd risked it all four nights ago for one night of pleasure. And she'd berated herself for that catastrophic mistake every night since. She never compromised her career; she always did the best possible job she could. And this assignment was important. To Temple and to her.

But as she sat on the stool in Luke's kitchen, her stomach weighed down by the pancakes he'd made her, his face an unreadable mask, just one thing he'd said to her—unbidden and unexpected—as he'd asked about her phobia reeled through her head.

'You're tough.'

And what that meant.

You have value.

It was the one thing no other man had ever said to her. Not even her father. Because no man had ever known her as well as this man had come to know her after only a few days.

And with that realisation came the knowledge that all her hard work—all the late nights, the missed weekends, the lost friendships, the dedication to her job above everything else which had minimised her personal life—didn't seem worth as much any more as it always had, because of one crucial reality that had only become clear in the last three days.

While trying to impress her father and make him realise something Luke had acknowledged without even being asked, she was in danger of *becoming* him. A ruthless workaholic who had nothing in his life outside his job. Maybe she wasn't there yet, because Ash's expansive friendship—the only social connection she'd managed to maintain in the last four years—had added joy and warmth and humour and an adorable flakiness to her life. But she couldn't rely on Ash for ever to stand between her and the threat of turning into the kind of sterile, soulless, embittered person her father had eventually become after her mother's death.

She had to find her own path, her own personal joy. And, while she knew what she had discovered in Luke Broussard's arms last night, and then in his bed, was not going to last, for the first time in as long as she could remember she felt fully alive. Fully engaged. Fully seen.

She didn't want to lose that. Not yet. Not until she had to.

And so she found the courage to say what she really wanted to say.

'I could stay here and check out other investment prospects online until you head back to the city. Unless you really want me to leave today?'

His eyebrows lifted, and she could see he hadn't expected the question. Then his brows flattened, his gaze becoming even more intense as he studied her… And a part of her—a big, empty part of her—immediately wanted to take the suggestion back.

What was she doing?

What if he said no?

How compromised would she feel?

Why was she giving him the power to reject her?

What was she really hoping to achieve by staying?

But before any of those misgivings had a chance to come out of her mouth, or even really queue up in her brain, his lips quirked on one side in that devastating half-smile—so hot, so confident—that she had become completely addicted to, and he said, 'I don't want you to leave today.'

Her heart leapt in her chest.

She didn't have to go. He wanted her to stay. Sort of…

So she gave herself permission to go with her gut again…for the first time since Friday night.

'Then I'd be happy to stay until the weekend, too,' she said. 'If you're okay with that.'

His eyes flashed with something so hot and fierce and possessive she was surprised it didn't burn her.

'I'm more than okay with that…' His smile sharpened as he reached out and hooked her hair behind her ear, the touch light but devastating, and added, 'On one condition. No work while you're here. This is a vacation. And we've got more than enough things we could be doing to occupy the time,' he said, the passion in his gaze making it crystal-clear exactly what those 'things' might entail.

Need throbbed at her core, but somehow she clung to the last remnants of practicality…and professionalism.

'But I have to work on an investment report that doesn't include Broussard Tech for Temple…' She began, but he pressed his finger to her lips to silence her.

'How long have you got before your trip finishes?' he asked.

'Until next Friday,' she said, her breath catching when his finger trailed down her neck to drift across her collarbone. She couldn't think when he was looking at her like that… As if he might jump her at any minute… As if he wanted to do things that would make her moan…

'That's heaps of time. I know some great start-ups ripe for investment. I'll put you in touch with them once we're back in the city. Okay?'

She found herself nodding, still mesmerised by the desire and purpose in his eyes. When had any man ever looked at her with such hunger…such promise?

'Okay…' she managed, because he seemed to require some kind of answer.

'But no talk of Temple or your job for the next five days? Understood?' he murmured, and that caressing finger dipped to circle her nipple through the sweater.

She choked off a sigh as he plucked and played with the turgid peak.

'Understood, Cassandra?' he demanded, still watching, his smile sharpening with devastating intent.

'Yes, absolutely…' she said, not even sure what she was agreeing to any more as need exploded at her core.

'Good girl,' he said. 'We're gonna have a great vacation,' he murmured, lifting his caressing hand to circle her neck and draw her closer. 'As long as you understand, *cher*, that when we leave here it's over.'

It was what she'd assumed—what she'd always known to be true. All he'd done was say what she was already thinking. This connection between them wasn't about love, or anything romantic. It was more prosaic. It was about need, and desire, and maybe—for her—about changing priorities which had held her prisoner for too long. It was about going with her instincts, giving herself permission to live a little… Heck, to live a lot.

But even so, once he'd said it with such finality, she felt a hollow tug in her chest.

She dismissed it. Forced it back where it belonged, in the box marked *This is just a sexual adventure*, and let the hunger reign.

'I know,' she said, so desperate now she could hardly breathe. 'I wouldn't have it any other way.'

'Bien,' he said, then threaded his fingers through her hair and angled her face for his kiss.

Anticipation shimmered down to her core as she grasped his waist. His hot breath skimmed over her cheek and her heart soared.

'Let's take this upstairs,' he murmured. 'Where it belongs.'

She barely had a chance to nod before he'd lifted her into his arms and headed out of the kitchen, leaving their dirty dishes and the last of her sanity behind.

Excitement rushed through her, blasting away the last of her thoughts about anything other than feeding this hunger. She would take this chance. Take everything Luke Broussard had to offer over the next five days. Not just spectacular no-strings sex, but the chance to indulge in all the things she'd denied herself for so long.

Freedom, exhilaration, excitement, fun.

But as he marched up the stairs, holding her in his arms, she couldn't quite ignore the weight in her chest warning her she was already more invested in this moment—this man—than she had any right to be.

CHAPTER TEN

'ON YOUR FEET, Cassandra!' Luke's shouted command carried across the roar of the surf. 'Now.'

Cassie tensed, her tired muscles straining as she leant forward on the board the way he'd instructed her. *You can do this. Get off your knees.*

But her fingers refused to obey her. She had only seconds before the wave would barrel past her and she'd miss her chance.

'Look at me, *cher*. Don't look at the board.'

She raised her gaze to find Luke standing a few hundred feet away, thigh-deep in the water.

The surfing lessons had been her idea—why the heck had she suggested them again…? Oh, yeah, because otherwise she and Luke would never have left the house, or rather his bed, in the last four days.

But still her fingers refused to relinquish their death grip on the board.

I can't do this... I just can't.

'Cassandra, you've got this.'

The words carried over the tumble of water—powerful, provocative, confident. Confident in her. And in her ability to finally get this right.

And as if by magic the inadequacy which had been

holding her back all morning finally let go its stranglehold on her body.

There's no pressure here except the pressure you put on yourself.

This wasn't about pleasing Luke. It was about pleasing herself.

The thought was like a light, blasting the last of the doubts out of her brain—and her fingertips.

The tired muscles in her thighs relaxed. She pressed her toes into the board and finally let it go…

Determination surged through her as she rose to a standing position in one fluid movement. Her legs strained, her knees shook, but she stood upright, instinctively assuming the stance Luke had taught her over the past two days—one leg forward, the other back, her arms outstretched to steady herself.

Her body absorbed the kick of power as the board skimmed across the water. The wave broke behind her and the board shot forward.

Suddenly she was flying. And shrieking. Her joy collided with the rush of triumph.

Her knees trembled, but instead of throwing herself into the sea, this time she adjusted her arms to balance her stance.

Still up…still flying.

Luke shouted and punched the air. 'Way to go, Cassandra. You're surfing.'

She had one blissful moment to absorb the glory of her achievement. It seeped into her soul and made her heart pound as she flew across the water.

This is what living is actually about.

Then the board wobbled and she tipped, sliding into the surf. She went under, swallowing a mouthful of brine.

But it didn't matter because she had already achieved the impossible.

Cassandra James—surfer extraordinaire!

Strong arms took hold of her and yanked her up, back into the air. Exhilaration joined the joy charging through her veins as she spluttered.

'You did it, *cher*.'

A broad smile split Luke's features, making her heart race fast enough to win The Grand National.

'Does it still count? Even though I wiped out?' she said, still not quite able to believe she'd actually stood upright and rode the wave.

'Of course it counts,' he said, while he unstrapped the board from her ankle and strapped it to his own wrist. It bounced and bounded behind them as he swung her over his shoulder and marched back to shore.

She giggled as he carried her back through the waves, then deposited her on her feet.

'Good?' he asked, the twinkle in his eyes even brighter than the sky.

'Never better,' she managed around the emotion forming in her throat.

With his wet hair plastered to his head, the afternoon light gleaming on his tanned face, he was so strong and steady and magnificent in his full body wetsuit.

'That was fantastic,' she added.

'You sure looked fantastic, riding that wave like a pro,' he said.

'I'll just bet I did.' She choked out a laugh, matched by his rough chuckles, as her racing heartbeat galloped into her throat. 'I want to do it again,' she said, still struggling to catch her breath.

But her knees buckled.

He gripped her waist to hold her upright.

'No way,' he said, hooking her wet hair behind her ear, the gesture so tender her knees still refused to cooperate. 'You're beat and we've still got to kayak back to the house.'

She blinked furiously, stunned by the sudden sting of tears that came at the look in his eyes. Not just approval, but respect, admiration, protectiveness. Her heart swelled, pushing uncomfortably against her larynx.

'Fair point,' she said.

She stepped back, out of his embrace. Her swollen heart swooped into her stomach and suddenly she was tumbling again—but this time she was in free fall, and she knew there would be no one to catch her.

She rubbed her eyes to stop the stinging. Tried to steady herself again, but her balance was shot even though she was standing on dry land.

The last four days had been amazing. More than amazing. Everything she had wished for and so much more. The sex had been spectacular. Her body was still humming from all the orgasms, some compelling, some searing and seductive, every one of them more intense and unsettling than the last.

But she'd been ready for that, knowing they shared a rare chemistry. What she hadn't been prepared for when she'd made the decision to stay on Luke's island and grab this moment with both hands was how good the time they spent out of bed would become.

She'd discovered a side of Luke and a side to herself that felt like more than just a physical connection.

He'd been so patient, so protective and focussed on her. They hadn't talked again about anything deep or personal, both far too aware of the end date this moment out of their real lives had, but even so she'd discovered something about him that only made him more compelling, more exciting, more…wonderful.

Luke Broussard might think he was a rebel, a loner, an outsider. And he was a man whom she knew had defied all the odds to make such a staggering success out of his life. But underneath all that ruthless determination and ambition he was a born nurturer.

He'd taught her every one of his mother's signature dishes—she now knew how to cook everything from crawfish étouffée to a mean batch of blueberry pancakes. He also had an encyclopaedic knowledge of the local flora and fauna, which he'd been determined to share. After dragging her off on a couple more hikes through the island's interior he'd taught her the difference between a hawk and a raptor, a red alder and an Oregon white oak. His boundless patience and energy had also paid rich dividends when he'd dedicated their final two afternoons in Pirates' Cove to teaching her how to surf.

There had been no judgement, no cutting remarks, no impossible demands, no ultimatums—even though she wasn't the most able student. Instead there had been only encouragement and excitement at her achievements, however meagre.

The stinging in her eyes got worse. She blinked furiously.

Don't you dare cry. It's just the salt water. You have nothing whatsoever to cry about.

He caught her wrist, dragged her fist away from her face. 'Rubbing them will only make it worse,' he murmured.

Leaning down he grabbed the bottle of water from his pack, uncapped it.

'Here, hold steady.' He cupped her chin, tilted her head back and held one of her eyes open, then the other, to douse them with clean water. 'Okay?' he asked, as he handed her a towel to wipe her eyes without re-contaminating them.

'Yes, thanks,' she said, trying to smile as her stomach bottomed out.

What had she done? And how did she take this yearning back? They were flying to San Francisco tomorrow. This moment was almost over.

'Let's head home,' he said, gathering up the surfboards to lock in the container he had at the far end of the beach. 'How about we hit the hot tub, then nuke one of Mrs Mendoza's pot roasts or something?'

'Sounds like a plan.'

She made herself smile as she packed up the rest of their stuff for the kayak journey back around the point. But her swollen heart had already snagged on the word 'home'.

Luke Broussard might be a natural nurturer at heart. But he wasn't hers—could never be hers.

She swallowed past the raw spot forming in her throat. Somehow or other she was going to have to hold it together tonight, because tomorrow she had to return to reality.

'Hey, come here.'

Luke gripped Cassandra's wrist and tugged her into his lap. They'd done some heavy petting in the hot tub, and filled their stomachs with Mrs Mendoza's enchilada bake, but he'd been itching to make love to her again ever since that moment when she'd stood triumphant on the board and a swell of pride had burst in his chest.

But as he cupped her cheek, leaned in for a kiss, she braced her hands against his chest and pushed him back.

'Problem?' he asked, surprised by the edge in his voice.

He didn't pressure women. But he'd got used to her instant response. That spark of hunger, of need, that had become as natural as breathing—for both of them—every time he reached for her.

Her golden eyes searched his face. 'No, it's just… I'm

exhausted. I thought I'd head to bed now. In… In the guest bedroom. I've got a busy day tomorrow,' she added hastily. 'As soon as we get back to the city, I need to check in at the office and start working on my investment report so I can take something tangible back to Temple in a week's time.'

She was babbling, her nerves evident in the way her body was vibrating under his hands. He stroked her waist, far too aware of the need still thrumming through his system and the instant spurt of anger at the mention of her boss.

Her job was important to her. He got that. And he thought he knew why after spending the last week in her company.

Cassandra was sharply intelligent, focussed and loyal. She was also extremely conscientious. He'd noticed that about her after teaching her everything from how to make a gumbo to how to spot the difference between an oyster-catcher and a cormorant. She had an adorable way of processing every single instruction as if her life depended on it… He could imagine she made a brilliant executive assistant. Even if he'd generally tried not to think about her relationship with Temple.

But they'd had an agreement. No work on the island. And she'd broken it. He hadn't wanted to mix this…whatever *this* was…with their professional lives.

The truth was, he didn't want to think about her returning to the UK. And to Temple. Up to now it had been easy to lose himself in the sex and the companionship—which had surprised him more as each day passed. But as she shifted, ready to get off his lap, he found his grip tightening on her waist. He knew he didn't want to let her go—wasn't ready to let her go. Not yet.

And, weirdly, he knew it wasn't just because of the sexual connection that had blindsided them both. Sure, that had been diverting—and intensely pleasurable. But what had captivated him more was *her*. Her willingness to try new things, to overcome what he'd begun to realise were some fairly major insecurities. Insecurities he suspected she'd hidden behind a shield of competence and capability.

He already knew her father had been a bastard, but when he'd watched her this afternoon, overcoming her fear of failure as she came shooting towards him on the board, her face a picture of pure and uninhibited joy, he'd known he could easily become addicted to that look.

'I should go to bed…' she said, sounding exasperated, but he could hear the uncertainty she always made such an effort to hide.

'I told you I would help you with the report,' he said.

'I know, but there's still a lot to—'

'How about I introduce you to the start-ups I have in mind in person once we're back in the city? And you can come with me to the product launch Tuesday next,' he added, cutting off her argument. 'Because everyone who is anyone in the tech industry in the US will be there.'

Adrenaline surged as he made the offer off the top of his head and realised that tonight didn't have to be the end. Not yet. Not if she agreed to his proposal.

Why the hell *not* continue this liaison? They'd enjoyed themselves on Sunrise. She wasn't due back in the UK for another week. The product launch was a big deal for Broussard Tech—a chance to take his company to the next level. And, again weirdly, he wanted her by his side for the events he had planned. Not just the launch itself, but the lavish reception afterwards at one of the city's hippest nightclubs.

'But…' She blinked. '*Really?* Are you sure? I… I thought we weren't going to see each other once we got back to San Francisco,' she said, blunt as always.

'That was the plan, but the plan can change.'

He hitched his shoulder. He couldn't let this matter to

him—not too much. But even so his gut twisted when she stared back at him and did that lip-chewing thing again, which had always driven him nuts.

'No reason why we shouldn't enjoy the time we have left,' he added, deciding that mixing *this* with his professional interests and hers didn't have to be a bad thing, if it gave them both what they wanted.

Her brow puckered; her thoughts transparent as always. She was torn—he could see that. Torn between taking what she wanted and doing what was right for her boss.

He stifled the prickle of annoyance.

He didn't like Zachary Temple much, even though he'd never even met the guy. And he liked even less having to help the guy out in order to keep Cassandra with him for a while longer. But if Temple wanted to invest in the US tech scene—as long as it didn't mean any involvement in Broussard Tech—he would throw the guy a bone just to have Cassandra where he wanted her for the next week. Until this need had run its course.

'An endorsement from me will give Temple a huge advantage when it comes to getting investment opportunities in Silicon Valley,' he added.

'I… I don't know,' she said, still tugging on her bottom lip—and making him ache.

'What don't you know?' he asked, not quite able to keep the snap of frustration out of his tone any more. Why was she being so difficult about this? He knew she still wanted him, as much as he wanted her, so what exactly was the issue?

'I'm not sure what Temple will make of it if he finds out I attended the launch as your guest…'

He hadn't invited her as a guest, but as his date. His gut knotted, the snap of frustration becoming something darker and more painful.

He pushed it back. Forced himself not to overreact. This was about her job. She was scared of messing up, of looking unprofessional, because that was the kind of woman she was. This wasn't about him. Or her loyalty to Temple. Not really.

'Hey… It's not that big of a deal,' he said, ignoring the bitter taste in his mouth and the unhappy shaft of memory of all the times he'd been ostracised as a kid, for something he hadn't been able to change and had no control over.

He captured her chin, lifted her gaze to his. He saw uncertainty and concern.

Yeah, so not about you, Broussard.

'This is just a chance to enjoy ourselves for a couple more days,' he said, with a nonchalance he didn't quite feel. 'And ensure you get your job done while we're at it. That's all. But if you want to call it quits tomorrow, when we get back to the city, I'm good with that, too.'

He waited for her reply, and as he watched the emotions cross her face—concern, confusion, and finally conviction—a weird sense of relief overtook his irritation. Her answer really shouldn't matter that much. He wasn't that ostracised kid any more… He didn't need Cassandra to accept him—or validate him.

'I… Okay, I'd like that,' she said, not sounding entirely certain.

But that didn't stop the surge of vindication rising up his chest and making his stomach bounce.

'If you're sure it's not a bother,' she added.

'A *bother*?' He grinned—he couldn't help it. The question was so quintessentially Cassandra, he found it unbearably charming. '*Non, cher*, it's not a bother.'

She smiled. It was a tentative curve of her lips—as if she still wasn't sure, but she was willing to take a chance—both brave and sweet. 'Okay, then. I guess we have a deal.'

His ribs tightened and he had the weirdest thought that if he'd ever had the chance to date Cassandra James in high school, *she* would have acknowledged him the next day in class. No question.

He dismissed the dumb sentiment.

And the burst of pride and exhilaration at the thought of having Cassandra James on his arm at the product launch.

Still just a booty call.

'Cool.' He cradled her cheek, then swept his thumb across her bottom lip to stop her worrying it with her teeth—and driving him the rest of the way out of his mind. 'How about we celebrate?'

He grinned at the flush that lit up her cheeks as she nodded. Damn, but she was adorable when she blushed. He tucked her hair back, pulled her in, then slanted his lips over hers, not able to wait a moment longer to taste her.

She opened for him instinctively and he feasted on the soft sob of pleasure, the gentle sigh of surrender. When they finally parted she looked dazed, arousal darkening her eyes.

'You still want to sleep alone tonight, *cher*?' he asked, glad he could tease her about it now.

She shook her head. 'I never really did.'

His heart punched his ribcage the same way it had that afternoon, when she'd stood shaky but upright and ridden the wave towards him.

He stood, scooping her into his arms and heading up to his bedroom. *Their* bedroom.

Hunger flowed through him like the wave that afternoon—strong, steady, unstoppable—but, best of all, it destroyed all the other emotions in its path.

CHAPTER ELEVEN

'YOU LOOK SPECTACULAR, *cher.*' Luke's arms wrapped around Cassie's waist as he drew her into his embrace. 'It's a good thing this gown gives you a lot more coverage than the last one.'

She huffed out a laugh at the audacious comment. She'd bought the bronze silk creation at a luxury clothing consignment store in the Tenderloin yesterday, while channelling her inner Ashling. She hoped the dress was just as hip as the first, but Luke was right—it was a lot less revealing than the gold dress now tucked into her luggage in need of repair.

'I don't want to have to punch anyone for staring,' he added.

He nuzzled her neck, his lips trailing to her earlobe. Her heartbeat hammered against her throat at the possessive comment—which was pretty much where it had remained for the last three days.

She cleared her throat and tried to smile as the mirrored reflection of his hot, mocking smile sent a heavy pulse deep into her abdomen. 'Very funny,' she said, sure he was just teasing her.

She stared at the shimmering silk. So much more demure than Ash's dress. The dress that had caused her so much trouble... Although she was afraid this dress wasn't going to make tonight any easier to negotiate.

She should never have agreed to Luke's invitation to extend their affair for another week. Because after four more days with Luke this felt too much like a real relationship. And tonight… Tonight she was already losing her grip on reality. Thanks to the searing gaze making her cheeks burn.

She didn't know what she'd expected, but somehow she hadn't expected Luke to be quite so…attentive.

After flying them back to the city on Saturday morning, he'd had her luggage moved from the hotel to his apartment in the Presidio. Then he'd arranged meetings for her with a string of CEOs from a series of dynamic new start-ups. The information they'd given her was like gold dust for investors, and she knew Temple would be pleased with the report she had been working on while Luke was out of the apartment preparing for the product launch.

She had finally had the chance to speak to Temple yesterday, to update him on her progress. Thank goodness he hadn't seemed remotely fazed when she'd told him Broussard Tech wasn't looking for investment so she was lining up other prospects. The truth was he'd seemed surprisingly preoccupied.

She hoped it had nothing to do with the astonishing message she'd discovered from Ash after switching her phone on again when she'd got back to San Francisco—and her phone charger.

Gwen's still off sick with her back issues. So I'm running errands for Temple.

Seriously? Ash was working for *Temple*? After being so reluctant even to deliver a tuxedo to him a week ago? And managing to screw that up, according to the last time she'd checked in with her friend?

But Cassie hadn't really had time to investigate. Especially as Ash had seemed more than a little evasive about the arrangement when they'd spoken—and more interested in quizzing Cassie about developments with Luke. But as Cassie had no desire to talk about *that* topic, she'd decided not to press Ash on her new temporary job.

She had much bigger things to worry about right now than whether Ash was going to flake out on Temple again. Such as how she was going to keep her heart from shattering when she had to return to the UK in three days.

The product launch itself that morning had been a spectacular success. But she'd found it increasingly hard to concentrate on business with Luke never far from her side. She'd expected to be anonymous at the launch, one of the many invited guests. But she'd been anything but…

She shifted round. 'Are you sure I should be going to this party tonight?' she asked. 'I haven't told anyone except Ash about…about us. I don't want to seem unprofessional,' she said, knowing she was lying to herself as much as Luke.

She'd crossed that line twelve tumultuous days ago—and keeping their affair a secret had nothing to do with her job and everything to do with keeping her own feelings in check.

'Ashamed to be seen with me?' he asked.

But even though his lips had curved into that confident sensual smile she adored, his eyes had suddenly lost their twinkle of amusement.

'Of course not,' she said instantly, and her heart squeezed at the thought she might have insulted him.

However much being Luke's date might compromise her business reputation—especially when she was forced to explain the situation to Temple—that wasn't the real reason she was struggling.

'I just... I didn't expect for us to be so...' *Right.* She swallowed the word down, tried to unthink it. 'So much like a couple,' she managed.

This relationship wasn't right—it wasn't even real. Not for much longer anyway.

He stared back at her. 'You've got to come. You don't want to waste this dress.'

He pressed his palms into the fabric, letting the shimmering material rasp over her already over-sensitised skin.

'Even if it's gonna be torturing me all night, knowing how much I want to get you out of it,' he added provocatively, skimming a finger over her breast.

Her nipple squeezed into a tight peak from the tantalising caress. She shuddered, enthralled all over again—the way she had been for nearly two weeks now. Every time he touched her, every time he looked at her with that searing approval in his eyes, every time he made her feel more than she'd ever felt before...

He dropped his hand back to her waist and tugged her close to press a kiss to her temple. 'Don't worry,' he said. 'We won't be staying long.'

He clasped her hand and led her out of the penthouse apartment.

'Which is why we need to get there before midnight,' he added as he stabbed the private elevator button. 'So we can leave early.'

She let the familiar hunger surge. His urgency was as intoxicating as the devilish gleam that had returned to his eyes. But it did nothing to cover the frantic beat of her heart, which was still rammed in her throat.

It wasn't until Luke stepped out of the limo at the venue, with her hand still clasped firmly in his, and headed through the barrage of paparazzi to the legendary nightclub hired for the event—three floors of the world's hottest DJs, housed in an iconic nineteen-hundreds redbrick canning factory in Fisherman's Wharf—that she realised her professional reputation was the least of the things she had already lost to Luke Broussard.

And the only person to blame for that was herself.

'Damn, I thought we'd never get out of there.'

Luke spun Cassandra around as they walked back into his apartment. *Finally.* The sun was coming up over the bay through the penthouse's windows as he pressed her lithe body to the glass and placed his mouth on the hammering pulse in her neck.

He wanted her. *Now.* Had been frantic to have her all evening. Dancing with her had been tortuous…feeling her body move in time with his and knowing he couldn't claim her the way he wanted to claim her without getting arrested.

But he'd branded her as his for all the world to see tonight in every other way that counted.

'I haven't told anyone except Ash about us...'

The quiet words she'd spoken earlier ricocheted through his head again, taunting him the way they'd been doing all evening, tying his gut into tight, greasy knots and making his insides hurt.

To hell with that.

She was *his*. And he'd be damned if he'd let her hide that from anyone.

The echo of her words had faded when he'd paraded her in front of the photographers outside the club, when he'd kept her anchored to his side while everyone came up to congratulate him on the launch, when he'd lost himself in the throbbing bass beat of a retro rap anthem and celebrated his success with her in his arms.

But now what she'd said shouted across his consciousness again, as he grasped the dress that had been keeping her from him and yanked it down.

The sound of rending fabric tore through the quiet apartment and she bucked against his hold.

'Luke…' she said, her voice trembling with arousal, and shock. 'Is something wrong?'

'Not any more…' he said, cupping the breast he'd exposed and capturing the swollen nipple in his mouth.

She jerked, her ripe flesh engorging in a rush as he suckled strongly. He lifted his head to watch as he shoved the remnants of silk off her, leaving her naked but for the swatch of lace covering her sex.

'I need you,' he said, palming her sex through the lace.

The desire to own her, which had been building like wildfire all night, ever since she'd challenged him, was turning into a need so fierce it all but consumed him. Wet heat flooded into his hand as he delved beneath the gusset, found the slick nub of her clitoris.

'Tell me you need me, too,' he demanded.

She nodded, her eyes dazed, and yet she was focussed solely on him as he hooked her leg around his waist and fumbled with the zipper of his pants.

His fingers were clumsy, frantic, as he freed his huge erection, ripped away the last barrier between them, and then lifted her to plunge in up to the hilt.

She took him in on a shocked sob.

The penetration was deep, but not deep enough. He needed all of her—every single inch, every single millimetre. Claimed, conquered, branded.

Her head fell back against the glass as he rocked out, thrust back, harder and faster. But still it was not enough. Her first orgasm hit as her sex massaged his, nearly sending him over too, but he held on, held back. He needed more. He needed her total surrender to make this right.

The terrifying realisation barrelled into him as a titanic climax gathered at the base of his spine, more pain than pleasure. Too raw, too desperate. Suddenly he was that boy again. Needing approval, needing validation, needing respect, needing love.

'More,' he groaned. 'Come again, just for me.'

Holding her up with one arm, still thrusting like a mad man, like an insane person, he found the heart of her pleasure, circled the swollen nub with his thumb. She came around him, pulsing hard, the orgasm even more intense than the first, and he yelled and finally let himself shatter too, body and soul, pouring himself into her.

They sank together to the carpet. Her naked limbs were tangled with his. Her face was pressed into his neck, and the shattered gasps of her breathing matched his as he cradled her body.

And knew he'd made her his, the only way he ever could.

Cassie sat on the carpet, struggling to capture her breath and make sense of what had just happened. It had been like a whirlwind. She felt so raw, so...owned. So exhausted.

It was six in the morning and she knew despite everything, despite all her warnings to herself, that she'd fallen hopelessly in love with the man whose head now rested on her shoulder as they both tried to claw back the sanity they'd lost so comprehensively.

This wasn't just sex. Had never been just sex. Not for her.

The sound of her phone buzzing crashed into the terrifying thought. She reached for her bag, suddenly desperate to escape the painful pressure in her chest which had been there for days but was now threatening to crush her ribcage.

She couldn't be in love with Luke. It would force her right back to where she'd been all those years ago. With her self-worth, her security, tied to a man who didn't love her back.

'Hey…' He grasped her wrist as she retrieved the phone from her bag, her fingers trembling. 'You're not taking that,' he said.

It was a command, not a question. And something deep in her heart twisted. She'd let so much of herself go for this man, and none of it made sense any more. She had to leave—had to get out. Before the damage was irreparable.

'I have to. It might be important.'

She eased herself off the floor, grasped the remains of the silk dress which he'd torn off her only moments before, held it to cover her nakedness. Panic at what they had just shared—so urgent, so basic, so uncontrolled—gathered in her gut alongside the need to run before Luke realised the truth.

Her hand shook as she pressed her thumb to the home screen to unlock her phone and read the message from her boss.

I need you. Can you get an early flight back?

She blinked. Temple's text was so out of character it barely registered for a moment. But when it did, she knew she had a way out.

It was cowardly, weak, pitiable—she knew all that—but as she tapped out a reply on her phone, still trembling from the orgasms which had shattered her, the panic controlled her.

This was a fight for survival now. If she stayed another minute, another day, all it would do was crush what was left of her spirit, her independence and her self-respect.

She'd had misgivings about going to the launch as Luke's date—she'd told him that—and he'd introduced her to everyone—including all the people she'd interviewed for her investment report—as if they were properly dating. As if they were a couple.

Had he known how that would make her feel? Had he done it deliberately? Or did he simply not care enough about her to be cautious.

She suspected it was just Luke being Luke—commanding, arrogant, nurturing, but also possessive—but she also knew that he didn't understand how deep her feelings went…how delusional she had become in the last few days. So he had no idea the damage he was doing.

Still holding the torn silk to cover her nakedness, she said, 'I have to book a flight home.'

'What's wrong?' Luke asked, coming up behind her. He placed his hands on her hips to turn her around.

Humiliation washed over her. He was already dressed—all he'd had to do was zip his flies. And she was still naked and shivering, with the afterglow still racking her body, making her want what she couldn't have. Shouldn't need.

He gently cupped her chin to lift her gaze to his. 'Who's the message from? Has something happened?'

Her heart shattered a little more at the concern in his eyes. He cared about her—just not in the way she had come to care for him. Why did that make it hurt so much more?

'Temple. He needs me,' she said.

The thunderous frown on his face came from nowhere. And when he spoke, the lash of contempt in his voice shocked her.

'You have got to be kidding me! What are you—his lap dog?'

She stiffened, reeling from the unprovoked attack, and

from what she could see in his eyes—which wasn't anger so much as…jealousy?

'He's my boss,' she said slowly, feeling exposed and small. 'This is my job. It matters to me.'

'Oh, come on. This isn't about your damn job. He clicks his fingers and suddenly you're hightailing it across an ocean to do his bidding?'

She pressed the torn material to her breast, shaking now… But somehow, from somewhere, she found the courage she needed to cover the hurt and humiliation burning in her gut.

'What are you implying?' she said, her voice surprisingly calm given that everything she knew about him, about herself, was imploding.

'Just tell me one thing—have you slept with him?'

'You bastard,' she said, his accusation slicing through her heart. 'You're the only man I've ever slept with.'

'What?' he asked, his face a picture of shock. 'What did you just say?'

'Nothing—it doesn't matter,' she said, desperate to claw the words back, their truth making her feel so insignificant, so foolish.

'Damn it, Cassie. Was I your first?' he said, as if it mattered to him.

But she could hear the demand in his voice. And she knew that if she admitted the truth it would only make her more lost, more vulnerable, more unequal.

'Tell me the truth,' he said.

She shook her head. She didn't owe him an explanation. Didn't owe him the truth. Because it wouldn't change the real truth. That she'd given him far too much of herself and all the time she had never meant that much to him.

'It isn't important anyway,' she said, wanting desperately to believe it. 'Because you certainly won't be my last.'

He tensed as if she'd struck him. 'Why the hell did you lie about it?' he said.

But when he reached for her arm, she jerked it out of his grasp. 'Don't touch me, Luke,' she said, knowing she had to protect herself now. She couldn't worry about him and his demons, because her own were already consuming her. 'I don't want you to touch me,' she added. 'I'm leaving, and I won't let you stop me.'

She knew she'd hurt him—saw him flinch as he dropped his arm. But she turned, ran into the bedroom and locked the door, before the great gulping sobs could overtake her.

How could she have given so much of herself and been prepared to get so little in return? She'd succumbed to his will all the way along and lost herself in the process. Opened herself up and told him things about herself that had given him a power over her she couldn't get back. And he'd never done the same. He'd remained closed off—in control the whole time.

All that was left to her now was to run away and own the fact that she'd fallen far too easily.

She dropped the torn dress and tugged on other clothing, her silent sobs making her fingers clumsy, her body convulse.

After throwing everything she could reach into her case, she forced herself to open the bedroom door—and found the room empty.

She knew she couldn't survive another confrontation with him, that he'd done her a favour, but the relief she wanted to feel refused to come.

She scribbled a note, to apologise one last time. She hadn't meant to hurt him. But it would be just one more thing to regret of so many.

She managed to hold herself together until she was sitting in a cab on her way to the airport. But as she booked a flight, and sent a message to Temple to say that she was on her way home, the tears fell unbidden to splash onto the phone. Because London didn't feel like home any more.

The urge to call Ash, to draw her friend into this titanic mess, to lean on her unqualified compassion and solidarity was immense. But she tucked her phone back into her bag as the cab took the exit onto I-80 and the Golden Gate Bridge disappeared in the rear window, her throat still raw from the look on Luke's face the last time she'd seen it.

She didn't deserve Ash's support now…didn't deserve her comfort.

She'd made this mess all by herself… And now she would have to live with it.

CHAPTER TWELVE

'I NEED TO know where Cassandra James is.' Luke stared down the man standing behind the mahogany desk. He'd had to barge past two security guards and an assistant he didn't recognise to get to him.

'Who the hell are you and how the hell did you get into my office?' Zachary Temple glared back at him.

Dressed in a three-piece suit, his height an inch above Luke's own six-foot-three, Cassandra's boss looked as stuck up as Luke had expected. The furious expression on the guy's face would have intimidated Luke once upon a time, when he was a green kid from the wrong side of the tracks, but it didn't bother him now. Not after an eleven-hour flight, a mad dash from the airport and enough fury and frustration and hurt to keep his temper at fever-pitch for the foreseeable future—especially where this arrogant bastard was concerned.

He never should have let Cassandra leave. But he'd needed time and distance to control all the feelings roiling in his gut at what she'd blurted out.

'You're the only man I've ever slept with.'

How much that admission had disturbed him. And the same confusing emotions continued to churn now. Panic, regret, but most of all…terror. Terror that he'd already lost something he hadn't even known he had.

How ironic was it that those same dumb emotions had got him into a load of pointless fights as a kid?

He wanted a chance to explain. To apologise…to see if her admission meant what he thought it meant. But he had to find her first. And the only person standing in his way was this guy.

'Gwen, get in here,' Temple shouted at the woman he'd barged past five seconds ago.

The middle-aged assistant appeared at the door, looking just as concerned as she had a few moments before. 'I'm so sorry, Mr Temple. He said he had an appointment.'

'Like hell he—'

'I'm Luke Broussard of Broussard Tech.' Luke interrupted the man's diatribe as it occurred to him that Temple—despite his three-piece suit and his carefully manicured appearance—looked almost as harassed as Luke felt.

'Terrific,' the guy announced with biting sarcasm as he thrust his fingers through his hair. 'The man who managed to lose me the best executive assistant I've ever had. What are you doing here? Have you come to gloat?'

'What do you mean, "lose you"? Where is Cassandra?' Luke asked, feeling anxiety tightening around his throat. The anxiety which he'd been busy trying to control for over fifteen hours—ever since he'd returned from a walk around the block to cool off and found an empty apartment and Cassandra's note.

I can't stay, Luke. And it has nothing to do with Temple. Or my job.

I lost perspective on what this is...or rather what it was. I let myself believe that it could be more. And that's on me, not you.

In answer to your question, you were my first

lover. I shouldn't have lied about that because it gave it much more significance than it deserves.

Please don't feel you owe me anything. You don't.

The note had damned him—because he'd been able to read the pain and humiliation he'd caused in every scrawled word. But at least it had finally forced him to stop and think long enough to figure out a lot of stuff he should have figured out days ago.

The truth of her virginity had shocked him, but more than that it had humbled him. But what had humbled and shocked him more was the fact that she had lied about it. And what had bothered him was *why*.

One thing was for sure—nothing about their situation had ever been simple. What astonished him, though, was the knowledge that he was pretty damn sure he didn't want it to be simple any more.

Right now, though, he felt as if he'd just wiped out on his board and capsized the kayak at the same time. And the only way he knew how to come back up for air was to see her again.

'I expect she's at home,' Temple murmured. 'Being head-hunted by one of my rivals. So thanks for that.'

'She resigned?'

Luke gaped. He couldn't believe it. The guilt that had been riding him for hours took another sharp twist. She loved her job—why had she left it? Was that on him too? Because paparazzi photos from the launch had been all over the press this morning. And after seeing them he'd finally had to acknowledge another home truth. It had felt *right* to introduce her as his date. He'd *wanted* her on his arm… And it had never just been about getting vindication for that troubled kid who had once been shunned by his whole hometown.

His guilt at the news she had left her job—that this was one more thing he'd robbed her of, as well as her pride and self-respect—was accompanied by something else.

Hope.

If she isn't tied to the UK any more, maybe...just maybe...

The hollow ache in his stomach knotted and the flicker of hope guttered out.

Getting way, way ahead of yourself, buddy.

Opportunism had once been his strong suit, but all it did now was shame him more. He'd given Cassandra nothing of himself, and that had to come first—before anything else. She needed to know why he'd guarded his feelings while exploiting hers. Why he'd taken from her and given nothing back. She needed to know the truth about that kid. The kid he'd thought he'd left behind a lifetime ago but who was still inside him, always ready to fight, but not ready to heal… Until now.

'You need to give me her address,' he said, jettisoning his pride. 'Please, man. I need to talk to her… To explain.'

So much.

Temple looked unmoved. 'What the hell makes you think I'd give you my executive assistant's address? Why should I? Not only is it unethical, but it's also quite possibly illegal. And I really could not care less if—'

'Because…'

I think I might be in love with her… The words echoed in his head, shocking him right down to his core. But he had the peace of mind to hold on to them. He couldn't think about that now. Couldn't contemplate it or it would just terrify him more. And Temple sure as heck wasn't the person to talk to about it.

'Because *what*?' Temple snapped, his impatience clear.

Luke resisted the urge to grip the guy by the throat and force the information out of him. *Just.*

'Because I know why she resigned her position here. You want her back? You need to let me speak to her—so I can explain.'

Like hell was he going to help Temple get Cassandra back in his employ. He didn't like the guy. But if he had to lie to him to get Cassandra's address, he'd do it in a heartbeat.

'And because this is personal,' he said, when Temple still looked unmoved and unconvinced. 'I hurt her and I want to make it right,' he added.

Temple stared at him for the longest time, considering. And then—just when Luke was sure he'd blown it and debased himself in front of the guy for nothing—Temple grabbed a pad and jotted something down.

He ripped the note off the pad and handed it to Luke. 'Take it. But if you hurt her again, in any way, I'll destroy you.'

Luke saluted the man, so grateful he would almost have been willing to kiss him. *Almost.*

He dashed out of the office, past the assistant and the two security guards who had just arrived on the top floor of Temple Corp's offices.

Now all he had to do was figure out what to say to Cassandra to make things right… Or at least not so wrong.

Cassie's head lifted as the loud buzz of the doorbell drilled into her frontal lobe.

Ash? At last. It had to be. She was for ever losing her key.

Cassie had managed to hold off contacting her BFF on the flight back. But when she'd got home to find Ash gone, having left some garbled note about going to a family event in Ireland, and she hadn't answered any of her texts, the last reserves of Cassie's strength had collapsed and she'd been crying ever since.

Sniffing loudly, she wiped her eyes, which were red raw, and managed to pick her aching body off the couch. She headed down the hall, feeling as if she were walking through a fog. Who knew heart-ache could be so exhausting? This was like having the flu and jet lag and a hangover all at once.

She undid the chain, her bruised and battered heart squeezing. Maybe Ash could make it better? Because crying for twelve hours solid had only made her a wreck.

She opened the door, her sore heart beating painfully, then gasped. 'Luke?'

Was she hallucinating? Surely she had to be.

But then the vision spoke, his husky voice raw with emotion and reaching right down into her soul. 'Cassandra, we need to…'

It was all he managed to get out before the fog cleared, her heart hit warp speed and she tried to slam the door shut.

Too late. He stuck his foot in the gap.

She managed to stop the door hitting him, her terror she might hurt him more devastating than the shot of pain arrowing through her heart.

'Please, I can't…' she said, but he had already eased the door open, stepped into the entrance hall and closed it behind him. She stepped back. 'I can't do this.'

'I know,' he said. 'I'm not here to hurt you again, I promise.'

He looked as if he meant it, but she couldn't seem to focus on his words—only his face. How could this man—less sure of himself now than before, but no less overwhelming—still make her pulse race and her heart leap in her chest?

'Why did you lie to me about being a virgin?' he said.

She could feel her heart collapsing all over again. *Oh, no.* Was that why he was here? Because he thought somehow he owed her something? Hadn't she explained all that in her note?

She could minimise the fact of her virginity again, but that would give the truth too much power. More power than it should ever have possessed.

'Because I didn't want it to be a big deal…' she said, suddenly feeling unbearably weary. Was this another mistake she'd made?

'Even though it was,' he said, so softly she almost didn't hear him. 'And still is.'

'No, it's really not,' she said, needing him to leave now, before she went totally to pieces again.

He cupped her cheek, ran his thumb over the sore skin where her tears had burned. 'You're a terrible liar—you know that, right?'

She forced herself to pull away, even though she still yearned for his touch. This wasn't fair. How much more was she going to be forced to endure?

'Just because you were my first, it doesn't make this special, or different…' *If only that were true*, she thought miserably. 'I understand that.'

'But it matters to me,' he said, cutting off the anger she wanted to feel at the knees.

'Why?' she said, not even able to muster the energy to be angry with him any more.

His hand sank to her waist and he pulled her close to touch his forehead to hers. He touched her neck. 'Because you trusted me,' he said. 'And I never trusted you.'

'Okay…' she managed—because what else could she say? Her foolish broken heart was beating double-time again.

'You gave me something precious, Cassandra, and I threw it back in your face because of my own insecurities.'

She breathed in, the tightening in her chest almost as painful as the aching pain in her heart. She didn't want to hope, didn't want to believe…

'It's okay, Luke. I know where those insecurities came from,' she said, remembering the few things he'd told her about his past, and all the things she suspected he hadn't told her. 'I understand them. I have a few fairly massive insecurities of my own,' she added.

'Don't let me off the hook,' he said. 'Because I don't deserve it.'

He kissed her eyelids, kissed her cheeks, in an act of worship that staggered her and had her heart swelling in her chest, making her sore ribs ache even more and her breathing uneven. What was actually happening here? Because it felt like more than she could ever have hoped for.

He placed a tender kiss on her lips. But then, just as she let out a small sigh, feeling the hunger still there, despite everything, he drew away and let her go.

Sinking his hands into the pockets of his leather jacket, he took a step back. He dropped his chin to his chest, looking more nervous than she had ever seen him—and yet more open, too.

'You need to know…' He huffed out a breath. 'I didn't tell you the truth either.'

'About what?' she said.

'I told you I didn't remember my old man…'

His gaze met hers, and what she saw in his eyes had her heart thundering into her throat before he looked away again.

'It's not true. He was sent to the pen just after I was born. But he came back when he'd served his time. Just arrived at our trailer one day, out of the blue. I was fifteen, and I already hated him, but she thought…'

His shoulders rose and fell, and the pain in his face when he hesitated seared Cassie's insides.

'My mama…she thought he had come back because he loved her. Because she had never stopped loving him. He beat the crap out of her…'

Luke touched his thumb to the small scar that bisected his eyebrow, the one that she'd wondered about often, and she realised that his mother wasn't the only one who had been hurt.

'And he took the money we'd been saving to put a down payment on a house.'

'Oh, Luke, he sounds like a hideous man…' she murmured.

'He was.' He glanced up, then stared back at his toes. 'But the hell of it was she refused to press charges… Because she didn't want to screw up his parole.'

His head rose again, and his eyes were fierce and unguarded for the first time since she'd known him. She could see it all now. The pain, the regret, the fury and the deep grief—for his mother and for the love she'd had for a man who didn't deserve it.

'I'm so sorry, Luke,' she said, reaching up to cradle his cheek.

She wanted to soothe, wanted to destroy the demons that still lurked in his eyes the way he had destroyed hers. Was this why it had been so important for him not to feel anything? Not to trust her or any feelings he might have for her?

'He sounds like an even bigger bastard than my father,' she added. 'And that's saying something.'

'Ain't that the truth?'

He chuckled. The sound was rough and raw, but still her heart swelled and beat heavily against her ribs.

He gripped her hand, brought her fingers to his lips and kissed the palm. 'But I don't care about him any more, or what he did. Do you know why?'

'No,' she said, her wayward heart beating double-time at the look in his eyes. Not just approval, not just arousal, but so much more.

'Because I finally figured something out. A part of me always blamed her for being a sap, for falling for a guy who didn't love her back. I swore I would never be so dumb. Which was why, when I started falling for you, I did every damn thing I could to try and deny it.'

'*You...* You fell for me?' Her heart slammed into her throat.

'Yeah… I think I started falling the first moment I spotted you at Matt and Remy's wedding. Busy chewing off your lipstick like your life depended on it.'

He rubbed his thumb across her bottom lip and she realised she was doing it again. 'Really?' she asked, because she couldn't believe it. *Love at first sight was actually a thing?*

'Yeah, really.' He chuckled again. 'Why are you so surprised?'

'Because… But *why* did you?' she said, still not quite able to let go of the fear that had always consumed her as a child. That she wasn't good enough—would never be worthy of love.

He laughed, the sound low and husky this time, and hot enough to warm the last of the cold, empty spaces that still lurked in her heart.

'Well, that's the easy part.' He brushed his thumb across her cheek. 'Because you're smart and cute and loyal and honest—'

'You make me sound like a puppy.' She interrupted, astonished that she could joke with him when her heart had expanded to impossible proportions and got jammed in her throat.

He laughed again. 'And hot as hell,' he added.

'That's better,' she said, euphoria infecting her soul and making her lips lift up in what she was fairly sure was a mile-wide grin. 'Keep going…' she added.

'I love the way you bite your lip when you're nervous, or concentrating, or doing something you're scared to fail at but are determined to try nonetheless. I love your bravery and your boldness and your ingenuity, and how, even though you have a veneer of efficiency and purpose, it really isn't that hard to turn you into mush.'

A laugh burst out, riding the wave of euphoria right out of her mouth. How wonderful, she thought, to realise that so much of what she had considered her weaknesses, were her strengths…to him.

He took her hand, threaded his fingers through hers and tugged her slowly into his arms, until her hands were settled on his waist and she was staring into his eyes.

'And I love that you're gonna forgive me for being a jerk.'

His gaze roamed up to her hair and over her face, the light shining in his eyes for her and only her.

'You weren't a jerk,' she said, touching his cheek. 'You were just cautious.'

'Not any more,' he said, covering her hand, then bringing her fingers to his lips. 'Not with you.'

She blinked, felt the tears threatening again, but this time they were tears of joy.

He wrapped his arms around her, tucked her head under his chin to whisper against her hair. 'I'm sorry I lost you your job…but how would you feel about finding a new one in San Francisco? I have some great contacts. And I know an island that wants you to call it home.'

The giddy beat of her heart hit hyperdrive. She'd only known him two weeks. This was a big step—a huge step—a decision she couldn't make on the spur of the moment. But somehow, as mad as it was, it already felt right.

After all, it would just be another crazy adventure—and she was getting surprisingly good at those.

'I'll consider it,' she said, being coy two weeks too late. Then she leaned back to stare up at him. 'But don't you want to know if I love you too first? Before you ask me to move in with you?'

He shook his head and framed her face with his hands. 'Nuh-uh,' he said, with the confidence she had come to adore. 'I already know you do, *cher*.'

And before she had a chance to be outraged, or indignant, or to dispute the inevitable, he covered her mouth with his lips and sealed the truth with a soul-searing kiss.

* * * * *

THE BILLION-DOLLAR BRIDE HUNT

MELANIE MILBURNE

MILLS & BOON

To all the wonderful people out there
who adopt or foster children
and give them a happy and loving home.

And a special message of love and heartfelt empathy
to those who can't have their own biological child.

CHAPTER ONE

EMMALINE WOODCROFT WAS basking in the glow of yet another successful match between two of her dating agency clients when her secretary-cum-receptionist, Paisley, came into her office and informed her she had a walk-in who insisted on seeing her immediately.

'Male or female?' Emmie asked, putting her mobile phone back down on the desk.

Paisley pressed her back firmly against Emmie's office door, as if worried the client would stride in without waiting for permission. 'Male.' There was a slightly breathless quality to her voice and she added, 'Tall, very tall, good-looking. Italian, I think, going by the accent. Designer suit. But why he would want to engage a professional match-making service is beyond me. I'd have him in a heartbeat if I wasn't already engaged.'

A tingle of intrigue tiptoed across Emmie's scalp on tiny stilettoed feet. A new client was always a good thing and a handsome one a bonus. And, given he was a walk-in, it confirmed to her that setting up a small bricks-and-mortar London office as well as her online platform had been a good idea. Spontaneous decisions to engage her match-making services often produced the best results. It was when people let their guard down, inspired by an in-the-moment impulse. 'Send him in.'

Paisley's eyes sparkled and she said *sotto voce*, 'Brace yourself, Emmie. You're not going to believe how off-the-scale handsome he is. He quite took my breath away.' She disappeared out through the door. A few moments later the door opened again, and a tall suited man stepped into Emmie's office and closed the door behind him with a firm click that sent a shiver coursing down her spine.

'Ms Emmaline Woodcroft? Matteo Vitale.'

If his looks hadn't been enough to send her senses spinning, the mellifluous tone of his voice with its distinctive Italian accent more than finished the job. At least six-foot-four but possibly half an inch or so more, he made her office seem tiny. Well, tinier than it already was. He had olive-toned skin and thick jet-black hair that was neither short nor long but somewhere in between. He was clean shaven but his late-in-the-day stubble was generously distributed along the lean landscape of his jawline and around his nose and mouth.

His mouth…

Emmie's breath stalled in her throat and a quiver went through her entire body. His mouth was the sort of mouth that would have sent Michelangelo rushing off to sharpen his chisels and restock on marble—a fuller lower lip with a thinner top one that was perfectly balanced by a deep ridge below his long, straight nose. It was a sensual mouth tempered by a hint of stubbornness, perhaps even a streak of ruthlessness. He had prominent ink-black eyebrows that would have met in the middle except for the two-pleated shallow groove of what looked to be a perpetual frown.

But it was his eyes that stopped Emmie's heart. With his Italian, olive-toned colouring she had expected dark-brown or hazel eyes, but they were an unusual shade of blue. They reminded her of an uncharted ocean, the unknowable depths giving no clue whether danger or buried treasure were hidden beneath.

Matteo strode across the carpet to stand in front of her desk, proffering his hand across the top. She slowly rose from her chair, because for some strange reason her legs were decidedly unsteady, and slipped her hand into the firm, warm cage of his. His long, tanned fingers pressed against hers and she gulped back an involuntary swallow. A tingle scuttled down the backs of her legs like a small startled creature.

'How do you do? Oh, and please call me Emmie.'

'Emmie.' Matteo said her name unlike anyone had ever said it before, his accent leaning a little heavily on the second syllable, making it sound more like *Em-meee.*

She had to remind herself to take back her hand because she was tempted to let it stay exactly where it was—captured in the warm, dry enclosure of his. She eased out of his light grasp, but her fingers tingled and the palm of her hand fizzed as if some strange energy had passed from his body to hers.

The energy moved further through her body like the powerful rays of a heat lamp, searing warmth that lit tiny spot fires in each of her erogenous zones. Zones that had lain dormant for so long it was a shock to feel them stirring into life now. Every millimetre of her skin was intensely aware of him. Aware of his towering presence, his penetrating gaze, his arrant maleness, his commanding, take-charge air.

Emmie waved her hand towards the velvet-covered chair opposite her desk. 'Please, take a seat.'

'Thank you.' His deep voice sent another shockwave of awareness through her, so too did the sharp citrus top-notes of his aftershave. Lemon and lime with a hint of something a little more exotic in the base notes that made her nostrils flare and her pulse throb.

Emmie sat back down before her trembling legs gave way beneath her. She had no idea why this man was having such a potent effect on her. She met dozens, hundreds, of men in her line of business and not one of them had caused her body to react like a star-struck teenager in front of a rock star. Even seated Matteo Vitale was so tall, her neck muscles pinched as she craned her neck back to maintain eye contact.

'So, how may I help you, Mr Vitale?' She activated her best business-like tone but something about the glint in his dark blue eyes was cynical, perhaps even a little mocking.

'You're a professional match-maker, correct?'

'Yes. I individually profile my clientele and help them to find a partner who will be perfect for them in every—'

'I need a wife.' His blunt statement and the determined set to his mouth made her sit up straighter in her chair.

'I see. Well, then, you've come to the right person because I have successfully matched many couples who to date are still all happily together. Emmie's Magical Match-Ups has a track record I'm enormously proud of, and I know it's because I take the time to get to know each of my clients personally before I find them the love of their life.'

One side of his mouth lifted but it would be a stretch to call it anything near a smile. If anything, it matched the cynical glint in his eyes that seemed as perpetual as his frown. 'I don't want a long-term wife. Only one who will stick around long enough to provide me with an heir.'

Emmie blinked, wondering if she'd heard him correctly. She moistened her suddenly paper-dry lips and shifted slightly in her chair. 'So…you're not looking for love?'

'No.' His flat tone and cynical expression seemed to suggest he didn't believe the concept even existed. 'My father died recently and, unbeknownst to me, added a codicil to his will. I will not be able to inherit my father's large estate in Umbria, which has been in my family for generations, unless I marry and produce an heir within a year.'

'I'm sorry for your loss—'

'Save your condolences. We weren't close.' His dismissive tone irked her and intrigued her in equal measure. What sort of relationship had he had with his father for his father to have added such an unusual codicil to his will? A large Umbrian estate meant there was a lot of money at stake, but Matteo Vitale didn't look like the sort of man who had to rely on a family inheritance to get by. His suit was bespoke, his shoes hand-stitched Italian leather, his beguiling cologne certainly not one of those cheap knockoffs you could pick up at any discount outlet.

His name rang a faint bell in her head… Hadn't she seen an article about him in the press a few months back about his work as a forensic accountant? He had uncovered a massive fraudulent operation during a high-profile divorce case. It had involved millions of pounds of cleverly hidden money but Matteo had uncovered it all. How galling it must have been to find out his father had hidden this codicil from him until it was too late to do anything to change his father's mind.

Emmie still had both her parents and, while she wasn't as close to her father as her mother since their divorce during her teens after her cancer diagnosis, she couldn't imagine not grieving for him. Nor could she imagine her father adding such a codicil to his will, because he of all people knew the last thing she could ever do was provide an heir.

'Look, Mr Vitale, I don't think I'm the right person to help you after all. My focus is on finding true love for my clients, not finding a womb for hire.' She began to push back her chair to bring the meeting to a close but something about his expression made her sit back down again.

The silence was palpable. It seemed to press in from all four corners of the room, robbing the air of oxygen until Emmie found it hard to expand her lungs enough to take a breath.

'I'm prepared to pay well above your normal fee.' His tone was coolly business-like. She knew she should inform him that no price would allow her to compromise her professional reputation by taking on a brief so far outside what she normally did for her clients. But something about that ever-so-brief flicker of pain in his gaze captivated her.

Emmie studied him for a moment, scanning his features for any further sign of vulnerability, but there was none. He could have been carved from stone. 'How do you know I won't name a price more than your family estate is worth?'

'I've researched you. You're expensive but your clients get what they pay for. And, as you say, your success rate is commendable. I'll pay you three or four times what you normally charge.'

Emmie had done well with her business, better than she had expected, but it was an expensive service to run with increasing overheads. Plus, she had a mortgage, and she was helping her mother pay for her younger sister Natalie's therapy for an eating disorder that had started during Emmie's battle with cancer. It would be crazy not to at least consider Matteo's offer. His request might be a little outside her normal range of service but it was surely worth a try? Never let it be said she shied away from a challenge. Her history of chemotherapy was proof of that. 'You're a forensic accountant, right?'

His eyebrows lifted in mild surprise. 'Was that a wild guess?'

'I saw something about you in the press a while back,' Emmie said. Although the photo hadn't done him justice. Matteo Vitale had a commanding presence that no camera lens could ever capture. It wasn't just his imposing height or brusque manner—something about his eyes hinted at deeply buried pain. Pain that was so cleverly, determinedly hidden it took a special skill to recognise it.

And Emmie had that skill in spades. Her pain radar had been finely tuned by life's disappointments. There was a lot of truth in that old maxim 'it takes one to know one.' She saw in others what she hid so cleverly in herself. It caused other people pain to know about hers, so she had excised it. Denied it. Buried it. She could walk past a pram, smile at the mother and no one would ever guess the searing agony inside her heart that she would never hold her own child in her arms.

Her ovaries had been damaged during her chemo and no amount of wishing and hoping and bargaining and praying for a miracle was ever going to restore them. IVF and donor eggs had been mentioned by her doctors, but Emmie knew it wouldn't be the same as holding her own baby, seeing her own features and that of other members of her family in the child's features and personality. Emmie had decided that, if fate had decreed she was infertile, then she would accept it, as painful and heart-wrenching as it was. She had even convinced her parents and sister she had put that bitter disappointment behind her once and for all. It was too upsetting to see them worrying about her. Pitying her.

Emmie placed her hands on the desk in a clasped position. She felt compelled to find out everything she could about Matteo Vitale. He was like a complicated puzzle someone had presented her with, and she wouldn't rest until she solved it. 'I must admit, I'm finding it hard to understand why you even need my services, Mr Vitale. I mean, you're good-looking, and apparently rich enough to afford to pay me handsomely. I would have thought you'd have no trouble convincing any woman to do anything you asked her to do.'

'Do you include yourself in that statement?' His eyes held hers in a lock that sent a shower of unfamiliar sensations to her feminine core.

Emmie raised her chin a fraction and forced herself to hold his challenging gaze. 'No, I do not. I'm quite immune to charming men.' Or so she'd thought until he had walked through the door.

He glanced at her left hand, presumably to see if she was wearing a wedding or engagement ring. His gaze came back to hers, the dark slashes of his eyebrows slightly elevated. 'So, the premier match-maker is herself unattached. Interesting.' His tone was smooth, his expression again just shy of mocking.

Emmie stretched her lips into a tight smile and unclasped her hands and placed them on her lap beneath the desk. 'Mr Vitale, allow me to assure you my currently single status is a choice, not an unfortunate circumstance. My career is my focus and I pride myself on being totally available to my clients in order to give them the best possible service.'

Matteo continued to hold her gaze to the point of discomfort. Emmie was determined not to look away first but, as each microsecond passed, her heartrate increased and her breathing quickened. 'Good, because I don't have a lot of time to waste,' he finally said. 'I need to get this sorted as quickly as possible.'

'I'm tempted to say you can't hurry love, but clearly that's not applicable in your case.' Emmie rose from her chair and went to her filing cabinet and took out one of her glossy brochures and handed it to him over the desk. 'There are various packages you can sign on for, which are detailed in this brochure. The top-level package is probably the best option, given your time-pressure issue.'

Matteo held the brochure in one hand and with the other took out a pair of black-rimmed reading glasses from the inside pocket of his suit jacket and put them on. If anything, they made him look even more heart-stoppingly attractive. He leafed through the brochure, at one point pushing his glasses further along the bridge of his nose with his index finger, his forehead creased in deeper lines of concentration.

He lowered his glasses further down his nose and glanced up at her from over the top of them, his gaze so compelling she couldn't have looked away if she'd tried. She was vaguely conscious of holding her breath, wondering if he was going to walk out of her office without a backward glance, yet desperately hoping he wouldn't. Finding him a wife according to his brief would be a challenge but she had faced bigger ones—surviving Hodgkin's lymphoma as a seventeen-year-old being the primary one.

'I'll take the top-level package.' He closed the brochure and placed it back on the desk, taking off his glasses and slipping them back inside his jacket pocket. She caught a glimpse of his broad chest as he opened his jacket, his light-blue business shirt stretched over toned muscles.

Emmie blinked rapidly and tried to refocus. She resumed her seat and smoothed her skirt over her knees. 'As you can see from the outline there, I usually spend a bit of one-on-one time with my clients to get to know them. That way I can judge what sort of person would best suit them. I have a detailed questionnaire I ask my clients to fill in but I've always found it much more informative to actually see them in action, so to speak. Like at work, at leisure, socialising with their friends and family, if possible. Would that be agreeable to you?'

A hard light came into his gaze and his jaw shifted like a heavy lock clicking firmly into place. 'No can do the family. I'm an only child and my father is dead.'

'And your mother?'

He made a dismissive sound, part-snort, part-sigh.

'Haven't seen her since I was seven years old. She decided marriage and motherhood weren't for her.' He gave a 'couldn't care less' half-smile and added, 'I have no idea where she lives or even if she's still alive.'

Emmie frowned. 'I'm sorry. That must have been very upsetting and destabilising for you as a young child.'

He shrugged one broad shoulder in a negligent fashion. 'I soon got over it.'

Emmie wasn't so sure that was entirely true. There was an aura of guardedness about him that suggested he wasn't comfortable allowing people too close. The walk-out of a mother at such a young age and with no contact since would be highly traumatic for a child. It would have created bonding issues, uncertainty, emotional withdrawal or lockdown and numerous other coping mechanisms that often, if not always, played out in adulthood. She had found the walk-out of her father when she'd been seventeen traumatic, but at least she still saw him occasionally. How much worse for a seven-year-old boy who had never seen his mother again?

'Some children are more resilient than others,' she offered. And then, on an impulse she couldn't quite account for, she added, 'How soon would you like to start with my programme? I'm fairly busy just now but—'

'Tonight.'

Her heart slipped from its moorings. 'Tonight?'

'Have dinner with me. You can pick my brain at your leisure.'

Emmie had an unnerving feeling he would find out more about her than she would about him. After all, he had built his hugely successful career on uncovering well-hidden secrets. His piercing gaze held hers and her pulse sped up again. 'Lucky for you, I happen to be free tonight. Would you like to invite a couple of friends along so I can see how you relate to them?'

A steely glint appeared in his eyes. 'Let's do this alone.'

Alone. Somehow the way he said that word made a frisson skitter over her flesh. Emmie disguised a swallow. Dinner alone with a client was not out of the norm for her. What was out of the norm was her reaction to the prospect of dinner with this particular client. Excitement, intrigue, nervous anticipation—all were fluttering about in her stomach like frenzied moths. 'You do have friends, yes?'

He gave an indolent smile that completely transformed his features, making him seem less serious, less tense and less guarded—more approachable and even more devastatingly attractive. 'But of course.'

'Are you worried what they might think of you engaging the services of someone like me?'

'Not particularly, but I would rather keep my private life out of the press as much as possible.'

'You don't trust your friends?'

He gave a stiff quirk of his lips, his gaze inscrutable. 'I don't trust anyone.'

'That must be an occupational hazard of yours, I guess.'

'Perhaps.'

Emmie tucked a strand of her hair behind her ear, trying to disguise how much he was affecting her. Never had she been so interested in finding out more about a man's character. He was complex and closed off and compelling. She was as giddy as a teenager anticipating her first date. She had to get a grip. She was a professional match-maker and he was engaging her services to help him find a wife. She had no business being interested in him herself other than in a professional sense.

Getting to know him was essential to the success of the mission of matching him with a suitable partner. But, right at that moment, Emmie couldn't think of a single one of the female clients currently on her books who would suit his unusual requirement. Her clients wanted love. Didn't most people? They wanted connection and commitment and continuity.

'Yes, well, you'd be surprised at how few friends some people have these days, which is why finding a partner can be so difficult. Meeting someone through friends used to be a sure, safe way to meet a potential partner.' Emmie painted another smile on her lips and added, 'I've designed my business model by becoming that mutual friend for my clients. It's much more appealing to most of my clients than using a dating app.' She paused for a beat and added, 'I suppose you've tried the dating app approach?

'Not for my current situation.'

Emmie could feel a blush stealing into her cheeks at the thought of him hooking up with casual lovers via an app. She had no problem with casual sex, although she hadn't had a sexual partner for so long she was starting to wonder if her body would still know what to do if she happened to find someone she was interested in enough to do the deed.

You're interested in Matteo Vitale.

The random thought sent another wave of heat through her cheeks and she lowered her gaze from the disturbing intensity of his. 'Yes, well, your...erm... unusual specifications might attract the wrong sort of person. People often talk themselves up on social media apps.'

'Indeed.'

Emmie opened her desk drawer, pulled out a selection of forms and laid them in front of him on the desk. 'If you could fill in your details—phone number, email address, social-media channels and home address—I'll enter them into my system. I can assure you of absolute privacy. No one but myself has access to the personal information of my clients. And I only give your contact details to a potential partner once I've discussed it with you first. The only thing I outsource is the personality questionnaire, to a team of experts who analyse my clients' responses. It's a well-researched personality model that helps me decide who would best complement you.'

She handed him a card with a web address printed on it. 'Here's the link to the questionnaire. It takes about forty-five minutes and I get the results back in a week or so.'

Matteo took the card from her and slipped it into his jacket pocket. He took out a gold pen before she could pass him one off her desk and began to fill out the forms with enviable speed and efficiency. Emmie examined the dark scrawl of his handwriting. The bold strokes spoke of a man who had a determined streak, but the light flourishes on some of the consonants hinted at a romantic element to his nature. The other thing she noticed was he was left-handed. Approximately ninety percent of the world's population was right-handed, which to her made him seem even more unique.

But when he passed the completed forms back across the desk he did so with his right hand. 'There you go.'

'Are you mixed-handed or ambidextrous?'

'Mixed. I write with my left but do a lot of other things with my right.'

Emmie could only imagine what some of those things might be and how skilled he might be at doing them. He had broad hands, tanned and long fingered with neat, square nails and a dusting of dark hair along the back and each of his fingers. She found herself imagining his hands on her…not just a 'pleased to meet you' handshake but on her face, on her breasts, on her hips, on the most intimate part of her body.

Her female flesh stirred, tensed and tingled, as if every sensitive nerve was preparing itself for his touch. She squeezed her legs together under the table, but if anything, it made it worse. She pushed back from the desk and stood, hoping her cheeks weren't as pink as they felt. 'I mustn't keep you any longer, Mr Vitale. I'll get my secretary, Paisley, to book a restaurant for eight this evening. I'll text you the details and meet you there.'

He rose from the chair and his imposing height made her snatch in another breath. For someone so tall, he moved with leonine grace. He had a rangy rather than gym-pumped build, an endurance athlete rather than a sprinter, which gave her another clue to his personality. Driven, disciplined, goal-oriented, he wouldn't be afraid of hard work—in fact, he'd most likely thrive on it.

'I'll book the restaurant. And I'll pick you up.' His voice had an edge of intractability about it, which was another clue to his take-charge, stay-in-control personality.

Emmie decided against tussling with him about it, for she quite fancied seeing what car he drove and what sort of restaurant he would choose. Those would also be important clues she could use to assess his character. So, too, would visiting his home at some point.

'Fine. Just as well I don't live too far away.' She leaned down to scribble her address on the back of one of her business cards and handed it to him. He took it from her with the slightest brush of his fingers against hers and a jolt of electricity coursed through her body. She pulled her hand back and gave him a stiff smile. 'Till tonight, then.'

He gave a mock bow. 'I'm looking forward to it. *Ciao*.'

Emmie was looking forward to it too, far more than she had any right to.

CHAPTER TWO

MATTEO PULLED UP in front of a smart white Georgian town house in South Kensington and whistled through his teeth. Who knew operating a dating agency could be so lucrative? Emmie Woodcroft must be raking it in, even if she was just renting this place, let alone if she owned it. But all power to her, as long as she achieved what he was paying her to achieve—finding him a wife in a hurry.

He opened and closed his clenched hands on the steering wheel and took a steadying breath. He was still recovering from the shock of finding out about his father's last-minute addition to his will. Of course, he could buy several Umbrian estates and have money to spare, but he wanted his family estate. Wanted it so badly he was prepared to do whatever it took to secure it. He had spent years and more money than he wanted to think about restoring the rundown estate, and it was now producing olives, and grapes for award-winning wine. The crumbling villa of his childhood had been completely renovated and he had paid for all of it, his father having struggled financially for as long as Matteo could remember.

But, more importantly, it was the land on which

Matteo's wife and child were buried and he would not be able to forgive himself if he let them down again by allowing the property to be sold. Eight years had passed since his pregnant wife had driven off to attend a pre-natal appointment he should have accompanied her to. They had argued about it that morning. He had been under time pressure from a complicated case he'd been working on for the Supreme Court in London, and had chosen to fly to London rather than stay in Umbria one extra day.

Matteo closed his eyes in a tight blink and clenched his hands around the steering wheel again until his knuckles protested. He opened his eyes and let out a ragged breath. His father had no doubt orchestrated the codicil on his will to force Matteo to marry again, even though Matteo had always sworn he would never do so. He wouldn't have married Abriana in the first place, but when she'd become pregnant during their brief on-again-and-off-again fling, he had offered her and their unborn child the protection of his name. It had seemed the right thing to do at the time but he often wondered if Abriana's unhappiness during their short time together had stemmed from knowing he hadn't been in love with her.

And now he must marry again without love being part of the equation. Because how could it be? He had no desire to love someone the way his father had loved his mother. The way *he* had loved his mother. He had learned from an early age how destructive deep love could be. He wanted no part of it. He cared about people, cared enough to put himself out for them, but he would never fall in love with anyone. He wondered if it was one of the few traits he had inherited from his mother. She'd given the appearance of love but hadn't felt it. The only time Matteo had come close to feeling it was when he'd seen the first ultrasound photo of his child. A flicker of something had stirred in his chest…

Matteo removed his hands from the steering wheel and unclipped his seat belt but he stayed seated in the car, taking in deep breaths that snagged at his throat like claws. His gut was in knots, his chest tight, his mind swirling with images of the scene of the accident that had killed his wife and tiny unborn son. Could he even face having another child, knowing there was a possibility it too could be taken away from him? Marrying again without love being part of the equation was asking for trouble. What if his new marriage ended up causing the same pain and destruction as his first? How could he bear it a second time—inflicting hurt and despair on someone who deserved so much better?

He could not forgive his father for putting him in such a painful and impossible situation. It smacked of meddling and manipulation and a cruel type of emotional torture he hadn't thought his father capable of. Yet here he was, doing all he could to fulfil the wretched terms of his father's will.

There was a sudden tap on the passenger window and Matteo was jolted out of his torturous reverie. He turned his head to see Emmie standing there dressed in a light-blue dress with a lightweight navy trench coat over the top. Her straight blonde hair was loose around her shoulders, reminding him of a skein of silk. Her periwinkle-blue eyes were highlighted by smoky make-up, including eyeliner, and her full-lipped mouth was a soft, rosy pink.

He'd had trouble keeping his eyes away from her

mouth earlier that day. It was a mouth built for sensuality, its contours lush and soft and beautifully shaped. Her nose was straight with a slight elevation at the end, like a gentle ski-slope. Her cheekbones were another striking feature of her face—regal, aristocratic—and her skin was as clear and pure as cream.

He opened his door and went round to help her into his car. 'You should have waited until I knocked on your door.'

'I saw you pull up and thought I'd save you the trouble.'

What else had she seen? Matteo was starting to suspect Ms Emmie Woodcroft saw too damn much. He comforted himself that his car windows were tinted. She might not have seen much at all. He normally kept his self-recrimination sessions for when and where he could not be observed.

Emmie moved past him to get into the passenger seat and he caught a whiff of her perfume—a fragrant blend of bergamot and geranium with a base note of patchouli that danced past his nostrils, causing them to flare. He was so close to her he could have touched her, and was surprised at how much he wanted to. Ever since they had shaken hands in her office earlier that day, he had been able to feel the soft, gentle imprint of her hand against his. It had sent a shockwave through his blood, kicking up his pulse in a way he had not expected.

Matteo closed the passenger door for her, strode round to his side of the car and got back behind the driver's seat. 'Nice house. Do you rent it or…?'

'The bank owns most of it but I'm making good progress. Well, better than I expected when I first started in the business.'

He glanced at her as he put the car in gear. 'How long have you been in the business of match-making?'

She flashed a smile, showing brilliant white teeth that made something in his chest slip. 'Informally since I was a teenager, actually. I recognised I had a natural flair for understanding which people suited each other and decided to make a career out of it. I've been in business five years now.'

Matteo checked his rear vision and side mirrors and then pulled out into the street before he asked, 'What sort of qualifications have you got?'

'I've done a couple of online counselling courses. I would have liked to do a psychology degree and a master's after I left school but things didn't work out that way.' Something about her tone made him glance at her again.

'Why?'

Emmie gave a shrug of her slim shoulders, her gaze trained on the road in front, but one of her hands was fiddling with the clasp of her evening purse in a restive manner. 'My schooling was interrupted during my teens.' She paused for a beat and continued, 'I spent a bit of time in and out of hospital.'

Matteo wondered what would have put her in hospital for an extended period but didn't want to pry. Some conditions were deeply personal. 'I'm sorry to hear that. Anything serious?'

There was another beat of silence.

'Nothing too serious.' She gave another smile that seemed a little forced and added, 'But it gave me a lot of time to learn stuff about people. To listen and observe. I even helped two young doctors to get together.

They're still married with a couple of kids now. They send me a Christmas card each year.'

'So, you're a romantic at heart.'

'For other people, not for myself.'

'Which begs the question, why?'

Emmie opened and then closed the latch on her bag, the *click* as it shut overly loud in the silence. 'I'm helping you find a wife. You don't need to worry about my single status. I'm perfectly happy with my life as it is.'

Matteo knew better than to think that all women wanted the marriage and babies package. Many lived happy and fulfilling lives with neither partner nor children but something about Emmie's body language was out of tune with her words. It was like hearing the wrong note in a piece of music, the discordant sound jarring, off-putting. 'Point taken,' he said with a wry smile. 'Is there anyone on your books who you think would be interested in the post?'

Emmie gave a snort of laughter. 'The post? You're making it sound like a job.'

'But it is.'

'It should be a partnership, not a posting.'

'Under normal circumstances, that may well be true, but nothing about my situation is normal,' Matteo said, trying to suppress the desire to grind his teeth. 'I have no desire to marry or have children. My father knew that, and adding that ridiculous codicil to his will was his way of trying to control me beyond the grave.'

'What sort of person was he? I mean, were you ever close to him?'

'He was weak.' Matteo pulled up half a block from the restaurant he'd booked and turned off the engine. He turned to look at Emmie and continued. 'He allowed my mother to walk all over him, and when she left him he completely fell apart. He gave her everything she asked for in the divorce, way more than she was entitled to, compromising his own finances in the vain hope she would come back. But of course, she never did. If anything, his pathetic attempt to please her probably drove her further away.'

'Okay, so I get the aversion to marriage thing, but what about kids? Why have you never wanted them?'

Matteo unclipped his seat belt and picked up his phone from the console below the dashboard. He had wanted one child—his tiny son—and yet he had been taken away from him. Poor little Gabriel had not even taken a breath before his life had been cut short. 'We'd better claim our table. It was a late booking, and if we don't show up on time they might give it to someone else.'

It was a paltry excuse for terminating a conversation but he was done with talking about marriage and kids. His wife's and child's deaths were not common knowledge, given they had happened in Italy and not in England, and he wanted to keep it that way. He was an intensely private person, and besides, he hated talking about his failure. He had failed to protect those who'd needed his protection the most. He had failed to love them as they'd deserved to be loved. He had failed as a husband and father and he was not comfortable with the prospect of becoming either again.

But, with his father's will written the way it was, he had no choice. It was marry and produce an heir or lose everything, including the sacred ground on which his wife and tiny son were buried.

* * *

A few minutes later Emmie sat opposite Matteo in one of London's top restaurants. Nothing but the best for Matteo Vitale, she mused. But she didn't think he'd chosen this particular restaurant to impress her. He didn't seem the type of man to resort to such tactics but rather a man who enjoyed good food and wine and pleasant surroundings and didn't mind paying well for it.

'Would you like wine?' he asked, looking at her over the top of the drinks menu, his glasses perched on his nose.

'I'm not a big drinker,' Emmie said. 'But you go ahead.' Ever since her cancer diagnosis, she had avoided anything that might trigger a relapse. She ate as cleanly as possible, tried to keep her stress levels down, exercised gently but regularly and avoided using chemicals or known carcinogens. She knew it was obsessive at times, but the thought of going through another cancer battle was so terrifying, she was prepared to do whatever she could to avoid facing it all again. She had already caused her family so much stress and heartache by becoming ill in the first place. If she didn't take care of herself to the best of her ability now, she might end up inflicting even more pain on those she loved.

Matteo put the drinks menu down, a wry twist on his mouth. 'I suppose it helps to get your clients drinking so you can draw out their secrets, *si*? *In vino veritas*.'

'In wine lies the truth.' Emmie gave an answering smile. 'Sometimes it helps but I rely on other tactics.'

'Such as?'

She held his penetrating gaze, her heart giving a pony kick against her breast bone. He had such beautiful eyes, she could so easily drown in their bottomless depths. Mysterious, with shifting shadows that intrigued and fascinated her in equal measure. 'I can tell a lot about people by how they move their bodies, what amount of eye contact they're comfortable with, whether they smile a lot or rarely, whether they talk more than they listen—all sorts of stuff.'

'And what is your assessment of me so far?'

'You're not the easiest person to read but I think you're unhappy.'

He gave a bark of humourless laughter. 'I've not long buried my father, so that's hardly a surprising observation.'

'Maybe, but you said you weren't close to him.'

Something flickered through his gaze like a breath of wind across the surface of a deep mountain tarn. His mouth tightened just a fraction and a tiny muscle pulled tighter in the lower quadrant of his lean jaw. 'I'm not happy with how his will is written, that's all.'

'Did you love him?'

He flattened his lips and moved them from side to side, as if deciding whether to respond. After a moment, he let out a short breath. 'I loved him but I didn't respect him for some of the choices he made with his life. He refused to move on from the divorce. To my knowledge, he never had a relationship with another woman. He neglected his duty as a father and as an employer. He allowed the family estate to fall into ruin. It took millions of euros to restore it to what it is today.'

'Your money?' Emmie guessed.

Matteo heaved out another sigh. 'I was happy to pay for everything. If only it would have made him take back control of his life, but no, it was as if he wanted to hurry up his death.'

'What did he die of?'

'Cancer.'

Emmie suppressed a shudder. The *C* word, even after all these years, still triggered her. Memories rushed into her mind of the follow-up appointment a biopsy of her lymph nodes. The doctor's blunt way of delivering the news, her parents' shock and her own fear at what lay ahead. The gruelling chemo regime that had worked for a time, sending her into remission, only for the cancer to flare up again. And again. And again. Months and months of her life locked away in hospital, unable to see her friends in case of infection. Unable to live a normal life for so long, she'd felt like a pariah when she'd finally been released from hospital.

She'd been out of step with her peers. They had all moved on, had finished their education while she had been having toxic chemicals infused through her veins to try and beat the cancer. The shadow of cancer followed her to this day. There was no certainty it wouldn't reoccur. In fact, there was an increased risk she could acquire other cancers as a result of having had Hodgkin's.

And then she had received the most devastating news of all. The high price of saving her life was she would never give life to a baby of her own.

Emmie pushed her gaze up to meet his, hoping he couldn't see any of her inner turmoil. 'What type of cancer?'

'Lung. He smoked even though his doctors were at him for years to give it up.' Matteo's mouth twisted again. 'I know it's an addiction, and a hard one to overcome but there's so much help available these days. He just didn't want to try.'

'It must have been so frustrating for you, watching him slowly kill himself.'

Matteo picked up the food menu. 'Let's talk about something else. What do you like to eat? The seafood is excellent here.'

Emmie busied herself with studying the menu, but she was just as busy covertly studying him. Like a lot of people, he changed the subject when things got uncomfortable. Clearly talking about his father frustrated and upset him. Watching a parent slowly destroy themselves would have been incredibly painful to watch, and would have made him feel out of control.

She had watched her sister Natalie do much the same thing as his father had, denying her body the food it craved to sustain life, becoming so ill she'd had to be hospitalised time and time again. Emmie had watched on in despair, feeling out of control, unable to help, feeling powerless and useless, and also feeling partly to blame for her sister's illness. Her battle with cancer had consumed her parents' time and energy and then, with their divorce, poor Natty had been pushed to one side, almost becoming invisible as the doctors had fought to save Emmie and her parents and their lawyers had fought over assets and custody arrangements.

Emmie was starting to realise how much control was also incredibly important to Matteo Vitale. It was deeply rooted in his character. That was why the sudden change to his father's will would have been so terribly shocking. He hadn't been expecting such a thing to occur, especially a condition attached that involved him doing something he clearly had no desire to do—marry and have a child. Lots of men of his age were not ready to settle down but when the right woman came along were more than happy to do so. And Emmie's job was to find the right one for him. But how hard was that going to be when he was not looking for love and all of her clients were?

The waiter approached to take their order, and a short time later Emmie sat back with her glass of freshly squeezed orange juice. 'So, tell me what you do in your free time.'

Matteo gave a slanted smile, as if the concept of free time was amusing. 'I work.'

'But surely you relax sometimes?'

He gave a one-shoulder shrug and picked up his glass of white wine. 'The work I do is very time consuming. I often have a lot of cases on at once, many of which involve the preparation of court documents. I pride myself on making sure I uncover where any discrepancy or fraudulent behaviour has occurred.'

'It sounds very intense.'

'It is.'

Emmie took a sip of her juice and put it back on the table, flicking him a glance. 'Tell me about your family's estate in Umbria. Why is it so important to you? Apart from the money you've spent on it, I mean.'

There was a slight pause, as if he was carefully rehearsing his answer. A screen came down in his gaze and he put his wine glass down with almost exaggerated precision. 'Generations of my family have lived and worked there. I owe it to them to keep it going for generations to come.'

But how would those generations come about if Matteo was so against settling down and having a family? It didn't make sense. If Matteo loved the place so much and wanted it to continue being in the family, surely, he would have considered marrying and producing an heir without having to be forced to do so?

'Presumably that was your father's plan, then, to ensure there was a generation after you. I mean, given you were so against marrying and having a family,' Emmie pointed out.

Matteo frowned so heavily the pleat between his eyebrows could have held a pencil. His hand tensed where it was resting on the table, the fingers opening and closing repeatedly. 'My father could have left it to one of my cousins but he added another condition—if I don't fulfil the terms of his will, the estate can only be sold to someone not connected in any way to the Vitale family.' His hand clenched into a tight fist. 'It was his way of ensuring I did what he wanted. He knew I would never allow it to be sold to a stranger. Someone who might turn it into a hotel or something.'

Emmie chewed her lip, wondering why his father had felt he had to go to such lengths to get Matteo to do as he wished. But she knew all about difficult fathers and the lengths they went to in order to get their way. 'Manipulation is a cruel tactic some parents use to get what they want.'

'That sounds like the voice of experience.' His gentle tone was disarming, so too his unwavering gaze.

She gave a rueful twist of a smile. 'My parents divorced when I was in my late teens. My dad was like a spoilt child who couldn't get his way.' She sighed and added, 'It made a bad situation so much worse.' Emmie was a little shocked she had disclosed to him—a client—such personal information about herself. She normally kept her own issues out of the conversation with clients.

Her mission was to get to know him, not have him get to know her.

'Is that why you're not interested in finding love yourself? Only for your clients?'

Emmie tore a small piece off the fresh bread roll on her side plate and dipped it in the olive oil and balsamic vinegar in a tiny dish on the table. 'I'm not cynical about love. I believe in it and love to see it happen between my clients and friends. But I'm not sure I'd make a great partner myself. I'm too much of a workaholic.' She popped the morsel of bread in her mouth and chewed and swallowed.

'Why are you so driven?'

Emmie gave a light laugh. 'Interesting question from someone who claims he doesn't know how to relax.'

'Takes one to know one.' His lazy smile made something in her stomach swoop.

She lowered her gaze from his, her cheeks suddenly warm enough to toast the rest of the bread roll on her plate. After a moment, she looked up to find him watching her with an inscrutable expression. Her breath caught, her heart tripped and her stomach nosedived again. She hastily pulled herself back into line. She was acting like a fool, getting all het up over being in his company. She'd had dinner with loads of clients and had never felt so undone before. Her job was to find out everything she could about him so she could find him a suitable partner. 'Where do you live in Italy? At your family estate or somewhere else?'

'I have apartments in Rome and Milan but I spend most of my time at the estate.'

'Is that where your father lived too?'

'No. He lived in an apartment in Florence to be closer

to health services, but retained ownership of the estate.' A ripple of tension travelled across his features. 'He always assured me it would pass to me. I had no reason to doubt him.'

'Did you think of challenging the will? I mean, was he in sound mind when he made the change to it? Maybe if you could prove he wasn't, then you'd have a chance of—'

'I've wasted enough time already trying to challenge it,' Matteo said. 'It's iron-clad and I have no choice but to do as it states. He might have been dying of cancer, but he was in full control of his mind right up to the last. All of his doctors confirmed it.'

Emmie wondered how far the apple had fallen from the tree. The stubborn determination of his father to achieve his goal beyond the grave was reflected in Matteo's grim determination to do whatever he could to secure the estate—even something he clearly didn't want to do. 'Would you be open to having me visit you at the estate at some point?'

'Is that what you would normally do? Travel abroad to visit a client's family home?'

'Sometimes. It depends.'

'On what?'

'On whether I think it will help me to get to know a client better,' Emmie said. 'Would you be agreeable? I know you're a busy man and all, and it's terribly short notice, but you're in a hurry to find a wife and I want to make sure I give you the top-level service you're paying for.'

'How long would you want to stay?' There was a guardedness about his tone that made her wonder if she had overstepped the mark. But she felt compelled to see him at his estate. It was the reason he was so intent on finding a wife to fulfil the terms of his father's will. She refused to acknowledge she had any other reason for wanting to spend more time in his company.

'Two or three days should be enough.'

'I'll see what I can do.'

Emmie smiled. 'Great. I'll get my secretary to clear my diary once you let me know which days suit you. But in the meantime, I'll go through the list of clients on my books to see if there is someone who might suit your requirements.' But, right at that moment, she couldn't think of a single one. Which one of her clients would agree to his unusual request?

Matteo continued to hold her gaze for a beat or two but then his eyes drifted to her mouth for a heart-stopping moment. He blinked and then lifted his eyes back to hers, his expression cast in a deep frown. 'You're not worried about spending time alone with a man you've only just met?'

Emmie was worried but not for the reasons he probably thought. It wasn't him she was afraid of—it was herself. She was drawn to him in a way she couldn't explain. He was like a wounded wolf that was hiding its pain in order to survive. How close would he allow her to get to him? How close did she dare get to him? She gave him an arch look. 'Should I be worried?'

His eyes dipped to her mouth for a brief moment before meshing again with hers. 'Not at all.'

Once their meal was over, Matteo walked Emmie back to his car. He was still mulling over her request to visit him at his family estate. It seemed an odd request and yet he had decided against refusing. He was intrigued by her approach to finding him a wife. He was intrigued by her, full-stop. There was something about her that drew her to him in a way few people did. He was a loner, and preferred his own company, and yet he found her company…interesting. Interesting company, but not exactly relaxing, given her propensity to ask questions he would prefer not to answer. But she was only doing her job—the job he was paying her handsomely to do.

Matteo opened the passenger door and Emmie brushed past him to get into the car. He had to drag his eyes away from the slim length of her legs and he had to ignore the delicate waft of her perfume dancing past his nostrils. He had to ignore the quickening of his blood as she flicked her trench coat out of the way of the door and smiled up at him.

'Thank you.'

'You're welcome.'

He walked round the front of the car, got behind the wheel and started the engine, pulling down his seat belt and finding her looking at him with a small frown on her face. 'What's wrong?'

Her frown smoothed away and she gave a quick on-off smile. 'Nothing. I was just wondering if we could do a detour before you take me home.'

'Where to?'

'Do you stay in hotels when you come to London or do you have an apartment here?'

'I have a house. I travel back and forth a lot—I have an office here in London.'

'Can I see it? Your house, I mean. I'll save your office for another time.'

Matteo put the car in gear and frowned. 'Does all this research you do actually work?'

'If you don't want to take me to your home, then don't.'

That was the whole trouble right there in a big, fat crinkly nutshell. He wanted to take her home and see if that rosy pink mouth felt as soft as it looked beneath the pressure of his. He gave himself a mental shake. Emmie was off the market—or so she'd said. 'Fine. I'll take you to see my house but I can't see what the point is. It's just a house I stay in while I work in London.'

'Yes, but it's a house, not an apartment, which tells me a lot about you.'

Matteo harrumphed and pulled out into the street. 'I had no idea I was such an open book.'

'You're not,' Emmie said with another smile. 'But I like nothing better than a challenge.'

'Just as well, because finding me a wife in such a short time frame is going to be one hell of a challenge.'

'You don't think I can do it?'

Matteo clenched his teeth and his hands. 'I'm counting on you to do it.'

CHAPTER THREE

A FEW MINUTES LATER, Matteo parked his car in front of a beautiful, three-storey Victorian house in Chelsea. 'This is my home,' he said, turning off the engine.

Emmie studied the neat exterior, then glanced his way. 'Is it really a home, though, or just a place to sleep at night?'

He met her look with a frown. 'Has anyone ever told you, you ask a lot of questions?'

She gave him a winning smile. 'It's my job.'

He grunted and opened the driver's door and came around to her side of the car. He opened the door for her and she stepped out, taking care not to touch him on the way past. Emmie was determined to keep things professional and impersonal between them. This wasn't a date with a new man—this was a fact-finding mission with a new client. She had a job to do—a challenging job—and she couldn't afford to be distracted by Matteo Vitale's brooding good looks and magnetic mysteriousness of manner.

Matteo led her inside the gorgeously appointed mansion. It had a functional and masculine feel about it but there were softer touches here and there that perfectly balanced the overall look. 'Is there any particular room you'd like to see?' he asked.

'Where do you spend most of your time when you're here? Apart from your bedroom, of course.' Emmie wished she hadn't mentioned his bedroom. She was dying to take a peek at it, but the thought of entering it with him made her feel hot all over. She could only imagine how many women he took in there and made mad passionate love to. Not that she had read anything about him being an out-and-out playboy, but what woman wouldn't want a night in his arms? There was a sensual energy about him that spoke to her body in a way nothing had ever done before. Her awareness of him increased with every moment she spent with him. She could easily have waited for another day to ask to see his home but she had felt compelled to extend the evening with him, to delve a little more deeply into his enigmatic personality.

'I spend most of my time in my study.'

She rolled her eyes. 'I should have known.'

A half-smile flirted with the corners of his mouth. 'Come this way. It's through here.'

Emmie followed him upstairs to a bookshelf-lined room on the second floor. She walked over to the mullioned windows that overlooked a neat garden at the back of the house. The garden was a mostly formal affair, illuminated by subtle lighting set in sandstone flagstones. There was a small water feature in the centre, complete with water lilies floating on the top, that was also illuminated. It looked like a peaceful place to spend a summer evening entertaining friends, or even to sit in quiet reflection on one's own. She suspected Matteo did the latter far more frequently than the former.

Emmie turned back from the window to cast her eyes over the study. There was a large leather-topped desk in dark wood in front of one row of bookshelves, and it had a leather Chesterfield-type chair. A slim-line desktop computer was situated on the desk and a printer set up on a lower shelf of the bookcase that kept them out of sight.

Emmie ran her gaze along the bookshelves to see what sort of books he liked to read. There were many Italian titles as well as English ones, and numerous financial tomes, including some hefty tax law volumes. There were a few crime fiction novels and biographies and even some art history. Not surprising, given the art work on the walls looked like originals. But there were no personal photographs of friends or family although, given what he'd told her about his parents, that too wasn't all that surprising.

'Seen enough?' Matteo asked.

Emmie turned from examining the bookshelves to face him. 'It's a nice study. It's got an old-world atmosphere, suggesting you're a bit of a traditionalist at heart.'

A cynical light entered his gaze. 'On some issues, perhaps. Others not so much.' He walked over to the door. 'I'll go and put some coffee on and let you have a wander around on your own.'

'Are you sure you'd be comfortable with me doing that?'

'If I find something valuable missing after you leave, I know where to find you.' His tone was playful, his smile teasing, and it made her heart give an extra beat. It was the first full smile he had given her and it transformed his features, making him appear younger and even more attractive.

'I can assure you, I am completely trustworthy.'

'There's nothing here you could steal that couldn't be replaced.'

But what about your heart?

The errant thought shocked Emmie into silence and, within another moment, he had gone.

Matteo went to put on some coffee, wondering if he had made a mistake in engaging Emmie's professional services. Her approach seemed reasonable on one level, but he was uneasy her mission to get to know him might reveal things about himself he would prefer to keep hidden. But any misgivings on his part would have to be shelved—he had to find a wife sooner rather than later. The deadline set out in his father's will was rapidly approaching and, while he could have cast his net via a dating app, he hadn't wanted to risk attracting the wrong person. A professional dating agency, especially one with Emmie Woodcroft's reputation for excellent service and results, was his best option.

What he hadn't expected was Emmie herself to be so alluring. Or so against finding a partner herself. It seemed a little odd for a professional match-maker to be single. After all, she knew how to find the right person for her clients—how much easier to find one for herself? He admired her ambition, the focus on her career, but something about her adamant stance on singledom didn't ring true.

His job was to spot irregularities, to uncover secrets and hidden information. Was there some other reason Emmie wasn't interested in finding love? Had she been hurt in the past? Had her heart broken by a lover? Been frightened off commitment because of the fear of losing herself in a relationship and not being able to follow her dream career the way she wanted to? She certainly put a lot of her time into her clients. Her willingness to travel and spend time individually with them was commendable. It was no wonder she got the results she did. And, as long as she got results for him, he would be happy. Well, as happy as he could be under the circumstances, and as circumstances went they weren't exactly happy-making.

Emmie peeped into a couple of the spare rooms on the upper floor but the one room she was drawn to look at was Matteo's bedroom. She walked towards it as if pulled by a powerful magnet and gently pushed the door open. She stepped over the threshold and breathed in the light citrussy notes of his aftershave that lingered in the air. The king-sized bed dominated the room and drew her gaze as if the same powerful magnet was at work. The bed linen was a blinding white, but there was a dark-blue throw on the end of the bed, as well as three scatter cushions in the same hue propped against the array of snowy-white pillows. Twin bedside lamps and tables were at either side of the bed. The left-side table had a book with a bookmark poking out of the top, which told her Matteo slept on the left side of the bed.

She moved across the room and took a peek in the walk-in wardrobe. His clothes were neatly organised, even colour coordinated, which suggested either he was a little pedantic or obsessive or his housekeeper was. She assumed he had one. The place was immaculate and, given he was such a busy man who travelled a lot for work, she couldn't imagine him wandering around his many homes flicking a duster over the furniture and doing his own laundry.

She slid the pocket door closed and went to have a peek at the *en suite*. It was stylishly and luxuriously appointed in white Italian marble with veins of grey and black running through. The large shower area triggered her thoughts into imagining him in there naked, hot water from the shower attachment splashing over his toned and hard male flesh. She suppressed a shiver and moved further into the *en suite* and picked up a bottle of his aftershave from the marble counter, unscrewing the cap and holding it up to her nose. It was intoxicating but not half as intoxicating when it was mixed with his own personal scent. She closed her eyes and took another sniff…

'Found anything interesting?' Matteo's deep voice sounding from the *en suite* doorway startled Emmie into dropping the cologne bottle on the marble floor. It smashed into several pieces and she gasped in horror at the mess she'd created.

'I'm so sorry!' She bent down and began to pick up the pieces, but the first shard of glass cut her finger and large droplets of blood began dripping to the floor. *Eek!* How could she have been so clumsy?

'Leave it.' Matteo snatched up a snowy-white hand towel and crouched down beside her, holding her hand and inspecting her finger for fragments of glass before he wrapped her hand in the towel to stem the flow of blood. 'Are you okay?'

Emmie was sure her cheeks were as bright red as the droplets of blood on the floor. Never had she felt so hideously embarrassed. What must he think of her, snooping round his bathroom? She was hardly acting like a consummate professional. She was acting like a star-struck teenager let loose in a celebrity's house, hunting for a souvenir to take home. Seriously, what was wrong with her? She had never acted so out of line before. Never.

'I'm fine. I'm really sorry. You startled me and I… I shouldn't have been snooping around in your bathroom, but I really like your cologne. It's one of the nicest ones I've ever smelt and I…' She scrunched her eyes closed and opened them again to say with a self-conscious grimace, 'I'll shut up now. Nothing I can say can excuse my appalling behaviour. Please forgive me.'

Matteo helped her to her feet, his towering height all the more apparent in comparison to her smaller stature. The top of her head barely came up to his shoulder. He was so close she could feel his body warmth and she had to resist the temptation to move even closer. She hadn't been this close to a man for years. In fact, the only men who had touched her since her teens were her oncologist and the occasional male nurse.

Matteo was still holding her hand wrapped in the towel, his expression etched in lines of concern. 'There's nothing to forgive. I'd better take another look to see if it's stopped bleeding. Do you mind?'

'Go for it.'

He peeled the towel away and inspected the wound with a frown of concentration. The blood was still seeping, so he quickly bound it up again and applied more pressure. 'You're lucky you didn't sever a tendon or something. Does it hurt?'

'Not really.' What hurt was standing so close to him and wanting to lift her face to be kissed. Emmie kept her gaze lowered, worried he might see what she was trying so hard to suppress. The need to be held by him, to feel his arms go around her and bring her closer to the hard, warm frame of his body. It was as if her body was under some weird sort of spell, activated the first moment she'd met him.

'Do you feel light-headed? Faint?' His other hand slipped to her other wrist and measured her pulse. 'Your pulse is quite fast.'

'I—I always have a fast resting pulse. I'm not very… erm…fit…'

His thumb stayed on the blue-veined skin of her wrist, his eyes holding hers in a lock that made her insides twist and coil with lust. 'You don't look unfit to me.' His voice was deep and low with an edge of huskiness. His thumb began to stroke her wrist in a slow caress that sent her pulse rate soaring.

'I—I can't run up a flight of stairs without getting breathless.' Nor could she stand in such close proximity to him without becoming breathless. Breathless with longing, a longing she had never expected to feel with such intensity. A longing she *had* to suppress.

His lazy smile made something in her stomach turn over. His eyes were so dark she could barely make out his pupils from the sea of dark, bottomless blue. His gaze drifted to her mouth and she disguised a swallow… or tried to. The silence was so thick she could hear the up and down movement of her throat and, judging from his expression, so could he. His eyes went to her mouth again, lingering there for an infinitesimal moment.

Emmie didn't realise she was holding her breath until her lungs began to beg for more air. She snatched in a wobbly breath and pulled her hand out of his, holding the towel in place. 'Do you have a bandage I could borrow? I'm really sorry about this. I feel so foolish. I'm not normally so clumsy.'

'Stop apologising. I'm just glad you didn't do any worse damage.' He opened one of the drawers below the marble basins and took out a first aid kit and laid it on the counter. He opened the kit and took out a crepe bandage as well as antiseptic and cotton pads. He turned back to take her hand again, peeling away the towel to check the bleeding. 'We'd better give it a wash under cold water just in case there are any tiny fragments of glass embedded in there.'

'I can't feel any. It's just a clean cut.'

He held her hand under the cold tap and, even though his touch was gentle, it made her intensely aware of every point of contact with her skin as if she was being permanently branded by him. Her arm brushed his shirt sleeve and it was impossible not to notice the firm muscles the fine cotton covered. Her gaze drifted to his hand, holding hers under the water, his skin tanned, his fingers long and strong. She thought of his hands touching her in other places—places that hadn't been touched by a man in so long she had forgotten what it felt like.

She stole a glance at his profile while he was concentrating on cleansing her finger. The dark stubble surrounding his nose and mouth and running over his lean jaw made her want to reach up and stroke her fingers along its sexy roughness. She wondered what it would feel like against her softer skin. Her heartbeat increased as her thoughts ran wild, let out of a locked vault inside her head—thoughts of being kissed by his firm mouth, touched by his surprisingly gentle hands, possessed by his hard maleness. A soft flutter in her feminine core brought forth an involuntary gasp and he glanced at her with an apologetic look.

'Sorry if this stings.' Matteo turned off the water and dried her hand with a fresh towel and then proceeded to dab the wound with antiseptic.

'I've felt worse pain.'

He gave her another sideways glance as if something in her tone intrigued him. 'A broken bone?'

'No, just the usual cuts and bruises.'

Matteo continued to dress her wound and finished up with winding a bandage around her finger, padding it with cotton wool beneath to protect it from bumping. She found herself wishing she had a bigger wound so she could stay close to him longer. 'There you go.'

'You missed your calling as a doctor.'

He gave a soft laugh, which was even more breath-snatching than his smile. 'My bedside manner would need some work.'

'I don't know about that.'

His eyes met hers and time seemed to come to a standstill. The silence was so thick she could feel it pressing from all four corners of the room. Emmie could feel the colour pouring back into her cheeks and sank her teeth into her lower lip. 'I think I need to go home now. It's way past my bedtime.' Oh, dear God, could she just stop mentioning the word *bed*?

Matteo guided her out of the *en suite* with a gentle hand at her elbow. 'Careful—there's still glass on the floor.'

'I'll replace the bottle of cologne for you.'

'Don't be silly.'

'I insist.' Emmie moved away to put some distance between them before she made an even bigger fool of herself. 'And I'll catch a cab home. I've taken up too much of your time.'

'I'll take you home, and that's not negotiable. Understood?' He had an intractable light in his eyes that should have annoyed her but somehow didn't. She was looking forward to eking out the last few minutes of the evening in his company before the clock struck midnight.

Cinderella has nothing on me, Emmie thought. Just as well she wasn't wearing glass slippers or she would likely shatter them too.

Matteo pulled up in front of Emmie's house a few minutes later. He was out of the car and round to open her door before she had even undone her seat belt. Emmie stepped out onto the footpath and turned to face him. 'Thank you for dinner.'

'I'll walk you to your door.'

'I'm sure I won't sever an artery between here and my front door,' Emmie said with a self-deprecating smile.

Something flickered in his gaze and his lower jaw tightened. 'You should probably get a doctor to check your finger in the morning. It could become infected.' He placed a gentle hand below her elbow and guided her towards her door.

Emmie had so rarely been touched by a man she decided that was why Matteo's touch was doing such weird things to her. In fact, she couldn't recall the last time a man had got close to her, held her, kissed her, looked at her with desire gleaming in his eyes. Matteo's eyes were inscrutable most of the time but every now and again she caught a glimpse of something that looked like interest. The same interest she was trying so hard not to show in her own gaze.

Emmie took out her key from her bag but realised her cut finger was going to make unlocking the door difficult. But Matteo had already anticipated that and held out his hand for her key. 'I'll do it.' She slipped the key into the broad span of his palm but somehow her fingers brushed against his skin and a flicker of electricity shot through her body.

Matteo unlocked the door and pushed it open for her. 'There you go.' He handed her the key but it was impossible to take it without touching him again. The lightning bolt of awareness zapped from her fingers to her armpit and all the way down to her core like the fizzing wick of a firework.

Emmie closed her hand around her key and stepped across the threshold but then turned and faced him. 'Would you like to come in?' She issued the invitation before her rational mind caught up and warned her against spending any more time alone with him.

His dark eyebrows rose ever so slightly above his unreadable eyes, the only sign her invitation had surprised him. 'Sure.' He stepped through the door and closed it with a soft click behind him.

Emmie ran the tip of her tongue across her lips, her breath stalling when his gaze followed the movement.

'Erm, would you like a drink? Cocoa? Hot chocolate? Juice? I'm afraid I don't have any alcohol.' She knew she sounded as unsophisticated as she felt. She was offering him nursery-school drink options when no doubt he was used to complicated cocktails and nifty little nightcaps.

One side of his mouth came up in a half-smile. 'It's actually nice to meet someone who doesn't drink.'

'Would you like me to add that to your list of requirements in a partner?' Emmie asked.

'A moderate drinker is fine.'

Emmie turned away to hang her coat on the coat stand near the door. 'I guess your future wife will have to give up drinking anyway if she's to become pregnant as soon as possible.' Even saying the word made her heart ache for what she could never have. She imagined him holding a new-born baby. Somehow, she knew he would be an excellent father. Strong, dependable, protective.

'Yes.'

Emmie turned to face him again, not entirely confident her features were as neutral as she would have liked. 'But what if she doesn't get pregnant straight away? Some couples take many months to fall pregnant. Sometimes years. And others, never.'

'And others on their first attempt.' His expression was shuttered but his tone contained a note of something she couldn't quite identify. It sounded cynical and yet it had an undertone of something else.

Emmie searched his face for a clue but it was like trying to read a marble bust. 'I guess that would be ideal for your situation, but you can't guarantee it will happen.'

'It has to happen, otherwise I stand to lose everything I've worked so hard to keep.' The implacable quality to his voice was a reminder of his determined nature. Once he set his mind to something, he would not stop until he achieved it. But some things in life were impossible to achieve no matter how much you wanted them. She, of all people, knew that only too well.

'I have women on my books who desperately want to have a family, but they also want love,' Emmie said. 'And therein lies the problem, because you want the former but not the latter.'

'It's my experience that if you pay someone enough they will agree to whatever you want them to do.' There was no doubt about the cynicism in his tone now. Every word positively dripped with it.

Emmie gave him a tight smile. 'You're going to be a hard sell, Mr Vitale, but never let it be said I baulk at a challenge.'

Matteo held her gaze for a beat longer than she was comfortable with but she was determined not to look away first. His gaze drifted to her mouth and she had to resist the urge to moisten her lips. 'Do you live alone?' His gaze came back to hers and she could feel her cheeks heating.

'Yes.'

He cast his gaze around the spacious interior. 'It's a big house for one person.'

'I like my own space.'

'Fair enough.' He studied her for a long moment, his eyes moving over every inch of her face, as if searching for something. Emmie kept as still as she possibly could, barely taking a breath in case she betrayed how unsettled she was in his disturbing company. Not creepily disturbing, but disturbing to her sense of equilibrium. Everything about him made her feel on edge, worried he would see more than she wanted him to see.

'You're a very unusual young woman, Emmie.' His voice dropped to a low burr that reminded her of distant thunder. Nature signalling a warning of approaching danger. Danger that could upend her carefully ordered life and make her want things she had no business wanting.

Emmie glanced at the shape of his mouth and imagined it pressed to her own. Those firm, determined lips moving against hers, drawing from her a fervent response that she sensed would set fire to every cell in her body. She drew in a prickly breath and took an unsteady step backwards, and would have stumbled if not for the quick action of his hand coming out to stabilise her.

'Are you okay?' His brows snapped together in concern, his grip gentle but firm, his touch sending waves of awareness rippling through her body.

Not in your presence, I'm not. But she could hardly say it out loud.

'I—I'm fine.' Emmie pasted a bright smile on her mouth.

His gaze lowered to her mouth, his hand on her arm moving to press ever so gently on the small of her back, bringing her slowly, inexorably closer to the warm, male heat of his body. There was a dark intensity in his hooded gaze and her blood quickened, as if suddenly injected with a potent drug. A drug that pushed aside her normal inhibitions and sent her senses spinning out of control.

Emmie licked her lower lip, breathing in the intimate warmth of his breath that danced over hers, her eyes lowering to half-mast. She was drugged, dazed, dazzled by the ever-so-slow descent of his mouth, her breath hitching in the nanosecond before he touched down. His lips were firm and yet soft, moving against hers in a languid manner, exploring the landscape of her lips before lazily stroking the seam of her mouth with his tongue. A hot shiver coursed down her spine and Emmie parted her lips on a gasp of pleasure, hungrily responding to his erotic entry, the very hairs on her head standing up at the roots in sensual delight.

Emmie murmured against his lips, wanting more, needing more. But then a voice sounded in her head, reminding her of the danger she would drift into by becoming involved with Matteo. He was not just a healthy man in his prime but more importantly a client. What was she thinking? It was completely and utterly unprofessional. She had never crossed such an important line before, nor had she ever been tempted to do so.

With what little self-control she had left, she pulled away from him, her cheeks warm, her lips hotter from where his had pressed so expertly, so temptingly. 'Erm, I'm sorry. I—I don't want you to think I allow all my male clients to kiss me. I don't know how or why that happened, but it must *not* happen again.' She straightened her shoulders and painted on a formal expression. 'Now, about that drink?'

A crooked smile formed on his lips, his eyes glinting. 'Let's leave it for another time.'

It? What 'it' was he referring to? A drink or something even more potent to her senses? 'I guess hot chocolate or fruit juice isn't quite up to your sophisticated taste?' Emmie put in with an attempt at an I'm-not-flustered-by-you-one-little-bit smile.

'It's late and I should let you get to bed. We both have to work tomorrow.'

There was the 'bed' word again, and somehow hearing it from his lips made it even worse. Especially when she could still taste his lips on her own. Her mind conjured up images of her in bed with him, their limbs entangled, their naked bodies pressed together in the throes of passionate sex.

Emmie had never had passionate sex, only a teenage fumble and the hit-and-miss sort of mild pleasure that had left her disappointed and wondering what all the fuss was about. She hadn't been brave enough to have sex since her diagnosis and treatment. Sharing her body with someone post-cancer was too confronting. But, now that Matteo had kissed her, she was tempted in a way she had never been tempted before to experience competent lovemaking. To lie in a man's arms and be pleasured like she had never been pleasured before. For his lovemaking would be nothing if not competent, she was sure. Matteo Vitale had an aura of sexual competence about him and it called out to every hungry cell in her body.

But she could not be tempted. Must *not* be tempted again. It was completely unprofessional and would only waste valuable time for him to achieve his goal.

Emmie quickly did a mental scan of her clients and came up with a name. Karena Thorsby wasn't a perfect fit for him but she came reasonably close. 'Look, speaking of work, I wonder if I do have someone who might suit your requirements. Would you be interested in meeting her for a drink, perhaps tomorrow if I can arrange it? If she suits, I wouldn't need to come to Umbria after all. I mean, it will save time for you, not to mention money.'

Matteo's gaze held hers in a lock that made the backs of her knees tingle. His expression was impossible to read and it made her all the more determined to keep her distance. She had never met anyone so intriguing, so alluring and complex. So dangerously tempting.

'Fine. I'll clear my diary.'

Emmie licked her lips and was shocked at how sensitive they still were, as if his kiss had somehow changed them. Charging them with such sensual energy they could never be the same.

'So, I'll be in touch as soon as I speak to Karena.' She moved towards the front door, desperate to get him to leave before she changed her mind. She opened the door and stretched her lips into another forced smile. 'Thank you again for dinner and for the lift home.'

Matteo stood in the frame of the doorway and looked down at her with his inscrutable expression still in place. His eyes briefly dipped to her mouth before coming back to hold hers. 'Goodnight.'

Emmie was aware of every thudding beat of her heart, aware of the hum of sensual energy in the air passing from his body to hers, aware of the magnetic pull of his gaze. Aware of the silent throb of blood still coursing through her kiss-swollen lips. ''Night.'

She closed the door once he'd left, and leaned back against it and let out a long, serrated sigh. 'Don't even think about it.' She whispered the words but they rang in the silence like a clanging alarm bell.

CHAPTER FOUR

MATTEO SUPPRESSED YET another yawn as Karena Thorsby told him her sad relationship history and why she was now thirty-four and desperate to settle down and make babies with the man of her dreams. But, while he conceded that she was attractive and intelligent, and had every right to want to fulfil her dream of happy-ever-after, he'd known from the moment he met her he wasn't the one to give it to her. There was no chemistry, no electric spark, no longing on his part to see her again.

Unlike with Emmie Woodcroft.

Every time he thought of Emmie, he thought of her periwinkle-blue eyes and lush mouth. The sweet softness of her lips and how they had clung to his when he'd kissed her. He thought of her petite frame pressed closely to his as he'd attended to her cut finger. How soft her skin was, how small her hand in comparison to his. He recalled the fragrance of her, the geranium and bergamot scent that was as intoxicating as a drug.

From the moment he'd met her, he had been drawn to her in a way he had never experienced with anyone else. Of course, he had felt instant desire in the past, but somehow with Emmie it went further than primal urges. Way, way further. It was as if she had some other indefinable element to her personality that called out to his on a silent radar frequency that sent tingles dancing along his flesh.

Finally, his date with Karena finally ended, his only comfort being she didn't seem all that disappointed, or even surprised, when he said he wasn't interested in repeating it.

He drove home with his mind replaying his dinner date with Emmie—how he had been disappointed when the evening had finally come to an end. He let out a sigh and turned his car into his street. Was he strangely fixated on Emmie because she had made it clear she wasn't interested in finding a partner? Did his male ego see her as some sort of fresh challenge? He usually had no trouble finding casual partners, but right now he wasn't after a fling. He needed a wife in a hurry, and obsessing about a young woman who had no plans to marry any time soon, if ever, would only waste his valuable time.

And yet, that kiss between them had shown him she was as drawn to him as he was to her.

Could he get Emmie to change her mind?

Emmie caught up with Karena the following day when she popped into Emmie's office on her lunch break.

'So, how did your date with Matteo Vitale go?'

Karena plonked herself down in the chair opposite Emmie's desk. 'Don't get me wrong, he was polite and easy on the eye, but I didn't feel any connection with him at all. In fact, I found him a little intimidating—more than a little, if I'm honest. I kept babbling on to fill the awkward silences but I think he was bored the whole time we were together.'

Emmie should have felt disappointed it hadn't

worked out for Matteo with Karena but strangely she was not. Nor was she going to examine too closely why she wasn't disappointed. 'I'm sorry. I guess he can be a little intimidating when you first meet him. But I do have another client who might be better for you. I've only just finished entering his details into the system.'

She clicked on her computer screen and scrolled through the list till she came to a divorced man of a similar age to Karena. 'Colin Appleby is looking for all the things you are. His wife left him a couple of years ago because he wanted children and she didn't. I'll organise a meeting for you both if you like?'

'Please do. My biological clock is ticking so loudly, it keeps me awake at night.'

Emmie forced her lips into an empathetic smile, her heart twisting into a tight knot in her chest. 'I can only imagine how awful that must be but let's hope Colin is The One.'

Karena had only been gone half an hour when Paisley informed her she had another visitor. 'It's Mr Vitale,' she said in a stage whisper. 'He's insisting on seeing you now. He's making rather a habit of this, isn't he? Shall I insist on him making an appointment or send him in?'

Emmie tried to ignore the soft flutter around her heart and rose from her chair. She suspected anyone insisting that Matteo Vitale do anything would be an impossible task. He had an iron will and a steely resolve that would daunt most people. But she was not most people and, besides, he was paying her a large sum of money, so she had to make his needs a priority. 'Send him in.' She smoothed her hands down the sides of her skirt, her pulse already picking up its pace.

Matteo came in looking as dashingly handsome as ever, especially with his windblown hair, and dressed in a dark suit the same colour as his eyes. He looked like a brooding hero from a Gothic romance, the landscape of his face drawn into harsh lines, his unusually blue eyes as dark as a midnight sky.

'Really? Was that the best you could do?' His blunt question was delivered with a cutting note of disdain.

Emmie refused to be intimidated by him, somehow understanding his natural inclination was to push people away rather than draw them near. 'Look, these things take time and—'

'I don't have time. I'm paying you a truckload of money to find me a wife, but if you can't find someone even remotely suitable then please tell me now so I can make other arrangements.'

'I'm working on it. Please, take a seat. Paisley has organised my travel arrangements and I can be in Umbria next week. Spending time with you will give me a clearer idea of—'

'Next week?' His eyes flashed with impatience and he remained standing, his imposing height never more apparent. 'Why not this weekend?'

Emmie disguised a convulsive swallow. She needed time to prepare herself, to get her head round spending an extended period of time with him. That impulsive kiss between them at her house warned her of the danger in being alone with him. She took a calming breath and straightened her spine, eyeballing him as if she was a stern schoolmistress dressing down a recalcitrant student.

'Mr Vitale, it no longer surprises me you've found it hard to find a suitable partner. I understand you like things done quickly, but I can't just shuffle around my diary to suit you. I have other clients to see to.'

'You have staff, don't you? Get them to see to them.'

Emmie gave him a look so glacial she fully expected the glass of water on her desk to freeze on the spot. 'You know, you might have had a chance with Karena if you hadn't scared the hell out of her. You made her nervous.'

'She should be an anaesthetist,' he shot back, scraping a hand through his already tousled hair. 'She would save the NHS a fortune on drugs. I swear to God, she almost put me to sleep by telling me about every man she'd ever dated and why they hadn't worked out.' He dropped his hand by his side and continued in a less harsh tone, 'Not that she wasn't a nice person, but she's far from my type.'

'Ah yes, your type,' Emmie said with an arch look. 'And that type would be…?'

He held her gaze for a throbbing moment, his eyes so dark and unreadable her heart skipped a beat. 'The type of woman who would agree to marry me for a year or two, max, and provide me with an heir.'

'But what sort of woman do you normally date?'

'The no-strings type.'

'It's my experience there are a lot less of them around than most men think,' Emmie said. 'Relationships, even casual ones, rarely come without strings, or indeed consequences. Someone nearly always gets hurt.'

Matteo drew in a deep breath and turned away to go and stand in front of her window, looking at the sliver of a view she paid a fortune in rent to stand on tiptoe and crane her neck to see. One of his hands came up to rub at the back of his neck as if to loosen a knot of tension. He rolled his shoulders and released a long sigh, turning around to look at her. 'It's never been my intention to hurt anyone, but yes, it has happened in the past.'

'Have you ever fallen in love?'

'No.'

'But someone did with you?'

A flicker of pain passed through his gaze. 'Unfortunately, yes.'

'Unfortunately, because…?'

'We were totally unsuitable for each other.' His tone was flat, his expression bleak. 'You have no idea of the pain I caused and there's nothing I can do to change a damn thing about it. Not now.'

Emmie came round from behind her desk and laid a gentle hand on his forearm. 'Do you want to talk about it?' She kept her voice soft, her gaze searching his pained one.

He blinked as if to recalibrate his mood and his expression became shuttered. 'No. Talking about it won't change a thing.' His hand came down over the top of hers and a frisson passed through her body. At first, she thought he was going to remove her hand from his arm, but he seemed to change his mind and took her hand in his. His long, tanned fingers curled around hers and he began to stroke the fleshy part at the base of her thumb, his gaze locking on hers. 'You're good at this.'

'At what?'

'Finding out people's darkest secrets.'

'But you're determined not to tell me yours.'

His eyes went to her mouth for a heart-stopping moment. Was he recalling their stolen kiss? The heat of it, the warm press of flesh on flesh, the erotic tangle their tongues? 'Doesn't everyone have something they would rather keep private?' His gaze locked back on hers and a tiny shiver raced across her scalp.

Emmie looked down at their joined hands, her stomach swooping at the sight of his tanned skin against her lighter skin. 'Maybe.'

Matteo turned over her hand and inspected the bandage on her finger. 'How is it feeling?'

'It's fine. Oh, that reminds me…' She pulled her hand out of his and went back to her desk and opened the top drawer on the left side. She took out the bottle of cologne she'd bought to replace the one she had broken at his house and came back to him with it. 'For you.'

He took the cologne with a lopsided smile. 'You didn't need to do that.'

'Yes, I did. I still feel embarrassed about that night.' And not just about the broken bottle. The kiss. She had relived that kiss so many times since.

'Don't be. I can see you have an inquisitive nature.'

Emmie gave a rueful smile. 'That's a polite way of saying I'm a nosy busybody.'

He gave an answering smile that sent a warm flutter through her lower body. He passed the bottle of cologne from one hand to the other, his eyes still holding hers. 'I'll pay you double to come to Umbria this weekend.'

Emmie spluttered out a shocked laugh. 'Don't be ridiculous. You don't have to bribe me. I'll come. But I insist on making my own way there.'

'Fine.' He held the cologne bottle in his right hand and, taking a piece of paper off a sticky note pad on her desk, took a pen out of his jacket pocket, wrote down an address and handed it to her. 'I'll look forward to seeing you there.'

So will I, Emmie thought. Way more than she had any right to.

Emmie drove the hire car through the stone and wrought-iron entrance to Matteo's Umbrian estate. She had insisted on making her own way to Italy, wanting to maintain some independence rather than relying totally on him. The long driveway was lined on either side by rows and rows of lush grape vines, and on the slopes in the distance was an expansive olive grove. There were woods on another side of the property, and a lake, as well as a small river, with a stone bridge across it that led to the villa at the top of a steep hill.

Emmie could immediately see why Matteo was so keen to keep possession of the estate. The villa was centuries old but in wonderful condition with beautiful gardens, both formal and informal. The stunning view from the top of the hill where the villa was situated was enough to steal anyone's breath away, and she was no exception. Emmie turned off the engine and got out of the car and stood for a long moment, looking out over acres and acres of verdant land, imagining Matteo's ancestors tilling the soil. The sun shone down on her with delicious warmth, birds tweeting in the nearby shrubbery, the leaves of the trees rustling in the light summer breeze.

She shaded her eyes from the bright sun with one hand, then turned and caught a glimpse of Matteo coming towards her dressed in nothing but dark blue denim jeans and brown leather work boots. His hair was tousled by the breeze, and his broad, tanned chest shone with perspiration, and Emmie had never seen him look more heart-stoppingly attractive.

'You're early,' Matteo said, roughly finger-combing his hair.

'I—I was bumped forward to an earlier flight.' Emmie felt strangely shy and tongue-tied. 'And it didn't take me as long as I thought to find my way here.'

'I'll get one of the staff to get your luggage. Come inside out of the sun. You already look flushed from the heat.'

Emmie was flushed because seeing his toned chest and abdomen was doing serious damage to her heart rate. Coils of tight muscles rippled from his chest to the waist band of his jeans and her imagination did the rest as to what was below. 'It is a lot hotter than I expected.' And so was he. She had already suspected he had a good body underneath the designer suits he wore but not as breath-catching as this. Her fingers twitched, tempted to reach out and stroke his abdomen to see if it was as rock-hard as it looked.

'If you have staff, why are you working in the fields?' Emmie asked on their way to the villa's entrance.

'My job as a forensic accountant is a desk job with long periods of sitting. I like the exercise working on the estate, not to mention the fresh air.'

Emmie turned and looked at the view again before he caught her staring at his toned body. 'It's beautiful, Matteo. I can see why you love it so much and want to keep it in your possession. If I lived here, I would never want to leave.'

There was a funny little silence only broken by the whistling of the breeze and the twittering birds.

Emmie turned to look at him to find him looking at her with a frown. 'Is something wrong?' she asked.

Matteo gave a movement of his lips that was just shy of a smile. 'I need to take a shower before I give you the grand tour. I'll get my housekeeper, Valentina, to take you to your room and give you some refreshments.'

'Oh, lovely, I could do with a nice cup of tea.'

A short time later, Emmie was led upstairs to a beautifully decorated guest room on the second storey by the housekeeper, who unfortunately didn't speak much English. Emmie had to resort to sign language, as her smattering of Italian didn't extend much besides greetings and 'please' and 'thank you.' It was frustrating, because she had hoped to find out what she could about Matteo via his staff. How someone behaved as an employer was often a clue to how they behaved in other contexts. But, even without the benefit of talking to Valentina, Emmie could see the older woman adored him. Her black-button eyes all but sparkled whenever she mentioned his name.

Once Valentina had left, Emmie finished her refreshing cup of tea and then freshened up. The view from the window in her room drew her back yet again to gaze at the rolling fields and dense woods in the background. She was not a city girl at heart, and had spent most of her childhood in Devon three and a half hours from London in a small village. But her cancer diagnosis and subsequent treatment—not to mention travelling back and forth, overnight accommodation and other expenses—had made it impossible for her parents to keep up with the mortgage payments, so their lovely little country property had had to be sold.

It had been yet another casualty of her illness, one

she found hard to forgive herself for, even though she knew on an intellectual level the cancer hadn't been her fault. But in her heart, she still ached for what her illness had done to her family. No one had escaped the fallout and each in their own way was still paying the price.

There was a firm knock on the door and Emmie turned from the window. 'Come in.'

Matteo entered the room and her heart stumbled. He was freshly showered, his hair still damp and curling where it brushed the collar of his casual, open-necked white shirt. He had changed into navy chinos and black leather boots and, even though he was a couple of metres from her, she could pick up the citrus notes of his aftershave. Seriously, she was becoming addicted to that smell. She'd been tempted to buy two bottles when she'd bought the replacement bottle for him. One for him and one for her to sniff in private like a forbidden drug.

'All settled in?' Matteo asked.

'Yes, thank you. But I'm not sure I was able to communicate how happy I was with the room to Valentina. I'm afraid my Italian is a bit patchy.'

'I'll pass on your appreciation.'

'How long has she worked for you?'

'Fifteen years.'

'That's nice.' Emmie moved from the window to tidy the tea things on the tray the housekeeper had left, more to do something with her hands. Being in a bedroom with Matteo Vitale was having a potent effect on her, one she had to do her best to control. 'It shows you're a good employer.'

'But it also could be the money I pay her, *si*?'

Emmie shifted her lips from side to side, her arms crossed against her body, and studied his cynical expression for a moment. 'You don't think much of my powers of observation, do you?'

He came closer to stand within touching distance and she had to work hard to keep her breathing under control. 'Body language is not fool proof, and people's motivations can be easily disguised.' His voice was deep and rough and sent a shiver cascading down her spine. 'Like yours, for instance.'

'M-mine?' Her voice barely got above a cracked whisper and her pulse began to race. She was conscious of how close he was, the heat of his body stirring hers into a frenzy of want. She had to crane her neck to maintain eye contact but every now and again, as if of their own volition, her eyes flicked to his mouth. And, before she could stop the impulse, the point of her tongue came out and licked across her lips.

Matteo placed a gentle hand beneath her chin, his touch light but electric. Lightning bolts of awareness shot through her entire body and a liquid pool of longing stirred deep and low in her core. His eyes were as dark as midnight, moving between hers in a back and forth motion before becoming hooded and lowering to her mouth. 'Why are you so keen on finding a happy-ever-after for other people but not for yourself?'

Emmie called on every bit of willpower she possessed to step out of his light hold. She wrapped her arms even tighter around her body and moved so the bed was between then. *Oh, dear Lord, the bed.* It seemed to dominate the room. It seemed to be all she thought about—a bed with he and her in it, making mad, passionate love. 'I could ask why you find it so satisfying being a forensic accountant,' she threw back.

'I like righting wrongs.'

'And I like making people happy.'

He gave a slanted smile that didn't reach his eyes. 'But, sadly, that is not always possible. Some people can never be made happy.'

Emmie moved away from the bed and back to the window, adopting a casual pose against the windowsill she was far from feeling. 'Perhaps they feel they don't deserve to be happy.'

He gave a loose-shouldered shrug, his expression equally noncommittal. 'You're an idealist, I'm a realist. We don't speak the same language.'

'I'm an optimist and you're cynical, but that's understandable given how your mother left so early in your life,' Emmie said. 'You have attachment issues. You will never be happy with anyone until you address your fear of intimacy.'

Matteo came to join her at the window, standing so close to her she could see the dark points of stubble along his jaw. He lifted his hand to her face, trailing an idle finger down the curve of her cheek, from her ear to her chin, and every nerve in her face rioted in tingling pleasure. 'Ah, but is it me with the fear of intimacy or you, hmm?' His tone was gently teasing, his touch spine-loosening, his proximity spellbinding.

Emmie sucked in a breath, her heart threatening to beat its way out of her chest. She couldn't stop staring at his mouth, drawn to its sensual contours by a force as old as time. Her lower body began to throb with a primal beat of blood, swelling sensitive tissues, sending tingles and darts and arrows of greedy want through her flesh.

'I— It depends what you mean by intimacy.' She was annoyed her voice wasn't as steady as she would have liked. 'Anyone can jump into bed and have sex, even perfect strangers. True intimacy is much more than that.'

His thumb began a rhythmical stroke of her cheek, like a metronome arm set on the slowest possible time signature. 'Who is the person you are closest to?' His hand paused its stroking, as if waiting for her to answer.

Emmie looked at him blankly for a moment, her brain in a scramble to come up with someone. She hadn't felt close to anyone for years, not since her illness. Her best friend had moved on, her sister was a stranger to her, her parents were so at war with each other that even after all this time becoming close to either of them was out of the question. Each would see it as betrayal of the other. Those in her current friendship circle knew about her brush with cancer but not about her infertility. No one knew how much her heart ached for what she had lost.

She swallowed tightly and removed his hand from where it was cupping her face, annoyed she hadn't done so as soon as he'd touched her. 'This is highly irregular...you mustn't touch me...like that...not again...'

'Because you like it too much?' His gaze was pointed, his tone mocking.

Emmie raised her chin. 'It would be completely unprofessional of me to encourage your advances.'

He gave an indolent smile that sent another wave of liquid heat to her core. 'Forgive me for misreading the signals.'

Emmie bridled in affront. 'I gave you no signals.' She mentally crossed her fingers over her white lie.

His eyes twinkled knowingly and he gave a mock-bow. 'Come. Let's not quibble over it. I will keep my distance unless you expressly tell me not to.'

'I can assure you that will *never* happen.' Emmie's confident tone didn't quite match how she was feeling on the inside. Matteo Vitale was the most tempting man she had ever met. If he put his mind to seducing her, she wouldn't stand a chance of resisting him.

And she had a horrible feeling he knew it.

Matteo gave Emmie a tour of the estate but stayed well away from the private garden he had made for Abriana and Gabriel. It was in a secluded part of the estate, in an area where his late wife used to spend a lot of time on her own. The reason for that was she had been deeply unhappy, and that had been entirely his fault.

Emmie leaned down to smell one of the old-world roses in the garden closest to the villa. 'Wow, what a heavenly scent.' She straightened and smiled wryly at him. 'I can never decide if roses or sweet peas are my favourite flowers. Or freesias, or lily of the valley… So many to choose from.'

'You can have more than one favourite, surely?'

Her smile faded slightly and her gaze fell away from his. She trailed her fingers across the shell-pink bloom of the full-blown rose in a reflective manner. 'When I was a child, I used to have my own garden where we lived in the country. My parents gave me one plot and my sister the other.' Her hand came back to her side and she let out a long sigh. 'Pot plants aren't quite the same thing, are they?'

'No, not quite.' Matteo walked in step with her along the gravel path, conscious of keeping space between them. He sensed her attraction to him but wondered why she was so adamant not to pursue it. Maintaining a professional distance was advisable, but he had seen the way her gaze kept drifting to his mouth, and had felt the crackling energy that zapped between them from the moment they met. But indulging in a fling with professional match-maker Emmie Woodcroft was not going to achieve his goal of finding a wife. Not unless she herself volunteered for the position. But that was hardly likely—she had already insisted she was a card-carrying member of the single-and-loving-it club.

The question that bugged him was, why? He found it hard to imagine her spending the rest of her life alone. She didn't seem the loner type. Running a professional match-making service seemed an odd choice of career for a loner.

'Is your sister older or younger than you?' Matteo asked in the silence.

'Younger.'

'What does she do for a living?'

Emmie bit her lip and turned to look at the fields in the distance. 'Natalie isn't working at the moment. She's been…unwell for a long time.'

Matteo frowned, wondering if he should press her for more details. He didn't appreciate people prying into his background, but he found he really wanted to know more about Emmie and what had made her the person she was today. She had mentioned during the evening they'd had dinner together that she'd spent some time in hospital as a teenager. Did her sister suffer from the same unspecified illness? 'I'm sorry to hear that.' He figured if she wanted to tell him more, she would do so.

Emmie turned and gave him a stiff smile that wasn't really a smile. 'She has an eating disorder. Anorexia. We've almost lost her several times. It's been such a rollercoaster, trying to keep her from going over the edge.'

Matteo reached for her hand and gently squeezed it in his. 'I'm sorry. That must be terrifying for you and your parents.'

She looked down at their joined hands. He was relieved and secretly delighted she didn't pull away. 'Yes, well, we manage each in our own way…some of us better than others.'

He stroked the back of her hand with his thumb. 'It's a wonder your parents are still together. The stress of an ill child can—'

'They're not.' Emmie's tone was blunt but with a lower note of pain. She slipped her hand out of his and picked another nearby bloom, holding it up to her nose before adding, 'They divorced years ago.'

Matteo was starting to understand Emmie's need to make people happy. She hadn't been able to solve the problems of her sister and parents, so sought to do it for her clients. 'You mentioned when we first met that you'd spent time in and out of hospital. Did you have an eating disorder too?'

She looked at him for a moment before shifting her gaze back to the garden bed. 'No.' She paused for a beat and added, 'I had cancer.'

CHAPTER FIVE

EMMIE CLOSED HER eyes in a tight blink and wished she hadn't spoken. She had known some of her friends for years before she had mentioned the dreaded *C* word. Why, then, had she told Matteo when she had only met him a matter of days ago? Why was her guard slipping when for years it had stayed firmly, resolutely in place? She normally kept a professional distance from her clients. She didn't tell them much about herself because it wasn't about her—it was about her finding them a partner.

But Matteo Vitale was not just a client…he was the first man she had felt attracted to since she'd become ill all those years ago. Really attracted, intensely attracted, to the point where her stoic acceptance of her circumstances was being undermined, like a fine crack in a china tea cup. She had taught herself not to want the things other people wanted, for if she fell in love and then got a recurrence of cancer she would be hurting yet another person. She would have to witness them fall apart just as she had witnessed her mother, father and sister do. Her illness had irreparably hurt everyone she loved. Her mission in life now was to make sure others had the things she could no longer have.

Matteo came closer and laid a gentle hand on the top of her shoulder and turned her to face him. His expression was etched in deep concern. 'Cancer?' His tone was hoarse with shock.

'Lymphoma. Hodgkin's. I was in and out of hospital for two years.' Seriously, she had to learn to keep her mouth shut around him. Next, she'd be telling him all the gory details—how wretchedly ill she'd been with the chemo…how her sense of dignity had completely disappeared the moment she had gone to hospital and had never quite recovered. How guilty she felt about the break-up of her family and her sister's slide into anorexia. How everything had been blown up by the bomb of her cancer.

His hand gently squeezed her shoulder. 'You poor darling, but you're better now, *si*?'

Emmie stretched her lips into a smile. 'But of course. The chemo worked brilliantly… Well, eventually, that is.' A little too brilliantly but, as low as her guard currently was, there was no way she was going to tell him that little nasty detail.

Matteo's hand fell away from her shoulder as if he'd only just realised it was still lying there. 'Cancer is hard enough to face as an adult but for a child…' He shook his head as if in disbelief that life could be so cruel. 'It's unthinkable.'

'I was seventeen, almost an adult.' Emmie began walking along the garden path again, keen to avoid his gaze. 'I won't say it wasn't hard. It was, but it's in the past, and I rarely think about it now.'

And there was another big fat lie. She *always* thought about it. Every headache or painful twinge of a muscle sent her into a mad panic. Was the lymphoma back? Was she going to die of some other sort of cancer? Would she have to go through months and months of torturous treatment all over again? Would her family and friends fall apart around her all over again? The worries were like little gremlins that followed her wherever she went, reminding her she was on borrowed time and that, one day, her time might be up sooner rather than later.

They walked under an archway of the pendulous blooms of fragrant wisteria and Matteo pushed one section aside to let Emmie through. He was still reeling from her revelation about her illness. Cancer was such a frightening diagnosis for anyone to face, much less a teenager. He could only imagine how tough it must have been for her and her family. Facing one's mortality at such a tender age would surely leave an indelible mark on one's character? The more time he spent with Emmie, the more he was intrigued by her character.

'My father refused chemo,' Matteo said after a moment. 'Although, to be fair, the survival rate for lung cancer is abysmally low compared to other cancers, even with chemo or surgery. It's good that you came through with the all-clear. Your parents must have been so relieved.'

'They were but not enough to call off the divorce,' Emmie said with a sigh. 'I sometimes wonder if I hadn't got sick if they'd still be together.'

'Sometimes challenges thrown at a couple shine a light on the cracks that were already there,' Matteo said. 'You shouldn't blame yourself. It wasn't your fault you got cancer. That was sheer bad luck.'

Emmie stopped by the next fragrant garden bed, snapped off a blue love-in-the-mist bloom and twirled the stem between her index finger and thumb. 'I used to grow these in the garden I was telling you about.' She walked a couple more paces and continued, 'We had to sell and move closer to London when I got sick. I cried buckets when we left—not where my parents could see me, of course. But when I was alone.' Her teeth sank into her lower lip and he wondered if she regretted being so open and honest with him.

Matteo was starting to realise there was a lot more to Emmie Woodcroft than he'd first thought. No wonder he found her so intriguing—there were depths and layers to her personality honed out of suffering at such a young age. She had stared down death as a teenager and won, but no doubt there had been a lot of suffering in the process.

And didn't he know a little about suffering from a young age? Not anything as terrifying as cancer, of course, but the walk-out of his mother had been a life-defining moment. A moment he remembered so clearly, *too* clearly. Painfully clearly. If he allowed himself to dwell on it he could still picture her car disappearing into the distance...could still feel the empty ache of despair in his chest...the painful jab of rejection that had never quite gone away but still lay twisted and ugly, deep inside him like a wound, gnarled and ropey with scar tissue.

'Where was your country home?' Matteo asked.

'In Devon. We had a bit of acreage there, not a lot, but it was wonderful not being too close to neighbours.' She gave him a sideways glance and added, 'I'm sorry if I'm boring you.' She gave a self-deprecating laugh, her cheeks going a delicate shade of pink. 'I'm supposed to be getting to know you, not you me. It must be the heady scent of the flowers and the fresh air bewitching me. Tell me to shut up.'

Matteo smiled. 'I like hearing about you.'

She stopped walking to look up at him. 'But I've told you heaps more about myself than you've told me. Tell me something about yourself that no one else knows.'

There were many things Matteo had not told anyone about himself, and he was doing everything in his power to make it stay that way. Not that Emmie Woodcroft made it easy, though. She had a beguiling nature that had a potent effect on his resolve. But he considered his back story irrelevant to the task at hand. He needed her to find him a suitable wife and the sooner she got on with it, the better. Playing twenty questions was not his thing at all.

He glanced at his watch in a pointed manner. 'We'll have to save this conversation for another time. Can you find your way back to the villa from here? I have to see one of my staff about something before dinner.'

'Sure, but I'm going to ask you again over dinner, so don't think you're getting off so easily.'

Matteo forced a smile. 'You're a determined little thing, aren't you?'

Her eyes twinkled like the sunlight dancing on the water-lily pond behind her. 'It's how I succeed at my job. And you do want me to succeed, don't you?'

'But of course.' Matteo was paying her a small fortune to do as he requested. It was a pity her methods included digging for emotions he had long ago buried.

But he was going to damn well keep them that way.

Emmie was enjoying the early-evening summer sunshine too much to go back to the villa straight away. The air was fragrant with flowers and the scent of freshly mown grass and the light breeze had taken the harsh sting out of the sun's heat. She wandered along the crushed limestone path, past the water feature, stopping every now and again to smell yet another heady bloom of the exquisite roses. Blooms as big as saucers, petals as soft as velvet, the mix of fragrances so intense it was intoxicating to her senses.

Or maybe that had more to do with being with Matteo Vitale…

Emmie knew she had to stop thinking about him in that way—the way that would only lead to disappointment, if not heartbreak. She might sense his attraction to her, and she was in no doubt of her attraction to him, but it couldn't go anywhere. How could it? She couldn't provide him with the thing he most needed—an heir. But she could hopefully provide him with a wife from her list of clients, for that was what he was paying her to do.

The kicker was, what woman in her right mind would marry him when he had no intention of falling in love with her? Love was what her clients were seeking, not a marriage of convenience, even if it was to one of the most handsome and wealthiest men Emmie had ever encountered. Of course, it was true that occasionally marriages of conveniences worked out well for some couples, mutual love developing over time, and the relationship strengthening and growing into one of joy and long-term happiness.

Some distance from the path, Emmie noticed a small rivulet that fed into the river running through the estate. A family of wood ducks waddled near the banks and, dying for a better glimpse of the cute little fluffy ducklings, Emmie walked towards it through a wilder section of the garden.

The family of ducks had by now slipped into the water and was swimming away, but then Emmie noticed a chest-high hedge in the distance close to a thickly wooded area. The hedge enclosed a squared-off area that appeared to be some sort of private garden with a large shady tree in the centre. She had to step across the rivulet to get to it, which was not all that easy to do. There was no bridge, and the stones that were there were slippery with moss, but somehow, she managed it without falling in. When she got closer, she found a rustic wrought-iron gate set in the hedge. She turned the handle and pushed the gate open and stepped into the cool shady enclosure.

And then she saw the white head stones over two graves.

The leaves rustled above her head like the breath of a ghost and a shiver tiptoed over Emmie's scalp, and then all the way down her spine. There was an adult grave and a smaller one…so small it could only be that of a child. Her heart gave a painful spasm… A very small child—a baby. A tiny baby. There were fresh flowers in the brass vases and a teddy bear encased in a glass box on the baby's grave.

Emmie moved closer to the head stones and knelt on the soft grass to read the inscriptions.

Abriana Maria Vitale,
wife of Matteo Andrea Vitale,
loving mother of Gabriel Giorgio Vitale

The rest of the words were in Italian, but Emmie could see from the dates that Abriana had died eight years ago at the age of twenty-five. And the baby…she swallowed a thick lump in her throat…the baby had died on the day it was born, presumably at the same time as his mother.

Emmie sat back on her heels in shock, her heart contracting as though it was in a vice. Her fingers and toes went numb as if the blood had left her extremities to pump to her vital organs. Matteo had been married? He'd tragically lost his wife and baby and yet hadn't told her? Why not? It was the most important information about him and yet he had kept it from her.

A cold shiver coursed down her spine and her stomach churned with anguish. Such a terrible, heart-wrenching tragedy to go through and yet it explained so much about his personality. The harsh landscape of his face, his perpetual frown, the lines of pain etched into his skin, the shadows in his eyes, his set mouth that so rarely smiled, as if he had forgotten how to… No wonder he was furious about his father's will—Matteo was still grieving the loss of his young wife and child. No wonder he baulked at the idea of marrying. He wasn't ready to move on with his life but the will left him no choice.

But why were his wife and child buried here and not at the local cemetery Emmie had driven past on her way to the estate? There were no other graves, so this was not a family plot with the rest of Matteo's ancestors. His father had died recently and there was no sign of his grave here. Just these two lonely graves hidden in a secluded green area of the estate.

There was the snap of a twig behind Emmie and she jumped in alarm and scrambled to her feet to see Matteo only a few feet away, his expression hard to read, given the angle of light, for his face was entirely in shadow.

'So, you've found them.' His tone gave her no clue as to how he felt about her stumbling across his wife and child's graves. It was flat, toneless, empty.

Emmie brushed her breeze-teased hair back off her face. 'Matteo… I don't understand. Why didn't you tell me you were married and had a child?'

He moved closer to the graves and stood looking down at them with his hands shoved into the pockets of his chinos. 'I don't like talking about that period of my life.'

'I can only imagine how terribly painful it must be, but surely you see—'

'You can't possibly understand,' he said, turning to look at her with a savage frown. 'So don't insult me by pretending you do.'

'I understand grief is a very personal thing,' Emmie said. 'That it's painful, and a process that can takes years if not a lifetime to work through. Losing someone you love is one of the most devastating things that can—'

'But that's the point.' Matteo's voice hardened. 'I didn't love Abriana, not the way she deserved to be loved. Not the way she wanted to be loved.'

Emmie looked at him in shock, her mind whirling. Then why had he married her? She glanced back at the tiny grave next to his wife's and bit her lip, joining the dots herself. 'It was because of the baby? Your marriage, I mean? Because of Gabriel?'

He flinched as if the very sound of that tiny baby's name was an arrow to his heart. 'We had dated on and off for a month or two. She told me she was on the pill and, even though we always used condoms, she somehow got pregnant.' He scraped a hand through his hair. 'I understood and respected her wish to keep the baby. But I wanted my child to grow up with my name, so I offered to marry her.'

'But neither of you were happy.' Emmie didn't state it as a question for she could see there was no point. The answer was in the ravaged lines of Matteo's face, a road map of pain and grief and guilt.

'No, not for one moment.' He turned back to look at the graves of his wife and child, his shoulders hunched forward, tension visible in the muscles of his back and shoulders.

Emmie came up beside him and placed a gentle hand on the small of his back. He gave a light shudder, like a stallion shivering a fly off its hide. 'I'm so very sorry...' she whispered.

There was a long silence broken only by the tinkling of water nearby and the gentle rustling of the leaves above of the large tree casting its sheltering shade.

Matteo took a ragged breath and stepped back from the graves. 'Abriana was a nice person. A decent person. She would have been a wonderful mother, but even that was taken away from her. She never even got to hold our child in her arms.'

'What happened?'

'A car crash. She was driving back from a pre-natal appointment and a car crossed into her path on a narrow bend. She made it to hospital but died a short time later. They delivered Gabriel but he...' He swallowed and continued in a hollow voice, 'He only lived for two hours. I didn't get back from London until later that evening.'

Emmie blinked back the sting of tears and touched him on the arm. 'Oh, Matteo, how tragic. How terribly sad and tragic.'

Matteo covered her hand with his and gave it a squeeze, his expression still grim. 'I swore I would never marry again. I don't consider myself cut out for marriage and all it entails. If I had been a better husband, then maybe Abriana would still be here, and Gabriel too.' He removed his hand from hers and thrust it back in his trouser pocket. 'But of course, my father had other ideas, and decided to force my hand.'

Emmie frowned. 'So, that's why he wrote the codicil on his will? To force you to marry again and produce an heir?'

'Thoughtful of him, *si*?' His sarcasm wasn't wasted on her. She knew all about manipulative fathers. Her father had played a few manipulative games in his time and caused no end of stress in order to get his own way. But what if Matteo's father had acted out of concern for Matteo? Wanting him to move on with his life instead of being stuck in a deep well of grief and regret? Perhaps his actions were motivated out of love and concern, not a desire to cause further pain.

'You know, there could be another way of looking at your father's motives,' Emmie said. 'He might have wanted you to forgive yourself for what happened with Abriana and Gabriel and to move on with your life.'

'Forgive myself?' Matteo's frown was so deep it carved a deep trench between the dark flashing orbs of his eyes. 'And how am I supposed to do that with them both lying there in the ground?' He waved his hand at the graves. 'I blame myself for everything. How can I not?'

Emmie rolled her lips together, her heart aching for the pain she could sense in every fibre of his being. 'You told me it wasn't my fault I got cancer. It's not your fault your wife and baby died. You weren't driving the car and, besides, you said the other driver crossed to the wrong side of the road. It was their fault, if anyone's.'

'But I *should* have been driving that day,' Matteo said through tightly set lips. 'Abriana wanted me to attend that appointment with her but I chose to go to London instead. I had a court case I was working on for a client, but I could have waited one more day before flying back to London.' He muttered a curse and added with a bitter edge to his voice, 'So don't tell me it's not my fault.' He swung away, walked back through the gate in the hedge and disappeared from sight.

Emmie let out a long sigh but didn't follow him through the gate. She needed time to process what he had told her, to get her head around the tragedy that had shaped him into the man he was today. He was tortured by the grief and guilt of his wife's and baby's deaths, which was completely understandable. Some people never got over such a loss and carried it with them for the rest of their lives.

It seemed more and more obvious to her that Matteo Vitale's father had changed his will to force his son to marry again and produce an heir to continue the family line, knowing that without such an impetus Matteo would be stuck in a prison of self-blame for ever. And, while Matteo was reluctant, he was prepared to fulfil the terms of his father's will—some would say in rather a ruthless manner—in order to save the estate. The estate where his wife and child were buried in this sad little garden.

No wonder Matteo was so keen to keep the estate in his possession. The stakes were higher than Emmie had realised, and it all made sense now. How he had insisted she act with haste in finding him a suitable partner. She had thought him ruthless and a little unfeeling when he'd come into her office that first day, but now she understood his motivation and couldn't help feeling sorry for the horrible dilemma he faced. She wished he had told her from the get-go, but a part of her understood why he hadn't. He was a loner, a deeply private person who would not go public with his pain.

She was reminded again of the wounded wolf image—the alpha male taking himself away from the pack to lick his wounds in private, unwilling to show any hint of vulnerability. There was an element of that same behaviour in her own personality, an unwillingness to share with anyone the deepest agonies of her soul.

But, if Matteo married again without love being part of the equation, it would make it yet another marriage of convenience. Surely that wasn't wise? Such a marriage had already ended in tragedy. Emmie believed in the power of love and, while she had ruled it out for herself, she knew Matteo was someone who was worthy of being loved, if only he would allow himself to love in return. To open his guarded heart and allow it to feel the love she was sure he was more than capable of feeling. But the desertion of his mother when he'd been a young child had made him wary of engaging his emotions.

From the moment she'd met him, Matteo had given her the impression his heart was bricked up behind a thick wall of cynicism. He had told her he had never been in love and she suspected he would never allow himself to be. Matteo had experienced untold pain and loss and had come to her out of desperation to solve his problem. He was paying her a lot of money to find him a wife, to match him with someone who would provide him with an heir.

Emmie released another sigh and turned to look at the head stones standing side by side with only the sound of the birds and the breeze keeping them company in the cool, green shade. The clock was ticking. She had to find him a wife, otherwise he would lose everything, including this sacred ground where his wife and child were buried.

CHAPTER SIX

MATTEO WAS FURIOUS with himself for not realising Emmie might discover Abriana's and Gabriel's graves when he'd left her to make her way back to the villa. Her inquisitive nature, especially in finding out everything she could about him, should have been warning enough but he had ignored it.

But, strangely, there was a part of him that had wanted her to discover the secret pain of his past. Not that he felt any better for revealing it to her. If anything, he felt worse. Emmie would no doubt want to talk more about the tragedy and it would bring it all back—the harrowing guilt. It was a gnawing pain inside him, a constant reminder of how he had failed to keep safe those under his care and protection.

And now, his late father had demanded he commit to another marriage and risk the same happening all over again. But he couldn't walk away from the estate and see it pass into a stranger's hands. He had to do everything in his power to keep it in his possession—it was the price he must pay for having failed to keep his wife and child safe. He owed it to them to honour their memory.

Could Emmie be the answer? The thought was growing deeper roots in his brain. She claimed she wasn't looking for love. That her focus was her business, not finding happiness for herself. A marriage of convenience between them could work if he could convince her to agree to it. Their mutual attraction was undeniable and increasingly irresistible. But he would have to be patient in talking her round. He didn't want to pressure her but surely, she could sense the connection that had developed between them? He wondered if that was why she had been trying to keep her distance since they'd kissed at her house in London. Unless he was misreading the signals, the temptation to explore the chemistry between them was as tempting to her as it was to him.

And he was determined to act on it.

Valentina informed Emmie through a combination of sign language and broken English that dinner would be served in the smaller of the two dining rooms on the ground floor, overlooking the lake. Emmie changed into a dress and scooped up her hair up into a makeshift bun and applied some light make-up. On her way downstairs, she stopped to look at some of the art work, some of which included portraits of Matteo's ancestors. She could see the likeness, particularly in what appeared to be his grandfather Giorgio's portrait. She recalled Matteo's baby son's full name, and that Giorgio had been included in it. Did that mean Matteo had had a special connection with his grandfather? One he hadn't had with his father?

Emmie walked further along the gallery with an even deeper understanding of Matteo's reluctance to lose the estate, notwithstanding it being the final resting place of his wife and child. This was the home of his ancestors, the place where they had lived and loved for hundreds of years. She had found it devastating to move from her childhood home and she had only lived there for seventeen years. How much worse to lose the home that contained so many centuries of history, so many memories?

Emmie came to a door at the end of the gallery that was slightly ajar and her curiosity soon got the better of her. She gently pushed it open and stepped inside to find a library with floor-to-ceiling bookshelves, a mezzanine level and a wooden ladder for access to the higher shelves. There was a beautiful antique desk in polished walnut set in front of tall windows draped with heavy velvet curtains in a deep red the same colour as one of the roses she had smelled that afternoon.

Emmie moved closer to the desk and ran her fingers along the polished surface. She sat on the studded leather chair and swung it from side to side, wondering why Matteo had no photos or sentimental artefacts on his desk as so many people did. There was only a laptop and a blank notepad and a collection of pens and a glass paperweight.

'Looking for more of my secrets?' Matteo's deep voice at the door startled her into standing upright, her cheeks instantly flooding with heat.

'I'm sorry. I was just having a look around. It's a beautiful room…so many books. Some of them must be so old. Have you had them valued? There might be first editions in that collection and they're worth a fortune.' Emmie knew she was rambling, desperate to fill the silence, desperate to avoid the censure and cynicism of his gaze.

'Yes, well, it will be a pain to have to move them if I am unable to fulfil the terms of my father's will in time.' He glanced around the room before bringing his gaze back to hers. 'But, all being well, it won't come to that.'

Emmie moved out from behind the desk. 'Your situation is…complicated. I can see that now. I understand your reluctance to marry again but this time around might work out brilliantly. Lots of cultures rely on arranged marriages and using a dating agency is a little like that. Matching people who are most likely to fall in love.'

'I'm not interested in falling in love. All I'm interested in is fulfilling the terms of my father's will.'

'But surely you could do both?' Emmie said. 'You shouldn't rule it out. Love can strike when you least expect it.'

Matteo came to where she was standing and her senses reeled at the force of energy he brought with him. Sensual energy, a dark, brooding energy, that sent livewires of awareness flickering across her skin. She had to hyper-extend her neck to keep eye contact and her stomach swooped at the deep blue of his glinting eyes.

'And has love ever struck you?' His voice was low and deep, and caused a riot of sensations to flutter in her core.

Emmie disguised a swallow, her pulse hammering, her heart racing. 'No. I haven't been in love before…'

A cynical light gleamed in his gaze. 'And why is that, do you think?' He ran an idle finger down the curve of her cheek, setting spot fires in her flesh.

'I—I'm too busy finding love for my clients…' Emmie was annoyed her voice was so whispery and her heart rate so erratic and her resolve to resist him so absent. She was acting like a love-struck schoolgirl in front of a much-adored celebrity. The sheer magnetism of him overwhelmed her, bewitching her into a mesmerised trance. She couldn't drag her gaze away from his mouth, the sculptured perfection of it, the firm lines of his top lip and the fullness of his lower lip that hinted at a potent, bone-melting sensuality.

Matteo sent the pad of his thumb across her bottom lip in a spine-tingling stroke. 'You have such a beautiful mouth…' His voice had lowered another semitone. 'I keep thinking about how it felt to kiss you that evening at your house.'

Emmie wasn't aware of moving but suddenly she was pressed against him, chest to chest, thigh to thigh, her gaze locked on his, her heart threatening to punch its way out of her body. 'Matteo…' She could barely get her voice to work, barely think straight—all she wanted was to feel his mouth press down on hers. It was a burning need inside her, a fervent need that would not be tamed any other way. 'Kiss me.' She could hardly believe she had spoken her need out loud, even if it had only been a whisper—a desperate whisper.

The smouldering heat in his gaze intensified, as if the fire he had stirred in her flesh had travelled to his. His thumb passed over her lower lip once more, slowly, torturously slowly, making her flesh tingle with increasing want. A want so agonisingly intense it consumed her, controlled her, overpowered her.

'I've had a burning desire to do so almost from the first moment I met you and every moment since.' His warm breath mingled with hers in the intimate space between their mouths.

Emmie stood on tiptoe and laced her hands around his neck, worried he might change his mind and pull away. Her breasts were crushed against the hard wall of his chest, her thighs pressed into the firmness of his, her senses doing cartwheels as she felt the stirring of his erection against her body. Desire rippled through her in a torrent, a flash flood of fiery heat that left no part of her unaffected. Her inner core pulsed with longing, a deep, throbbing pulse that turned her to molten liquid. 'Then do it. Do it now. Kiss me. I want you to.' She didn't care that she was close to begging—all she cared about was feeling his sensual mouth pressed to hers again, feeling the desire he felt for her against her lips.

He gave a low groan deep in his throat and then his mouth came down on hers, his lips firm, urgent, masterful, demanding. Emmie responded with the same urgency, hungry for the exquisite taste of him, the incendiary heat and fire of his mouth sending shock waves through her body. Delicious, shuddering shock waves that awakened every nerve in her flesh.

Emmie murmured her approval against his lips. His tongue stroked the seam of her mouth in a spine-loosening movement and she welcomed him in with a whimper of pleasure. His tongue touched hers and an explosion of sensations shot through her, sending waves of heat to her core. He deepened the kiss, stirring her into a fervent response that was so erotic, so electric, so exciting, it set her pulse madly racing.

One of his hands came up to cup her face and the other went to the small of her back, bringing her body closer to the hot, hard heat of his growing erection. Emmie whimpered again in excitement, relishing the feel of his aroused flesh against her. Nothing could have prepared her for the magic of his explosive kiss, the potent power of his lips and tongue making every cell of her body shout in rapturous joy.

Matteo angled his head to shift position and another guttural groan came from his throat, his lips firmer, more demanding, signalling an escalating need so similar to the one pounding through her flesh. One of his hands went to the back of her head, his fingers clutching a handful of her hair, not roughly, but not gently either, just somewhere delightfully, thrillingly, in between. Ripples of pleasure ran down her spine, her inner core throbbing with the need for his erotic, intimate possession.

'Are you okay with me doing this?' He spoke just above her mouth, the movement of his breath like a caress on her sensitised lips.

'More than okay,' Emmie said against his lips. 'It's just a kiss, right?' She wanted more, much more, but didn't know if it was wise to take things that far. She had for so long ignored her body's needs. They hummed occasionally, in the background, but she had taught herself to ignore them. But now, in Matteo Vitale's arms, she caught a tempting glimpse of what making love with him would be like—thrilling, mind-blowing, earth-shattering.

If she succumbed to the temptation, nothing would be the same again. *She* would not be the same.

Matteo framed her face with his hands, his gaze searching. 'Is it?'

Emmie stroked her hand down the length of his lean jaw, her soft skin catching on his light stubble, sending another wave of shivering sensations down her spine. 'You're a very attractive man, and I'm only human, but anything more than a kiss or two is probably not wise under the circumstances.' She removed her hand from his face but he captured it and held it against his chest instead, his eyes smouldering.

'Because?' he prompted.

Emmie moistened her lips with the point of her tongue, her stomach swooping when his gaze followed the movement. 'I need to maintain a professional distance in order to do what you're paying me to do.' She tugged her hand out from underneath his and stepped back. 'I came here to find out everything I can about you so I can match you with the perfect partner.'

'Allowing me to kiss you is part of your research, *si*?' There was a sardonic light in his deep-blue eyes.

'No, it is not.' Emmie could feel her cheeks heating and turned away to regain her composure. She picked up the paperweight from his desk and tested its weight in her hand. 'Why don't you have any photos of your wife in the villa?' She put the paperweight down and turned and faced him. 'I've looked in most of the rooms and there's nothing. Only portraits of your ancestors.'

'We didn't have that sort of relationship.' He moved across the room to straighten a couple of books on the bookshelves, his back turned towards her.

'Describe your relationship with her.'

Matteo turned to face her, his expression grim. 'It wasn't intimate.'

'Did you share a room? A bed?'

'No.'

Emmie frowned. 'Why not? You were husband and wife.'

He gave a movement of his lips that was one-part

smile, three-parts grimace. 'I didn't think it was wise or indeed fair to encourage her feelings for me.'

Something tightened around Emmie's heart—a painful tug of invisible stitches. 'She was in love with you?'

A shadow moved through his gaze and his jaw tightened. 'So she said, but I could not return her feelings. I liked her, cared about her, but as to love, that sort of love…' He gave a one-shouldered shrug. 'It's not an emotion I've felt for her or for anyone.'

'Would you recognise it if you did?'

A cynical smile slanted his mouth. 'Romantics such as yourself would say so, would they not?'

'But what do *you* think?'

Matteo came back over to her and lifted her chin with the end of his index finger, locking his gaze with hers. 'I think you ask a lot of questions that you would not answer yourself.'

Emmie's heart began to thump, her breath stalling in her throat. 'I think I would recognise it if I fell in love with someone.' Her voice came out scratchy.

His hand cupped one side of her face, his eyes still unwavering on hers. 'What do you think you would feel? Describe it for me.'

Emmie sent her tongue across her lips again, her pulse racing so fast she felt light-headed… Or maybe that was because she was mesmerised by the deep, rumbling tone of his voice, the warm cradle of his hand against her face, the proximity of his tempting body and her own body's craving, driving need for more of his touch. Never had she been so aware of a man. Aware of every nuance of his expression, every soft, warm waft of his breath against her mouth.

'Having never been in love, I can only go on what

other people have said. That you just know with a certainty that this person is the only one for you. You know it like it was written in stone. That it was meant to be from before you were even born. That this person is the one who completes you, complements and fulfils you in a way no one else can do.'

His gaze was unwavering. 'So, you believe there is only one perfect partner for each person?'

Emmie eased out of his hold and made a point of putting some distance between them. 'What I tell my clients to concentrate on is being a perfect partner themselves rather than expecting to find someone who is perfect for them. Working on yourself first is key. Too many relationships fail when one partner shines a light on the other's imperfections without examining and working on their own.'

Matteo gave a rueful movement of his lips. 'Wise words.' He picked up a pen from his desk and stroked his fingers along its slim barrel, his forehead creased in a frown.

Emmie studied him for a long moment, wondering if he was thinking about his late wife. 'Were you overly critical of Abriana?'

He put the pen down and met her gaze head on. 'Not at all.'

'But she was critical of you.' Emmie didn't phrase it as a question.

'And why shouldn't she have been? She wanted me to fall in love with her the way she had fallen in love with me.' His lips twisted into another grimace. 'It's not a comfortable feeling, knowing you've broken someone's heart.'

'But you were honest with her from the get-go? I

mean, you didn't say things you didn't mean to get her to marry you once you knew she was pregnant?'

'I was brutally honest.'

Emmie could well believe it. 'And you were absolutely certain Gabriel was your child?'

'Absolutely.'

'You asked for a paternity test?'

'No.'

Emmie raised her brows. 'Why not? How well did you know her? She might have been—'

'I didn't ask, but she insisted on having one done so there was no question over paternity.'

'I guess, given your forensically trained mind, she felt she had to.'

'Perhaps.'

There was a silence that was so thick Emmie could almost hear the tiny dust motes moving through the air.

Matteo moved to the door, his expression inscrutable. 'Come. Valentina will be waiting for us with our dinner.'

Emmie followed him out of the library, conscious of him walking by her side down the long, wide corridor… conscious of the brush of his arm against hers…conscious of the taste of him still lingering in her mouth. And conscious of the needs he had awakened that still hummed in her flesh.

CHAPTER SEVEN

DINNER WAS A beautiful meal prepared with fresh produce from the estate, and Emmie delighted in every dish that was brought to the table. Valentina's cooking took the whole pasture-to-plate trend to a whole new level. Succulent asparagus in a creamy hollandaise, trout caught from the river and pan-fried, served with an Italian-style salsa, and to follow a delectable honey-flavoured panna cotta garnished with plump strawberries.

'Your housekeeper could open her own restaurant,' Emmie said, finally putting down her cutlery with a sigh of pleasure. 'Seriously, that was one of the best meals I've eaten in ages.'

'Don't tempt her to leave me,' Matteo said with a wry smile, pouring a fresh serving of mineral water into Emmie's glass.

Emmie leaned her head on one side to study him. 'So, you can form deep attachments to people, then?'

He made a harrumphing sound. 'Valentina and I go a long way back, even before she came to work for me.'

'She's old enough to be your mother,' Emmie mused.

'Precisely.'

'So, she's kind of a maternal figure to you?'

'*Si*, and one I deeply admire. She was unable to have children of her own and her husband left her because if it.' He picked up his glass of ruby-red wine but didn't raise it to his lips. 'She never got over it. She hasn't had another relationship and instead has devoted her life to working for me.' He took a token sip of his wine and put the glass back on the table.

Emmie wondered if Valentina's infertility was the most heart-breaking thing for her or the rejection of her husband. Was that why she had never married again? 'That's sad… I mean, that she hasn't had the family she longed for. She must have been devastated when you lost your wife and baby.'

Something flickered across his face. '*Si*, she was, but unfortunately she and Abriana did not get on well.' His lips moved in a grim twist. 'Valentina didn't think Abriana was the right partner for me.'

'Because you weren't in love with her?'

'That and other reasons.'

'Such as?'

Matteo gave his mouth another twist. 'I don't wish to speak ill of the dead. Abriana did her best under difficult circumstances.'

Emmie secretly admired him for not spilling all about his late wife's shortcomings. Too many of her clients spoke at length about how awful their previous partners were and it always rang alarm bells for her. The talking down of a previous partner often showed her far more things about the client than their ex. But Matteo had clearly respected Abriana even if he hadn't loved her the way she had wanted him to. 'Can I ask you something?'

'Go ahead.' His tone was bland but his gaze was watchful. Guarded.

'Why didn't you bury Abriana and Gabriel at the cemetery in the village? Why here, on the estate? And in that particular spot?'

Matteo's expression clouded and she got a glimpse of the pain he was so good at hiding most of the time. 'Abriana loved that shady area away from the villa. She used to go down there with a book and read for hours.' His broad shoulders slumped, as if weighted down by the burden of sad memories and painful regrets. 'I didn't think she would want to spend eternity in a cold impersonal graveyard amongst strangers, but rather somewhere she felt at peace.'

His actions showed a deeper sensitivity than Emmie had given him credit for. 'It's a beautiful spot…so tranquil and serene.' She picked up her water glass for something to do with her hands. 'Do you go there often?'

Another shadow passed through his gaze. 'Every day when I am home.' Another rueful twist of his mouth. 'Abriana would find it amusing that I have spent far more time down there now than I did with her when she was alive.' His attempt at wry humour fell a little short of the mark and it showed in his tone and on his features.

Emmie put her glass back down and reached for his forearm where it rested on the table. She gave his firm flesh a gentle press. 'I'm sure she would appreciate the respect you pay her and Gabriel.' Her own voice betrayed her see-sawing emotions. She was not normally a teary person—facing down death at a young age had taught her that tears couldn't change difficult circumstances. But Matteo's situation was so tragic, and the self-recrimination he flayed himself with was painful to witness. Her heart ached for Abriana who had died so young, and for little Gabriel, who had never felt the shelter of his mother's arms in the two-hour span of his tiny life.

Matteo placed his hand on top of hers. *'Grazie.'* His voice was deep and husky, his eyes dark and tortured.

Emmie bit down on her lower lip, trying to contain her feelings, but the sting of tears at the back of her eyes made her vision blur. 'Did you get to…to hold him? To hold your son before he…?' She found she couldn't say the word, that dreadfully final word—*died.*

Matteo's dark gaze shone with moisture and her heart twisted again. '*Si*, I held him.' His throat moved up and down over a tight swallow. 'But not while he was alive. I got there too late. It is my biggest regret, and I cannot escape it, no matter how much I try.' He suddenly scraped back his chair and stood. 'Will you excuse me? Valentina will show you to your room. It's been a long day and I'm sure you're ready for bed. Goodnight.' A shutter had come down over his features like a curtain on a stage, his tone polite but formal, distant and unreachable.

'Goodnight…' Emmie could barely get her voice above a mumble and, right at that moment, she didn't trust her legs to get her out of the chair. She sat in silence for endless minutes, staring sightlessly at the remains of their meal and the flickering candle on the table, wondering if Matteo would ever come to a point when he would forgive himself and finally move on with his life. Or would he be chained to the past with shackles of regret and self-blame for ever?

* * *

Matteo strode out of the villa and into the moonlit garden, desperate for air, desperate to escape the pain of his failure to protect his own flesh and blood. It was a gut-wrenching pain that tortured him daily and never more so than when he was home on the estate. Every time he visited the graves of his wife and son, he revisited his failure. To think their lives had been cut short because he hadn't been there when they'd needed him was an inescapable reality. He should have been driving Abriana to that appointment. She hadn't been a confident driver and she had spoken to him about having 'baby brain,' when she lost concentration at times. How could he forgive himself for not doing all he could to keep she and the baby safe?

He was shocked at how much he had revealed to Emmie in the short time he had known her. She had a way of getting under his guard with her active listening and gentle questioning, making him *want* to tell her more. Making him want to relieve himself of the burden of carrying this load of guilt that never seemed to lessen even though eight years had passed. But Emmie Woodcroft was not a grief counsellor, she was a professional match-maker, and he needed her to do her thing so he could keep the estate secure.

But his attraction to her was proving harder and harder to resist. Emmie had asked him to kiss her and he had done so with such ardour it had shaken him to the core. She stirred in him a ferocious lust that stormed through his body like a red-hot fever. Her mouth was sweet, yet dangerously tempting. Everything about her was dangerously tempting. But his ardour was more than matched by hers for him. It had been electrifying to hold her in his arms, to explore her soft and yielding mouth with his own. His body still hummed with the need she had awakened. It was distracting to have her here, to say the least, especially when she was supposed to be finding him a wife.

A wayward thought drifted into his mind… *You could have a fling with her in order to convince her to marry you.*

The more he thought about it, the more attractive the prospect became—and all the more deliciously tempting. There was a definite spark between them, a hot, bright spark he hadn't felt quite as intensely with anyone else. Emmie Woodcroft, with her luscious mouth and spine-tingling touch, made him hard as stone and aching with forbidden longing. But perhaps, after offering her a short fling, Emmie might be more open to the idea of marrying him, thus helping him fulfil the terms of his father's will.

For, if he didn't marry soon and gain an heir, he would lose the estate for ever. And that didn't bear thinking about.

Emmie was sure she would never be able to get to sleep that night but she drifted off more or less as soon as her head landed on the satin-covered pillow. But some time during the wee hours she heard a sound that had her sitting bolt-upright in her bed. She shivered even though the room wasn't cold. The moon shone in from the windows, and she strained her ears to listen out for a repeat of the sound.

The night was silent for so long, she thought she must have dreamt the sound or maybe even uttered it herself. But then, just as she was about to settle back down, she heard it again—a low, deep howl of pain that tore at her heartstrings. She pushed back the covers and grabbed her wrap and hastily put it on over her nightgown, tied the waist ties and padded out to the corridor. The sound had come from Matteo's suite a little further down the long, wide corridor, and before she could stop and think about what she was doing, or why she was even doing it, she went towards his closed door and gave it a soft rap with her knuckles.

'Matteo?'

There was no sound other than the rustling of bed linen, as if he was thrashing about. Emmie turned the handle and pushed the door open a fraction, the moonlight shining a wide, silver beam across Matteo's rumpled bed, where he was lying in a state of agitation, although he was obviously still asleep. Emmie had had nightmares for years after her cancer scare, so recognised the signs immediately.

She padded over to the bed and gently stroked him on the shoulder. 'Matteo. Wake up. You're having a bad dream.'

He suddenly sat up and one of his strong hands flashed out and gripped her by the wrist. His hold was almost cruelly tight and a flicker of fear whipped through her. His hair was tousled, his upper body naked, the lower part covered by the sheet. *Was he completely naked under that sheet?* The thought sent a delicious thrill through her body. The ripped and coiled muscles of his abdomen made her fingers itch to caress them, to see if they were as hard as they looked.

Matteo blinked as if to clear his vision but his hold was still painfully tight around her wrist. 'What are you doing in my bedroom?' His voice was a low growl, his eyes dark and brooding, the generous peppering of ink-black stubble around his jaw making him look menacing, almost dangerous.

Emmie tried to ignore the leap of her pulse, the hot spurt of longing that smouldered in her core and the crackling of dark sexual energy that sparked in the air. 'I heard you call out… I—I was worried about you.' She tugged at his hold, wincing slightly. 'Could you relax your grip a bit?'

A flicker of shock passed over his features and his fingers fell away from her wrist. 'I'm sorry.' His voice was hoarse, his expression tortured with self-loathing. 'Did I hurt you?' He snapped on the bedside lamp and Emmie quickly covered the noticeably red marks on her wrist with her other hand.

'No. Not at all. I'm fine, really.'

'Let me see.' His voice brooked no resistance and she meekly raised her wrist for his inspection. He swallowed deeply and ever so gently cradled her wrist in his hand, as if it were a fragile piece of blown glass. One of his fingers traced over each of the red marks, and then he lifted her wrist to his mouth and pressed a barely touching kiss to her skin. She shivered as his lips caressed each mark, her heart beginning to thrum with excitement, her lower body stirring with feminine longing.

Matteo's eyes met hers and the atmosphere tightened with an almost audible click. He released her wrist to stroke his hand down the curve of her cheek. 'You shouldn't have come in here.' His voice contained a note of reprimand that somehow made her flesh tingle all over again.

'Why?'

His eyes drifted to her mouth. 'I think you know why.'

Emmie stroked her hand down his face, her soft skin catching on his stubble, making another frisson of delight course through her body. 'What do you think might happen?' She was a little shocked at how flirty she sounded, so recklessly flirty.

His eyes moved between hers in a back and forth fashion, every now and again flicking to her mouth as if drawn there by an irresistible force. The same irresistible force that was drawing her gaze to his mouth, aching for him to press it to her own. 'You might regret this in the morning.' His voice was still pitched low and deep, so deep it sounded like the rumble of distant thunder.

Emmie trailed her index finger across his top lip, slowly outlining the firm contour before moving to his fuller lower lip. 'What is there to regret between two consenting adults who desire each other?'

One side of his mouth tilted, his eyes glinting. He placed his hands on her hips, drawing her closer to him on the bed. 'Nothing, if both adults agree on the terms.'

Emmie licked her lips, her heart going like a hyperactive jackhammer in her chest. The smell of him was intoxicating, the press of his hands on her hips sending her senses into a tailspin, the thought of being intimate with him driving her wild with desire. 'The no-strings thing?' She injected her tone with playfulness, keen to show him she wanted nothing more than this stolen moment in time. Their relationship couldn't go anywhere. How could it? She couldn't give him what he most wanted and needed. 'I'm okay with that.'

Matteo pressed the thick pad of his thumb against her lower lip, then he moved it back and forth in a slow caress that sent buzzing sensations through her flesh. The wizardry of his touch was mesmerising. She had no thought of resisting him, no thought of putting a stop to this madness—all she could do was relish the throbbing energy that vibrated between them. 'I can't afford to be distracted right now,' he said but she got the feeling he was saying it for his own benefit rather than hers.

'I know, so why don't we just enjoy the moment?' Since when had she been a living-in-the-moment girl? Never. But this felt right. It felt necessary. It felt important enough to put all other counter arguments to one side. Emmie *wanted* him. Wanted to be wanted by him. Wanted to experience a stolen moment in his arms so she could feed off the memories later. She hadn't been touched by a man other than a doctor or nurse since she'd been diagnosed all those years ago. Why shouldn't she indulge in this moment of madness? This passion had unexpectedly flared between them and she desperately wanted to explore it, even though it was completely out of character for her to do so, especially with a client.

But Matteo Vitale was not just a client—he was the first man who had made her feel powerful as a woman. He awakened in her a sensuality she hadn't known she possessed.

His frown deepened a fraction. 'What happens in Umbria stays in Umbria. Is that what you're saying?'

Emmie moved her mouth closer to his, so close she could feel the warm waft of his breath against her lips. 'That's exactly what I'm saying.'

Matteo made a rough sound in his throat and closed the distance between their mouths in a drugging kiss that made her gasp in delight. His lips moved with urgency against hers, his tongue demanding entry, and she opened to him with another whimper of pleasure. Their tongues met like two hot flames from separate fires, causing a combustion of sensual energy that flared throughout her body in molten heat. His taste was both familiar yet exotically strange—a taste she was rapidly developing a hunger for like an addict does a forbidden drug. It sent her blood racing through her veins at breakneck speed, making every inch of her skin tingle with the need to feel his hands gliding over it.

He pressed her down to the bed, half-covering her with his weight, his mouth still clamped to hers in a hungry kiss that spoke of a man only just holding on to control. How could she ever have thought she could resist him? The need he stirred in her was almost frightening. It was like a storm rampaging through her flesh—a storm of need and aching want that begged to be assuaged no matter what the consequences.

Matteo lifted his mouth off hers to blaze a trail of red-hot kisses down her neck, his lips moving against her sensitive skin, sending a shower of shivers down her spine. 'I want you so badly.' His voice was a low, primal growl of male need that sent her heart rate soaring.

'I want you too.' Emmie could barely speak louder than a whisper, so intense was her need to feel his possession.

He peeled away her wrap and slid a hand under the V-neck of her nightgown to access her naked breast, his touch sending her into raptures. Her nipple hardened like a pebble, her skin tingling as his warm hand cupped her breast. He bent his head and kissed the skin of her upper breast, his tongue moving against her in a teasing flicker that made her back arch off the bed. He took her nipple in his mouth, teasing it with his tongue, sending sparks of fire through her tender flesh. 'So beautiful…' His voice was sexily husky, his teeth grazing her skin as he moved to her other breast, subjecting it to the same exquisite torture.

Emmie stroked a hand down the marble-hard muscles of his chest and abdomen, her heart thudding like a tribal drum. She could already feel the rise of him against her thigh and desperately wanted to touch him. He made a growling sound of pleasure and it emboldened her to pull away the sheet that was draped over his hips. She took him in her hand and gazed down at his magnificence, her own body preparing in its secretive, sensual way. The liquid dew of arousal formed between her thighs, a persistent throb of want that intensified with each heart-stopping moment. 'You're so…so big…' Her voice caught as another frantic wave of longing swept through her.

Matteo cupped her cheek in his hand, his gaze locking on hers. 'I won't hurt you. I'll go slowly.'

Emmie stroked her hand down his length again. 'I don't want you to go slowly. I was ready for you ten minutes ago.'

He smiled against her mouth. 'I was ready the moment I met you.'

'Really?'

'Really.' He pressed a hard kiss to her lips and she opened to him, and the kiss deepened, softened and then became urgent once more. He lifted his mouth off hers after a heady moment or two. 'You felt it too that day, didn't you?'

How could she deny it while she was lying in his arms with her body on fire? 'You certainly got my attention, being so demanding and all.' Emmie adopted a playfully reprimanding tone. 'Most of my clients make appointments to see me. They don't barge in insisting on seeing me right then and there.'

His smile was crooked, his eyes gleaming with desire. 'Am I forgiven?'

'Not unless you make love to me right this minute.'

'Now who is being demanding?' His tone was teasing and his smile made her blood sing. His mouth came back down on hers and she was swept away on a tide of longing that thrummed deep and low in her body.

He peeled back her wrap to expose more of her flesh to his hungry gaze. Under any other circumstances, Emmie would have been shy. She would have snatched at the edges of the wrap and tried to cover herself, thinking her curves too small to incite lust in a man. But, with Matteo, she felt gloriously desirable and delighted in watching his smouldering gaze sweep over her as if she was the most beautiful woman he had ever held in his arms.

He kissed his way across her décolletage, his tongue tracing the delicate scaffold of her collar bone and dipping into the shallow dish between it. Emmie shivered under his caresses, her spine tingling in anticipation, her feminine core pulsating with need. Matteo lifted the hem of her nightgown and she wriggled out of it, hauling it over her head and tossing it over the side of the bed.

He ran his gaze over every inch of her and she wondered again why she wasn't shrinking away from him in embarrassment. 'So beautiful…' His voice was a caress in itself, its low rumble rolling down her spine.

'I was thinking the same about you.' Emmie stroked

his hard length with her hand and watched as his face contorted with pleasure.

His hand came over hers to still her caress, his expression sober. 'You're using a reliable contraception?'

The question blind-sided her for a moment. Contraception was something she never had to think about. 'Erm…yes, of course. Completely and utterly reliable.' Emmie figured her damaged ovaries counted much the same as any contraceptive.

Matteo reached for a condom in the bedside drawer and she watched in breathless excitement as he applied it. He came back to her and stroked a lazy hand down the length of her thigh. She quivered under his touch, her need for him so intense it vibrated like a plucked cello string deep in her core. She instinctively opened her thighs, but he didn't respond to her invitation in the way she'd expected. Instead, he moved down her body with a hot trail of kisses from her breasts to her abdomen and then to her feminine mound.

She sucked in a breath and grasped him by the head. 'I haven't let anyone do this before…'

'Relax. Let me be the first then to pleasure you.'

Emmie gave a gulping swallow. She'd had fantasies about this sort of scenario but never had she thought she would have the courage to allow herself to be so vulnerable. But somehow with Matteo it felt as natural as taking her next breath. She sighed with delight as his mouth came in contact with her swollen flesh, his touch gentle, worshipful, respectful, and her senses went haywire. Tension grew in her tissues, cords of tension that travelled throughout her pelvis in tingling pathways that set her body on fire. His tongue flickered against the tight pearl of her womanhood, the central trigger of female pleasure.

And, suddenly, the storm broke and she was swept up in a vortex of ecstasy that roared, rippled and rumbled through her body. Emmie was shaken to the core by the waves of release that pounded in her flesh, a mind-blowing release that was beyond anything she had ever imagined let alone experienced. It stunned her into silence, only the sound of her heavy breathing audible in the room.

Matteo moved back up her body to kiss her on the lips. She tasted her own essence and was a little shocked at the sheer intimacy of the moment. 'You enjoyed that?' he asked with a knowing smile that set her pulse racing all over again.

Emmie could feel her cheeks growing warm. 'It was beyond anything I've experienced before.'

He brushed a wayward strand of hair back from her face. 'I'm not done with you yet.'

A shiver coursed down her spine at the dark intensity of his gaze. 'Oh, really?'

'Yes, really.' And his mouth came back down on hers like molten fire.

CHAPTER EIGHT

MATTEO HAD MADE love to many women over the course of his adult life, but none had stirred his senses quite like Emmie Woodcroft.

Waking to find her sitting on his bed had turned his nightmare into a dream he knew he wouldn't mind revisiting every night. Her taste was on his tongue, her touch lighting fires over every inch of his skin, his need for her a pounding ache in his groin. He stroked the slim length of her thigh as he deepened his kiss, delighting in the way she whimpered in encouragement. Her legs were tangled with his, her hands playing with his hair in little tugs and caresses that sent tingles racing down the backs of his legs.

'Don't make me wait any longer...' she whispered the words against his lips.

Matteo needed no other inducement and he parted her folds and entered her with a deep groan of pleasure as her slender body gripped him like a fist. He tried to go slowly but her gasps and movements of approval made holding back impossible. He drove into her with increasing speed, going deeper, harder, the primal lust taking control of him like never before. Sensations rippled through him, the delicious friction of her body driving him wild.

He slipped a hand between their rocking bodies, wanting to share this moment of pleasure with her. She was wet, swollen and sweetly fragrant and his senses were intoxicated, drugged, dazed by her. She gave a whimpering cry and arched back sinuously, like a cat, her body quaking, shaking with release. Matteo knew he couldn't hold on much longer. Her body was triggering his with its rippling contractions around him.

He snatched in a breath and then expelled it in a harsh-sounding groan as he finally let go, his scalp tingling, his spine melting, his body shuddering from head to foot with the earth-shattering, planet-spinning pleasure that rocked through him.

Matteo slumped over Emmie in the aftermath, his breathing still ragged, his senses still spinning from a passionate encounter unlike any he'd had before. It was physical pleasure at its finest and, although he'd had plenty of sexual pleasure in the past, something about making love with Emmie had taken it to a whole new level of enjoyment. The cynic in him wanted to point out he hadn't had a lover for a couple of months. His father's death and Matteo's stress over the terms of the will had not exactly been a climate in which to seek a casual lover.

And that was all Emmie wanted to be—a casual lover. The sort of lover he had only ever sought and the sort of lover she only wanted to be—or so she said.

But another less cynical part of him wanted to understand why this encounter with Emmie had been so off-the-charts fantastic. What was it about her that spoke to his flesh and made it wild with lust unlike any he had felt before? Was it simply that breaking his recent sex drought had upped the impact on his senses?

Emmie's hands stroked over his back and shoulders and Matteo shivered in reaction. Her touch was like silk against his skin, soft and gentle, and yet it created a tumult of sensation in his flesh. Electric sensation that made him want her all over again.

Matteo eased away from her to dispose of the condom and then came back and propped himself up on one elbow, gazing down into her pleasure-riven features. 'You left me speechless,' he said with a wry smile.

Her periwinkle-blue eyes sparkled. 'Well, that's only fair, since you did the same to me.'

Matteo trailed a lazy finger down between her breasts. 'When was the last time you had a lover?'

Twin spots of colour bloomed on her cheeks and her smile faded, her gaze lowering to stare at the juncture of his collar bone. 'Why are you asking?' A note of self-doubt crept into her voice. 'Did I act like a novice or something?'

He tipped up her chin to mesh her gaze with his. 'No, not at all. I just wondered, that's all.'

'How long since *you* slept with someone?' She threw his question back at him with a challenging light in her eyes.

'Couple of months.' He didn't tell her the rest—that since his wife and child had died his forays into casual dating hadn't started until a full year after Abriana's death, and only sporadically since then.

Emmie ran the tip of her tongue across her lips and her gaze fell away again from his. 'Well, I've had a bit longer between drinks, so to speak.'

'How long?'

Her teeth began to chew her lower lip. 'I'm too embarrassed to say…'

He bumped up her chin again, locking his gaze on hers. 'Don't be.'

Emmie gave a self-deprecating grimace. 'I haven't had sex since I was a teenager.'

Matteo went completely and utterly still. It was as if every muscle and sinew in his body had been snap frozen. Not since she was a teenager? How could that be? She was an attractive young woman with the same sexual needs as any full-blooded man. Had something happened to her? A sexual assault? Rape? The possible scenarios were ugly, and his gut roiled at the thought of someone abusing her. 'But why on earth not? Did you have a bad experience? Did someone hurt you or…?'

She picked at the edge of the sheet with her fingers, her gaze seemingly unwilling to stay connected to his. 'After I came out of hospital, I felt completely out of step with my peers. I'd stared down death, faced my mortality and dealt with issues most people only face decades later. I couldn't relate to my friends any more. The guys seemed so immature to me, like boys instead of young adult men. The girls weren't much better, although to be fair a couple of friends tried hard to relate to me, but with all the stuff going on at home with my parents and my sister… It…it got too difficult…'

Emmie brought her gaze back up to his and continued, 'I decided to concentrate on my business instead. The only dates I was interested in were other people's. I didn't consider myself a very sexual person until…' Her cheeks were tinged with a faint shade of pink.

'Until now?' he offered.

Emmie gave a wry smile. 'Yes, well, you do have a way of making a girl feel pretty amazing, but no doubt that's because you've had loads and loads of practice.'

Matteo coiled a strand of her silky hair around his finger. 'Sex is not always this good.'

Her eyebrows rose ever so slightly. 'Are you saying you found it amazing too? I mean, more amazing than usual?'

'Why are you so surprised?'

She gave a shrug of one slim shoulder. 'I just thought… I don't know… I've just never seen myself as the sort of woman a man would feel particularly attracted to. Or at least, not enough to have earth-shattering sex with.'

Matteo pressed a brief kiss to her soft mouth. 'I've been fighting my attraction to you from the moment I met you.'

A smile flickered across her lips but it didn't travel the full distance to her eyes. 'That's not going to help your mission to find a wife, though, is it? I'm a distraction you don't really need right now.'

'Maybe I want to be distracted.' Matteo brought his mouth to the side of her neck where her skin was soft and fragrant, sending his senses into mayhem. Would he ever forget the fragrance of her skin? The soft silk of her body lying against his? The hot, tight grip of her feminine muscles around him?

'Maybe I want to forget all about my father's will and enjoy this moment instead.' Matteo wasn't a live-in-the-moment person by nature. He was organised, a planner, his time was structured and never a minute wasted.

But right now, all he wanted was to forget about the clock ticking on the timeline of his father's will and indulge his senses with the most responsive lover he had ever bedded. Besides, his plan to suggest Emmie become the wife he needed was still in place. He was biding his time—the little time he had—because he wanted to wait until he was sure she would say yes.

Emmie murmured under his caresses, her slim body moving against his with enthusiasm. 'I think you're the one doing the distracting,' she said with a breathless sigh as he placed his mouth to her soft breast. 'I can't think straight when you do that.'

'I don't want you to think,' Matteo said, rolling his tongue across her tightly budded nipple. 'I want you to feel.' He circled his tongue around her nipple and then gently took it between the soft press of his teeth. She gave a soft moan and ran her hands down his abdomen to caress his erection. Hot, dark need thundered through his flesh, a need so intense it made every cell in his body throb.

And then, it was Matteo who couldn't think straight. Primal desire drove every thought out of his mind and he gave himself up to the sensual heaven of her touch…

Emmie woke early with one of Matteo's arms flung across her tummy. He was soundly asleep, his hair tousled from where her fingers had clawed through it last night in the throes of mind-blowing sex. She gazed at him for a long moment, memorising every feature of his face. The dark shadow of stubble that was sprinkled across his jaw and around his nose and mouth. The leanness of his face. The chiselled jaw bone. The prominent eyebrows and the permanent trench between them that, right now, was not quite as deep. In sleep he looked more relaxed, younger, less serious, less burdened.

As much as Emmie longed to reach out and stroke him awake, she kept her hands to herself. She knew she had crossed a line by sleeping with him and, while she could never regret the experience of making love with him, she had a job to do, and indulging in a fling was not going to achieve anything but waste his valuable time. Not to mention stirring up a host of longings she had locked away many years ago. But those longings would have to shut the hell up and get back into the vault she had constructed for them and stay there.

Emmie carefully eased out of the bed and slipped on her wrap but in her effort and haste not to wake Matteo, she was unable to find her nightgown. She went back to her own room to give herself a moment to reflect on what had happened during the night. She straightened her barely slept in bed, fussing over the pillows, tempted beyond measure to go back to Matteo's room and enjoy the magic of spending more time in bed with him. But when she reached down to unplug her phone from the charger by the bed she noticed a text message from her mother.

Natty back in hospital.

Emmie's heart sank and guilt washed over her. Her sister's illness was a reminder of how much suffering her own illness had caused to her family and it only reinforced her decision to steer clear of intimate relationships.

And, as timely reminders went, it was certainly bang on time.

Emmie quickly typed a message back, assuring her mother she would be back as soon as she could to offer support. The same support she had been offering for years—hoping, praying, that this time Natty would move a step closer to conquering her illness. The mortality rate from anorexia was the highest of any other mental disorder, a fact that never left Emmie's thoughts. Natty had been in and out of hospital for years, in fact she had spent more time in hospital than Emmie, which seemed ironic under the circumstances.

Ironic and sad, not to mention guilt-inducing.

How could she stay a minute longer with Matteo in Umbria when her sister was fighting for life in hospital? Knowing that, while she was in bed with Matteo Vitale—a client, no less—her mother had been shouldering the burden of her sister's mental health crisis? A crisis that Emmie had caused by becoming ill in the first place. She was doing something she had told herself she never would do—putting her happiness before her family's.

How could she have been so selfish to cross a boundary she had sworn never to cross? Her body still hummed with the pleasure Matteo had evoked. She suspected it would last for days, weeks—maybe for ever. How would she ever forget the magic of his touch? The mind-blowing orgasms that had shaken her from head to toe? The stroke and glide of his hands on her skin, the pressure of his mouth, the taste and texture of his lips, the heat and hardness of his possession?

Emmie slipped her phone in her tote bag and quickly dressed. She left her overnight bag by the door, planning to pick it up once she collected her nightgown from Matteo's room, having only taken her wrap earlier. She told herself it was because she loved that nightgown, it was too expensive to leave behind. But another part of her knew it had more to do with her wanting to see him one more time.

He was still sound asleep and she stood looking at

him for a moment or two. Then, with a silent sigh, she bent down to scoop her nightgown off the carpet close to the end of the bed. There was a rustle of bed linen and the sound of Matteo's hand scraping over his stubbled jaw. 'You're up early,' he said. 'Going somewhere?'

Emmie turned to face him, stuffing the nightgown into her tote bag. 'I have to go back to London today.'

His frown deepened and he tossed the sheet aside and stood, and it took every bit of willpower she possessed not to lower her gaze to the perfection of his male body. 'Is something wrong?'

'My sister is unwell. She's been admitted to hospital. I have to get back to support my mother.'

'I'm sorry to hear that.' He stepped into his jeans and zipped them up, then came over and took her by the hands. 'Give me half an hour and I'll come with you.'

Emmie pulled out of his hold. 'No, that's not necessary.' She straightened her tote bag across her shoulder and gave him a tight smile. 'My goal in coming here to see you in your own environment was to get to know you better. I think I've achieved that, and so now I need to get back to the job you're paying me to do. Finding you a wife.'

Matteo's face froze as if every muscle had been paralysed. He stared fixedly at her for a long moment. 'Thank you for taking the trouble to come.' Somehow Emmie suspected there was a double entendre lurking in his curt response.

'Thank you for having me.' Two could play at that game. 'Will you thank Valentina for me? It was a lovely meal last night.' Emmie moved towards the door. 'I just have to get my overnight bag from my room… I've already packed.'

Would the housekeeper be surprised that Emmie hadn't spent the whole night in the room she had prepared for her? Or perhaps Valentina was used to a bit of female-guest bed-hopping. No doubt Emmie wasn't the first woman Matteo had bedded here. He was a virile man in the prime of his life—every intimate muscle in her body could vouch for that.

'I'll take your bag down for you,' Matteo said in a firm tone that quickly dispensed with any notion of her arguing with him.

'Fine. That's…kind of you.'

A short time later, Matteo carried Emmie's bag down to her hire car and placed it in the boot. He knew she had a valid excuse for leaving earlier than he had expected, but it still niggled him that she might have decided to leave early in any case. She had planned to stay three days and was leaving after only one. How could he not feel short-changed, especially after last night? He'd been looking forward to spending more time with her, and not just in bed. There were things he wanted to show her on the estate, and he wanted to tell her some of the history of the place that went back centuries.

He opened the driver's door for her, aching to touch her before she got behind the wheel, but somehow summoning up the self-control not to. The lines of their 'relationship' were blurry enough. Maybe this was the right way to go—let her leave without any hint of regret on his part.

It stirred a memory of the day his mother had left. But back then he had bawled and begged her to stay, his gut had hollowed out, his chest so tight, as if a clamp had been on his ribs, his eyes streaming, nose running, hopes fading. But, of course, his mother had not changed her mind. She had driven away down the driveway without once looking back.

'Drive safely,' Matteo said, closing the door for Emmie.

She started the car and pressed the button to lower the window. 'I'll be in touch with some potential dates. And I should have your personality profile results back early next week. That will make things a lot easier.'

He arched one eyebrow. 'What? You don't know me well enough by now?' He injected his tone with a hint of mockery.

A flicker of something passed across her face, and then her lips pressed together. 'Thank you again for your hospitality.' Her voice was as polite and formal as a robot's and just as impersonal.

Matteo stepped back from the car and turned back to the villa. He was damned if he was going to watch her drive away.

But he *would* see her again. He would not leave things so up in the air between them, not after last night. Emmie was upset about her sister and needed some time to be with her family. But, once the time was right, he would present her with a proposal she could not possibly refuse.

CHAPTER NINE

EMMIE SAT BY her sister's bedside while a naso-gastric tube fed Natty essential nutrients to keep her organs from failing. Her sister was shockingly thin, little more than a skeleton tightly wrapped in greyish-hued skin, with bruises all over her body, sores where she had been picking at herself, her nails bitten down to the quick.

Emmie fought back tears, her chest so tight she could barely breathe. How could she not feel responsible for the illness that ravaged her younger sister's body and mind? How could she not feel guilty that it was her cancer that had torn apart her family, throwing poor little Natty into the grip of a deadly condition even more deadly than Emmie's? Over the last couple of months, there had been some improvement in Natty's condition. Not much improvement, only a smidgen, but still, anything was better than nothing.

But now this heartbreaking backward step…

It was hard to cling on to hope that her sister would one day turn a corner, that this dreadful illness would somehow lose its grip on her and allow her to live a more normal life. It was so sad to think that, like her, Natty was infertile—not from chemo, but from years of malnutrition, particularly as it had started in young adolescence.

Emmie knew anorexia was a mental health condition, that Natty's starved brain caused the disordered thinking that perpetuated her disease. But she was still angry at her sister for not responding to the costly treatment she had been given over the years. Time was running out; her sister's ravaged body could not take too much more. It intensified Emmie's feelings of powerless and guilt for her part in her sister's illness.

Their mother, Gwen, sat on the other side of the hospital bed, looking a decade older than she should. Her blonde hair was streaked with grey, her skin was sallow, her eyes hollow with dark circles below and there were deep lines on her face that hadn't been there the last time Emmie had seen her.

'Has Dad been in yet?' Emmie asked in a low voice.

Her mother shook her head, her shoulders slumping. 'You know what he's like. He finds hospitals too upsetting.' The disdain in her voice was unmistakable. 'And do you think I don't too? But here I am, week after week, month after month, year after year, wondering if it will ever come to an end.' Gwen brushed at her eyes with the back of her hand, her chin trembling as she fought back tears.

Emmie came round the other side of the bed and knelt down beside her mother's chair. She took her mother's hands in her own and gently stroked them. 'Oh, Mum, you've had to deal with so much pain and stress, it's so unfair.'

Her mother sniffed and looked at Emmie through watery eyes. 'Do you think it's my fault? I wasn't a good enough mother?'

'Stop it,' Emmie said, squeezing her mother's hands. 'You heard what the psychologist said during that session we had. That mother-blaming stuff was what they thought in the past, but they don't now. It's a mental illness and not at all your fault.'

Gwen sighed so deeply, her shoulders went down another notch. 'It's hard not to blame myself when both my daughters have been so ill. I keep thinking I must have done something wrong during my pregnancies. Was it something I ate or drank? Chemicals I consumed in processed food? Not enough exercise? Too much? The guilt never goes away.'

Tell me about it.

Emmie had been accompanied by guilt every day of her life since her diagnosis. Had she done something that had caused her cancer? Had that one cigarette she'd tried when she was fourteen triggered rogue cancer cells in her body? Had the sip or two of vodka at a party when she was sixteen done it?

The one thing she did know was that her illness had caused unbearable stress to her parents and in consequence her sister. Natty hadn't coped with the long absences of their mother during Emmie's hospital stays. She hadn't coped with their father's emotional distance, or his constant criticism over her not doing her homework or her chores. It had been too much for quiet, overly sensitive Natty, whose life had spun so quickly out of control that she'd controlled the only thing she could—her eating.

'I guess that's how most loving mothers would feel…' Emmie said. Not that she would ever know that feeling now. Motherhood was an impossible dream, a shattered dream. She would never have a child of her own. IVF with a donor egg was an option but she would never see aspects of herself or her sister or parents in a tiny baby's face in the way biological parents did.

Gwen grasped Emmie's hand. 'Darling, thank you for being with me. But you said you were in Italy. What for? You never mentioned going on holiday when we spoke a couple of weeks ago.'

'It wasn't a holiday. I went for work.'

Her mother looked at her expectantly, obviously wanting more information. Emmie was reluctant to give too much away. There was client confidentiality, for one thing, and then there was the agreement between her and Matteo that what happened in Umbria stayed in Umbria. But as long as she didn't reveal his name, Emmie comforted herself, her mother would never find out who he was.

'I was visiting a client at his villa in Umbria.' Emmie filled in the silence. 'A high-end client. He's in rather a hurry to find himself a wife.'

'Sounds intriguing. What's he like?'

Emmie wondered what her mother would say if she told her that only hours ago she had been in bed with him. That even now she missed him as if a part of her had been left behind in Italy. She had relived every moment of their night together since, her body tingling all over as each erotic scene played out in her mind. 'He's a widower. He lost his wife and baby eight years ago.'

'Oh, how terribly sad.'

'Yes…' Emmie got up from the floor and forced a smile. 'But he's keen to marry again and it's my job to find him a suitable partner.'

Gwen smiled back. 'You bring happiness to so many people, sweetie. I'm so proud of you.'

But Emmie wasn't able to bring happiness or healing to her family, and that plagued her constantly. Her parents were bitter enemies, her sister was creeping closer and closer to death's door and Emmie was unable to do anything to help.

'Thanks, Mum.' Emmie bent down to drop a kiss on the top of her mother's head. 'I'm proud of you too.'

A few days later, Emmie finally got the results of Matteo's personality profile. It didn't reveal much more than she had already surmised. He was a man who preferred his own company to that of others. He was goal-and achievement-oriented and he had strong personal values. He thought before he spoke, he reflected before he acted, he was not driven by emotions but by logic. He sought organisation and efficiency, and took pride in doing any job he set out to do and doing it to the best of his ability. But he wasn't without sensitivity and emotional intelligence—the feedback showed a broad band of those qualities, although it wasn't his primary strength.

Emmie went back through her database and selected the female clients she thought would be most suitable for him. She ended up with four on her shortlist but she felt none of her normal excitement about finding a match for a client. In fact, she was jealous that someone else would experience the passionate press of his lips on theirs. Someone else would experience the magic of being in his arms, the mind-blowing magic of making love with him.

Jealousy was an emotion she had never experienced before, or at least not in this context. Sure, she was jealous when she saw young women pushing prams, or stroking their bulging tummies during pregnancy. How could she not be envious of a state that fate had decided she would never experience? Every time she saw a baby or a young child, her heart would ache as if it had been pierced with an arrow. Several of her happily married clients had come in with their new babies and Emmie had cuddled and cooed over those precious little bundles, displaying an acting ability that was worthy of an award. No one would ever guess how gut-wrenching it was for her to smell a new-born's beautiful smell, to look down into their little, scrunched-up pixie faces, to listen to their cute little snuffles and sighing noises, knowing she would never give birth to her own child.

Emmie reached for her phone to call Matteo and organise some potential dates but, just then, Paisley popped her head round the door.

'Guess who's come to see you?' She waggled her eyebrows and added, 'Your favourite client.'

Emmie's heart stumbled like a foot missing a bottom step. 'He's not my favourite but he's certainly my most difficult.' Difficult to resist, difficult to forget, difficult to put out of her mind. She had replayed their night together so many times, her body aching for him like it had never ached before. He had triggered desires and needs in her she had no way of satisfying now. Not without him. Self-pleasure was an option, of course, but it would be a paltry substitute now she had experienced the explosive fire of his touch.

Matteo entered her office a moment or two later, his dark-blue gaze meeting hers. 'How is your sister?'

'A little better, thank you.' Natty had marginally improved now that she'd had some intravenous nutrition, but how long she would stay that way once she went home was anyone's guess.

'Still in hospital?'

'Yes, she will be for another week or so.' Emmie waved at the chair in front of her desk. 'Please, sit down. I was about to contact you with some potential dates now that I've read your personality profile. You received a copy of the report via email?'

'Si.'

'Did anything surprise you in it? Anything you didn't already know about yourself?'

'No.'

Emmie forced a stiff smile. 'A lot of my clients are quite surprised. They find it helpful to understand how they come across, what personality traits or ways of relating to people might be getting in the way of them finding a partner—that sort of thing.'

'Have you had yours done?' His gaze was unwavering on hers.

'Yes, as a matter of fact I have.'

'And?'

Emmie moistened her suddenly parchment-dry lips, the penetrating beam of his gaze making her feel as if she were under a microscope. Could he see how much his presence stirred her senses into overdrive? Could he sense how hard and fast her pulse was beating? 'And what?'

'Were you surprised by what you found out about your personality?'

'Yes and no.'

A lazy smile tilted his mouth. 'Let me guess what it said.'

She pressed her spine more firmly back into her

chair, desperately trying not to look at his mouth. The mouth that had kissed hers and set it on fire, leaving smouldering embers in her body that his mere presence now fanned into leaping flames. 'Go ahead.'

His chair creaked as he changed position, one ankle crossing over his bent knee in a relaxed pose. 'You're warm and compassionate and like helping people. You rely on your gut rather than your head when you decide about something. How am I doing so far?'

'Not bad.' Rather brilliantly, actually. But there were things he could never know about her and she was going to keep it that way.

His smile broadened and her heart tripped and flipped. 'You're observant and dedicated with strong personal values. You don't enjoy the company of people who show little regard for other's feelings.' His eyes darkened and his gaze dipped to her mouth before he added in a deeper, huskier tone, 'You're a very sensual person, passionate and fiery, although you try to hide it.'

Emmie tried to ignore the hot flutter of desire between her thighs, tried to ignore the way her lips were tingling, aching to feel his mouth upon them. She pushed back her chair and stood, folding her arms across her chest, fixing him with a cool stare. 'Mr Vitale, I think—'

'Mr?' His dark eyebrows rose cynically and he stood from his chair and strode over to where she was standing. 'Surely, after our time in Umbria, we have moved past such formalities, *sì*?'

His deep baritone was a caress that glided down her spine and left a warm pool of longing in its wake.

Emmie had plenty of time to move out of his reach but found herself unable to move a muscle. She was spellbound by the glint in his eyes, mesmerised by the sensual energy that passed like a current between their bodies. Her gaze drifted to his mouth and her stomach swooped and her pulse raced. She caught the citrus notes of his aftershave, the sharp lemon and lime drugging her senses. 'We agreed that what h-happened in Umbria stayed in Umbria. We—we need to forget about it and move on.' Her voice wasn't as steady as she'd hoped, and nor was her heartbeat—it was going at a hit-and-miss pace.

Matteo placed a gentle finger beneath her chin and lifted her face so her eyes meshed with his. He was close enough for her to see the black, bottomless depths of his pupils and the tiny flecks of different shades of blue that made his irises look like a mysterious labyrinth. 'I haven't forgotten a moment.' His thumb began a slow stroke of her lower lip, setting every nerve in her mouth on fire.

Emmie tried to disguise a gulping swallow but the sound was clearly audible. 'It shouldn't have happened. *I* shouldn't have let it happen.'

His brows snapped together. 'You regret it?'

She chewed at one edge of her mouth. How could she regret the most amazing experience of her life? It was right up there with the day she'd been declared cancer-free. But how could she allow herself to take it any further? It would be stepping outside the parameters she had set for herself. Other people's happiness was her business now, not seeking her own. 'No. I don't. It was...wonderful, amazing, unforgettable...but it can't happen again.'

'Why can't it?'

Emmie's brain was scrambled by his proximity,

addled by his touch, dazed by the desire she could see gleaming in his eyes. She was *supposed* to be able to resist him. She was *supposed* to avoid tricky emotional entanglements, because that was the only way to appease the guilt she carried around how her cancer had ruined her once-happy family. But as soon as Matteo stepped into her presence a tidal wave of longing swept her up and carried her into a fantasy world where she promised herself, *just one more time.*

'You know why not.'

He held her gaze for a long, throbbing moment. 'Let's pretend I'm not a client right now. Just for a couple of days—a week.'

'But you don't have time to waste and—'

'I can afford a week or two.' His hands came down to settle on her hips, bringing her closer to the tall, hard frame of his body. The body that had possessed her and thrilled her and was now making it hard—nay, impossible—for her to rustle up the willpower to say no.

'You mean…continue our fling?'

His finger stroked from her ear to the bottom of her chin in a caress that made every knob of her spine shiver in reaction. 'I want you.' His statement was blunt, bold, and it spoke to every cell in her flesh, causing her to vibrate with desire deep and low in her core. 'And I know you want me.' He brought her even closer, his body so hard against her belly she almost came on the spot.

Emmie drew in a rattling breath and released it in a shuddering stream. 'I don't suppose there's any point in me denying it?'

His smile was knowing, his gaze glinting. 'I could kiss you right now and prove it.' His gaze lowered to her mouth and her heart leapt in anticipation. 'But I'm going to make you wait until tonight.'

Disappointment flooded through her. He was going to make her *wait*? Tonight was hours away. 'Tonight? What's happening tonight?'

He stroked a slow-moving finger across her tingling mouth, the top lip and then the lower one, ramping up her need for him with every sexy graze of his finger. His gaze was still as dark as a midnight sky, the sparks of male desire like winking stars from an outer galaxy. 'I think you know what's going to happen.' He dropped his hand from her face and stepped back. 'I'll pick you up at eight. Bring a toothbrush and a change of clothes.'

Emmie arched one eyebrow. 'What about a night-gown?'

He gave her a smouldering look that made every intimate muscle in her body fizz like shaken champagne. 'You won't need it.' And, without another word, he left.

Matteo had to stop himself from turning up at Emmie's house an hour earlier than he'd said. Anticipation thundered through his blood, the need to make love to her again driving every other thought out of his head. He knew he was acting out of character by putting to one side his mission to fulfil the terms of his father's will, but he was compelled to explore the blistering sensuality between himself and Emmie Woodcroft. How he had stopped himself from kissing her in her office earlier today still surprised him. Who knew he had such iron-clad self-control? She had tested it, though, tested it almost beyond its endurance.

Emmie was the most alluring woman he had ever met and the thought of making love to her again made him ache and pound with need. He was unable to get the memory of their passionate lovemaking out of his mind. It was the first thing he thought of when he woke, the last thing he thought of before he slept, and it filled his thoughts throughout the day. He was a man obsessed and he had to get control of it otherwise he was going to lose even more valuable time.

Matteo was determined not to fall in love, but he had nothing against having a short fling with Emmie in order to convince her to consider his proposal, because the combustible chemistry between them was beyond anything he had experienced before.

They had only had one night together and that wasn't enough. No way was it enough. The disappointment he'd felt when she'd left him that day at his villa had made him all the more determined to see her again. She had stirred a bone-deep longing in him that was making it difficult to think about anything but making love to her again.

But he was acutely aware of the time frame in his father's will that added a whole other level of urgency to his relationship with Emmie.

One that was impossible to ignore.

CHAPTER TEN

EMMIE OPENED THE door to Matteo right on the dot of eight p.m. 'Hi.' She was strangely tongue-tied, feeling as shy as a girl going on her first date. 'I—I just have to get my toiletries bag. Make yourself at home and...'

Matteo stepped over the threshold and closed the door, taking her by the upper arms before she could step away to collect her things. He brought his mouth down on hers in a blistering kiss that lifted every hair on her head and sent sparks of electricity shooting through her blood. His tongue entered her mouth in a bold thrust that had distinctly erotic overtones, the flickers and darts of tongue-play making every female hormone in her body do a happy dance, like an over-pumped cheerleading squad. His hands moved from her upper arms to glide down to her hips, bringing her closer to the proud jut of his arousal. Desire flooded her being, dousing her in molten flames of lust that licked at every inch of her flesh.

He finally lifted his mouth off hers and gave one of his crooked smiles. 'I would have done that earlier today, but I wasn't sure your receptionist would be able to handle it if she happened to come in on us having red-hot sex on your desk.'

Emmie licked the salty taste of his lips from her own, a frisson passing over her body at the sexy scene he had just planted in her mind. 'I'm not sure I would have been able to handle it either. Desk sex sounds a little uncomfortable.'

His eyes smouldered. 'I'd make sure it wasn't.'

That she could well believe. Emmie linked her arms around his neck and planted a soft kiss to his lips. 'I'll hold you to that some time but not here. The desk I have in my home office is an heirloom ladies' writing desk that used to belong to my great-grandmother. She would probably spin in her grave if I used it in such a way.'

Matteo smiled and placed his hands on the curve of her bottom, his hardened length stirring her female flesh into a madcap frenzy. His mouth came back down to just above hers. 'Do you know how crazy with desire you make me? I can't think of anything but how much I want to be inside you again.'

Emmie gave an involuntary shudder, her body already hot and damp with desire. 'You drive me more than a little crazy too.'

He closed the distance between their mouths, his lips moulding to hers in a mind-altering kiss that swept her up into a vortex of thundering longing. Need pulsated throughout her lower body, a desperate, clawing need that made her feel hollow and empty without his thick, hard presence. Now that she had experienced his possession, her body craved it like a drug. Needed to feel the ecstasy of his earth-shattering lovemaking.

Matteo placed one hand in the small of her back and the other slipped up behind her head, his fingers tangling in her hair, sending shivers cascading down her spine. His kiss became more urgent, more intense, more spellbinding. Emmie groaned against his mouth, delighting in the hard pressure that signalled his desperate need for her—the same need that was consuming her.

Matteo finally tore his mouth away, his breathing heavy, his eyes shining brightly with unbridled lust. 'As much as I'd like to finish this here and now, I have a special evening planned for you.' He gave a rueful twist of his mouth and added, 'Besides, I'm mussing up your hair and make-up and giving you beard rash.' He touched a gentle finger to her chin.

What could be more special than being ravished inside her front doorway? Never had such thrilling excitement thundered through her blood. Never had she experienced such giddy anticipation. 'I gotta admire your self-control,' Emmie said. 'It's a whole lot better than mine.'

Matteo smiled and brushed her cheek with his bent knuckles in a light-as-air caress. 'Go and get your things. I'll wait for you here.'

Emmie scooted away to get her toiletries bag, her heart still thudding like a mad thing in her chest, her lips still tingling from his kiss, desire still pounding in her body. She caught a glimpse of herself in her bathroom mirror and was a little shocked at what she saw reflected back at her. Her hair was tousled where Matteo's hands had played with it, her eyes were bright as headlamps and her lips were swollen, without the coating of lip-gloss she had applied earlier that evening. And there was a reddened patch on her chin where his stubble had grazed her. She touched it with her finger, her stomach freefalling at the thought of his stubbly face buried between her thighs.

Emmie took a breath and released it in a shuddering

stream. She had not thought it possible to be so madly attracted to a man that nothing else would matter other than getting naked with him as soon as humanly possible. If anyone had told her even a couple of weeks ago that she would be in such a giddy state of arousal, she would have rolled about the floor laughing. But now all she could think about was rolling around a bed, a floor and, yes, even a desk with Matteo Vitale.

And the sooner, the better.

A short while later, Matteo led Emmie into the restaurant he'd booked in Mayfair. He had been in two minds over whether to skip dinner altogether and go straight back to his house and make passionate love to her. But he wanted this evening to be special because he'd been thinking about her lack of dating experience.

He wasn't sure how he felt about being her first lover since she'd been a teenager. Honoured? Privileged? Touched? None of those words adequately summed up how he felt. He mostly dated women with loads of experience, so it was certainly a novel experience to sleep with someone who was practically a virgin. He was used to worldly women who played the same game as him—casual dates with no-strings sex.

Emmie was hardly worldly, but she wasn't unsophisticated. She was naturally elegant, and poised and articulate. And, while she hadn't had a lot of sexual experience, he would never have guessed from her responses to him. She responded with such enthusiasm, receiving him as if her body had been designed especially for him and his for her.

The more time he spent with her, the more he longed to know about her. Emmie was the first woman he had wanted to get to know on a deeper level. His relationships in the past had been short, some might even go as far to describe them as shallow. Even his relationship with his late wife had hardly been what anyone could call close. It had been a convenient solution to marry for the sake of their surprise pregnancy.

It saddened him that he had been unable to return Abriana's feelings for him. She had deserved better, but how could he have given her what he hadn't had? His ability to form a deep and loving attachment had no doubt been blighted by the walk-out of his mother when he'd been such a young age. Which was why he had been so careful not to raise anyone's expectations in relationships since.

Matteo cupped Emmie's elbow as they made their way to their table. Her petite frame brushed against him. The flowery notes of her perfume drifted past his nostrils and a wave of desire washed over him in a hot tide. She glanced up at him with a small smile and he fantasised about kissing her soft lips again. She had covered the beard rash with some make-up but just knowing it was still there made his groin tighten.

'Here we go.' He pulled out a chair for her and waited for her to be seated. He rested his hands on the tops of her shoulders for a moment before going to his own chair opposite.

'This is nice,' Emmie said, glancing round at the other tables which were situated some distance from theirs. 'Oh, there's a dance floor…' Her teeth sank into her lower lip.

'You like dancing?'

Her cheeks grew pink and she made a business of spreading her napkin over her lap, her gaze not quite meeting his. 'I love it but I'm hopeless at it. I'd have to be tipsy to get on a dance floor and, since I don't drink, that's not going to happen any time soon.'

'Did you ever drink alcohol?'

'If you can call having a sip or two of vodka at a party when I was sixteen drinking, then yes, I used to.'

'But nothing since?'

She shook her head. 'I don't mind other people drinking in moderation but it's not for me.' She waited a beat and added in an altered tone, 'I'm too scared...'

'Of making a fool of yourself?'

Emmie met his gaze with a sombre one. 'Of getting cancer.'

A knife-like pain suddenly hit him in the chest. *Emmie was terrified of getting cancer again.*

He could only imagine how hard it would be to live with the threat of it hanging over her. He knew about the carcinogenic properties of excessive alcohol use and that even drinking in moderation contained some element of risk. He was a moderate drinker himself. He hadn't been drunk or even tipsy since he'd been a teenager, and even then, it had only been the once. He admired her stance. It showed discipline and the ability to resist peer pressure. But it also showed how much her cancer diagnosis had impacted her. 'It sounds like you made the right choice, then.'

'Yes. I don't ever want to go through chemo again. It was ghastly.' She gave a little shudder and picked up her glass of water. 'Let's talk about something else. I hate thinking about that time in my life.'

'But in a way, it's made you who you are today.'

'Yes, but I often wonder who I might have been if I hadn't got sick,' Emmie said, frowning slightly as she looked at the ice cubes in her glass. 'And if my parents wouldn't have split up and my sister get an eating disorder.' She glanced up at him and asked, 'Do you ever wonder what you would be like now if your mother hadn't left when she did?'

Matteo gave a one-shoulder shrug. 'Who knows?'

'Do you think it's affected you in any way?'

'A bit, perhaps.'

'Do you want to know what I think?' Emmie asked, and without waiting for him to answer continued, 'You find emotional intimacy difficult because you were abandoned as a young child by a primary carer. And, since your father struggled when your mother left, you taught yourself to be independent and emotionally distant. But you can train yourself to be more open emotionally. It's hard, but it can be done. Otherwise relationships, particularly intimate ones, will always be fraught with difficulty.'

'But what if I don't want that sort of relationship?' Matteo said with a cynical smile. 'What if I'm perfectly happy with being independent and emotionally distant?'

'But you're not.'

Matteo arched an eyebrow. 'So you believe, but you've only known me a week or so.'

'Maybe, but I'm pretty good at reading people.'

'So...' He glanced at her mouth before meeting her gaze once more. 'Tell me what I'm thinking right at this very moment.'

Emmie's cheeks went a deeper shade of pink. 'You're uncomfortable with my line of questioning, so you're trying to distract me.'

'And how I am distracting you, hmm?'

'By looking at me as if you want to forget about dinner and go straight to your place and have mind-blowing sex. Am I right?'

Matteo smiled. 'You're good.'

Emmie smiled back. 'It's how I make my living.' Her smile slowly faded, her gaze fell away, and she began to make a circular pattern with her fingertip on the tablecloth near her glass. 'I've made a shortlist of candidates for you to—'

'I thought we agreed to forget about that for the next few days?' Matteo asked. The thought of dating anyone else while he was indulging in a fling with Emmie seemed a little weird, if not downright distasteful. He couldn't imagine wanting to talk to another woman, let alone date anyone else. Nor did he want his so-called fling with Emmie to be over any time soon, which was unusual in itself. He was normally formulating an exit strategy on the second date. But not with Emmie.

'Fine but, given the time pressure, I need to have a plan in place. It takes time to get to know someone and—'

'Not according to what you said a few moments ago,' Matteo said with a sardonic look. 'You claim to know everything about me and we only met less than a fortnight ago.'

'Yes, but that's me. Someone else might not have the same ability to see you for who you are. They might be turned off, like Karena Thorsby was, thinking you were intimidating—which you are, by the way.'

'But it doesn't seem to bother you.'

She shrugged and gave him a crooked smile. 'You know what I thought when I first met you? You reminded me of a wolf with a wounded paw.'

Matteo held up both his hands. 'As you see, no wounds.'

'You hide your pain because to reveal it to anyone would make you feel too vulnerable. Like a lot of men, you see vulnerability as a weakness, but I see it as a strength. Admitting you haven't got it all together and need the support of others is an admirable quality.' Emmie leaned forward across the table and placed a hand on his chest, right over the top of his heart. She looked directly into his eyes with her own periwinkle-blue ones. 'There's your wound.'

He held her gaze for a long beat, the warmth of her hand seeping into all the cold corners of his chest, threatening to melt the cage of ice around his heart. Or maybe it wasn't the physical touch of her hand that threatened to chip away the thick layer of ice. It was the way she looked at him—*really* looked at him. Emmie wasn't someone who was satisfied with what she saw on the outside. She went deeper, the way he did as a forensic accountant. Looking for discrepancies, looking for clues, looking for things that didn't add up. She had looked at him that way from the very first day, seeing through his emotional armour like a security scanner, somehow intuiting that all was not right in his life.

Over the short time he had known her, he had told her more about himself than he had told anyone and, yes, it did make him feel vulnerable. When she'd stumbled across the graves of his wife and child he had opened up his world of pain to her, and he had been touched that she seemed to understand in a way few people could.

Matteo captured her hand and brought it up to his

mouth, pressing a kiss to each of her fingertips. 'And where is your wound, *cara mia*?'

Her eyelids flickered as if his question had momentarily thrown her. 'I—I don't have one.' Her slim throat rose and fell, and even with the background noise of the restaurant he heard the sound of her tight swallow.

Matteo kept hold of her hand, his thumb stroking across the soft skin of her palm. 'Ah, but that is not quite true, is it? We all have some hoof print of hurt from the past, often from some event in our childhood or adolescence. And you've had cancer, which is one hell of a wound to deal with—one, I suspect, that would leave a much larger hoof print than most.'

'But I was cured, so I don't have that wound any more.'

'But you still worry about getting cancer again.'

Her gaze lowered to the collar of his shirt. 'Yes, but so do most cancer survivors. Every ache or pain, you wonder… *Is it back*? Every annual check-up and blood test are an anxiety fest until the results come back normal.'

Her gaze crept back up to his. 'It's a heck of a way to live, but I'm glad I'm still living. There were a couple of other teenagers on the ward with me who didn't make it. I made a promise to myself back then that I would make the most of my life to honour them. And I believe I do that every time I match up two people and they fall in love with each other and get their happy-ever-after. Nothing gives me more pleasure.'

Matteo hooked one eyebrow upwards, his thumb circling her palm in a caressing manner. 'Nothing?'

Emmie's cheeks went pink again and she gave a wry smile. 'Well, apart from *that*.' She paused for a moment and added, 'But I don't regret waiting this long to…to have a fling. I needed to concentrate on my business and it might not have been as successful as it's been if I'd been distracted by my own relationship. An intimate relationship takes time and commitment. I've put that time and commitment into my career.'

'There might be a time when a career isn't enough for you any more.'

Emmie pulled her hand out of his and picked up her water glass, shooting him a look from beneath her lowered lashes. 'Not every woman wants the husband, the kids and the white picket fence, you know.'

'Do your parents pressure you and your sister to give them grandchildren?' Matteo asked, thinking of the endless nagging his father had gone on with over the years, about Matteo producing an heir.

Emmie put her glass back on the table, but seemed to misjudge where the cutlery was. The stem caught the tines of her fork and the glass fell over, spilling water across the tablecloth. 'Oh, shoot. I'm sorry for being so clumsy.' She began to mop up the spill with her napkin but a waiter soon rushed across and took over.

Matteo couldn't help feeling his question had unsettled her and wondered if her parents were the traditional sort who expected their offspring to date, get engaged, marry and then produce children in that order, as they had. He had lived experience of parental pressure, and if anything, it had achieved the opposite, making him even more determined not to settle down. Which was no doubt why his father had gone to the lengths he had to get Matteo to do what he wanted.

The waiter replaced the tablecloth and poured Emmie

a fresh glass of water and then discreetly melted away again.

'Will you excuse me?' Emmie said before Matteo could resume the thread of conversation. 'I need to freshen up.'

'Sure.' He watched her weave her way through the tables, a frown deepening on his brow. If her parents had pressured her the way his father had pressured him, then Emmie and he had more in common than he'd thought.

No wonder he felt such a deep connection with her.

CHAPTER ELEVEN

EMMIE WAS GLAD the rest room was empty so she could pull herself together in private. Matteo's question had caught her off-guard, not because she hadn't been asked such a question before—she had, many times, too many times to count. Her parents were the last people who would ever pressure her to produce grandchildren, because they knew she couldn't. Nor could Natty, unless her condition was cured, and unfortunately, with every year that passed, that was looking more and more unlikely.

It pained Emmie every time she saw her mother's wistful glance at a pram or a pregnant woman, or when she walked past a children's wear boutique. Her mother was careful to do it covertly but Emmie had seen it enough times to know her mother grieved deeply for the shattered dream of one day holding her own grandchild in her arms.

It was why Emmie didn't add to her mother's grief by openly expressing her own sadness at not being able to have a baby. She pretended it would have been her choice to be childless regardless of her chemo-induced infertility. What good would it do to dump even more pain on her already overburdened mother? It wouldn't be fair, nor would it achieve anything but inflict more emotional distress. Her cancer had taken so much away from her but it had also stolen so much from her family. The future they had once envisaged, the happiness and healthiness all of them had taken for granted until it was snatched away.

Emmie could no longer be the daughter her parents had once pictured as the mother of their future grandchildren. How, then, could she dare to picture herself as someone suitable for Matteo? It was an impossible dream. A fool's dream.

Emmie finger-combed her hair, reapplied her lip-gloss and took a deep breath to compose herself. Spending time with Matteo Vitale was exciting, exhilarating and erotic, and yet he threatened everything she had worked so hard to finally accept in her life. She knew it was hypocritical of her to call out his fear of vulnerability when she was covering up her own. His laser-like focus, his forensically trained, sharply intelligent mind and his assiduous attention to detail were qualities she deeply admired in him, and yet they were the very qualities that most unsettled her. While she didn't believe vulnerability was a weakness, *her* vulnerability was nobody's business but her own.

And she intended to keep it that way.

The band had taken up position next to the dance floor by the time Emmie got back to the table. Matteo rose from his chair and held out his hands. 'How about we try out those two left feet of yours?'

Emmie fought back a smile. 'Are you wearing steel-toed shoes? Don't say I didn't warn you.'

'I have a high pain threshold.'

Emmie didn't for a moment doubt it. He had lost his wife and child and, while he claimed not to have been in love with Abriana, he most certainly felt enormous guilt and sadness at the loss of her life and that of their child. It struck Emmie then how similar he and she were. Both dealing with deep personal sadness, pretending to everyone they were fine when they were not. They had each buried their sadness and carried on the best way they knew how.

Matteo led her to the dance floor, held her in the waltz position and began moving with her to the slow ballad. Emmie moved with him, a little surprised at how natural it felt, as if they had been dancing together for years. Three other couples joined them but to Emmie it felt as if she and Matteo were completely alone. His hand on the small of her back sent tingles down the backs of her legs. The fingers of his other hand were warm and gentle around hers. His navy-blue eyes held hers in a mesmerising lock, communicating a sensually charged message that made her skin tighten in anticipation.

'You're a natural,' Matteo said, bringing her closer to his body, close enough for her to feel the impact she was having on him. It thrilled her to feel his reaction, the stirring of his body sending a hot wave of desire flooding through hers.

'I don't know about that. Maybe it's because you're such a good partner,' Emmie said, gazing up at him.

His eyes darkened and dipped to her mouth and her heart missed a beat. Her words seemed to ring in the silence. *Such a good partner*. The perfect partner in so many ways. But her job was to *find* him someone, not to be that someone herself.

There was no way anyone could describe her as the perfect partner for him. She could not give him what he most wanted. He didn't want love or even long-term commitment. What he wanted, needed, was an heir. There was no magic wand or benevolent fairy godmother that could ever bring that about for her. Her fate had been decided eight years ago, the day she had first been diagnosed with cancer.

Eight years ago…

And there was another similarity between her and Matteo. Eight years ago, his life had changed for ever when his wife and child had died in a car crash. The same year Emmie had been fighting for her life, his wife and child had lost theirs.

Matteo brought one of his hands to the small frown on Emmie's forehead, smoothing it out with his finger. 'So serious all of a sudden. Is something wrong?' His tone had a note of concern.

Emmie gave a vestige of a smile. 'I was just thinking that eight years ago we were both going through terrible times on opposite sides of the world. It's kind of spooky how two strangers' lives can intersect.'

Matteo brushed his fingers beneath her chin in a feather-light caress. 'Have you heard the saying, "strangers are friends you haven't yet met"?'

'No, but I like it.' She paused for a beat before asking, 'Is that how you see me? As a friend?'

His eyes moved between hers for a pulsing moment, his expression inscrutable. 'That's what you like to be for your clients, isn't it? The friend that facilitates a perfect match for them.'

Emmie sent the tip of her tongue out over her lips. 'Yes, that's exactly what I try to be. Someone they can rely on to be there for them, to help them identify and then push through the emotional barriers that have prevented them from finding love in the past.'

Matteo turned her away from one of the couples who were coming a bit close. His arms around her were strong and protective, the warmth of his body heating every tissue in hers. 'Some people find love only to lose it. My parents, your parents, numerous others.' His tone was more reflective than cynical, merely stating what he had observed.

'I know, and it's often the fear of losing love that prevents people from seeking it again.' Emmie looked up at him again. 'My mother is a case in point.'

'You haven't tried matching her with anyone?'

'I mentioned it a couple of times but she was pretty adamant she was never going to get involved with anyone ever again.' Emmie sighed. 'It's funny how I've been able to help so many people find happiness but I've not been able to do it for my mother and sister.'

'What about your father? Has he got a new partner?'

Emmie twisted her mouth. 'I've lost count of how many he's had since he broke up with Mum. He seems to be in a new fling just about every month.'

'Maybe he prefers to live his life that way.'

'I guess, but I can't help thinking he's going to end up a lonely old man in the end.'

There was a lengthy silence as they continued moving about the dance floor.

'We all make choices we have to live with,' Matteo said and led her back to the table now the band had stopped their bracket.

And some of us don't get a choice at all, Emmie thought with a deep twinge of sadness.

* * *

A few minutes later, Matteo led Emmie into his house and drew her into his arms, his mouth coming down on hers in a surprisingly gentle kiss. Emmie responded by linking her arms around his neck, leaning into his warmth, relishing in the proud rise of his hard male form against her. Her lips moulded to his, moving with the same perfect timing as their dancing had only half an hour ago. Their tongues met and danced a sexy tango that made her blood tingle and race through her veins. His hands went to her hips, pulling her closer to his hardness, a low, deep groan sounding in his throat that vibrated against her lips.

Emmie shivered as his mouth moved from hers to trail a scorching pathway of fire down the side of her neck from below her ear to the framework of her collar bone. His tongue grazed her sensitive skin, sending shooting sparks down her spine.

'I want you.' His blunt statement sent another thrill through her body, an electric thrill that made her inner core coil and tighten with lust.

Emmie licked her tongue along the fullness of his lower lip, a frisson passing through her as her tongue encountered the pinpricks of stubble below his lip. 'Then have me,' she whispered against his lips. 'Because I want you too.'

Matteo pressed an urgent kiss to her lips, his tongue mating with hers in another erotic dance that made her heart race with excitement. After a few breathless moments, he led her upstairs to his master suite, loosening his tie with one hand as he walked her to his bed.

'Here, let me help you with that,' Emmie said, taking

his tie in her hand and using it to pull his head down for another kiss.

Matteo groaned against her lips and she opened again to the silken thrust of his tongue, her body quaking with desire. He walked her backwards to the bed, only lifting his mouth long enough to dispense with his tie, tossing it to the floor. His mouth came back down on hers, firmer, with more passionate urgency, one hand going to the back of her dress and releasing the zip all the way to just above her bottom. Her dress slipped away from her like a sloughed skin, and his other hand stroked down the length of her back and then to the curves of her bottom.

Emmie set to work on his clothes but not with quite the same skill and efficiency. She was sure she heard a button on his shirt pop but she was beyond caring. She wanted him naked. *Now.*

Within a few moments, they were both naked, and Matteo glided his hands upward from her waist to cradle her breasts. She had never considered her breasts the sort that men would want to pay too much attention to, but right then, with Matteo's dark blue eyes gazing at her small form, she had never felt more feminine and desirable. He bent his head to caress her right breast with his lips and tongue, making her almost delirious with lust. His tongue circled her nipple, then he took it in a gentle press between his teeth, releasing it to sweep his tongue around it again. He did the same to her other breast, sending shivers of reaction across her skin.

Matteo guided her to the bed, laying her down. He knelt one of his knees on the bed, his hands resting either side of her hips, a determined look in his eyes. A smouldering look she recognised all too well which sent a river of heat to her core. 'This is all I've been thinking about this evening—tasting you, pleasuring you.' His voice was gravel-rough and so deep she could feel it reverberating in her body as if an invisible wire tied her to him.

Emmie wasn't capable of speech just then. Her anticipation was at fever pitch and, as soon as his mouth came to the heart of her female flesh, she shuddered in reaction. His tongue played her tender tissues like a maestro fine-tuning a delicate instrument, and she came apart in a rush that swept through her like a pounding wave.

Her gasps, cries and whimpers shattered the silence but she couldn't suppress them…nor could she suppress the burgeoning feelings deep inside her. Feelings she had promised herself she wouldn't feel for anyone, must less Matteo Vitale. Feelings that were like tiny fledglings perched high up in a nest, wanting to fly free but sensing the danger of doing so. She had to keep them in the nest. She had to secure the nest, reinforce it, concrete over the gaps so none of those feelings could escape.

They must *not* escape.

Matteo lay beside her on the bed once he had sourced and applied a condom. He ran his hand down the length of her body from her shoulder to her thigh, his gaze focussed intently on hers. 'You are so delightfully responsive.'

Emmie could feel her cheeks warming. Had she been too loud? Too enthusiastic in her response? But how could she help it? He triggered in her such incredible sensations…such forbidden feelings. 'You make it easy for me to respond. I didn't know my body was capable of some of the things you've made me feel.'

He smiled and stroked his hand across her stomach, a lazy finger circling her belly button. 'I could say the same about you…' He bent his head and captured her mouth in a bone-melting kiss, the intimacy intensified by tasting her own essence on his lips. The kiss deepened and then he rolled her over so she was lying on top of him, his hands resting on the curve of her bottom, gently encouraging her to take control. 'This way can increase your pleasure. You can control the pressure and depth.'

The one thing Emmie couldn't control was the growing need for his possession—it was a tight ache inside her flesh, clawing at her with increasing desperation. She lowered herself onto him, shuddering with pleasure as her body wrapped around his steely length. It was erotic, excitingly erotic, and she didn't shy away from it but moved in a perfect rhythm with him. The friction was electric, sending fizzing sensations through her flesh, exquisitely tightening her tissues until there was nowhere to go but off into the stratosphere. The orgasm hit her hard, rocking her to the core of her being, an explosion of sensation that rippled throughout her pelvis. She threw back her head, her hair wild about her shoulders, her cries of pleasure shockingly primal.

Matteo's release followed on the heels of hers and she rode every pounding second of it with another wave of pleasure flowing through her flesh. The bucking and rocking of their joined bodies delighted her all over again. The intimate smells of their lovemaking, their perspiration and body essences overlaid with their colognes and hair products, mingled in the air like a bewitching vapour. Emmie collapsed over his chest, burying her head against his neck and breathing it all in, storing it into her memory.

Matteo stroked his hand down from her neck to the base of her spine and back again. Slow strokes that made her skin tingle and tighten in delight. She had not realised how gentle a man's touch could be. Her first and only foray into sex as a teenager was with a partner who had rushed and, in his hormone-driven enthusiasm, had been a little rougher than she would have liked. There had been small moments of pleasure but nothing like she was experiencing with Matteo. The earth-shattering release he triggered in her was off the scale.

Matteo's touch seemed to read her flesh like someone reading Braille. He sensed all her erogenous zones, seemed to know exactly what pressure and speed she needed to feel maximum pleasure. And she knew it would be a long time, if ever, before she experienced such pleasure with anyone else.

Matteo rolled her over so she was lying on her back, deftly disposing of the condom before taking her in his arms again. His eyes were dark and glinting, his hand coming up to cup one of her breasts. 'I can't get enough of you…' He brought his mouth back down to hers in a skin-tingling kiss, his hand caressing her breast, at the same time sending her senses into overload. He raised his mouth from hers to gaze down at her again, one of his fingers moving in a slow caress along her bottom lip. 'I have to go to Vienna next week for work.' He captured her hand and brought it up to his mouth, his gaze unwavering on hers. 'Come with me.'

Emmie was a little shocked at how much she wanted to go. But was it wise to keep spending time with him? Intimate dinners, dancing cheek to cheek, making love, staying in luxury hotels, as if they were a normal couple. Nothing about their relationship was normal. It never could be. 'Matteo…' She aimed her gaze at his neck. 'I have a business to run and I can't keep flying off to—'

'Look at me.' He tipped up her chin with his finger. 'Tell me what your heart is telling you, not your head.' His eyes held hers in a tight lock, his expression grave.

Emmie moistened her lips, her pulse suddenly unsteady. 'My heart is telling me it would be dangerous to spend too much time with you. And my head is telling me exactly the same thing.'

He frowned heavily. 'Dangerous in what way?'

She eased out of his hold and got off the bed, grabbing at his shirt in order to cover her nakedness. She slipped it on and did up a few of the buttons, her fingers barely able to complete the task. 'I don't want to blur the boundaries with you.'

'We've stated the boundaries,' he said, standing up from the bed and, unlike her, not seeming too bothered with his own nakedness. 'We agreed on a short fling.'

'I know, and I think the shorter, the better.'

He ran one of his hands through his hair from his forehead backwards, his expression a road map of tension. 'Emmie…' There was a grave note in his voice and he came over and took her by the hands. 'The thing is… I think we could make this more than a short fling.' He gently squeezed her hands, his eyes holding hers. 'And I think you do too.'

Emmie pulled out of his hold and began to hunt for her own clothes. 'We might be sexually compatible but that's all.' She found her knickers but couldn't find her bra and pulled back the bed sheets to hunt for it. 'Have you seen my bra? I can't find it.'

'Will you stop for a minute and listen to me?' His frown carved a deep trench between his eyes.

She scooped up her dress and wriggled back into it, twisting her arm behind her back to pull up the zipper. 'I think it's time for me to go home. I'll call a cab.'

'I'm not taking you anywhere until we've talked.' Matteo pulled on his trousers and zipped them up. 'We are more than sexually compatible. I enjoy being with you. I haven't enjoyed someone's company as much as yours before. I've talked to you in a way I have never communicated with anyone else.'

Emmie shoved her feet into her shoes. 'It's my job to make you feel comfortable talking to me. You're reading way too much into it.'

'Are you saying it's all contrived? That you tell everyone all the things you told me about your cancer and your sister and your parents' divorce?'

'Not everyone, but you're a good listener.' Too good a listener. Emmie had told him nearly everything. Shared so much that it was hard to imagine a time in her life when she wouldn't be able to talk to him any more.

He took her hands once more, his fingers wrapping around hers in a gentle but firm hold. 'Why do I get the feeling you're pulling away from me? Not just physically, but emotionally?'

Emmie painted a false smile on her lips. 'You're the one who doesn't talk about emotions in relationships, remember?'

Matteo brought her a little closer, the warmth of his body reminding her painfully of the cold reality of her situation. 'But I'm talking about them now. I'm asking you to marry me, Emmie. I know you said you didn't want to marry but we could make a go of it. I know we could. We're well suited. You surely can't deny it?'

Emmie wrenched her hands out of his and moved out of his reach, hugging her arms around her middle. 'Please don't do this…' She could barely speak for the anguish rising in her throat. 'We could never be happy.' How could she ever make him happy when she couldn't give him an heir? They might have a great sex life together but how could that ever be enough for a man who needed a wife and heir so badly? She would only hurt him the way she had hurt her family.

'Are you crazy?' Matteo asked in a disbelieving tone. 'Every minute I've spent with you has shown me just how happy we could be. I care about you in a way I have never cared about anyone else.'

'You're not saying you're in love with me?'

His throat moved up and down and a shutter came down in his eyes. 'I'm saying I want to be with you for longer than a fling. I want us to marry and have a family. Not just because of my father's will—although it's part of it, of course—but because you and I make a great team. I know we can make a good life together.'

Emmie raked one of her hands through her hair, her heart threatening to split in two. Pain spread throughout her chest, sending its stinging tentacles to every region of her body. 'Matteo… I can't marry you. It wouldn't be fair to you.'

'Look, I know my proposal is not the romantic declaration of love most women want, but—'

'It's got nothing to do with your proposal,' Emmie said. 'Nor is it because you're not in love with me…or me with you.' Not quite true. She was more than halfway to being in love with him. Her feelings for him had developed robust wings and were desperate to fly free. But she would clip those wings so they couldn't.

'Then what is it?'

Emmie met his gaze. 'I can't marry you because I am unable to have children.'

CHAPTER TWELVE

MATTEO LOOKED AT her blankly for a long moment, his thoughts twisting and twirling into a tangled knot, strangling his hopes, choking his plans, blocking the pathway he wanted to be on.

He wanted to marry Emmie.

He needed an heir.

Emmie was unable to have children.

He needed an heir.

He cared for Emmie. They were good together. A great team.

He needed an heir.

Emmie was infertile.

He needed an heir.

The whirling of his brain matched the churning in his gut. A strangely painful, burning churning unlike anything he had ever felt before. He wanted Emmie so badly, not just physically, but because the connection he felt with her made him feel whole for the first time in his life.

But he couldn't be with Emmie and keep his family's estate.

He had never felt more blindsided than by her revelation. How could he not have guessed before now? She had told him about her cancer but she had said she was cured. Cured but at a price—the price of her fertility. A huge price for a young woman to have to pay and one he could only imagine caused Emmie great sadness. Was that why she said she never wanted to marry? Was that why she concentrated on finding her clients their happy-ever-after but insisted she wasn't interested in finding her own perfect match?

But there were ways around infertility, many options available that hadn't been there before for couples in their situation. And he wanted them to be a couple, damn it. They already felt like a couple. The camaraderie, the closeness, the connection was not just in his imagination.

He *felt* it.

'But we can have IVF treatments.' Matteo finally found his voice. 'There are so many options these days.'

'But it won't be *my* child,' Emmie said, pressing the heel of her hand against her heart. 'It would have to be someone else's egg. I will never look at a child and see something of myself in its features. None of my DNA will be passed on to him or her.'

'I understand that would be difficult for you but—'

'How can you *possibly* understand?' Her voice rose in despair—a despair that was almost palpable. 'You can father as many children as you like. You haven't had cancer and had all your dreams and hopes taken away. You haven't walked past a pregnant woman or a woman pushing a pram and felt your heart was going to shatter into a million pieces. You haven't held a friend's baby and ached with every fibre of your being because you know you can never hold your own baby in your arms.'

'I might not understand totally but I have lost a child,'

Matteo said in a weighted tone. 'And I have grieved every day since for him and for his mother.'

Emmie's arms were wrapped around her body as if she was trying to contain her emotional pain. A pain he recognised because he could feel it grabbing at his guts every time he thought of his late wife and child. His two closest companions were grief and guilt. They followed him wherever he went.

'I know and I'm sad for you. It was a terrible tragedy and one you have to live with for the rest of your life. But, if I married you, I would only add to your pain. You're under enough time pressure as it is. You have to be married and have an heir within a year. Even if I agreed to IVF, it would take far longer than that to become pregnant, let alone deliver a child, and there's no guarantee that will ever happen for me. I don't even know if my body could cope with a pregnancy after all it's been through.'

Emmie's shoulders slumped and she added, 'Even the most in-love couples struggle when going through fertility issues. We don't have the magic ingredient to start with—love. We just have lust, and that is not enough.'

The magic ingredient. Matteo had never been a fan of 'the magic ingredient' of love after the damage he'd seen it do to his father. The magic ingredient caused pain and heartache and vulnerability and he wanted no part of it. But that didn't mean he didn't care about Emmie. He did and he had hoped she would be the solution to his problem. He had started to see her as the *only* solution. But her bombshell revelation gave him pause. He needed an heir. There was no escaping that fact. He had to marry and produce an heir otherwise his family's estate would be lost for ever. It was an impossible situation to be in, a torturous choice—happiness with Emmie and losing his heritage, or keeping his family's estate and losing Emmie.

Matteo picked up the shirt Emmie had discarded and shrugged himself back into it. He needed time to think. He needed a workable solution, one where he didn't have to choose between the two things he wanted so desperately. But how could he think when his emotions were in a state of chaos? His brain was flooded with unfamiliar emotions, ambushed by feelings he didn't know how to handle, let alone identify. 'Why didn't you tell me about your infertility before now?'

Emmie gave him a chilly stare. 'I don't usually discuss my health records with my clients and, at the end of the day, that is what you are—a client.'

Her words were like a cold, hard slap in the face. But any offence taken on his part was hardly justified. She had always been clear about the boundaries. They had drifted into a fling and foolishly, misguidedly, he'd thought it could become something more.

It couldn't.

Matteo searched her features but her expression was stony. The irony was he had used the very same expression many times in the past when a casual lover had asked for more than he was prepared to give. The drawbridge up, the shutters closed, the fortress secure.

'So, it looks like this is the end for us.' He delivered the statement in an impersonal tone. The same impersonal tone he had used many times before when ending a fling. But this wasn't the same as ending any other casual fling. It wasn't supposed to hurt. It wasn't supposed to claw at his chest and shred his guts and make him ache to hold her in his arms and beg her to rethink her answer.

Emmie gave a stiff nod. 'I'll be in touch with a list of potential dates for you.' Her tone was as impersonal as his. 'Thank you for dinner and…everything else.'

Matteo only just managed not to curl his lip. 'Everything else' meaning the best sex he'd ever had. The most intimate lovemaking. Now it was over. Finished. He turned to pick up his car keys and wallet, determined not to show the turmoil of emotion he was going through. A turmoil that made it impossible for him to think of a future with anyone else. 'I'll drive you home.'

'Please don't bother. I can call a cab.'

'It's no bother,' Matteo said, holding the bedroom door open for her.

She moved past him without another word and every muscle in his body wrestled with the temptation to touch her. To hold her. To never let her go.

But he wasn't the sort of man to hold on, to never let go, to beg and plead and fall apart because someone didn't want to be with him.

He was the man who didn't do emotion. He didn't feel romantic love.

And he wasn't going to start now.

Emmie sat silently beside Matteo in the car on the way back to her house. What else was there to say that hadn't already been said? His proposal had come out of necessity, not heartfelt love, and it had been promptly withdrawn as a result of her informing him about her fertility issues. She derided herself for having been tempted into a fling with him. It had only made things a squillion times worse. A fling with a client. How could she have been so stupid? So reckless and foolish to think there wouldn't be a price to pay?

There was *always* a price to pay.

Emmie had taught herself not to want the things most other people wanted and she had been successful in suppressing those desires until she'd met Matteo Vitale. He had upended her life, tempted her into thinking she could have more.

But she couldn't.

That option had been taken from her as a teenager and there was no way of getting it back.

But if he had loved her…

The thought drifted into her mind but she slammed the door on it. There was no way she could marry him knowing she would be stopping him from having what he most wanted. No amount of love could ever change that. In fact, it could even drive a wedge between them in the end. They might have formed a connection, grown closer than she had expected and had amazing sex, but the bottom line was he needed a wife and heir in a hurry and, while she could be that wife, she couldn't provide the heir.

And the biggest heartbreak of all was that Emmie wished with all her heart she could.

Over the next month, Matteo ignored the list of potential partners Emmie sent him via email. He wasn't in the mood for dating. He began to mentally prepare himself for the loss of his family's estate, knowing it would be impossible to find someone who would suit him more than Emmie. Even if she had said yes to his proposal, he couldn't have Emmie and have the estate too. He loved the estate in Umbria—it was his birthright, the sacred place where his wife and child were buried—but, unless he could fulfil the terms of his father's will, it would be lost. He needed an heir to secure the estate.

But he wanted Emmie.

He could not imagine a time when he wouldn't want her. It was as if his body had decided she was the missing link to his. He couldn't imagine feeling the same intense level of attraction to anyone else.

Matteo threw himself into work but it failed to enthral him the way it usually did. He was in danger of letting down his clients if he didn't pull himself together. He prided himself on his meticulous attention to detail, to finding out the truth behind every account he cast his gaze across. But all he could think about was Emmie's situation, how sad it was for her not to be able to have a child. How cruel life was that so many children were born to inadequate parents and ended up in foster care, while other people like Emmie could not have what they most wanted—their own child. He had seen his own flesh and blood on an ultrasound image, and then only a few months later he had held that tiny, lifeless body in the mortuary. There was no grief like that of losing a child, but close by was surely the grief of not being able to have a child in the first place, especially if it was what you most wanted.

And Emmie did want a child—she wanted one desperately.

Matteo pushed back his office chair, went over to the window of his London office and stared at the crowds of people walking in the streets below. Businessmen and women, people of all shapes and sizes, couples, families—all going about their daily lives while he was up here brooding in a new type of grief state.

Loss and sadness were not unfamiliar feelings…but there was something else that was lurking in the shadowy corners of his mind. From the moment he'd met her, Emmie had encouraged him to talk about his feelings. But talking about them was not the same as actually *feeling* them. He could talk about anger without feeling angry. He could talk about happiness without feeling happy.

But now, he couldn't talk about love without feeling something…something that flickered with a faint pulse in his chest every time he thought of Emmie. As though his frozen heart was slowly thawing, the layers of ice melting away to reveal a confronting truth about himself.

He was not incapable of feeling love.

He had deluded himself into believing he wasn't cut out for commitment. He had fooled himself into thinking he was only interested in casual encounters. He had convinced himself he was more profligate playboy than permanent partner.

But it was all lies.

Self-protecting lies that had shielded him from facing the love for Emmie that had silently, steadily, stealthily grown in his heart. He loved her. Truly loved her. It wasn't just a concept but an actual *feeling*. A state of being. It spread through his chest like something that had finally been set free after a long imprisonment. Free of its restraints, it had planted a seed of hope in the soil of his soul. All he needed now was the sunlight of Emmie. For wasn't she the light in his darkness? Without her, he would wither and fail to thrive. Sure, he could still have an all right life, but it wouldn't be the blossoming, blooming, blissful life he wanted unless she shared it with him.

He could deal with the loss of his family's estate. Lots of people lost their beloved homes, Emmie included. She'd spoken of her childhood home in Devon with great fondness, sold in order for her parents to move the family closer to London. He would learn to speak of his family's estate in the same way and put his regrets to one side. A property was not as important as a person and the only person important to him was Emmie.

But then a doubt raised its head in his brain… Emmie hadn't expressed her feelings for him. She hadn't confessed to loving him. Would he be showing more vulnerability than he had ever shown before by repeating his proposal, by telling her how much he loved her?

But vulnerability was a strength, not a weakness—or so Emmie said. It was a feeling like any other feeling. He could talk about it but it was important for him to *feel* it. To embrace it with courage.

Emmie had a long session with a new client who had a particular request for finding a partner. Harriet McIntosh was a young woman of twenty-nine who had been adopted at the age of two months old. 'I'd really like to meet a man who is also an adoptee,' she said. 'It would be great to have that in common.'

'So…your adoption worked out well?' Emmie asked.

Harriet beamed. 'Brilliantly. I got lucky in the adoption family lottery. My parents couldn't love me more than if they had physically given birth to me.'

'Have you met your biological parents?'

'Only my mother,' Harriet said. 'She was a homeless girl of fifteen when she had me. She left me on a community health centre doorstep with a note attached to my blanket, but the authorities were able to find her through DNA matching later on. She wanted the best for me but knew she couldn't provide it herself. It was a huge sacrifice on her part. I am forever grateful that she loved me enough to do that.'

Emmie had spoken to a few adopted people, some of whom still carried deep sadness about being relinquished, but it was so refreshing…so positive and uplifting…to hear of someone like Harriet who couldn't be happier about being adopted. It made Emmie start to wonder if she was *too* adamantly opposed to adoption as an option. But what if she adopted a child and then got sick again? She would be setting up innocent children for hurt and sadness they didn't deserve.

But you might not get cancer again. Many people go on to live full and healthy lives after cancer.

It was as if two sides of her brain were in deep debate. Could she be the sort of adoptive mother Harriet had been blessed with? Could she embrace the role of parenting without sharing DNA? She loved children. It was hard not to love a child and didn't every child deserve a loving home? The doubts inside her head were less strident, the positives more insistent.

You can be a loving adoptive mother, like Harriet's mother—the sort of mother who cherishes the children in her care. Who loves them as her own, protecting them, shielding them, treasuring them.

Emmie could do that with Matteo…except he didn't love her. And surely the happiest environment for a child would be one in which both parents loved each other? Families came in all shapes and sizes these days.

She had made the mistake of thinking there was only one way to be a mother and, because it had been taken away from her, she had ruled out ever doing it any other way.

But there was another way, a wonderful way, to be a mother. Harriet was living proof of it, speaking so lovingly of her adoptive parents.

'I'm so glad you had such a wonderful experience,' Emmie said. 'I think I have someone on my books who is perhaps a little less happy about his adopted family, but maybe meeting you will help him reframe how he sees them.'

'Oh, great. I can't wait to meet him.' Harriet waited a beat before adding, 'Do you believe in love at first sight? I mean, my parents fell in love with me from the moment they met me. Do you think it's possible in a romantic context too?'

Emmie smiled. 'Yes, I really do.'

After all, she had lived experience of it.

CHAPTER THIRTEEN

HARRIET HAD ONLY just left Emmie's office when Paisley poked her head round the door. 'Your father is here.'

Emmie rapid-blinked. 'My father?' Disappointment trickled through her. It was silly of her to have hoped it might be Matteo instead.

Paisley nodded and added *sotto voce*, 'Maybe he wants you to help him find a partner.'

'He needs no help from me,' Emmie said sourly. 'He's had numerous since Mum.'

'Will I send him in?'

'Yes. But tell him I only have five minutes.'

Emmie stayed behind her desk when her father came in. She couldn't remember the last time they had hugged or shown any affection. It wasn't how their relationship worked these days. Gone were the days of hugs and kisses and playful tickles and words of affection. Her cancer diagnosis had changed her father overnight as well as her.

'Dad, what brings you to my neck of the woods?'

He gave her a sheepish look and placed a hand on the back of the chair on which Matteo had once sat. 'Do you mind if I take a seat?'

'Go ahead.' She leaned her elbows on the desk and

steepled her fingers together. 'So, have you visited Natty yet, or has that been a little too uncomfortable for you?'

A dull flush appeared like two flags high on his cheekbones. 'Actually, I was there yesterday and again today.' His throat moved up and down and he continued, 'She seems to be getting a little better.'

'Yes, but it's too early to hope it's permanent.'

'Not much in life is…'

'Parental love is supposed to be,' Emmie tossed back with a speaking look.

Her father seemed to slump in the chair as if an invisible weight he was carrying had suddenly become too heavy. 'You think I don't love you and Natty?' His mouth twisted. 'I think the problem has been I loved you too much. That's why the prospect of losing you hit me so hard.'

'Your timing is way off.'

His mouth twisted again. 'Yeah, I know this is eight years too late, but I still need to get this off my chest.'

'So you can feel better about yourself?'

'So we can be a family again.'

Emmie pushed back her chair and stood with her arms crossed across her middle, glaring at him. 'Are you for real? How can we be a family again when you and Mum can't be in the same room as each other without it turning into World War Three?'

'Your mum and I have been talking over the last couple of weeks and—'

'What?' Emmie stared at him in shock. 'Over the phone? In person?'

'Both.'

'And?'

He took a deep breath and released it in a stuttering stream. 'I told her some stuff I should have told her when we first met. Important stuff about my childhood.'

'You said you had a happy childhood.'

'It was mostly happy.' He swallowed again and scrubbed at his face with his hand. 'My parents, your grandparents, were busy running a business together but they did their best to be there for me when they could. I was close to my grandmother because she took care of me most of the time. She was everything a grandmother should be. That's why I gave you her writing desk. She was a very special person to me. But one day she became ill and was rushed to hospital, and I went with her in the ambulance.'

He blinked back tears and continued, 'I was with her when she died. I was nine years old. I've hated hospitals ever since. I missed her so much. Life was never the same without her. I had to go to boarding school after that, but that's another story.'

Emmie stared at her father as if seeing him for the first time. Seeing the frightened little boy behind the distant and overly critical father he had become. The loving little boy who had lost the person he loved most in the world. 'Oh, Dad, I wish I'd known…'

'It was terrifying when you got diagnosed with cancer. I could see it all playing out again in my mind. I'd be sitting there one day holding your hand, just like I held Gran's, and then you'd be gone…' He lowered his head into his hands and gave a muffled sob. 'And then there's Natty…'

Emmie came over to him and knelt beside his chair, taking one of his hands in hers. 'But I'm still here and Natty is getting the best help possible. We have to keep hoping she'll make it.'

He raised his bloodshot gaze to hers. 'Can you forgive me for not being there when you needed me? For not keeping us all together? I'm doing all I can to make it up to your mother. She's been marvellous about it. But then, she always was the most amazing person, which was why I married her in the first place.'

'Of course I can forgive you, but why hasn't Mum said anything to me?' It was hard not to feel a little miffed her mother hadn't given her the heads up.

'We're taking it a day at a time, that's why.'

'You mean…you're *seeing* each other?'

Her father gave a wobbly smile. 'I can highly recommend falling in love with the same person twice. I've made some terrible mistakes in my time but the best thing I ever did was fall in love with your mum. And this time, I am not ashamed to tell her every day how much she means to me.'

'But what brought you to this point? I mean, something or someone must have helped you see…'

'I took a good hard look at myself about a month ago. I didn't like what I saw. I'm not sure what triggered it—maybe Natty's relapse. I knew I had to face my demons before they destroyed me.'

'Dad…' Emmie reached for him in a hug at the same time he reached for her. 'I'm glad you're back. I missed you.'

'I missed you too, sweetie.'

It took Emmie a good half-hour to repair her make-up after her father left. She no sooner put on more mascara when she would start crying again. Bittersweet tears for the lost years and the lost opportunities. But she was hopeful her father was on the right track now, learning to embrace vulnerability and show the love he felt but had denied for so long. Emmie glanced at her reflection in the mirror and dabbed at a speck of smeared mascara below her left eye. Maybe she had to do the same thing—stop denying her feelings and embrace them instead.

Paisley tapped on the door and poked her head round again. 'You have another visitor.'

'Let me guess. My mum?' She might as well give up on her make-up repairs.

Paisley's eyes sparkled like twirling tinsel. 'It's *him*.'

Emmie's heart almost leapt out of her chest and landed on her desk. She pushed herself out of her chair on unsteady legs. 'Okay…' She didn't dare harbour any fledging hopes that this visit was anything but a client visit. Not that Matteo had contacted any of the women she had selected as potential partners. She had tried not to read too much into his reluctance to engage with any of the women. She had tried not to think that he might well have found his own potential partner since they had ended their fling. It had happened to other clients of hers. A chance meeting had turned into something else. Had Matteo's problem been solved? Had he found someone who could give him the thing he most wanted?

Matteo came striding in and Emmie had to stop herself running to him and throwing herself in his arms. Her body reacted to his presence the way it always did—flickers of awareness racing across her skin, her heartbeat accelerating, her pulse racing. She hadn't seen him in a month and it looked as if time hadn't been all that kind to him. He looked as though he had lost weight and his eyes had dark circles beneath them, as if he hadn't been sleeping well. Not that she could talk.

It wasn't only smeared mascara that had left panda circles around her eyes.

'Emmie.'

His voice was a caress that sent a frisson through her body. *Em-meee.* Oh, how she had missed the sound of his voice! How she had missed seeing him in the flesh.

'Hello.' Emmie adopted her best business-like tone. 'You haven't contacted any of the women I selected for you.'

He came over to her and took her hands in his. 'That's because I only want one woman and that is you.'

Emmie stared up at him, not daring to take another breath in case she was getting ahead of herself. 'But I can't give you a child. And you don't love me.'

His hands gently squeezed hers, his eyes soft with tenderness. 'I do love you. I'm ashamed to admit it took me this long to realise it. You have taught me so much about myself, about identifying my feelings, helping me talk about them. But the one step I missed was allowing myself to actually feel them. But I know what I feel for you is the real deal.'

He drew her closer to his body. 'I know we can be happy together. We can't have the perfect family you dreamed of but we can be together. And that's all I want.'

Emmie flung her arms around his waist, squeezing him so tightly he gasped. 'Oh, Matteo, I can't believe you're prepared to sacrifice so much for me. I love you too. I think I fell in love with you the first time I set eyes on you.' She looked up at him again with a growing frown. 'But your family's estate? Won't you lose it without an heir?'

Matteo stroked her cheek with a gentle finger. 'I

would rather lose the estate than lose you. You are enough for me, more than enough.'

Emmie was trying not to cry but failing miserably. 'Oh, my darling, maybe we can have a family. We can adopt or foster. There are so many children out there who need loving homes. We could provide a wonderful home for our children. And they would be ours, wouldn't they? Because we would commit to them the same way we commit to each other—for ever.'

'You'd be open to that?' Hope shone in his gaze. 'Really?'

Emmie smiled and hugged him again. 'I made the mistake of thinking, if I couldn't be a biological mother, then I couldn't be a mother. But I realise now being a mother is primarily about love, not just sharing some DNA. And I can't think of a person I would rather be a parent with than you.'

'You'll be a wonderful mother.' Matteo kissed her lingeringly, leaving her breathless and boneless in his arms. He lifted his mouth from hers to gaze down at her. 'I can't wait to marry you. Don't make me wait. This last month has been torture, not seeing you, not touching you. Every day felt like a lifetime.'

'I won't make you wait,' Emmie said, linking her arms around his neck. 'I feel like such a hypocrite telling you to be open about your feelings when I'd locked my own away. I told you to be vulnerable but I didn't want to be vulnerable myself.'

Matteo cradled her face in his hands. 'I took a gamble that you loved me but were hiding it. I can't say it was easy allowing myself to feel so vulnerable, but I figured losing you would be so much worse.'

'Loving someone is all about facing the prospect of

losing them one day,' Emmie said. 'That's why it's so frightening to open your heart. I just had my father here half an hour ago. He explained why he became so distant when I got sick. He was so terrified of losing me that he pulled away. It was a self-preservation move, an unconscious coping mechanism to prevent further pain. He's seeing my mum again. Can you believe that? After eight years of bickering and all-out war, they're actually seeing each other.'

'I'm glad you understand him better. And it just goes to show you should never lose hope.'

Emmie gazed up at him dreamily. 'I didn't realise I could be this happy. I thought I would be alone for the rest of my life. I had even convinced myself I would be happy that way. I had starved myself of intimacy, just like my sister has starved herself of food. It disordered my thinking for so long but meeting you changed everything. You made me realise how much I wanted to love and be loved, no matter what.'

Matteo stroked her cheek again. 'I was the same. Telling myself I was satisfied by casual hook-ups and only finding fulfilment in my work. But we will fulfil each other now. We'll be an awesome team. And we'll need to be, because we'll have a lot on our plate travelling back and forth to Devon and London and Umbria.'

Emmie frowned in puzzlement. 'But why will we be travelling to Devon?'

Matteo's eyes twinkled and he slipped a hand into his jacket pocket and handed her a folded piece of paper. 'For you, *cara mia*, with all my love.'

Emmie took the paper and unfolded it, her eyes rounding to the size of dinner plates, her heart swelling in her chest. 'Oh, Matteo… You bought my childhood home?' Tears sprouted in her eyes. 'I can't believe it, it's like a dream come true. It's just so generous of you.'

He smiled and wrapped his arms around her. 'You are my dream come true. I love you. And I will shower you with gifts for the rest of our days.'

'I love you so much, it's impossible to put into words.'

Matteo lowered his mouth to hers. 'Then let's put it into action instead, *si*...?'

EPILOGUE

One year later...

EMMIE SAT SURROUNDED by her little instant family and wondered how she could ever have thought she would be any less of a mother for not having physically given birth to her children. Pepe and Paolo, the two-and-a-half-year-old twins, were playing with their father. For Matteo *was* every bit a father to them, as she was their mother, even though they didn't share a single speck of DNA.

Emmie looked down at the sleeping infant in her arms, Isabella, and silently promised Isabella's and the twins' late mother and father she would love and protect these precious children with all her heart for the rest of her days.

The children's biological parents had been tragically killed in a car crash and, with no immediate family Matteo, as the twins' godfather, had stepped forward and been awarded full guardianship. The children had adjusted well to the new living arrangements, being so young, and Emmie was so grateful that, out of such an unspeakable tragedy, she and Matteo were able to provide a loving home for the children.

Matteo came over to Emmie and laid a gentle hand on her shoulder. His gaze was loving and tender, and her heart swelled with love. 'You have the magic touch with Isabella.'

Emmie laid her hand on top of his and gave him a wistful smile. 'It seems wrong to be so happy when the children will never know their real parents.'

'I know.' He pressed a kiss to her forehead. 'Life is a journey between happy and sad moments, but we will make sure our little family has more happy than sad ones.' He stroked a gentle finger over the sleeping baby's petal-soft cheek, then glanced back at Emmie. 'There is no greater gift than promising to love and cherish someone else's children as your own. And these little *bambinos* are very lucky indeed to have you as their mama. And I am the happiest man in the world to be your husband.'

Emmie smiled. 'That's what my father keeps saying to Mum now they have remarried. I still can't believe it, you know. How two people who were at war for so long finally put their differences aside and reclaimed what they'd lost. And Natalie too…' She gripped his hand in gratitude. 'We all have you to thank for her recovery. That private clinic you paid for made all the difference. I have never seen her so healthy or so happy.'

Matteo leaned down to brush her lips with his. 'I would do anything for you, *tesoro mia.* You are my heart, my home, my future, my perfect match. My for ever love.'

For ever love sounded just perfect.

And it was.

* * * * *

MILLS & BOON

Coming next month

THE SECRET BEHIND THE GREEK'S RETURN
Michelle Smart

Marisa opened her eyes, going from heavy sleep to full alertness in an instant.

Nikos.

He was alive.

Or had she dreamt it?

A look at her watch told her it was four in the morning.

She threw the soft blanket off and her stockinged feet sank into thick carpet.

Rubbing her eyes, she stared at the sofa. At some point while she'd slept, Nikos had put a pillow under her head, laid her flat on her side and covered her.

She hadn't dreamt him.

Heart in her throat, she found herself in the adjoining room before she even knew she'd opened the door and walked into it.

The light in there was incredibly faint, the little illumination coming from the lamp Nikos had left on for her in the living area. It was enough for her to see the shape of his body nestled under the covers, breathing deeply.

She definitely hadn't dreamt him.

Nikos was alive.

The relief was almost as overwhelming as it had been the first time, and, eyes glued to his sleeping shadowed face, she stretched out a trembling hand and lightly pressed her fingers against his cheek.

The relief was short-lived. A hand twice the size of her own flew like a rocket from under the sheet and wrapped around hers.

'What are you doing?'

Her heart jumped into her throat, the beats vibrating through her suddenly frozen body.

Nikos raised his head and blinked the sleep from his eyes, trying to clear the thickness from his just awoken brain, and stared at the motionless form standing beside him.

'Marisa?' His voice sounded thick to his own ears too.

As his eyes adjusted he saw the shock in her wide eyes before his gaze drifted down to notice the buttons of her dress around her bust had popped open in her sleep to show the swell of her breast in the black lace bra she wore.

Arousal coiled its seductive way through his bloodstream to remember the taste of her skin on his tongue and the heady scent of her musk. He tugged her closer to him, suddenly filled with the need to taste it again, taste *her* again, to hear the throaty moans of her pleasure and feel the burn of their flesh pressed together. It was a burn he'd never felt with anyone but her.

Her lips parted. Her breath hitched. Her face lowered to his…

His mouth filled with moisture, lips tingling with anticipation. He put his other hand to her neck and his arousal accelerated.

It had been so long…

Then, with her mouth hovering just inches from his, she jerked back and snatched her hand away. It fluttered to her rising chest.

'I'm sorry for waking you,' she whispered, backing away some more. 'I was just checking I hadn't dreamt you.'

Continue reading

THE SECRET BEHIND THE GREEK'S RETURN

Michelle Smart

Available next month

www.millsandboon.co.uk

COMING SOON!

We really hope you enjoyed reading this book. If you're looking for more romance, be sure to head to the shops when new books are available on

Thursday 8th July

To see which titles are coming soon, please visit

millsandboon.co.uk/nextmonth

MILLS & BOON